JUST AN ORDINARY FAMILY

FIONA LOWE

PRAISE FOR FIONA LOWE

"Set to be the next *Big Little Lies*. Part-Liane Moriarty, part-Jodi Picoult, *Just an Ordinary Family* is a compelling drama about a seemingly 'ordinary' family that implodes after a domino effect of lies, betrayals, disappointments and regrets."—Mamamia on *Just An Ordinary Family*

"The undisputed queen of Australian small town fiction ... Fiona's trademark mix of engaging, well described characters and interesting social issues will draw you in."—Canberra Weekly on *Just An Ordinary Family*

"Fiona Lowe's ability to create atmosphere and tension and real relationship dynamics is a gift." —Sally Hepworth, bestselling author of *The Mother-in-Law* on *Home Fires*

"Fiona Lowe is the queen of Australian country town fiction ... another well researched and compassionate tale."—Canberra Weekly *on* Home *Fires*

ALSO BY FIONA LOWE

Daughter of Mine

Birthright

Home Fires

Just An Ordinary Family

A Home Like Ours

Coming in 2022

A Family of Strangers

Join My Newsletter

For a free novella, *Summer of Mine;* Doug and Edwina's summer of 1967, please join my VIP Readers newsletter. You'll also be the first to hear about new releases, book sales, competitions and giveaways. Register at

fionalowe.com

Did you know **BookBub** has a new release alert? You can check out the latest deals and get an email when I release my next book by following me at

bookbub.com/authors/fiona-lowe

JUST AN ORDINARY FAMILY

DEDICATION

For my sister, Sue
Thanks for the cheerleading, your wise counsel and the straight talk.
Love you lots!

A single lie discovered is enough to create doubt in every truth
expressed.
Anonymous

Betray a friend, and you'll often find you have ruined yourself.
Aesop

PROLOGUE

THE DAZZLING DANCE OF SUNSHINE ON WATER SO ENTRANCED Karen Hunter, she misjudged the width of the double baby stroller. One moment the outside wheels were firmly connected to the concrete path and the next they were suspended in midair. The stroller teetered violently. Red hot fear streaked through her. Throwing all her strength behind it, she wrenched on the handle, hauling the heavy stroller back to safety. The ensuing momentum vibrated through the tightly coiled suspension springs and it bounced wildly.

With her heart pounding as fast as if she'd just run a race, Karen frantically peered into the stroller to check her precious cargo. Both babies remained tucked up under their hand-embroidered blankets, sound asleep and utterly unperturbed by their rocky ride. She slumped in relief.

"No one ever tells you how hard these things are to drive, do they?" a voice said behind her.

Karen turned to see a woman of similar age pushing a regular stroller. "No one tells you that being a mother's both exhilarating and terrifying. Today's the first time I've taken them out on my own and I almost tipped them onto the road."

The woman laughed. "Don't worry, that's what the straps are for."

Karen envied her easy manner. "You sound a lot more experienced than me."

"Perhaps on stroller pushing. Dan gets colic so we walk a *lot*. We're on our way to the new mom's group." She pointed at the building farther down the street. "You must be Karen."

Karen's heart began to pound again. How did this woman know her name? Recently arrived in Kurnai Bay from Melbourne, she wasn't used to her neighbors knowing her name, let alone a complete stranger.

But the woman didn't seem to notice Karen's unease. "I'm Hilary van den Berg. It's great to meet you. Eileen said you were joining our group. I made you a welcome casserole four days ago, though it turns out the hardest part isn't the cooking, but actually getting into the car to deliver it to you." The woman leaned in conspiratorially. "If Eileen asks about it, can you tell her you got it? I promise Ken will drop it over to you tonight."

Hilary's rapid-fire speech generated so many questions, Karen didn't know where to start. Granted, she was sleep deprived and she and Peter had spoken to a parade of realtors, tradesmen and utility providers during the previous ten days, but she was certain she hadn't met an Eileen.

"Who's Eileen?"

"The health center nurse." Hilary laughed. "I'm not surprised you can't remember who's who. With twins, you must have double baby brain."

"Something like that," Karen said faintly. Most days she had no idea if she was coming or going.

"Twins have always been my secret wish." Hilary stroked her own baby's head. "I'll never tell Dan, but I was disappointed when I found out I was only cooking him. You're so lucky!"

Karen winced. Luck was such an arbitrary event—one person's luck was too often another person's misfortune, but she couldn't think about that. Couldn't dwell on the heartache and regrets. Her focus must be her daughters and creating opportunities for them both to thrive.

"I thought I was only having one baby right up until two minutes after I delivered Libby."

Hilary's eyes widened. "Crikey! Have you gotten over the shock yet?"

Karen thought about the rollercoaster ride of the last nine weeks, including the unexpected move. "Not really."

"Can I peek?"

Apparently, it was a rhetorical question, because before Karen could say a word, Hilary was pushing back the stroller covers and peering in.

"Oh, Karen," she breathed. "They're gorgeous. What are their names?"

"Libby's the eldest and she's under the lemon-colored blanket."

As if Libby knew she was being discussed, her blue eyes popped open, her lips widened into a beatific smile and then she gurgled.

"Aren't you a bright spark," Hilary cooed. "You look like you know what you want."

Karen thought anxiously about Libby's intensity—she was either in a fury or laughing in delight. "She knows what she likes and dislikes."

"It's a bit scary the way they arrive with their own distinct personalities. I wasn't expecting that. I thought I'd have more of an influence in molding Dan's character but after six months of motherhood, I'm already wondering if parents have any say in their children's personality."

Karen's gut churned. "Of course we have a say. We must have a say!"

Hilary blinked, momentarily startled by the emphatic response. "Let's hope you're right and I'm wrong, because right now, Dan thinks all he has to do in life is bat his baby blues and everyone will drop everything and come running." She turned her attention to the second twin. "And who's this cutie?"

"Alice. She's our precious surprise." Unlike Libby, Alice didn't stir, although her eyes roved under her almost translucent lids.

Hilary glanced at Karen; unasked questions clear in her eyes. "She's a lot smaller than her sister."

"Yes." Karen left it at that as a familiar guilt pulled tightly around her. It was her fault Alice had failed to thrive.

The pediatrician's words were never far away: "With such a low birth weight, there's a high risk of developmental delay."

"Do you mean brain damage?" Her husband, Peter had asked the question Karen had been too scared to voice.

"I'm constantly surprised by the remarkable resilience of the human body," the doctor said. "The fact Alice is alive is a miracle in itself. The best thing you can do is take her home and love her."

Karen slipped her finger against Alice's palm, welcoming the tight and reassuring grip of her tiny hand. Once again, she silently made the promise she'd made each day for weeks.

I'll make things better, Alice. I'll keep you safe and protect you. Always.

CHAPTER ONE

JANUARY

Alice Hunter sneezed into her shoulder three times and then, despite the warm summer day, shivered. It was a sure sign she was sick. These were the moments when she missed being a kid.

When she was growing up, her mother had strict rules about illness and one of Karen's favorite sayings had been, "If you can stand and argue with me about going to school, you're well enough to go." Many times, Alice had reluctantly stuffed her bag with books and stomped out the door. But whenever Alice had spiked a temperature, Karen had always tucked her up in bed and fed her chicken soup.

"Table seven." Jake, the chef and owner of the restaurant, slid hot plates onto the pass-through and frowned. "You look like crap. Don't give whatever it is to the customers."

"Gee, thanks. And here I was thinking you might make me some immune boosting soup."

"You're lucky I'm not making you work a double shift."

Not for the first time, Alice wondered how the life she'd envisioned for herself had come to this. Despite her best laid plans, she was back in Kurnai Bay, living in her childhood home and working four part-time jobs. Waitressing during the summer crush was the worst of them.

Alice carried the pasta bowl and the fish plate to table seven, offered pepper and parmesan cheese and smiled against aching teeth. Great. She probably had sinusitis on top of the cold. She considered dropping into the medical practice on the way home in case Libby could squeeze her in for an appointment. Then again, Libby's patients had to be halfway to septic shock before she prescribed antibiotics. Her twin would recommend saline nasal spray, steam inhalations and a review in three days.

"We need another bottle of water." The woman at table seven gave Alice the empty bottle.

"Absolutely. I'll be right back."

Alice hip-swiveled her way between the closely set tables. When she was halfway to the bar, someone grabbed the back of her T-shirt.

"We're ready to order. We've been ready for ten minutes."

Get your hands off me, you fat, ugly pig. "Excellent."

Alice didn't point out that their menus were still wide open, which signaled to her they were still prevaricating. Nor did she mention she was on an errand for another table and she'd be back in a minute— she'd learned it was faster to just take the order. Then she'd deliver it to the kitchen, collect table seven's water and return. Waitressing, she had down pat. It was the rest of her life that was a shambles.

Her nose tickled in a raft of irritation and she sneezed into her shoulder.

The customer leaned back, his face aghast. "We're on vacation. We didn't come here to get sick. Should you even be working?"

Probably not, but she didn't have the luxury of not working today. No one in Kurnai Bay did. They had four months to earn a year's income so they could survive the slower winter months. Once Easter was over, the town returned to the sleepy fishing village it had been since whalers and sealers plied their trade, the sea had been the highway to Melbourne and Sydney, and Canberra wasn't even a twinkle in Australia's eye.

Released from work a few hours later, Alice slumped on the same couch she'd lain on as a child—albeit reupholstered—only unlike when she was a kid, no one was home to fuss over her, stroke her forehead and tell her a favorite story. Although it had been years since either Karen or Peter had recounted the story of her birth—her surprise arrival twenty minutes after Libby's—it was part of the Hunter family's folklore. Not once as either a kid or an adult had Alice ever begrudged Libby her first-born status. Her theatrical soul preferred the story of her more exciting birth.

Her parents were out of town on their annual Melbourne vacation. They maintained that the big city in January was far more peaceful than Kurnai Bay, and they had a point. In previous years, Karen and Peter had stayed with Alice in her beloved Victorian terrace house in leafy Albert Park. This year, they'd rented a two-bedroom apartment in Docklands through Airbnb. They'd wanted Alice to come with them and although part of her appreciated their invitation, she'd rather walk over shards of glass than visit Melbourne. It hurt a little that her parents didn't understand that.

Alice's bug, which had been busy lobbing its fever and energy-stealing weaponry on her body, finally reached her mind. It easily breached the defenses she'd spent months bricking into place. Helplessly, she felt herself tumbling back into the quagmire of despair that had claimed her once before and she'd fought so hard to leave. A sob rose to the back of her throat and combining with her snot-clogged nose, she choked. Coughing violently, she sat up fast. Tubby, the family's elderly cat, meowed indignantly and sank his claws into Alice's thighs to stall his slide off her lap.

"Ouch! Play nice, Tubby." She leaned over the cat and grabbed tissues before lying back on the cushions. So, this was what her wonderful life had been reduced to? She was thirty-three and a half, ambivalently single, back living under her parents' roof, working minimum wage jobs, and so full of goop she couldn't cry and breathe at the same time. Hell, she couldn't even be sick right.

Her phone rang and she snatched it up. "Hi, Libs."

"You sound like death warmed up," her twin said.

"Summer cold."

"Poor you. It's going around. Thank God, I'm on a half-day. The clinic's been full of sad-sack tourists for two days and I'm over the monotony of doling out tissues and sympathy. By 11:00, I found myself daydreaming about broken bones and chest pain."

Alice laughed, immediately coughed and imagined Libby holding the phone away from her ear. She managed a strangled, "Sorry."

"I was calling to invite you for dinner. Nick's barbecuing and Jess is coming, but it sounds like you need to stay in bed."

Libby didn't say, "and not infect the rest of us" but it was there in her doctor's tone. Her twin had always been direct and never put up with any nonsense—not even when they were children. Unlike Alice, Libby had always known exactly what she wanted and set out to make it happen. When Alice was compared to Libby's single-minded determination and competitive streak, she came across as dreamy, vague and aimless.

"Do you need anything, Al? I've got some soup in the freezer I could drop-off."

"Thanks, but I'm fine."

"If you're sure. Yell out if you change your mind. I'll call tomorrow."

The line fell silent and Alice lay picturing tonight's dinner. Her nieces and Jess's little boy would charge around playing on the soft Santa Ana lawn while Nick cooked and kid wrangled. He'd pour Libby and Jess a glass of wine and insist they relax and "catch up," as if the two women rarely saw each other. The reality was Libby and Jess talked every day and met face-to-face at least three times a week.

A pale green snake slithered through Alice, although she didn't know if it was headed toward the children, Nick—a prince among men —or Libby's twenty-year friendship with Jess. Didn't all the twin studies prove that twins are each other's best friend? And yet, she and Libby were the exception to the rule.

For the first thirteen years of her life, Alice had struggled to keep up with Libby, who was smarter and more coordinated than she'd ever be, but the one thing that had sustained her was being her twin's best friend. Everything changed the day Jess arrived in Kurnai Bay and Libby's focus shifted away from Alice. Suddenly, her twin was just a sister. It was the first time Alice experienced true heartache. Now she was a pro, although she wasn't certain she was any better at dealing with it.

Karen had tried consoling a sobbing Alice, telling her it was normal for girls to have a wide circle of friends with different interests and that Libby's friendship with Jess didn't mean she loved Alice any less. But Alice didn't see it that way. Jess was everything Alice wasn't: worldly, street smart, edgy and confident. Dangerous even, although only Alice thought that. Her mother had dismissed her concerns as "nonsense'"

Karen, usually so cautious about people outside of their social circle, happily welcomed Jess to Pelican House. Once, when a frustrated Alice complained that Jess was "always here," Karen had replied firmly, "Her life hasn't been as easy as yours."

Alice's early years had been a continuous round of therapies—speech, occupational, physiotherapy—with Karen constantly pushing her to practice her reading, writing and times tables. She hadn't thought her life was particularly easy. She'd gone to bed each night hoping the intense friendship would burn out and that Jess would tire of Libby. But far from fracturing, the friendship deepened, leaving Alice firmly on the outside whenever Jess was around.

Now all three of them were grown and back in the bay, Alice was finding it harder than ever to catch her twin on her own. Not that Nick was the problem—it was Jess who left Alice feeling thirteen again and a third wheel. Or did she just allow herself to feel like that? Was she the problem? She got a definite vibe from Libby that her twin believed she was. Judging by the therapy podcasts she'd been bingeing recently —it was voyeurism catnip—feeling this way was probably due to some deep-seated insecurities from childhood. It seemed *everything* stemmed from childhood. The problem was, Alice's childhood had been rock-solid stable and full of love. It was her adulthood that was proving the challenge.

Six months earlier, everything Alice believed to be true about her adult life had blown up with the force of a terrorist's bomb, shattering her life in ways she'd never thought possible. Lawrence, the love of her life, her partner of three years and the future father of her brown-eyed, curly-haired children, had taken her to their favorite restaurant—the venue of their first date. Giddy with excitement, Alice had spent the day anticipating a proposal and an engagement ring. Instead she got, "It's not you, it's me. I just don't love you enough."

Whenever she looked back on that cold July night, facing Lawrence across the table as he worked through his printed list of their shared possessions, she still couldn't fathom how she'd managed to eat a meal and participate in the destruction of their thirty-six months together.

"You take the Creuset cookware and I'll keep the DeLonghi coffee machine," he'd suggested.

"Because you don't cook and I don't appreciate coffee?"

"Exactly."

"What about the Emily Kame Kngwarreye? We both appreciate that." They'd bought the canvas at auction a year before. It was Alice's first big art investment, but it had also been an investment in Lawrence.

"I don't want to sell it just yet."

Through the anesthetizing shock, Alice had managed a moment of clarity. As much as she loved the painting, she couldn't afford to buy Lawrence out and she needed money to eat. "Then we get it independently appraised and you pay me half."

Lawrence's grimace had been the first sign that their separation might leave a flesh wound.

Lawrence still lived in the house Alice had lovingly decorated, only now he shared it with another woman who wore his great-grandmother's antique diamond. The effect of "not being loved enough" had hit Alice with the devastation of a tsunami. Within hours, she'd lost her home, her job in Lawrence's family's high-end art auction house and her friends. That had felled her as much as losing Lawrence. She hadn't anticipated the loss of their friends, but as they'd been his friends first, they'd closed ranks after the separation and locked her out. Alone and jobless, she homed like a pigeon, desperately seeking reassurance that someone still loved her.

Her life had been officially declared a train wreck by everyone who'd heard the story. And since this was the bay, not only had *everyone* heard the story, they'd gleefully discussed it at the Returned Soldiers League—RSL—the supermarket, the marina—hell, she was surprised it hadn't gotten its own segment on Kurnai Bay community radio. People greeted her with sympathy for her circumstances, but it was always overlaid with sheer relief that they weren't being forced to start over when societal rules declared that your thirties were prime time for career advancement and personal success.

Her parents and Libby had tiptoed around her for a couple of weeks, her mother hovering like a hawk. Then the advice kicked in.

"Today's the perfect day to get up, shower and go for a walk along the coast." Her mother threw open the bedroom curtains. "Spring sunshine and a calm sea soothes the soul. I'll come with you."

Her dad handed her a piece of paper with a phone number scrawled on it. "The RSL needs a part-timer at the bar."

"Don't give him your power," Libby instructed with the certainty of a woman who'd never been dumped.

Alice had hunkered down, concentrating on getting through each day. For the first time in years, she'd embraced the prohibitive distance between herself and Melbourne. If it wasn't for those 280 miles, she'd likely have stalked her old home, been caught standing in the yard at 02:00 screaming "Why?" and been arrested for slashing the tires on Lawrence's and Laetitia's cars. Who knew isolation was protective?

By the time December arrived—those festive weeks that shine a spotlight on singledom and mark it out as failure—she didn't fall apart.

Her New Year resolutions didn't include "meeting someone", but did include plans to pursue her own interests so she was a fully evolved woman. She didn't need a man to be happy, and besides, she was far too busy juggling four jobs. Who had time to date, let alone the energy?

But on this hot January day, illness was shooting its DNA into her cells with the accuracy of an archer, and its message overrode her single life convictions with targeted precision.

You're not pursuing any interests and you're so far from being self-actualized, Maslow would boot you to the bottom of his pyramid. You haven't contributed any money to your retirement fund in six months. You're lonely. You're scared. Alone. Childless. Just an auntie. Abject failure.

McDougall, her parents' border collie, wandered in and, sensing Alice's mood, laid his head on her chest. Tubby stretched out a paw as if to bat the dog away but his claws stayed sheathed. Doleful brown collie eyes and challenging green cat ones stared up at Alice—sympathy and provocation. Tubby was having none of her wallowing.

Whether it was the cat's disdain for her pity party or the pseudoephedrine kicking in with its can-do attitude—or a combination of the two—she unceremoniously dumped Tubby off her lap, sat up and flipped open her laptop. If she wanted a shot at what sixty-four per cent of the adult population took for granted, there was nothing wrong with taking control of her life. She'd be more of a cliché if she sat around eating ice cream than being proactive. Bringing up a browser, she typed in, "best dating sites." 760,000,000 results came up. Her heart raced and she snapped the lid shut. Tubby gave her a death stare.

"Okay, fine." She reopened the computer and clicked on a site that explained ten of the most popular dating sites and apps. She quickly ruled out Boomer Singles, LGBTIQ Matchmaker and Hookup Heaven. She was looking for love, commitment and the promise of children. One site boasted over 25,000 marriages so she clicked on the link.

A box appeared on the screen. Name? Email? Zip code? Too easy.

How many children do you have? As she typed 0, the ache she'd fought to banish reappeared.

Date of birth? Alice typed in the unforgiving truth and then her finger hovered over the delete key. Her thirty-fourth birthday was six months away. Was that old? Was the truth overrated? But lying on the fifth question didn't seem to be best practice so she left the year unaltered. Ethnicity? Boring white Anglo-Saxon, although her father's swarthy skin hinted at something a little more interesting at some point back in the day. Perhaps she should be answering questions on Ancestry.com instead of here. Religion? Not really. Education level? Post grad. Her fingers flew. She could do this.

Occupation? Alice's fingers paused, drumming lightly on the keys. What to write? Unemployed art catalog designer? Not quite fully qualified art auctioneer? Waitress? Boat cleaner? She typed "journalist," justifying she was writing the community events notices for the *Kurnai Bay Gazette* and the occasional interview and opinion piece.

Income? So much less than it had been.

Height? 5'5".

Smoke? Never. Karen's drug education had terrified Alice so much she'd never even been tempted to try a cigarette.

Drink? If you're offering. She got up and poured herself a glass of wine.

What are you passionate about? World peace. *Now you sound like Miss Universe.* She hit backspace and gulped down half the glass of wine. What was she passionate about? Once she would have said art history, but that led straight back to Lawrence. Staying solvent didn't sound attractive nor did sorting the recycling. That was her current passion—bug bear really.

How hard was it for people to sort the bottles and the papers from the waste? Judging by the restaurant bins, which she dealt with at the end of each shift, and the hash the tourists made of the bins in the main street and the caravan park, it was very hard indeed. Did they want the white sand beach and the ocean they loved so much to be a flotilla of plastic bags?

Thinking of the sea, she typed "sailing" as her passion and vowed to dust off the Laser, which she hadn't sailed in years. Or ask Nick if she could tag along as crew on the Wednesday afternoon race.

The dots at the bottom of the screen did a flashing run and then the words *Compatibility Quiz* appeared accompanied by seven buttons of graduated colors with the words *Not at all, Somewhat* and *Very well* strung under them. Above the buttons it said, *How well does this word describe you?* Beneath the sentence red words dominated. Stable? Energetic? Affectionate? Intelligent? Compassionate? Loyal? Witty? Very well. Very, very well!

Stylish? Sensual? Sexy? She looked down at her old shorts and stained T-shirt. Had once been all three, although not necessarily at the same time. Was not currently but could be again. Would be when her nose stopped dripping.

Athletic? Compared to Libby, not at all. Compared with the average Australian, very well. Heck, she walked to work.

Content? Very well. The bug mocked her. She changed it to the next button down and refused to alter it again.

Patient? *This quiz is testing me.* God, there were six more sections like this to complete.

How well does this word describe you: Bossy, irritable, aggressive, outspoken, opinionated, selfish, stubborn? Who in their right mind would ever admit to these things when they're looking for a prospective partner, let alone a date?

The next section was titled, *Talk to us about your feelings* and the choices for the seven buttons changed to *Rarely, Occasionally and Almost always.* In the last month have you felt happy, sad, anxious, fearful of the future, out of control, angry, depressed, misunderstood, plotted against? Do your palms sweat when you meet new people?

Her entire body was a dripping mess of sweat. She closed the laptop and switched on the air conditioner, fanning herself with a copy of the latest edition of the *Gazette*. It was open on an advertisement for a new resort and the photos showed a family romping on the giant inflatable jumping pillow and swimming in the pool. The three children had curly hair.

The ache inside Alice burned. She wanted children and technically in today's progressive society she could have a child and raise it on her own without stigma. Women did it all the time, although she had a sneaking suspicion that only a very small percentage—either straight or gay—chose to do it that way. Jess was one of those women and strident in her conviction that she was better off having a child on her own instead of involving a man who, would invariably let her down.

But Alice wasn't Jess. She wanted a partner—she wanted to be part of a team like her parents, and her twin. She'd watched Libby and Nick in action often enough to know that even with a hands-on partner and grandparents to fall back on, there were times when parenthood was a hard slog. Alice wanted more than just to endure motherhood, she wanted to enjoy it. She wanted to share the experience with someone who wanted it as much as she did.

Whether it was being sick or just the inevitable outcome of circumstances, Alice's New Year's resolutions that had defended her single life now fell away, exposing a battered but intact belief. Yes, there were happy women actively choosing to live a single life and Alice admired their convictions. Good for them. But Alice wasn't one of them. They weren't her tribe and she'd erroneously hitched her wagon to their cause, thinking it would give her strength and purpose.

The problem was she hadn't chosen to be single—that decision had been forced upon her. In her fevered state she saw two roads in front of her. The popular and oft-quoted road: "One day when you least expect it, Alice, you'll meet somebody." But she couldn't imagine the odds of randomly meeting The One would be in her favor in a city of four million, let alone in a town of roughly 3,000, even when she factored in the 30,000 summer swell.

The second road was the online match. Why had she been so stridently opposed to it before? She had a vague memory of lecturing some poor bloke at the RSL who'd kindly—albeit misguidedly—tried to make her feel better by telling her about his son who "did the on the line dating, love. Met a lovely girl." After all, how was using a website to find a match any different from cultures who used a matchmaker? Or family and friends? Most importantly, the website she'd chosen was backed by science!

Social science, not real science.

Alice ignored Libby's voice in her head and reopened the laptop. She faced the next quiz statement—I am looking for a long-term exclusive relationship.

Absolutely agree.

Then channeling the "fake it till you make it" mantra, she tackled the dreaded profile.

AliceIsWonderland33

I find adventure all around me in the big and little things. The silver flash of a dolphin, the shriek of corellas as they dart across a pink sky and the way a painting can transport me to a different place. I love living the outdoor life on the coast and when I'm not sailing or hiking, I'm enjoying novels and doing the quiz in the weekend papers. Are you up for a trivia showdown? I love robust conversations over cups of tea and debates over red wine. I can't hold a tune but I don't let that stop me.

The real Alice was buried in there somewhere.

Libby hung up the phone and chewed her lip. Even when Alice was a hundred per cent well, she didn't always accept her invitations, but should she be taking her twin at her word that she was fine? Alice hadn't been fine since that bastard broke her heart and destroyed her dreams. Libby still couldn't believe what Lawrence had done to Alice, let alone how he'd done it. Against Nick's advice, she'd texted the scumbag, telling him exactly what she thought of him. He'd replied with an infuriating "Sorry." It had left her enraged for days.

Sorry was so easy. So glib. So *not enough*. Lawrence wasn't the one watching Alice barely existing and just going through the motions. Worrying about her. Recently though, her twin did seem happier, but on a scale from devastated to content, it wasn't that big a shift up the line.

Of course, it could be that right now Alice was frantically paddling under the surface like the rest of the town. The irony of living in a tourist destination was that summer was far from relaxing. It brought sunshine and a shipload of stress for the locals as they created a laid-back environment for vacationers. It didn't leave much time to think about anything other than the job at hand. Not thinking about things was a new approach to life for Libby, but one she'd been perfecting for almost two and a half years.

It had been a revelation to her how much easier it was to focus on other people's problems instead of dealing with her own. Thank goodness for patients—they had plenty of problems to keep her occupied. She thought about Jess. Her best friend was far from being a problem—she was a blessing—and her return to the bay had been the lone bright spot in a very dark time. Jess's company always filled Libby with a mixture of joy and exhilaration. Unlike Alice, who either procrastinated until Libby was ready to scream or acted impulsively, Jess always knew what she wanted and went for it. It was a character trait Libby recognized in herself and she'd admired it in Jess from the first day she'd watched the thirteen-year-old sauntering through the school gates on a hot November morning.

Wearing foundation and eyeliner, a far-too-short school dress and her long black hair cascading across her shoulders in a mass of unrestrained curls, the new girl had broken at least three uniform rules. But that wasn't the reason everyone took a second glance. Jess's utilitarian school uniform clung to her curves, leaving nothing to the imagination. It was in stark contrast to Libby's dress, which fell sack-like from her shoulders, because Karen had insisted on buying a dress one size too big. "It's expensive and you'll grow into it." But her mother's practicality hid breasts that filled a bra and Libby chafed against the uniform that stripped her body of all signs that she was no longer a child, but a woman. Why couldn't her mother see that?

But it wasn't Jess's sense of style that impressed Libby the most, it was the fact she was her own person. She refused to accept a hard time from anyone and she didn't conform or care what the other girls thought of her—she walked her own path. Jess's "I don't give a damn" attitude was intoxicating. It was a freedom Libby had never experienced. She'd been raised to always consider how her actions might affect others, especially her twin. But recently, she'd had intense moments when she wanted to scream and break free. Do what she wanted without having to worry about anyone else's feelings.

To be a separate person from Alice.

Libby had made the first friendship move, inviting Jess to Pelican House. After the successful first visit, she'd expected a return invitation, but Jess had continued walking home with the twins and whenever Libby hinted that they go to Jess's house, her new friend ignored her. This frustrated Libby, because she wanted alone time with Jess and that was impossible at Pelican House. Eventually Libby took the situation into her own hands. Telling her mother she was visiting the van den Bergs, she bicycled to where she thought Jess lived—her friend had been vague about her exact address. At first, she thought she must have the wrong house—weeds dominated the few scraggly plants, the car in the driveway looked like an old clunker and the paint on the clapboards was peeling off in strips—but the other houses in the street didn't look much different. Libby knocked hesitantly and relaxed the moment Jess answered the door.

"Hi!"

Jess scowled from around the barely open door. "What are you doing here?"

"I thought we could hang out. You know, just us."

"I didn't think you went anywhere without your shadow."

The need to be her own woman rose above Libby's guilt about leaving Alice behind. "We don't do everything together."

Jess didn't look like she believed her so Libby added, "I do surf lifesaving. Alice doesn't."

"Does she do anything except watch you do stuff?"

"Not really."

"Your twin's kind of a baby."

Although Jess had just articulated exactly what Libby thought, the need to defend her twin was instinctive. "It's not her fault she's immature. She was sick when we were little."

"What's that got to do with it?"

Libby hesitated and then gave in to the nub of the problem. "Alice does everything slower than me. She doesn't have her period yet."

"Or boobs. Does she even notice guys?"

Libby sighed. "No."

"Lucky for you, I came to town." But Jess still hadn't opened the door any wider.

Libby smiled. "So can I come in? I brought double chocolate Tim Tams."

Jess snorted. "Of course you did." But she accepted the packet and finally let Libby in, hustling her down a narrow hall lined with cardboard boxes. Libby glanced sideways into rooms, glimpsing a television balanced precariously on old wooden fish co-op boxes, cereal bowls from breakfast still on the kitchen table along with white bags from the drug store and a bottle of rum. Where were the cut flowers? The lace tablecloth? The computer in its dedicated corner? The books? The aroma of dinner cooking? Nothing about this house said home. Before Libby could think of a compliment—Karen had taught her to always say something nice—Jess pushed her into a room and slammed the door.

Jess's bedroom was as neat and tidy as the rest of the house was cluttered. Posters of Pink and Justin Timberlake were blu-tacked on the walls and there was a stack of *Seventeen* and *Cosmopolitan* magazines by her bed. This stack impressed Libby the most—it was the equivalent of finding a Bardot CD at the thrift shop. Karen had rejected her recent request to read *Seventeen*, telling her she needed to be fifteen. Libby hadn't dared ask how old she needed to be to read *Cosmopolitan*. While Jess curled up on her bed painting her nails black, Libby devoured every copy of *Seventeen* before moving on to the far more daring *Cosmo*.

If she'd flashed hot and cold thinking about her crush while she read "seventy-eight ways to turn him on," it was the "hotter sex for you" that sent her home determined to find something called her clitoris. Before that fateful afternoon, she hadn't known she had one. It was like stepping into a whole new world and she thanked the universe for introducing her to Jess.

The magazines and other forbidden things in Jess's room were the first secrets Libby kept from Alice. Her twin wouldn't understand—she was still drawing butterflies and fairies in her sketch book and watching *Saddle Club* when Libby railed to watch *Big Brother* and *E.R.* While Alice was content to stay a little girl, Libby wanted to date boys and experiment with the divine rush of feelings she got playing with herself in the bath.

When Libby asked her parents for her own bedroom, Alice cried. Libby didn't feel as bad as she should have for upsetting her twin.

Jess and Libby became inseparable. Although Karen acknowledged Libby's right to have her own friend, she frequently insisted Alice tag along. It hadn't worked particularly well when they were thirteen and by the time they were seventeen, it was a disaster. Alice always gave off a critical vibe that made Libby feel as if it was her fault her twin wasn't enjoying herself.

After one party, Jess said, "Your twin's such a killjoy. We always have way more fun without her."

And that was the problem—they did.

It wasn't that Libby wanted Alice to become best friends with Jess —she didn't want to share her friend that much. But as they grew into their twenties, she wished Alice could see past "party-girl Jess" and glimpse the Jess Libby admired the most: the woman who'd worked hard to move herself up, out and away from her poverty-ridden childhood.

The clink of the childproof lock closing on the side gate brought Libby back to the present. Thankfully, the three of them had matured and all that drama had faded. Real life had made sure of that, giving them far more important things to worry about. Despite the unhappy circumstances that had propelled Alice's return to Pelican House, Libby appreciated how much of an effort her twin was making with Jess. Leo helped. He was such a cute and engaging kid, and Alice was a sucker for babies.

Poor Alice. The Lawrence effect hadn't only stolen her hopes that she'd soon be a mother, it had stripped her of her security—emotional and financial. Unlike Jess, Alice didn't have a skill set Libby could employ at the medical practice. At least Nick had found Alice some work, but even so, her twin was still struggling to earn a decent wage.

"Daddy! Come for a swim." Her daughters' voices drifted through the open window. She couldn't quite make out Nick's rumbling reply, but it was probably something like, "Hang tight. I'll be there in a minute."

As she pressed a glass against the fridge's iced water dispenser, filling it for their Wednesday joke, Nick's shoes hit the boot box with a clunk and his keys dropped into the dish with a tinkle. Then he was walking up to her, his generous mouth creased in a familiar grin.

"Honey, I'm home," he said laconically.

Most days, Nick arrived home from work before she did so he only had a limited number of opportunities to use the line. He never missed his chance.

She rolled her eyes and stepped into his embrace. He smelt reassuringly of sunshine, salt and teak oil along with a hint of engine grease.

"Good day?" Libby handed Nick the glass of cold water. This was her side of the joke—pretending to be the dutiful 1950's housewife waiting to honor her man when he came home hot and tired after a long, hard day.

Nick kissed the top of her head. "Not bad. I had to rescue a tourist who'd gotten stuck on a sandbar, but it got me out of the office and onto the water, so that was a win."

"I bet you had to fight your dad for that job."

"Yeah. Lucky I took the call."

"And let me guess, you didn't rush straight back to base?"

"I might have thrown in a quick line."

She laughed, knowing him as well as he knew himself.

Salt spray ran in the Pirellis' veins. In 1923, Nick's great-grandfather had arrived in Australia from Italy with a battered suitcase and a dream. Over three generations, the family had transformed from the physically rigorous life of professional fishing to the less demanding one of charter fishing and small boat rental. Five years earlier, they'd added luxury yachts and motor cruisers to the fleet. Tourists paid big bucks to sail them around the largest navigable inland waterway in Australia—the Gippsland Lakes. Nick ran the company with his father Rick, who was technically retired, although only during the off season. During the summer, he worked as many hours as his son and the rest of their staff.

Nick gave a contented sigh. "The water's divine today and the breeze is just strong enough to make it fun. It's been ages since we sailed together. Let's go out for a couple of hours and kick back."

Libby glanced through the glass doors, checking the girls, who were occupied with a water play set. "It sounds great but I've already defrosted some meat and invited Jess for dinner."

Nick's dark brows pulled down sharply, carving a furrow across the bridge of his nose. "Why?"

His question surprised her. Hospitality was Nick's religion. Raised by two outgoing parents, he was always meeting people and inviting them round for a home-cooked meal or wood-fired pizza baked in the oven he'd built in the back yard. He regularly adopted the backpackers who worked for him, bringing them home and feeding them up before inviting them to lounge on the couch and use the laundry so they could pretend they were home for a night.

"Because it's my half-day. I thought it was a good time to catch up."

Nick drained the icy water, his Adam's apple bobbing quickly. "Catch up? Jess comes to dinner every Thursday and Sunday. Plus, we saw her last night when she picked up Leo and stayed for a drink."

"She moved down here to be close to us. We're her family."

"Yeah, but even with family, the fish goes off on the fourth visit in one week."

"Your mother's over more than that."

"Yeah, but she's babysitting."

"You were the one who suggested at Christmas that Leo spend more time with the girls to offset the fact he's an only child."

A sulky look entered his eyes. "All I'm saying is you could have checked with me before you made plans."

Irritation needled her—she hadn't done anything out of the ordinary. "And if you wanted to go sailing tonight, you could have given me a heads up and texted at lunchtime."

"Jeez, I thought it would be a nice surprise, okay?" Nick jerked his hand through his sun-bleached chestnut hair. "Remember spontaneity?"

She did. But it had been such a long time since they'd been spontaneous. Kids and jobs did that to a couple. So did grief, loss and sadness. An ache that had never completely vanished throbbed its dull pain through her. "We can go sailing tomorrow night."

"Since when are you home early enough on a Thursday? Besides, the weather's changing tomorrow. There's a big blow coming in." His tone oozed the disappointment of a kid whose kite kept slamming into the ground instead of soaring high and free.

These days, few things made Libby truly happy and despite Nick's reassurances that he was "all good," perhaps he wasn't doing as well as he professed to be either. The ache intensified and she fought it with a sudden desire to give Nick what he wanted. If he was happy, perhaps she would be too. "Okay, let's be spontaneous. Sailing's on."

"Yes!" He snaked an arm around her, pulling her in close before lowering his mouth to hers. His kiss overflowed with excitement, enthusiasm and optimism—just like his kisses of old. It was innocent of the heavy weight life had dropped on them two and a half years earlier. A weight that was too slow in relieving its pressure.

"If I get the girls sorted, can you do the food? I've got plenty of drinks on *Freedom* so we only need bread and sausages, some fruit and a packet of Tim Tams. We can go to Bunga Arm and barbecue on the beach." Nick winked at her. "Shame we can't stay the night, *tesoro mio.*"

Libby remembered the first night they'd slept on the beach. It was the third time she'd been out on *Andiamo* but the first time without the added company of Nick's mate, Will Azzopardi. They'd dropped anchor and swum off the yacht, but when it was time to return home, the wind had dropped. Nick had tried starting the motor but despite his legendary skills with an engine, it had failed to turn over. All these years later, Libby still didn't know if it had been a ploy of Nick's to deliberately maroon them on an isolated beach on a star-filled night or if it was just serendipity. Either way, they'd been together ever since.

Libby pressed her palm flat on Nick's chest. "Even if we didn't have to show up at work in the morning, I'm not sure sharing the beach with the girls, Jess and Leo would exactly recreate that night."

"I thought it was just us and the girls?"

"It can be next time, but I can't dump Jess for sailing at such short notice."

Nick crossed his arms. "She can't come."

"Wait? What? Why?"

"Leo is why. He's thirteen months and can barely walk on land."

Libby didn't understand. They'd taken the girls out on *Freedom* plenty of times when they were babies. "But you just said it's a divine evening and smooth sailing. We'll stick Leo in a lifejacket and put the girls' old harness on him. He'll be fine."

Nick's phone buzzed and he pulled it out of his pocket, read the text, then swore. "Looks like it's a moot point anyway. I have to go back to work."

Libby didn't ask why—she didn't need to. Whatever the minute details, the big picture was always the same: it involved a tourist. It was a common occurrence for them both in January. "I guess I'll see you when I see you."

He nodded, gave her a distracted kiss and grabbed his keys.

"Nick."

"Yeah?"

"The next perfect sailing Wednesday, I promise it's a family date. Or better yet, we can get Alice or Jess to mind the girls and go to Bunga Arm alone."

"Sure."

But the light in his eyes had extinguished and Libby got a sense of having literally missed the boat.

CHAPTER TWO

Jess filled Libby's wine glass. "Here's to my favorite time of day: when our children are fast asleep."

Libby clinked her glass against Jess's. "Amen to that but don't get too comfortable. The kitchen's a disaster."

Jess sat back on Libby's generously wide couch, settling comfortably into her usual spot with Monty the Jack Russell curled up next to her. She'd cooked the barbecue and made the salads so the last thing she wanted to do was rouse herself to do the dishes. "Won't Nick weave his usual magic when he gets back, you spoilt and pampered woman?"

Libby rolled her eyes. "You make it sound like I never wash up."

"I don't see you do it very often."

"That's because whenever you're over Nick treats us."

"Well, I'm over, so problem solved."

"He got called back to work tonight so it's not fair to expect him to do the dishes."

Jess wasn't certain Libby really knew all that much about fair. "Work? You're always saying Nick gets paid to do what he loves most, which is mucking about in boats. It's us who've been wrangling hot and tired kids."

"And Nick's dealing with a disgruntled customer who can easily have a tanty on TripAdvisor. Those sorts of reviews hurt the business."

"Sure, I get it. Someone stuffed up and it's a pain that Nick's got to sort it, but don't feel too sorry for him. This morning, Leo and I were walking along the pier just as he was sailing out. You should have seen the huge wave he gave us. We both know grumpy men don't do that. Judging by the Snapchat he sent you half an hour ago, he looks far from stressed."

"You think so?"

"I do." Jess stroked Monty's ears and he rested his head on her lap. "Why do you sound so surprised? Are you worried about him? I thought you said things were better?"

"Oh, I don't know. Sometimes it feels like even though Nick's standing next to me, he's very far away."

"You know that's just the normal January crazy. If I had to call it today, I'd say your husband's content."

The worried look vanished from Libby's eyes. "He really did look happy, didn't he? Thanks for talking me down."

"Any time. It's what friends do."

"And I really appreciate it. You do so much for me and I don't just mean cooking Thursday night dinner or being our emergency backstop with the girls."

"Oh, stop," Jess joked and then sobered. "You know I feel the same way, right? Without your help, I couldn't have come back to the bay."

Monty made a gurgling sound that was pure doggie delight. "I swear he loves you more than Nick or me."

"If you and Nick sat down more he'd snuggle up to you too."

"Maybe you're right." Libby stretched out on her couch and yawned. "Let's leave the dishes."

"That's the spirit." Jess refilled her glass, enjoying the Yarra Valley sauv blanc. She always drank the wine on offer in the Hunter-Pirelli household, because at home she'd reverted to the beverage of her youth

—rum and Coke. She preferred it to the less than stellar wine her budget could afford. During her years of working in Melbourne's then Sydney's finance sectors, the corporate functions had supplemented her lifestyle in a way her current salary never could. It had been far too easy to get used to the finer things in life—the top-shelf alcohol, the seventy-dollar rib eye and the junkets both domestic and international. That life had been so far removed from the privations of her childhood that if she didn't think about her first eighteen years—and she chose not to—it was easy to pretend they hadn't existed.

Dusty memories rippled across her mind. "Lib, remember the day we met?"

Her best friend smiled. "Funny! I was just thinking about it this afternoon. You walked into school like you owned it and every boy's head snapped round so fast it probably hurt. I felt like such a dork in comparison. I'm never subjecting Lucy and Indi to clothes that don't fit properly. You know I *never* grew into that school dress."

"Oh, yeah. Karen scarred you for life, for sure."

Libby flinched. "Sorry. That was a stupid and thoughtless thing to say."

"Don't be silly. Moving to Kurnai Bay and meeting you and your family was the best thing that ever happened to me." Jess shuddered. "I don't want to think about what my life might have been if Mom had moved somewhere else."

Unlike Libby, Jess didn't remember the exact moment they'd met, which was apparently just outside the school office door. She didn't even remember which eviction notice had precipitated her mother's fast move to the bay—over the years the many night-time departures had run together in a gut-churning blur—but she did remember her first day at Kurnai Bay High School. Thanks to her mother's flaky choice in boyfriends and her ability to run up debts and erode goodwill wherever they lived, the school had been her eighth. She knew the drill: 1. Show no weakness—any sign of neediness was social suicide. 2. Act as if nothing bothered her—fire back smartarse comments to any loser who tried to put her down. 3. Stay aloof just enough to be mysterious—use the time to work out who was who, which group ruled and who was worth knowing. 4. Wait for the cool group to approach her.

Jess pegged Libby as an annoying goodie two-shoes within ten minutes of their first class and not worth her time. The golden-haired girl had read the novel and shot her hand up to every question the dippy English teacher asked. A total suck-up. But at lunchtime, Jess watched in disbelief as Libby not only drifted easily between groups of girls but was welcomed by them all. Jess knew groups didn't usually operate that way. They demanded total allegiance and dropped any members who strayed. Yet Libby Hunter seemed to have amnesty and Jess couldn't work out why. The girl wasn't cool but then again, she wasn't a total dork like her twin sister, Alice.

When Libby approached Jess on her second day, she didn't know which way to jump.

"Jess! Wanna come to my place after school? We can do our homework and then hang out. It'll be fun."

Jess never wasted her own time doing homework—that was why first period existed. It was Libby's link between homework and fun that decided her. "I don't think so."

Libby's face screwed up in an odd mix of sympathy and frustration. "Is it cos your mom doesn't know us and you're not allowed? That's easy. My mom will call your mom. What's her number?"

Uncharacteristically lost for words, Jess had stared at Libby while outrage and confusion warred inside her. Who was this alien? Who had a mother who telephoned other people's mothers? It was the permission angle that finally released her indignant words.

"Of course I'm allowed to come!"

So, she went to Pelican House and it opened her eyes to a world she hadn't known existed. It was a place where food was plentiful, the kitchen was clean and women were respected. Jess wondered if that was what love looked like and then instantly dismissed it. She'd learned over many long years not to trust anything at first glance.

A couple of weeks later, during her first dinner at the Hunters' long red-gum table, she knew she'd been right to heed her instincts. The federal election was only a few days away and between mouthfuls of roast lamb, Karen Hunter announced that she was planning to vote for the Greens. Peter was unimpressed and the two argued, pitting their opinions and beliefs against the other's. Throughout the exchange, Alice placidly kept eating, Libby quoted statistics about wind-farms and Jess silently shrank into her chair, desperately wishing she could fade until she was invisible. Her breath solidified in her chest while she waited for Peter to land the inevitable blow—a sharp and stinging slap across Karen's cheek or a vicious shove that would push her to the floor.

But neither of those things happened. Peter eventually let out a long sigh. "If you want to waste your vote on a party with no real power that's not even ten years old—"

"It's hardly wasted." Karen gesticulated wildly. "After the debacle that was the *Tampa* incident, my vote's stating my immense disappointment with the Labor Party's stance on refugees."

"Fair enough." Peter looked down the table. "So, girls, who's up for ice cream?"

Jess's breath had rushed out of her lungs so fast she coughed, but her next drew in the possibility of change—was there a future for her that was very different from her mother's life? After that night, she'd listened carefully to the Hunter adults discussing all sorts of issues with the twins from budgeting pocket money to philanthropy, career advice and negotiating curfews. The idea of a curfew was utterly foreign to Jess. She came and went as she pleased and on the few occasions Linda bothered to ground her, she used the window instead of the door.

One afternoon in October, during her final year at school, Jess arrived at Pelican House to discover that Peter had taken the twins to the trampoline park as a treat after a weekend spent studying. Karen invited her in, offered her tea and cake then immediately put her to work helping her peel potatoes for the Sunday night roast. Karen did this sort of thing a lot and Jess was never sure how she felt about it. Part of her thought it was slave labor but another part enjoyed it, especially on the rare occasions she got Karen to herself.

"How were the practice exams?" Karen asked.

"Pointless. I skipped them."

Karen's hand paused on the knife she was using to peel a pumpkin, her breath seeming to slow. "They're a tool to show you where you need to concentrate your study."

"Study is sooooo boring."

"Anything that doesn't interest us is boring, but sometimes we have to play the game to get what we want. You're a clever young woman, Jess. If you think school is boring, how do you think you'll find life at the co-op shucking oysters?"

Jess thought of her mother. "There's no way I'm working at the co-op."

"Great. There's your first goal." Karen returned to the pumpkin. "But if you want options, you have to work hard for them. You need to create opportunities for yourself. Passing Senior Year is the first step to avoid working at the co-op. Passing it well enough to go to university is even better. You can do whatever you set your mind to, but it's totally up to you."

The thought of being stuck in Kurnai Bay while Libby and Alice got to live in Melbourne propelled Jess back to serious study. When she received an offer from Monash University, she suggested to Libby they share a house close to campus. Of course, the Hunters insisted Alice share too. Jess wasn't thrilled about that, because underneath Alice's arty and distracted personality was an obstinacy that had gotten in the way of her and Libby's plans more than once. Jess had never fully trusted Alice not to tell Karen and Peter about some of their wilder adventures.

But for once, Alice's obstinacy had worked in her favor and Alice had moved somewhere closer to the Victorian College of the Arts. The absence of her disapproving aura freed up Libby to join Jess in experimenting with everything student life offered. This included

Dylan, one of their housemates, who was also their first shared boyfriend. Those years in the house had been some of the best of Jess's life. They'd shared so many things they'd never told anyone else and Jess always got a fizz of delight knowing she was closer to Libby than her twin. She was the sister Libby had picked—she was finally part of a real family, one of her own choosing.

Those years were also the ones that chiseled Jess's determination that her future lay far away from her mother's debilitating demands and the isolation of the bay. She was going to live a financially independent life, free from the sacrifice men and her biological family demanded. She was never going back.

And for a time, she'd gotten exactly what she thought she wanted.

Libby's touch on her arm brought Jess's thoughts back to the present. "Sorry, what?"

"I said, I'm glad you moved here too but I'm even happier you're back for good. I'm so glad you actually listened to me for once."

"I always listen, I just don't always agree. But this time you were right. Every single parent needs the sort of backup you and Nick give me." A complicated mix of emotions—mostly appreciation, but with a pinch of ingratitude—snagged her. Libby's offer of work meant her return was possible and yet ... She took another sip of wine and gave herself a shake. She needed and wanted their help—the early months with Leo had taught her that. "Are you okay if I do the payroll tomorrow instead of Friday?"

"Sure, no problem. By the way, Nick mentioned that Enza's retiring. I almost suggested he hire you to do the books but I thought I better run it past you first."

"That's sweet of you, but I think I'd feel funny doing the Pirellis' books."

Libby sat up. "Why? You've done amazing things for the practice. And you got us up to speed on compliance. You've saved me money."

"Thanks, but if I do the books for Pirellis too, there's not much I won't know about your financial situation."

"So? We trust you not to blab the information all over town, which is more than we can say about some people."

"Thanks, but ..." She spun the stem of the wine glass between her fingers, not sure which words could explain it best.

"I thought you were looking for new clients and you'd jump at the chance for more work." Libby's confusion and disappointment hung in the air. "I know things are a bit tight for you at the moment, but if you're serious about buying your own place—"

"Of course I'm serious. I'm totally over renting. And I feel bad that Nick always ends up doing the repairs my landlord never gets around to."

"Don't waste any time worrying about that. You know he's always happy to help. So how far away from buying are you?"

Jess really didn't want to discuss her house plans. "There are so many variables it's not worth predicting."

Libby's face was a mix of love and frustration. "And one of those variables is money, right? So take the job."

"Lib, you and Nick are like family to Leo and me. I don't want anything to jeopardize that."

"You *are* family! And it won't jeopardize anything. In fact, it makes sense. Nick's already told you how impressed he is with what you've done at the practice. Call him tomorrow."

Despite Nick's compliments on her work, he was a clever business man and Jess wasn't convinced he'd be quite so on-board with the idea as Libby. There was an inherent safety net in employing someone else.

"Jess? Promise me?"

She swallowed a sigh, knowing Libby wouldn't let the topic drop until she agreed. "Okay. But I have conditions. I'll only call after you've told him it's your idea, otherwise he'll think I'm ambushing him."

"Of course he won't think that. But if it makes you feel better, I'll take it one step further and let him think it was his idea to employ you." Libby laid down again. "So, have you got big plans for the weekend?"

Jess gave a wry laugh. "Huge."

Libby's eyes sparkled with interest. "I hope it involves Will Azzopardi? Nick said he's on shore this week."

Jess fiddled with her bracelet. "It might."

Libby squealed, the pitch and the tone identical to when they'd been fourteen and Jess had told her that Jack O'Loughlin had not only kissed her, he'd gone down on her and been surprisingly talented for a ginger. Right from the start of their friendship, Libby had always quizzed Jess on her love life. When they were teens, Jess knew Libby was living vicariously through her, too indoctrinated by Karen to risk going beyond French kissing. At university, she and Dylan had taught Libby a lot, but even so, whenever she had a date, she'd always sought Jess's advice right up until she'd met Nick. Once they were a love-drunk couple, Libby had tried to partner Jess with Nick's best friend. Years later, she was still doing it.

Jess's fingers fell from her bracelet. "My weekend also might not include Will. Who knows?"

"Jess! Will adores you. He's adored you for years. Why are you holding back?"

"I've got Leo to think about now."

A casual observer wouldn't have noticed Libby's mouth tighten, but Jess had known her for twenty years. "If you'd waited instead of rushing into things, Will could have been Leo's father."

"I think you're conveniently forgetting that when I got pregnant, Will was shacked up with Sharnee Dixon."

"And you're conveniently forgetting the conversation we had when I flew up to Sydney for our girls' weekend."

Jess hadn't forgotten that conversation—it had set her on an unexpected course that changed her life. But she wasn't going to tell Libby that. Sometimes her best friend's competitive nature, which extended to her need to be right, needled like a burr.

Libby's first pregnancy had ironed a wrinkle in Jess's rusted-on belief that motherhood would never be part of her life. Up until then, being a mother wasn't something she'd ever wanted or needed. No way was she ever risking doing to a kid what her mother had done to her. But Libby's second pregnancy turned that wrinkle into an unexpected but permanent crease. Whenever she cuddled her goddaughters, the urge to hold a child of her own brought tears to her eyes.

The strong response shocked her. Sure, she'd shed a tear when the attorney's fees for Linda's shoplifting spree had vaporized her nest egg, but prior to that, the last time she'd cried she'd been twelve. She'd cut off the tears with brutal efficiency when she realized crying didn't stop the hurt or pain, dent her hunger, change her mother's behavior or lessen her longing. All it did was give her red and puffy eyes, churn her stomach and leave her feeling more alone than ever. She'd replaced crying with action. It was better to do something—anything—than sit sobbing like a weak and pathetic kid.

So, when she'd hugged Libby's daughters and breathed in their sweet baby scent, she'd been shocked and scared by the threat of tears. Her initial response was to throw logic at the problem. Children were a long-term investment with no fiscal return. They choked spontaneity. They were dependent and needy and she hated neediness in any form. They more than interfered with career paths —they killed them. The list of reasons *not* to have a child grew but none of them completely squashed the need. If anything, it strengthened it.

When Libby flew up to Sydney for their annual girls' weekend and announced she was pregnant yet again, something hard and soft and messy formed inside Jess. It took up a permanent position, sitting heavily behind her sternum. It featured elements of delight for her friend and heartache and disappointment for herself and all of it was wrapped in a massive and unexpected emerald bow of envy—the type and intensity she hadn't experienced since Libby had flashed a pavé-set diamond engagement ring at her, announced she was marrying Nick and asked Jess to be a bridesmaid.

The strength of the combined emotions had unwisely propelled her hand to the neck of a champagne bottle. Three glasses in, she was drunkenly touching Libby's belly, the bubbles of alcohol lobbing cannon balls into the steel-reinforced walls she'd erected long before she'd met Libby.

"Do you know how freaking lucky you are? You've got the trifecta. A career you love, a man who not only adores you but is a great hands-on dad and now, three kids."

Libby glowed in the way only a pregnant woman can—proud and just a tiny bit smug at her fecundity. "Almost three kids."

Jess rolled her eyes at Libby's scientific mind that always unnecessarily split hairs. "Most of my Sydney friends can't convince their man to have one kid, let alone three. You got the last good bloke."

Libby snorted. "Hardly."

"I'm not kidding. Men like Nick are mythical creatures."

"He's not that mythical. His dirty socks and jocks fall short of the laundry basket most nights." Libby poured Jess a glass of water as she'd done many times before and pushed it toward her. "I don't understand. You hate the idea of commitment. You consider three months a lifetime and if you're still with a guy after that, you dump him. Plus, you always tell me good men are dull and boring and you like bad boys, hot sex and excitement."

"Yes, but that was before I wanted a baby."

Libby's mouth fell open and Jess clicked her tongue. "There's no need to look quite so surprised."

"You—*you* want a baby? Since when?"

Jess shrugged, already regretting her disclosure. "Doesn't matter."

"Yes, it does. We don't only share clothes and shoes, we share everything."

Once they'd shared everything. "Remember how much Karen hated that?"

"You're changing the subject."

Sometimes a best friend knew a girl too well. "Okay, fine. I've been thinking about a baby for a year or so."

"Why didn't you tell me?"

"I was going to as soon as I found the right guy who wanted me, the mortgage and the kid." Jess threw a handful of peanuts into her mouth. "Problem is, he doesn't exist."

Libby's head tilted in disagreement. "Maybe you're not swimming in the right pool."

"What's that supposed to mean?"

"You only date alpha corporate suits."

"Duh! They earn heaps, which makes them good providers."

"Except, from what you've told me, they're all about the next merger or the next big float. That was fine when you were committed to no-strings-attached flings. If you want the whole soccer-mom scenario, you're better off dating a tradesman."

"This from a woman whose rule was to *only* date college-educated men!" And Jess had followed suit. It had shocked her that the choice hadn't completely protected her from the types of assholes her mother had paraded through her life.

"I was young and stupid when I said that," Libby said easily. "Besides, I married a man who dropped out of university."

Annoyance flashed. "Really? Is it dropping out if you leave to work in an established family business that's at the top of its game? And Nick finished his degree part time and then did an MBA."

Libby raised her hands in surrender. "Okay. All I'm saying is you need to think about dating men who work family-friendly hours instead of insanely long days. Better yet, date a teacher. They get school vacation."

Jess's hand trembled as she refilled her glass. "I've got a better idea."

"Is it a mail-order Russian oligarch?" Libby laughed, amused by her joke.

"No." Jess's jaw tightened. She didn't have a better idea, or any idea at all, but she'd had enough of Libby issuing dating instructions from the comfort of her marriage. Sometimes her friend's "doctor knows best" attitude collided with her general good fortune in all things, and the result thoroughly pissed off Jess. This moment was one of those times.

"What then?" Libby asked.

Jess suddenly remembered a conversation she'd overheard earlier in the week in the office tea room. One of the office clerks had been going on and on about her IVF cycles and discussing her husband's defective swimmers in great detail with anyone who was foolish enough to stop and listen.

"I don't need a man to have a baby."

"What?"

"I'll use donor sperm."

Libby's mocktail squirted out of her nose. "Jess, no! You do *not* want to have a baby on your own."

Jess bristled at the unwanted command and her annoyance with Libby moved closer to anger. "Why not? It's the perfect solution. I won't have to answer to a man and I can raise my child on my own. Heaps of women do it. My mother did."

Libby's eyes widened into two blue pools of sorrow. "And you've always said you'd never inflict the life of an only child onto a kid."

Jess gulped champagne, needing to dull the emerging memories of her mother, but at the same time wanting to demand her place at the motherhood table. "Too easy! I'll have two kids."

"Oh, God, you're drunker than I thought." Libby leaned forward, her face earnest. "Jess, listen to me. The easiest part of my week is when I'm at the clinic being Dr. Hunter. The hardest part is arsenic hour, which is really two to three hours when I'm trying to feed, bath and get the girls into bed without stringing them up or slashing my wrists."

White hot fury exploded behind Jess's eyes and she slammed her empty glass onto the coffee table. "Don't do that!"

Libby jerked back, surprise and hurt on her face. "Do what?"

"That exaggerating thing all mothers do. If the job's so frickin' hard and awful, why did you go back for a second let alone this third kid?"

"This one's a total surprise. To be honest, I cried when I saw the two pink lines on the stick. I didn't tell Nick for three days."

"Why? Problems in paradise?" It came out harsher than she'd intended.

"No, but we're already juggling two businesses and two kids under four. This time there'll only be fifteen months between Indi and the baby."

"So?"

"So, it's going to be tough. I wish it had happened next year or the year after."

"So, the timing's not perfect, but jeez, Lib! You're pregnant. I'd kill to have a baby." Dejection slumped Jess back against the couch. "Why can't I have that?"

Libby grabbed her hand. "I'm not saying you can't. I'm just trying to explain that even with a hands-on partner like Nick, there are times when being a mom is the toughest job you'll ever do. Your current job's not exactly flexible and when kids are involved, everything's a juggle. Being home alone with a baby can be long and lonely.

"When I had Lucy, some nights I stood in the yard waiting for Nick to walk through the gate so I could handball her to him the second he got home. Then I'd go for a walk to nowhere in particular just so I could be alone with my thoughts. I found it tough and I've got Nick, and Mom and Dad, as well as Nick's parents. Thank God, because we're really going to need them next year."

And there it was again. Lucky Libby. Although her friend had stopped short of saying, "And you don't have any family," the words hovered between them.

Libby rushed on. "You're barely thirty. You've still got time to meet someone and have a baby. What about Will Azzopardi? He adores you."

Jess's brows rose. "And living in Kurnai Bay. No thank you."

"Living in the bay in a lovely home by the water with a man you love who's earning a decent income is *nothing* like living there with your mother."

Did Libby realize she'd just described herself?

Excitement skipped in Libby's voice. "Plus, it's a fabulous place to bring up kids. Think about it. Will is to Nick what you are to me. Best friends. Family. Our kids would grow up together like cousins."

A picture formed in Jess's mind and a spurt of excitement sent jitters hurtling through her. "Perhaps I should come down and visit."

Libby squealed and clapped her hands. "When you do, I'll get Nick to invite Will out on the boat. Oh, wait! I've got a better idea. Nick can give Will a free hire and he can take you. The two of you alone on a yacht, job done!"

The past unexpectedly rose up and slapped her. "You mean just like you and Nick?"

Libby beamed. "Exactly."

CHAPTER THREE

The six o'clock sun bore down on the bowling greens at the RSL club, which were open to the public for the evening. Many barefoot tourists were attempting to master the fine art of lawn bowling with a drink in their hand. The sea breeze usually brought some relief from the heat, but this evening it was absent, leaving the tidal lake a still and silver pond, rippled only by the occasional cormorant diving deep for its fish dinner. The dry heat shimmered above the damp turf and even sitting in the shade of an umbrella, Alice felt rivulets of sweat running down her belly. Why had she allowed herself to be talked into volunteering tonight?

Because online dating's been going so well.

Calling it dating was a stretch. So far her "matches" were not striking. Three men had sent her identical messages: *Hello, Gorgeous. I love your smile.* They were either the same guy or all had read somewhere that this was the opener that guaranteed a positive response. It had such an opposite effect on her that when a fourth guy sent her the text, *S'up* she'd been tempted to respond.

Meanwhile, she'd carefully read the profiles of all the matches and written to two, starting with hello, reminding them who she was and asking a question based on the interests listed in their profile. She hadn't received a response from either of them. Had they been overwhelmed by three paragraphs of grammatically correct sentences?

Wishing she could shove her feet into the cooler full of ice, she bent down and plucked a cold can of beer from the drinks selection and rolled it over her hot skin.

The president of the bowling club shot her a disapproving look. "Hey , Alice love. No one's gonna buy hot beer."

She dropped the can back onto the ice. "Don't stress, Rod. We've already made a nice fat profit tonight and we've still got one very hot hour to go. Besides, I've got plans for that beer."

"Thought you were a gin and tonic girl?"

Alice didn't stop to question how Rod knew this about her. The topics of the Kurnai Bay grapevine were many and varied. She'd probably been spotted once, back in the day, drinking a G&T and the label had stuck, despite the fact she drank far more sauv blanc and pinot gris than anything else.

"The hot beer's for that obnoxious bloke on green six."

Rod squinted across the greens that were mostly dotted with family groups. "The bikers?"

"No. They were sweet and polite. It's the jet-ski mob. No manners on or off the water." Alice caught movement in her peripheral vision and turned. "Welcome to barefoot—Lucy! Nick! I didn't know you were coming."

"Daddy and I are going to play bowling," her six-year-old niece announced proudly.

"Sensational!" Alice jumped up and hugged them both. As she peered over the breadth of Nick's shoulder, she glanced down the path. "No Libby?"

"She's at the playground with the kids."

"Kids?"

"We're minding Leo tonight. Apparently Jess has a hot date."

The green snake stirred. "Lucky Jess," Alice said brightly. "Tourist or townie? Anyone we know?"

"Leo and Indi are too little to bowl," Lucy informed her with the superior glee of an older child.

Alice didn't mention that Lucy was barely old enough or strong enough to lift a bowl. That wasn't much of a consideration when the highlight for Lucy was having her father to herself for half an hour. Alice remembered those special childhood moments with her own father. Every now and then he'd say, "Ally-Oop, grab your sketch book," and they'd drive to his favorite spot on the Tambo River. While Peter fished, Alice would sit on the camp stool and keep him company, drawing birds and flowers or unicorns and clouds depending on her mood. She'd adored those quiet and companionable afternoons and now her fingers twitched with a sudden desire to grip a pencil. That hadn't happened in a long time—not since she'd moved in with Lawrence. Perhaps she should suggest a fishing trip to her father when he got back from Melbourne.

"You're having dinner with us in the restaurant after this," Nick said, adding when she gave him a blank look, "Libs did text you, right?"

Since Alice's foray into online dating, she'd been checking her phone far too often, but there hadn't been a text from Libby. Something about the way Nick asked the question—frustration overlaid with concern—made her wonder if Libby was having another rough patch. Alice wanted desperately to believe in the adage "time heals all wounds"—for them both—but the problem was that time was the unknown factor. If Nick was worried, then she should be too. Guilt needled her. Had she been so self-indulgent about her own hot mess of a life that she hadn't noticed? God, her twin radar needed recalibrating.

Protecting Libby, she said, "My bad. Ditzy Alice strikes again."

Nick was pulling out his wallet. "How much will this set me back?"

"Ten dollars for you and Lucy's free. Any drinks?"

"I'll have a pale ale. Lucy-Goose, do you want some lemonade?"

The little girl's brown eyes—so much like her father's—widened into circles of wonder. Alice knew Libby was anti all sugary drinks, having heard her sister's dissertation on the topic many times. Water was always the default choice of beverage for the children when they were out.

"Can I have lemonade?" Lucy breathed out, anticipation making her tremble.

Nick tapped his nose. "It will be our secret."

Alice laughed. "Good luck with that. She'll break the moment she sees Libby."

Nick gave a wry smile. "Yeah, you're right. No such thing as secrets in this family or this town."

"You're on green three. Ted's the man if you need a quick lesson."

"Great. Oh, and while I think of it, can you be at the marina at 8:00 in the morning? I've got a couple of quick turnarounds and you're my best cleaner."

Alice knew why her brother-in-law was turning on his legendary charm, even though she was grateful for the work. "Josie busy, is she?"

"You got me. But, seriously, Al, you do a much better job. The clients are mentioning how clean the boats are on TripAdvisor."

"Dad taught me well."

"Catch you at dinner."

Alice nodded and as they walked away she typed into the spreadsheet the amounts she'd taken for the game and the drinks. She had a flurry of arrivals and was kept busy counting in the borrowed bowls, noting down the free greens and handing out flyers about the upcoming Australia Day carnival. Just as the rush eased, her phone buzzed and a notification appeared on the multicolored heart-shaped dating app she'd parted with some precious money to use. Hoping it was from one of the men she'd contacted, she was opening it when she heard a sharp whistle followed by, "Hunter!" The shout made her look up.

It took her a second to realize the yelling man wasn't calling her surname, but calling to a kid.

"Hunter! Get down!"

A boy, who looked about nine, paused halfway up the cyclone fence before his shoulders drooped in resignation. He jumped down and sheepishly made his way back to his father.

"That one's full of beans," Rod commented drily.

"It can be boring waiting for your turn." Alice remembered long games of Scrabble where Karen, Peter and Libby took forever to create their words and how she quickly lost interest in the game. It didn't help that she lacked the competitive spirit that drove the rest of her family. She'd have preferred to be drawing.

Rod stood up. "I'll wander over and give him a lesson on green seven. That'll keep him off the fence and protect the garden."

"You're a nice bloke, Rod."

His sun-weathered face creased into deep smile lines. "Don't say that too loudly, love. I've got the committee foxed."

As he walked away, Alice clicked on the dating app and read, *Hey Alice! Paris is on the Seine, London on the Thames and Dublin's on the ...?*

A buzz of delight shot through her. Tim41 had read her profile. Her fingers flew across the screen. *Too easy, Tim! The Liffe. Challenge me. I promise not to cheat.* She hit send before she realized her mistake. She hadn't read his profile or looked at his photo.

Tapping through the links she found him and her insides sighed in both relief and anticipation. Although Aviator sunglasses sat on his shaved head—it wasn't a look she usually went for—it was his sparkling brown eyes creased in deep smile lines that captivated. They seemed to be looking straight at her. Tim was thirty-seven, worked in agriculture and lived in Lindenow, just under an hour's drive away. In the country, that was practically next door.

Her phone buzzed again and excitement leaped, quickly followed by disappointment. It wasn't a message from Tim41, but a text from Libby. *Can you come to dinner with us at the RSL?* It was immediately followed by a second text. *Al, I've booked for you. Hope you can come.* And a third. *Call me!*

Kurnai Bay's cell phone tower didn't always cope with the glut of communication inflicted on it by the summer crush. Occasionally it vomited a stream of messages, despite them having been sent hours apart. That her twin was getting snippy at Alice's lack of response was both annoying and comforting—it was a relief Nick was worrying over nothing. Not only had Libby sent the dinner invitation, she sounded her usual organized self.

Alice called her twin and two minutes later, Libby arrived with Leo on her hip and tugging a reluctant Indi by the hand.

"I didn't think you were working tonight."

"Technically, I'm not. Rod caught me at a weak moment. I'm volunteering and filling in for Dad." She smiled at the kids. "Nick tells me Jess has a hot date. Anyone we know?"

Libby's face lit up. "She and Will have gone to the jazz concert at Nyerimilang. Cross everything."

Alice didn't think Jess and Will were particularly well suited, but then again, she'd thought she and Lawrence were a perfect match. Obviously, she knew nothing. For as long as Alice could remember, Libby had been pushing Jess and Nick's best friend together, but they'd never really stuck.

"Don't you think it's time to let go of that dream? I mean, if those two were meant to be, they'd have gotten together years ago."

"Not necessarily. People change. Look at Jess. She always said she didn't want kids and she'd never come back to the bay, yet here she is."

"Even so, I don't think she's changed her views about not wanting a full-time man in her life. Isn't that why she used donor sperm? So she doesn't have to answer to anyone?"

"That conclusion's far too simplistic." Libby inclined her head toward Indi.

But it wasn't just talking about sperm in front of an almost four-year-old that was bothering her twin. Alice recognized the tone—the brusque one Libby always used whenever she thought Alice was criticizing Jess. It wasn't any of Alice's business if Jess wanted a life partner to co-parent Leo, or a friend-with-benefits arrangement—she assumed this was Will's role—or if Jess continued along the no-strings attached hook-ups path she'd always travelled. But despite all the people who loved Leo, she couldn't help feeling some sadness that he didn't know his father and he might never get the opportunity to meet the man who'd donated his DNA.

But that was another topic not to be mentioned, because even though Alice was convinced Libby felt similarly, she'd never admit it to her. The fact Libby had urged Jess to move back to the bay soon after Leo was born, and the amount of time Leo spent at the Pirelli house, lent weight to Alice's suspicions about Libby's beliefs. She also knew there were other compelling reasons for Libby to want to have her best friend living in the bay, but again, Libby wouldn't wish to talk about those either.

Alice changed the subject. "You look hot. Do you want a cold drink?"

"I've got water in my backpack." She lifted Leo off her hip and held him out to Alice. "Can you hold him for a sec?"

"I swinged high, Lis," Indi said, her fingers reaching for the cash box.

"Swinging high is awesome fun." Alice slid the box out of the way and then extracted Leo's pudgy hand from her sunglasses. "And did you have a swing too, Leo-the-Lion?"

"Up!" he said solemnly and made another grab for the sunglasses.

Alice got a hitch in her chest. With his dark curly hair and ebony eyes, he looked like the baby she'd always imagined she and Lawrence would have, except of course he looked like Jess—all bar his mouth. Jess had a small, bee-sting pout that Alice knew from experience could lurch from playful and sexy to hard and determined. Leo, on the other hand, had thick lips that stretched widely across his little face—a mouth he'd grow into one day far into the future. Meanwhile, it gave him a delightful albeit mostly gummy smile and Alice was a sucker for it. He was a gorgeous kid, but right now his body heat was raising her already elevated skin temperature.

"How about I get someone to man the cooler for the last fifteen minutes and we go inside to the air-conditioning? The kids can play in the ball pit and boost their gutter immunity and we can supervise and enjoy a G&T."

Surprise flitted across Libby's face. "Since when do you drink spirits?"

"According to Rod, I'm known for it, so I need to keep my reputation intact."

"Sounds great to me."

Thankful she could use her staff discount, Alice bought the drinks while Libby settled the kids. "I asked for plastic glasses so they look like lemon and soda. This way we can drink inside the play enclosure and keep your reputation intact."

Libby laughed. "You've got my back."

"Always. How are things?" Despite the broad question, Alice was hoping for some long-anticipated pregnancy news.

"Yeah, good. Busy. You?"

A curl of sadness rose into her for them both. "Same. Juggling jobs is keeping me sane and driving me crazy. I turned up to Jake's the other day when I was supposed to be here."

"That's what all those colors on Google Calendar are for." Libby sipped her drink. "Are you worried that straight after Australia Day most of your work will vanish?"

"It won't vanish. It will just slow. The weekends will still be busy, especially Saturdays."

"Don't you miss having a real job?"

Alice's hand tightened around the tumbler and the plastic creaked. "I waitress. I work behind the bar. I put up with crap from people who think they're the only ones on vacation in this town. And I clean boats and empty marine toilets. How much more real do I need to get?"

Libby held up her hand in surrender. "Okay, so "real" was the wrong word. But Alice, you've worked too hard and come so far to be content doing all these menial jobs."

Come so far. Unwanted sympathy cloaked Alice in a shroud of humiliation and she was wrenched back to when they were children; her watching Libby learn everything quickly and with ease, while she plodded and practiced until she was competent but never accomplished. Her parents had pushed cajoled and cheered her, but Libby had pulled Alice along in her slipstream, both championing and overshadowing her in everything except drawing. Art was where Alice aced her talented twin, but growing up, that had never felt enough.

"You wouldn't be happy doing these jobs," Alice said lightly, not wanting to discuss it any further. "But we both know I'm not you."

Her phone beeped again and a zip of excitement tingled through her. Was it Tim41, responding to her flirty message? It was probably just an ABC News update or the wildfire app—she really must assign the dating app its own sound.

"You can check it, I don't mind," Libby said, glancing at the children. "It's not like I don't do it to you all the time when I'm on call."

Alice knew she should say, "It's okay," but she gave in, desperate to know. Flipping her phone over, she read the first few words of the message on her screen and laughed.

Libby's head swung round, her face keen with interest. "I know that laugh. Have you been keeping secrets from me?"

"No."

"Liar." With the skill born from years of being nosey, Libby plucked the phone out of Alice's hand. "'Challenge accepted. How's your South American geography? Which river runs through San Paulo, Brazil?' Oh." Libby sounded disappointed. "Are you playing online trivia?"

Alice's heart was pumping just a bit too fast and she forced herself to sound casual. "It's more fun than Words with Friends."

Libby's eyes narrowed at the insult to one of her favorite games and Alice gave herself an internal high-five. Nice save!

Libby looked at the phone again. "Hang on. That's a heart logo..." She squealed. "Is this a dating app?"

Her twin might be a doctor and a well-respected member of the community but when it came to other people's relationships, she always acted like a teen, desperate to know all the details. Alice wanted to say no, but perhaps admitting to putting her toe in the dating waters might be the lesser of two evils—especially if it got her twin off her back about a real job.

"Yep. It felt right to try dating again."

Libby hugged her. "Thank God. Tell me everything."

Leo suddenly slid underneath the balls and Alice jumped to her feet. She plunged her hands under the moving sea of plastic and pulled him out and up into her arms. He gave a squawk of protest either from surprise or delayed shock and Alice hugged him before whispering into his curls, "Perfect timing, mate."

"I've got tickets to the Impressionists exhibition." Karen felt the heat of her phone against her palm and the agitation of Peter's one-handed charade of eating as she spoke to Alice. "And Dad's offering to take us to dinner at Verve even though he's seen the prices. Surely you're not going to pass on that?"

There was a moment of silence before Alice said wearily, "Mom, I'd love to but I can't get away."

Karen swallowed a tsk of frustration. "I've already cleared it with Nick and Dad's lined up Rod's nephew to cover your bar shift."

"I have shifts at Jake's and I don't think you can pull any strings there."

Karen didn't miss the tartness in her daughter's voice. "Sweetheart, we're not interfering. We're only trying to help. Libby says you've been sick and we thought a couple of days in Melbourne might be just what you need."

"I'm fine. Stop worrying about me and go and enjoy your vacation. I'll see you Friday afternoon." The line went dead.

Karen put down her phone with a sigh. "She's not coming."

Peter shoulder checked and changed lanes. "Not even for Verve?"

"Not for Verve, not for *Billy Elliot*, not for the art gallery and not even for Shakespeare in the Park." Karen stared out of the car window, her mind still on Alice, not the vista. "I don't know what else to try. I'm completely out of ideas."

"Perhaps the best thing to do is stop trying. Remember potty training? It turned into a battle of wills. You know how obstinate she can be."

"She gets that from you!"

He shook his head indulgently. "Go ahead and believe that if that makes you feel better."

"I'm worried about her."

"Kaz, that isn't news."

"I just wish Alice had an ounce of Libby's resilience to protect her, but you know she doesn't. She's too sensitive and takes everything to heart." Karen worried at the cuticle on her thumb. "And just when I thought she'd finally found her feet both with her career and with Lawrence, he went and did a number on her always wobbly self-confidence."

"She's not a teen anymore," Peter said firmly. "These days she's more robust than you think. I mean, look at Barry Corica's son. He's never left home and can't hold down a job. Despite Lawrence, Ally's working and paying her way."

"Cleaning boats is not working! She's scared of life and hiding out in the bay instead of using her talents. I can't help thinking if what happened to Libby had happened to Alice ..." Karen shuddered. "She wouldn't recover."

Peter frowned. "You're comparing apples with oranges. Besides, Libby has Nick."

"Exactly! And thank God for that. Libby chose a man who loves and adores her. Alice chose a man who loves and adores himself. But it isn't just men. You know Alice doesn't always think things through, how she can act rashly. Remember—"

"You can't accuse her of making any rash decisions today, otherwise she'd have accepted our invitation." Peter patted Karen's thigh. "How about you use this afternoon to take a break from worrying?"

Karen tried to shift the aching dread she permanently carried for her youngest daughter back into its well-worn box and concentrate on her husband's thoughtfulness. Like Libby, Karen had chosen a kind and loving man to share her life, although she knew her decision had been far more deliberate than her daughter's. "I'll try."

Peter shot her a smile. "Great. Sit back, enjoy the drive—and my surprise."

Karen noticed that houses had given way to manna gums, which lined the sides of the road. As the car climbed, large tree ferns came into view, nestled between the tall straight trees. A jolt of anxiety lodged in her chest. "Where are we?"

But she didn't need to ask. Despite the new signage and the fact that the police station was no longer the small clapboard building of her childhood, Karen recognized the intersection. She wondered if the people inside did a better job welcoming scared children today than they had fifty-five years ago.

"Two more miles and we'll be there." Peter slowed before turning right.

Karen's mouth dried. "You're taking me to Mt. Dandenong?"

Her snappish tone turned Peter's smile into a perplexed frown. "You said you wanted a drive to a surprise destination and I know you've never been there. I've booked us a decadent high tea so we can indulge ourselves while we enjoy the view. I thought we could visit Rickett's Sanctuary on the way down and you can tick it off your list."

"It was never on my list." Her jaw was so tight it hurt to speak. "I can't believe you thought coming here was a good idea."

He sighed and threw her a beseeching look. "A few weeks ago, I saw you looking at some old photos. I thought perhaps enough time had passed … Thought it might be an opportunity to remember the good times and create a new one."

Karen laced her fingers tightly in her lap. "There were never any good times, Pete. I thought you understood that."

He flinched at the accusation in her voice. "So that's a no to high tea?"

"Turn around and take me to the Windsor."

CHAPTER FOUR

February

Jess's life had a rhythm that was very much centered on activities for Leo—toddler gym, playgroup, story time at the library and music group. All the activities tired Leo out so he slept soundly for two to three hours in the afternoon, allowing her to work. This carefully thought out routine reduced her need to use paid childcare to one day a week. Leo was at home with her every day except Thursdays, when he spent six hours at daycare with Indi Pirelli. He adored Indi and toddled around after her happily. Libby often joked that Indi was his first crush. Jess always smiled but the notion unsettled her. Being dependent on anyone unsettled her and she didn't want her son to know the pain of rejection.

Leo loved all the week's activities, but what continued to surprise Jess was how much she enjoyed spending time with women who had children of a similar age. She'd discovered an unexpected camaraderie in sharing stories with other mothers in the toddler trenches. Of course, just like any group, there was an element of competition and while Jess consoled the women who struggled with some tasks, she couldn't help feeling a little bit smug about Leo's

JUST AN ORDINARY FAMILY   55

hand–eye coordination and his sure-footedness on the gym equipment.

"Were you sporty as a kid?" the instructor had asked her at the first session.

"Not really. It's why I chose a donor who was."

"A donor? I don't understand."

"Sperm donor. I'm doing the parent gig on my own."

"Oh, I see."

But it was obvious from the woman's face that she didn't at all.

From the moment Jess had announced she was having a baby, she'd learned from the almost universal response that it was easier for people to understand the decision of a woman who'd chosen the single parent path after unexpectedly falling pregnant than it was to relate to a woman who'd actively sought it. It was no different when she'd arrived back in the Bay, although by then Libby had accepted it and was championing her decision. It paved Jess's way, making her re-entry into the town smoother than she'd expected.

Most of the women she'd met since returning had moved to the bay in the years since Jess had last lived there. Many had partners who worked on the oil and gas platforms, which meant they were single parents two weeks out of four. They had more of an understanding of Jess's life with Leo than women whose spouses worked regular hours in town. There were only a handful of women from her high school days still living in the bay and their welcome ranged from enthusiastic to lukewarm, depending on who they'd married. Although Jess had made her peace with her wild years, people had long memories. The irony was that during her period of indiscriminate sex with boys, none of those women were dating them.

Jess had no intention of apologizing. Nor did she wish to revisit those lackluster moments of inexpert sex in the sand dunes or on broken couches in beach shacks, even if the boys were now grown men and had likely learned a trick or two. With a couple of exceptions, the sex had never been about the boys or the elusive hope of an orgasm. It had been about her mother's love of bourbon and rum ahead of her love for Jess. It had been about living life on her own terms and taking what she wanted and thought she deserved. It had worked right up until the terrifying moment at sixteen when she'd thought she was pregnant.

At first Jess had been paralytic with fury when Libby had disclosed her secret to Karen, but unlike Linda, Libby's mother hadn't hit her or screamed that she was a slut and a whore. Karen's eyes had dimmed, but all she'd said was, "Before we panic, let's find out what we're dealing with." Instead of taking her to the family planning clinic in town or even in Bairnsdale, she drove Jess the extra distance to Sale to protect her from the Kurnai Bay gossips. Libby had wanted to come and Jess had desperately wanted that too, but in that regard, Karen had been an immoveable force. Jess had spent the drive to Sale lurching between gratitude and shame, punctuated by moments of anger. She sensed Karen's disappointment and discovered that she much preferred being called a useless waste of space—her mother's favorite pejorative—than wearing Karen's sadness.

On the drive home, Karen raised the elephant in the car. "You've had a scare and this time you were lucky. Please take the pill and use the condoms the clinic gave you."

Jess stared out the window, burning with embarrassment. It had been bad enough when the nurse had banged on about it and demonstrated how to use the condoms on a carrot.

"There's nothing wrong with having sex, Jess, if you enjoy it," Karen said quietly. "But it comes with responsibility. I just want you to be happy, healthy and safe so you can achieve your full potential."

No one had ever talked to Jess like this before and although her insides were squirming, something made her say, "What if I don't enjoy it?"

"Sex?"

"Yeah."

Karen's hand left the steering wheel and she patted Jess's knee. "Then ask yourself why you're having it. If it's to hurt your mother, you're only hurting yourself."

"What would you know?" Jess hated that Karen understood.

Karen sighed. "My mother wasn't the mother I wanted her to be either and my father was worse."

Jess's head snapped round, stunned by this revelation. "Did yours drink too?"

Karen murmured something unintelligible before clearing her throat. "We don't get to choose our parents, Jess. Believe me, you can waste a lot of energy being angry and acting out, hoping it will shock Linda into cleaning up her act. But all it does is hurt you. I decided to live my life very differently from my parents. I chose to put myself first and protect the people I love. It didn't mean I wasn't angry. I was angry for a long time, but I channeled it into getting out and staying away."

Jess couldn't imagine Karen angry. "Does Libby know this?"

Karen shook her head, her face suddenly stricken. "Can it be our secret?"

For a moment, Jess considered telling her friend for no other reason than she could. But then the harsh truth broke over her and she realized what set herself and Karen apart from the twins. "Sure. There's no way Libby or Alice would get it."

"No, they wouldn't." Karen's mouth tweaked up into a rueful smile. "Thank you for understanding."

Warmth bloomed in Jess's chest. At that moment, she would have done anything for Karen and she tried hard to make choices Karen would approve of, but sometimes her anger with Linda flowed fast like a river in flood. She'd continued to take risks—drinking and using ecstasy at parties—but when she chose to have sex she used protection and insisted on a bed.

She still lived by those rules. Mostly. And if a few Kurnai Bay women were going to hold ridiculous grudges for something she'd done years earlier and gloss over their own teenage mistakes, then so be it. But her worries were unfounded, and the women welcomed her warmly. Although she'd never be as close to any of them as she was to Libby—they shared a once-in-a-lifetime friendship—Jess was enjoying her new circle of friends. They were more socially reliable than a busy doctor.

But the biggest surprise on her return to the bay was her desire to get involved in the community. For a long time, she'd taken Karen's advice to "put yourself first," but Leo had softened her. She'd discovered that giving came back to her three times over and her new friendships were all part of that.

"Thanks for organizing the playgroup sausage sizzle this weekend, Jess." It was the end of toddler gym and Jess and Genevieve Lawry were on packing up duty. Gen passed her a stack of orange cones. "How did you manage to get the Phelpses and the Lamannas to commit to an hour on the roster?"

Jess laughed. "I have secret powers of persuasion."

"I believe you! I get so frustrated sometimes. We make it really clear to people when they join playgroup they have to do some volunteering. Most people do it without quibbling, but not those families. They've always got an excuse to weasel out of it."

Jess stowed the collapsible play tunnels on a shelf. "I find it's amazing how people change their minds when they feel they or their kids have missed out."

"What do you mean?"

"Remember that article I wrote for the *Gazette* after the working bee? I left their names off the list and their kids weren't in the photo."

"Oh, that's clever."

"I thought so." Gen's admiration buoyed her. "And I might have told them the other families were donating food and drinks."

"No way!"

"Way. So the Phelps have paid for the sausages and the Lamannas have given us four cases of soda. Bread and sauce don't cost much so that means almost pure profit for playgroup. Nick's promised to cook lots of onions to bring in the crowds."

"He's so good! I wish more of the dads got involved. It's a shame Libby can't make it."

Jess shrugged, not overly bothered since the duty roster was full. "Doctors' hours."

"I guess. It's just I'm sure they used to do more stuff together." Gen handed Jess a box of name vests, her face wearing the eager look of a notorious gossip. "You're really close to them, aren't you?"

"Yep. We go way back. I knew Nick before Libby did."

"That's true friendship! I'm not sure I would have let my best friend anywhere near a guy like Nick. Are they okay? I mean, you know, after ..."

Jess didn't want to discuss the state of Nick and Libby's marriage, especially with Genevieve. "I don't think anyone ever knows the true state of other people's relationships."

Disappointment flittered quickly over Genevieve's face. "I guess not."

"Mom, Mom, Mom!" Leo ran over. "Cookie?"

She scooped him up and pressed her face into his curls, breathing him in. Some of the women in the group had confessed to taking days and weeks to feel love for their baby, but the moment the midwife laid Leo into her arms, the rush of love had been so strong and primal, she'd cried tears of joy. In the ensuing months, nothing had dented it—not colic or teething, three bouts of mastitis or the difficult decision to give up her corporate job and leave Sydney, even though it was professional suicide. If anything, her love for her son had widened and deepened. Leo was her world and she'd sacrifice everything for him.

A stab of old pain caught her by surprise. Had her mother ever thought she was worth it?

"Coffee time!" Tenika announced to the room. Post-toddler-gym coffee was an extension of the class. "I booked the couches at Jangles."

In a stroller convoy, they walked the short distance to the café and settled in for a chat while the children played at their feet.

"Anyone got any sexy plans for tonight?" Tenika asked.

A communal groan rolled around the couches. "Valentine's Day is such a load of crap," Eliza said. "Forget roses. I'd love it if Gav discovered how erotic I'd find it if he did the ironing or folded some laundry."

"Or the dishes," Kelly said. "When I asked Drew this morning if there was anything happening today, he reminded me he had cricket training. Mind you, he did offer to grab a bite to eat on the way home to save me cooking, so I guess that's my Valentine's present."

"Did you tell him you still had to cook for the kids?" Gen asked.

"Not worth it."

"Rob's on the drilling platform this week so it's Netflix for me," Michelle said.

"What about you, Jess?" Eliza asked. "Got a hot date?"

"I have actually."

Five sets of eager eyes swung toward her.

"Who with?"

"Where's he taking you?"

"I'm so jealous!"

"I envy your energy."

"Tell us everything so we can remember what romance is like!"

Jess laughed. "Stop salivating, ladies. You're way too excited. And I'm not doing anything you can't do for yourselves."

"What is it?"

"I have a date with myself."

"That's no fun," Kelly sank back on the couch, clearly disillusioned.

"Hang on, work with me. Remember Tenika's girls' night party?"

Gen giggled. "How can any of us forget? I had no idea vibrators came with so many moving parts."

"We all bought lingerie and candles and a couple of us bought some other toys." She tapped her reusable cloth bag. "In a piece of perfect timing, I just picked up my box from the post office. Once Leo's asleep, I'm putting on my silky negligee, lighting a candle, and opening a bottle of sparkling pinot for a date with the purple rabbit. Pure indulgence and orgasm guaranteed."

"Actually, that's a really good idea. I could FaceTime, Rob." Michelle grinned. "Or not."

"Exactly! There's nothing wrong with enjoying an orgasm all on your own," Jess said.

"At least you know you'll get one," Kelly grumbled.

"You've got time between the kids' bedtime and the end of cricket training."

"I'd feel guilty."

"*Never* feel guilty about taking something for yourself. You work hard and you deserve it." Jess stood up. "And talking about work, I better get going. Can't have the Kurnai Bay Medical Practice out for blood if their pay's late."

Libby kissed Nick in stunned delight. "Wow! This is a first. Not only did you remember it was Valentine's Day, you bought champagne, red roses *and* chocolates. The only thing missing is silky lingerie."

Nick grinned. "I did go onto the Victoria's Secret website—"

"And gotten distracted," she teased.

"There was that." His eyes twinkled at her the way they always had until their lucky lives had smashed headlong into the harsh reality of human existence. "But there were so many decisions. Color, size—it was overwhelming. I was going to ask Alice, but that seemed thoughtless, given it's her first Valentine's Day on her own in a while."

"You should have asked Jess."

He looked askance. "That would have been weird."

"Why? She helped you choose the dress you gave me for Christmas."

"Is that what she told you? It was more like she bought it for herself, changed her mind, told me you'd love it and then sold it to me. You know Jess. She doesn't like to waste money."

A ripple of annoyance spread through Libby. "She doesn't have money to waste. It's why she should be doing the Pirelli books."

"Not this again. I've explained that by the time you mentioned it, I'd already offered the job to Enza's niece and she'd accepted. I couldn't go back on my word."

"Not even for family?"

"Enza's as much family as Jess is."

Except Enza was a Pirelli friend and Libby didn't have quite the same allegiance. "Yes, but—"

Nick put two fingers against her lips. "Why are we talking about this now when it's Valentine's Day and the girls are asleep?"

"Fair call." She took his hand and kissed him before backing him down the hall to their bedroom. Feeling sexier than she had in weeks, she pushed him onto the bed, straddled him and whipped up his work polo shirt. Pressing her lips to his chest, she used her hands to release the waistband of his shorts. She smiled when she heard him groan. Then his fingers were tugging at her T-shirt before expertly releasing her bra and they wriggled out of the rest of their clothes. They rolled together, their mouths melding and skin touching glorious bare skin.

Later, as they rolled apart, panting, lightning lit up the room. A loud crack of thunder followed and they jumped. Libby laughed. "We started a storm. I hope it doesn't wake the girls."

"We were pretty good." Nick squeezed her hand. "You were on fire."

"I was, wasn't I?" She kissed him. "Who knew all it took was Chinese takeout, champers, chocolate and roses. Still, I feel a bit like I've let the sisterhood down by being such an easy lay."

"If I'd known that was all it took, I'd have done it years ago."

She propped herself on her elbow and studied him, his face as familiar to her as her own. "You've always said Valentine's Day's not only a rip-off, it's an insult." She deepened her voice to mimic his. "'If a bloke has to buy roses and chocolates to get into a woman's pants he's not working hard enough inside the house.' What changed your mind this year?"

"I thought it might be a fun surprise. You know, something we should do at least once. I'd planned to take you out to dinner too, but I left it too late to book." Nick brushed strands of hair off her cheek. "Sorry. Who knew Kurnai Bay had such a romantic streak?"

"Listening to this rain, staying in was a wise move. But I appreciate the thought." She covered his hand with hers. "Given how I leaped on you, I'm fertile. Hopefully we just made a baby."

A troubled look crossed Nick's face. "I thought you'd stopped tracking your cycle."

"I have. I promise I haven't been taking my temperature or peeing on ovulation sticks or even thinking about getting pregnant, but I know my body. When I get horny in a heartbeat, I know I'm ovulating."

"Don't go protecting my ego, *bella*. Here I was thinking that you were hot for me."

She laughed. "Always."

The word hung between them, not exactly false, because Nick was the love of her life and her best friend. But during the last twenty-four months, her sex drive had been hit and miss, and for a large part of that time she'd been focused on sex to make a baby rather than a way to increase intimacy or to have fun. Not that her priority had paid off the way she desperately wanted.

Three months earlier, when her period arrived yet again, Nick had come in late from a coast guard meeting to find her sorting clean laundry and with tears streaming down her face.

"I can't do this anymore," she'd said, blowing her nose on a tea-towel.

"Fold laundry?" Nick quietly removed the basket from in front of her and steered her to the couch.

"No! Try ... and g-get p-pregnant."

"Stop then!"

His harsh and unexpected words shocked her so much, she'd stopped crying. Blinking rapidly, she peered at him through blurry eyes, trying to bring his face into focus. "But we want a baby. We want another little boy."

Nick's hands fisted in his lap. "Not if trying makes you miserable month after month. Not when it turns sex into an event that has to be marked on the calendar along with paying the land tax and mowing the lawn."

Anxiety romped through her. "Are *you* happy like this?"

"Is that a trick question?"

"No! Why would you even think that?"

"Because if I say yes, you'll ask me how can I possibly be happy when our baby boy died. If I say no, you'll blame yourself."

A familiar combination of anger tinged with resignation bubbled and spat. "Am I making you unhappy?"

His arms flew into the air. "I didn't say that! All I'm saying is that one week you're happy and hopeful and the next you're desperately sad and upset again. It kills me every time shark week arrives and you're gutted all over again. If the solution's not getting pregnant, then let's stop trying. The girls are enough."

She hadn't really meant it when she'd said she wanted to stop trying and she didn't believe he wanted it either. "When you found out I was pregnant with Dom, you showed a side of yourself I'd never seen before. You went all macho-Italian on me, demanding we give him an Italian name. So don't lie to me now. I know you want a son."

His gaze fell to the floor and his shoulders slumped. Then the rest of him seemed to follow, folding in on himself as though he lacked the energy to hold himself upright. A long sigh rolled out of him. "Libs, all I want is for you to be happy again."

It hurt that he'd said "you" rather than "us."

Now, lying with Nick in a post-coital glow, she conceded that taking a break from trying to get pregnant had spun-off in positive ways. "Despite the busy summer, things have been better lately. With us, I mean."

"Yeah." He pulled her against him. "Things are good."

Recently Libby had been working extremely hard at concentrating on their blessings instead of their great loss. Whenever she thought about that awful time, she felt the strong drag of despair and it took monumental energy to dig her heels in hard so she didn't get pulled into the black morass. She'd taken the advice she gave to patients and was attempting to practice mindfulness—focusing on the moment instead of the past or the future. At first it had been hit and miss but lately, it was getting easier. Each night before she went to sleep, she journaled five things she was grateful for instead of railing against the one thing she'd been so cruelly denied. Among entries like, "I'm grateful for the crisp tang of a new season's apple, the sight of a peloton of pelicans flying low across the lake, Mrs. Giannopoulos's lemon cake," she recognized the obvious themes. She was grateful for a kind, patient, understanding and loving husband. Two gorgeous daughters and a caring extended family. The gift of a dear friend who was both a confidante and a sounding board. She was also immensely grateful that she and Nick had jobs they not only loved but that provided them with an income to live a comfortable—and some would say enviable—life. Enviable in all ways but one. After all her hard work, it pained her that Nick had just reduced their current closeness to "good."

"Just good?"

He shook his head indulgently at her need for affirmation. "Things are great. I love our Wednesday sails." After Nick's accusation of them no longer being spontaneous, Libby had arranged for her mother to mind the girls and she'd signed on to be part of Nick's crew for the twilight races. It wasn't exactly the definition of spontaneous, but it gave them couple time doing something they loved.

She pressed her finger onto his sternum. "You just enjoy bossing me around on the boat, captain."

"Nah, I only boss Alice. It's not my fault she looks so much like you."

"Nice try, but we're not identical."

"You pretty much are. It's impossible to tell when you're both wearing white shorts and blue polos and you've got your backs to me."

"Except I've got the cuter ass."

"No contest."

Rain continued to lash the windows and pound noisily on the roof.

Nick kissed her hair before winding some blond strands around his finger, his face pensive. "Just promise me you won't drop your bundle in a few weeks if you're not pregnant."

Libby instinctively tightened her pelvic floor and clamped her thighs together, knowing she couldn't promise him that. It was taking all her self-control not to throw her legs up over her head, but she knew if she did that, they'd probably argue. Being here together, snuggled up, talking, teasing, laughing and loving was just too special to risk.

"Libs?" Nick queried firmly, seeking the answer he wanted.

Thankfully, her phone rang. Despite not being on call, she automatically picked it up. "It's Jess."

"Don't answer it."

But she'd already swiped. "Hey, what's up?"

"I've got a leak in my roof."

Nick's mouth closed around Libby's breast, making her, "Oh!" come out as a high-pitched squeak. She gently pushed at his head but instead of deterring him, he moved his hand to caress her other nipple. Heat streaked through her and her belly clenched.

"Can you hear me?" Jess was yelling over the noise of the rain.

Nick was now pressing kisses between her breasts, trailing them downwards. Each flick of his tongue stole her concentration and she relaxed back into the pillows. "Hmm."

"Libby!" Jess's voice rose, urgent and commanding. "My bedroom ceiling's bulging with water!"

She pulled away from Nick and sat up. "Oh, God. That's awful."

"I know!"

"You need to drain the water before the plaster falls in. Do you have a drill?"

"No! And I've called the volunteer emergency service but so have heaps of other people. They can't tell me how long it will be before someone comes. By then filthy water and half my ceiling will be in my bed!"

"I'll send Nick."

Nick was sitting up now too, shaking his head and making an X with his arms.

"I can't ask you to do that. It's Valentine's night."

"You're not asking, we're offering," Libby said firmly. "Besides, you're not interrupting anything."

"Well, that's both TMI and far too sad," Jess joked. "But seriously, are you sure Nick's okay about coming out in this weather to rescue me?"

"Of course!"

"I guess I can wait for the emergency service if I have to."

"You won't have to but if it makes you happy I'll ask him. Hang on." Libby muted the phone and faced Nick. "Jess's bedroom ceiling is full of water."

"Sounds like a job for the volunteer emergency service."

"Nick!" She punched him gently on the arm. His lack of sympathy was surprising, especially as he often helped Jess out with general repairs like changing washers on faucets and high pressure cleaning her deck. He'd recently installed her new dishwasher. "She's already called them and there's a long wait."

"But tonight's our night," he moaned. "Surely there's someone else she can call? Someone on her side of the creek?"

"Will's on the platform this week. You know she wouldn't ask unless she was desperate. Do it for me," she implored, stroking his cheek. "Please."

He let out a groan, swung his legs onto the floor and grabbed his boxers. "Just for the record, Libs, I'm getting tired of being Jess's Mr. Fixit. We're giving her a tool kit and DIY classes for her birthday."

Libby laughed, knowing he wasn't serious, just a tad testy because of the timing and the wet weather. Nick loved his community and prided himself on being helpful. The widowed Italian nonnas in town adored it when he arrived on their doorstep with his tool kit. Once, one of the tech-savvy oldies posted a photo of a bare-chested Nick digging out her septic on the town's Facebook page. She'd tagged it #ifonlyIwasthirtyyearsyounger. Nick didn't have the heart to ask her to take it down and the blokes at the coast guard had ribbed him about it for weeks.

Libby scrambled to her knees and wrapped her arms around his waist. "Thank you for being such a wonderful man. I'll be right here waiting with my grateful thanks."

"I'll hold you to that." He gazed down at her, his face softening. "Love you, *bella*."

"Love you too."

THE HEADLIGHTS OF NICK'S CAR SWEPT INTO JESS'S LIVING ROOM, casting shadows on the walls, and then the light faded along with the throb of the diesel engine. Jess was surprised she'd heard the noise over the clamor of the rain, which didn't seem to be letting up. According to the weather bureau, Bairnsdale and Kurnai Bay were being hammered by a once-in-fifty-years storm. Luckily, she lived on a hill—the low lands would be flooding.

Despite the tumult and the racket Jess had made finding buckets, Leo was sleeping soundly. Even so, she didn't want to risk Nick ringing the bell and waking him so the moment she heard Nick's familiar tread on the veranda, she opened the front door.

"Hi."

"Seriously, Jess? Tonight?"

She forgave Nick his hostile greeting. Despite the short distance from the car, the man was wet through and rain droplets clung to his hair and eyelashes. "Come in before you get any wetter."

Kicking off his boots, he stepped inside and accepted a towel, burying his face in it before dragging it over his head. When he looked up he visibly startled. She glanced down at her rather boring dressing gown. It was identical to Libby's—her friend had bought two and given her one. Jess rarely wore it as it really wasn't her style, but she'd pulled it on to cover the berry-colored silk and lace negligee.

A flush of color was crawling up Nick's neck and washing across his face. It instantly took her back to the first time she'd met him, when he'd been an inexperienced eighteen-year-old boy at a beach party.

"Have you got a bucket to drain the water into?" he asked tersely.

"Yep and I've spread out drop sheets."

"Good." He walked down the short hall and Jess followed. While he stared up at the brown stain that was widening in concentric circles and looking a lot like tree rings, she set up the two-step ladder.

He balanced on the top step and pressed his hand lightly on the plaster. "I'll start with two holes. Be ready with the bucket."

"Aye, captain," she said, trying to get him to crack a smile.

The high-pitched whirl of the drill filled the room and then rank brown water poured into the bucket. Jess wrinkled her nose and shuddered at the lucky save of her new mattress.

"Thanks, Nick. I mean it. I appreciate you coming over."

He grunted. "Did you really call the SES?"

She shrugged. "I knew you'd be quicker."

"Damn it, Jess." But he no longer looked or sounded as ticked off as when he'd first arrived. He stepped neatly off the ladder. "If Costa's not going to sink any money into this place, you should move."

Jess was spreading out towels and adjusting buckets to catch the remaining drips. "Easy for you to say, Mr. Homeowner. I don't suppose you take any notice of the articles in the *Gazette* about how high rents are driving locals out and anything half-decent is up on Airbnb."

"So? Move to Bairnsdale."

He said it as if it was the perfect solution. As if it wouldn't change everything. "The next time I move, it will be into my own place."

"You're serious about buying in the bay?"

It annoyed her that it hadn't occurred to him. "Of course I am. Is it true Harry Sullivan's thinking of selling?"

Nick stiffened. "I dunno. But even if he was, that place isn't for you."

Old anger, forged in her childhood by small-minded bay residents, flared. "Are you saying my place is on *this* side of the creek?"

His gaze fell away. "I better get home."

She immediately regretted her confrontational tone—after all, he'd come out in shocking weather to help her. "Sorry, Nick. I didn't mean ..."

But his eyes were glued to his phone and he didn't appear to have heard her. "Bugger!"

"What?"

"The causeway's flooded."

"I guess you're stuck here for a bit."

He rubbed the back of his neck. "I've got the truck. I might be able to cross."

"Nick, no! I'm not letting my best friend's husband and the father of my goddaughters get swept down the creek. Libby will agree with me that the best thing to do is wait it out. Besides, the SES won't let you through."

"I guess." But he didn't look happy.

"Call her and I'll make tea." Jess walked to the kitchen, filled the kettle and switched it on. As she set out mugs and milk, she could hear Nick murmuring on the phone. She picked out the words, "at least an hour" and smiled.

By the time he walked into the kitchen, the tea was brewing and she was plating two slices of the cake her client had given her that morning when she'd dropped off some tax forms at the patisserie. She added some strawberries and a squirt of Chantilly cream.

Nick's eyes lit up. "Is that Patrice's chocolate indulgence cake?"

"The very same. But it's our secret. If Libby finds out I gave you a slice, we'll both get in trouble." She pushed a mug of tea toward him. "It's such a shocking night, I thought you might have already been called out by a hapless tourist."

"I asked Dad to be on call tonight."

"Oh, right. Valentine's Day." She licked some chocolate frosting off her finger. "I thought you and Libby didn't bother with it."

Nick looked over the top of his mug, his Tuscan eyes flinty. "You don't know everything."

Jess squashed a laugh. Was Nick really that clueless? How could he not know that women, let alone best friends, disclosed all sorts of intimate information to one another? She knew *everything* about his marriage. "I know the anniversary's going to be a tough time for Libby."

"Not just for Libby. My son died too, remember."

This time she stared him down. "You know it's not the same."

He held her gaze for a few more seconds before forking cake into his mouth. Steering the conversation into calmer waters, they chatted about the weather, the new barista at the marina café whose skills took coffee into the next realm and Alice's controversial article in the *Gazette* accusing the film festival committee of safe choices.

"What was she thinking? Didn't she know Claudia's Jake's silent business partner?"

"She does now," Nick said ruefully. "Jake told her a couple of days ago he doesn't have any more shifts for her."

"Typical Alice." Jess muttered into her cake.

"I'm happy," Nick said loyally. "It frees her up to work more for me."

Jess no longer wanted to talk about the twins. "While I've got you here, I need to ask you a favor." She laughed at Nick's wary face. "Settle, petal. I'm on the toy library committee and we're pulling together the annual raffle. I was wondering if Pirellis' would donate the main prize?"

Nick visibly relaxed. "What did you have in mind?"

"A three-day cruiser hire."

"Why not a yacht?"

"People feel safer on a motor boat."

The sailor looked baffled by the statement. "Let's give them the choice. Just make it clear the hire has to be taken between March and November but excludes Easter."

"Great!" She beamed at him. "Thanks, Nick."

"Too easy." He poured them both a second cup of tea and cut himself another slice of cake. "When the girls were younger, I used to take them to the toy library on Saturday mornings when Libs was at work. They loved all the big toys, like that huge molded plastic garden and the red car."

"Leo loves that garden! He's fascinated by the flowers and the butterfly."

"I bet he loves the mail box."

"So much. I gave him all my loyalty cards from the stores I can no longer afford to shop at. He uses them as letters and it's so cute! I took a video."

Jess pushed her phone toward Nick. Her heart turned over at her son's squeals of delight when he'd opened the mail box and found all the cards waiting for him.

Nick laughed. "And rinse and repeat, again and again. The girls do that. Guess it's how kids learn."

"I'm not complaining. It kept him occupied and happy for half an hour. No one tells you how your life changes once they start walking."

Nick grimaced. "Libby mentioned it. I know I did."

She let his comment go, not wanting to revisit the time she'd told Libby she was going ahead with assisted reproduction to create a child and raise it on her own. It was the only time in their long years of friendship that they'd endured a period of strained coolness. She'd hated it.

"Mom-mom!" Leo's cries broke the silence.

Jess sighed. "How can he sleep through the noise of the storm and wake up when it stops?" She pushed back her chair and walked into her son's room. "Nigh-nighs time," she whispered, laying him down and stroking his hair.

But Leo was having none of it. He struggled out from under the covers and stood, stretching his arms to be picked up. "Waa-waa," he demanded.

"Okay. A quick drink and then back to sleep."

As she carried him into the kitchen, Leo snuggled into her shoulder but the moment he saw Nick, his head shot up. "Ick!"

"G'day, mate. You should be asleep." Nick looked at Jess. "The causeway's open again so I'll get going."

"Ick!" Tears filled Leo's eyes as Nick walked away. "Deer!"

"Deer?" Jess had no idea what Leo was talking about.

"Reindeer." Nick fished his key fob out of his pocket. "It's a bouncing game I play with the kids when you and Libby are having a wine and a whine. You should do it with him. He loves it."

"Why don't you come over tomorrow and show me?"

All the tension Nick had carried into the house returned as if it had never left. "How about I show you on Sunday when you come over for dinner."

Jess's lips pursed at his captain's tone. "Tomorrow would be better."

"Jess—"

"While you're here, you can replace the two rotten boards on the back steps."

"There are no rotten boards! Jess, *this* has to stop. I've tried to be understanding. I've tried to be the good guy and support my wife's best friend, but this is getting ridiculous. If you're determined to keep it up, I'm telling Libby that many of your call outs are fake."

The sleeping dragon inside her lifted its head and blew a blaze of fury. "You could do that."

His eyes narrowed to slits as if he was desperately seeking the position of a tripwire in the dark. "What?"

"You could tell her, but just think about it. I'm not the only person who hasn't been completely honest with her, am I? So, perhaps one night after one drink too many, I let it slip exactly what happened that time behind the surf lifesaving club."

His laughter rained over her. "I didn't even know Libby then. You and I were just two teens fumbling in the dark."

Jess shrugged, not remembering very much fumbling at all. "All I'm saying is, when a secret comes out, people start wondering what else they haven't been told. That's not a road I want to go down. Do you?"

The large veins in his neck throbbed and he swallowed. "No."

"Good. We're on the same page then. See you at lunch tomorrow. Meanwhile, you better get going or Libby will start to worry."

Jess watched him stride out into the easing rain until his silhouette was consumed by the dark. Since she was fifteen, he'd been the one walking away from her without looking back. But she'd watched and waited long enough. It was time for things to change.

CHAPTER FIVE

ALICE READ THE NOTE ON THE KITCHEN TABLE. *HAVING DINNER at the RSL with Hilary & Ken etc. You're welcome too. Love Mom.*

It was Friday night and as much as Alice enjoyed the company of her parents' friends, spending time at the RSL on a night off wasn't up there on her bucket list of things to do before she died. Not to mention the message it sent to the town—poor Alice Hunter alone again on a Friday night and eating dinner with the oldies from the University of the Third Age set. She checked her phone again, telling herself she didn't have a problem—she had the ABC News app installed and she was merely keeping up with local and world events. Even so, she wasn't deaf to the mocking laugh in her head.

In a very short time, Tim had taken her from a woman who frequently had no idea where her cell phone was or even if it was charged and switched on, to one who checked it obsessively, seeking the thrill of expectancy and the jolt of heat when she read his texts. She was still pinching herself that her first attempt at online dating had brought this funny and interesting man into her life. After the initial flurry of flirty trivia-based texts, which had left her floating on air, he'd suggested they move off the dating app and exchange phone numbers.

Alice had read many online dating articles and they all said this was the "next step" and a great sign, so she'd eagerly sent him her digits on the app and waited for him to call. She knew Tim had received her number, because she could see the word "delivered" underneath the message. Thirteen days had passed since.

During the first three nail-biting days without a call or a text on her phone and matching radio silence on the dating app, she'd turned herself inside out second-guessing what she should do. Part of her had wanted to consult Libby, but there wasn't much point. The last time her twin had dated, it had all taken place in real life, not in this brave new online world. She'd spent days prevaricating. Should she contact him on the app now he'd asked her to move off it? Was that preempting him? Perhaps the moment she'd sent her number, his work had gotten crazy or something had happened like a family crisis or illness or ...?

The experience uncomfortably returned her to a teen again, reminding her of Tyler Hawkins kissing her at a party and promising to call and ask her out. He never did. Deep in her heart, she'd always known Tyler was far more interested in Libby and Jess, and he'd probably only talked to her to get intel on them, but that hadn't stopped it from being two of the most tortuous weeks of her seventeenth year. It had only been eclipsed two weeks later when she'd forced herself to go to another party on her own as Libby was sick. Alice had walked into the kitchen and found Tyler making out with Jess. Rooted to the spot and with her entire blood supply suffusing her face, Tyler had chosen that moment to come up for air and notice her.

"Oh, hey, Alice. Is it weird being a twin?"

As she'd fled, wet-eyed and dry-mouthed, she'd heard Jess's reply: "Only if you're the dorky one."

Alice hated how Tim's delay in calling brought all her teenage insecurities rushing back. How was that even possible? She was almost thirty-four and emotionally mature. *Are you though?* the traitorous voice in her head said. *Lawrence didn't think so, otherwise he wouldn't have dumped you for Laetitia.*

With Tim's failure to call, Alice wrenched back the control she'd fought so hard for after Lawrence pulverized her heart. She'd followed the online dating gurus' advice and gotten back on the dating app, if only to silence her mind. She'd traded messages with Lachlan, Brad and Corey, but their texts lacked the spark that made her fingers tingle every time she messaged Tim. When she'd woken this morning, she'd instructed herself calmly and firmly that thirteen was unlucky and it was time to let Tim go. She'd lasted until morning tea before checking her phone. But now she was facing a Friday night alone so she was definitely pulling the pin. Just as soon as she checked her phone one last time.

There was a text from Nick asking her if she could be at the marina by 7:00 tomorrow morning. One from Libby inviting her to Sunday night dinner with her parents and Jess. A text from Jim at the *Gazette* reminding her of the deadline for her "What's On in the Bay" column and an RSL shift swap request from Shay: *I'm desperate, Alice! He's so cute!*

There was nothing from Tim. Again. Dejection dragged at her, turning her limbs into dead weights and the voice in her head critically malicious. *You're the woman nobody wants.*

The phone rang and she stared at the unknown number before deciding to answer. "Hello?"

"Alice, it's Tim."

A delicious shiver raced across her skin and she twirled on the spot. His deep and melodious voice was the exact pitch her imagination had generated.

"Tim, hi!" Her own words were not modulated or melodious and they squeaked out in an unfamiliar register. She sucked in a calming breath and tried again. "How are you?" *Why has it taken you so long to call me?*

"Great. I've just cracked a bottle of Lightfoot & Sons pinot and I've got myself some Maffra cheddar. I was wondering if now was a good time to talk?"

Her heart leaped. "Give me a second to pour myself a glass of sauv blanc."

"Really? I thought you liked a bold red?"

Not for the first time, she regretted that hastily written bio. She'd only mentioned bold reds because of the general belief in the community that red wine and serious conversation went together. "I do but my—" *Do not say parents* "—friend left half a bottle last night. Can't let it go to waste."

"New Zealand or Australian?"

"I'm not sure I should admit to New Zealand when you're doing such a great job supporting local producers."

"My motto is drink what you enjoy. Have you got something to eat with it?"

Alice peered into the fridge and found a container of dip. "Olives and hummus."

"Excellent. I thought we'd jump right in. What's your take on the proposed mine at Fingerboards?"

Wine, cheese *and* conversation! Alice was dizzy with delight.

Their pre-dinner-drink conversation extended way past dinner time, finishing closer to liqueur, coffee and chocolate time. For almost three hours, they ranged from the political to the personal and many topics in between, leaving Alice energized, excited and hopeful. So, when Tim said, "Alice, it's been amazing. Let's do it again next week," she bit the bullet.

"Shall we try and do dinner next week?"

"You asking me out on a date, Alice is Wonderful?"

She heard the smile in his voice and the wordplay of her online handle, and the breath she'd been holding released. "I was thinking more along the lines of improving our health and wellbeing. Dips, cheese and wine for dinner every Friday's not sustainable."

He laughed. "How about I come to you? I've been wanting to try that seafood place on the barge, but I s'pose you've eaten there heaps already."

"I tend to avoid the local restaurants during the summer," she said neatly side-stepping the fact she'd been avoiding spending any money on eating out. "But as long as we avoid the long weekend, we won't have a problem getting a table."

"Do you mind making the booking?"

"Too easy. I walk past it every day. What time?"

Tim muttered something about packing the trucks, logging the paperwork and the hour's drive. "I should be able to make it by 7:00."

Excitement jittered deep in her belly. "I'll book for seven thirty just in case."

"Great. And I'll phone a mate and let him know I'll probably be crashing on his couch."

Probably? Did that mean just in case he drank too much and couldn't drive? Or just in case this palpable attraction that simmered between them didn't hold up in real life? She couldn't imagine that it wouldn't. They already knew they could talk for hours and they'd exchanged enough photos for her to see he had dimples and a cheeky smile. She was definitely attracted to him—his voice alone made her quiver.

Was this when she was supposed to say "You can stay the night at my place"? Except she couldn't offer that. The thought of having sex in her childhood bedroom was one humiliation too far.

"Sounds like a plan," she said brightly. "See you Friday!"

Alice spent the next six days in a lather of preparation and anticipation. She got her hair cut. Subjected herself to hot wax in places that hadn't been waxed in months and rummaged through the thrift shop desperate to find an outfit that fell between her Melbourne workwear, her hospitality uniform of black and white, and her boat-cleaning grunge gear.

"What do you think?" Alice asked Libby, feeling a little guilty that she'd dropped in unannounced at six o'clock. The girls were wired after swimming lessons and tickle-wrestling with Nick. Libby was throwing together a salad and fielding calls from her relief doctor.

"What do I think of what?"

Alice wafted her hands from her breasts to her thighs. "This outfit."

"It suits you." Libby's hand paused on the vegetable peeler. "Hang on. You never ask me for fashion advice. What's up?"

Alice's excitement bubbled over. "I've got a date. I'm terrified and thrilled all at the same time."

"Oh, Alice, that's wonderful." Libby hugged her. "Where's he taking you? It is a he, right?"

Alice couldn't tell if Libby was teasing her or being deadly serious. "It might be five years since I last went on a date, but I haven't changed teams since then."

"Just checking. More than one woman I know who's come out of a filthy relationship breakdown has switched sides. It's a trauma response."

"Lawrence didn't hit me or steal my money."

Libby muttered something that sounded a lot like *stealing self-esteem*. "All I'm saying is, I can see why some hetero women try a same-sex relationship. I mean, women offer one another so much emotional support." She leaned forward and dropped her voice. "In so many ways, Jess understands me better than Nick."

Alice glanced at her brother-in-law, who was lying flat on his back with his daughters sitting on him as if he was a couch. They were listening wide-eyed as he spun a story about a boat, a giant squid and an adventurous sea captain. Lucy insisted the captain was a girl. Indi was acting the story out with her pirate ship and a toy dolphin. Alice's heart squeezed and old pain trickled through her, not only because the scene was one she hankered to replicate with a man of her own, but because Libby was closer to Jess than she was to her own twin. Alice jerkily swiped a carrot stick through the pesto dip and tried to push down the hurt.

"You have the perfect situation, Libs. A best friend who gets you and a man who loves and adores you. Besides, you'd miss the sex."

"Lesbians do have sex, Al." Libby's tone was the same one she'd used back when they were sixteen and she'd decided it was time Alice learned about sex whether she wanted to or not. "According to the research, they have more satisfying sex, because they don't have to teach their partner where their clitoris is." She handed Alice a glass of wine. "You did a fine arts major. You were surrounded by gays. Surely you had the right-of-passage one-night lesbian stand at university?"

"No!" Alice sputtered as realization dawned and reinforced yet again how little she knew about her adult twin. "But I'm gathering you did."

"Don't tell Nick, but Jess and I tried it once or twice when we were filthy drunk." Libby laughed. "Close your mouth. I can't believe you're still so easily shocked."

"What can I do?" Nick walked into the kitchen and slid an arm around Libby's waist before scooping some dip onto a celery stick.

"Help Lucy set the table."

"Alice, you're staying for dinner?"

"I—"

"Just say yes and save us all from Nick badgering you until you finally give in."

"I don't badger." Nick threw them a mock-injured look. "Besides, Alice needs feeding up and my lasagna's perfect for that."

"Alice has a date on Friday night."

Nick's face broke into a smile and Alice warmed under its genuine delight. "That's fantastic. Who's the lucky guy? It is a guy, right?"

"That's what I said." Libby high-fived Nick.

"Oh, my God! Not you too." Alice glanced down at her clothes. "Am I putting out a vibe that's going to scare Tim off?"

"I only asked because my backpackers have taught me it's not PC to assume," Nick said. "Believe me, you're *not* going to scare him off."

After dinner, Alice left Nick and Libby tidying the kitchen while she put the girls to bed. She loved this routine and always took the opportunity when it arose. Cuddled up in the bottom bunk with a girl on each side, she told them the fairy and unicorn stories she'd written years ago when she was a dreamy kid.

"Sleep tight, munchkins."

"Love you, Lis," they chorused.

"Love you more."

Alice closed the bedroom door and walked into the living room. Libby and Nick were sitting on the couch—Nick's arm slung over Libby's shoulder, her hand on his thigh—looking like they were in the early weeks of dating instead of married for years. Rather than envy, Alice experienced relief that they'd found a way out from the crushing despair Dom's stillbirth had brought down upon them. Thankfully, they'd come through their grief stronger than ever, and this strength was helping them deal with their disappointment that Libby wasn't pregnant again with the child they both desperately wanted.

"Thanks for a yummy dinner, but I better get going. I promised Dad I'd watch that new detective series with him and I need a good night's sleep for my big date."

Libby eyed her over her mug of tea, zeroing in like only a twin could. "Tim knows you're living at home, right?"

"I haven't actually mentioned that."

"Alice! What's your plan? Introducing him to Mom and Dad as you cross the living room to the stairs? Or are you asking him to shimmy up the wisteria?"

"We might take things slowly."

Libby laughed. "Yeah, right. You glow just mentioning his name. You'll be lucky to make it to dessert."

"*Calypso*'s in dock, if that helps," Nick offered. "And if things go well, why not take her out over the weekend? Just make sure she's clean and ready to go first thing Monday morning."

Alice couldn't help herself—she squealed and twirled around in delight. "You're my best brother-in-law."

"I'm your only brother-in-law."

"If I had others, I'm sure they wouldn't come close to being as awesome as you."

Nick suddenly looked uncomfortable and she realized she'd

embarrassed him. "You're family," he said in a deep and heavily accented voice. "Of course I'm gonna help."

Libby laughed. "He thinks he's gangster but really he's a hopeless romantic."

"I'm right here," Nick said.

Libby kissed him on the mouth.

"That's way too much PDA and my cue to leave. You two have a fun night."

"Call me," Libby instructed. "I want a full report."

On Friday evening, buzzing with exhilaration, Alice walked into Pelican House's kitchen and twirled, letting the full skirt rise and fall. "Will I do?"

Her mother clapped. "You look beautiful, darling."

Her father whistled. "You'll knock his socks off, love."

I plan to knock more than his socks off. She kissed them both. "Thanks."

"Have a lovely time," Karen and Peter said simultaneously.

Alice would have appreciated the sentiment more if her parents hadn't exchanged a familiar anxious look—one that said Alice was expecting too much. Sometimes it felt like she couldn't win. If she sat at home, she was accused of letting life pass her by. Now she was being proactive, they worried she was putting her heart on the line to be hurt.

Tim's phone call came in just as she was at the marina putting the keys to *Calypso* in her handbag.

"Alice, I'm so sorry! I can't make dinner." His stress slammed down the line, knocking into her. "Half our pickers have come down with stomach flu so it's all hands on deck to get the broccolini picked."

"Oh, that's awful! The stomach flu, I mean," she quickly amended, hoping to cover her disappointment. She knew they picked vegetables at night because of the cooler temperatures and the crisper evening air was still a few hours away. "What if I brought a picnic? We could eat before you start."

"I love the idea, but I'm already at work and making a hundred calls trying to find healthy pickers on short notice."

Alice heard voices and machinery in the background. She refused to be one of those women who pouted when things didn't go her way so she tried hard to cover her dismay with relaxed acceptance. "Oh, well. These things happen."

"I'm gutted we're missing dinner."

"Me too."

"I promise I'll make it up to you as soon as this craziness is over, Alice is wonderful."

Ten seconds after he rang off, a gif of Tom Hiddleston saying "sorry" and blowing a kiss pinged onto her phone. A cartoon of broccoli followed, accompanied by *#greatbroccolinidisaster*. But as she laughed, the excitement that had buoyed her all week flattened like day-old lemonade and the colors in the world that had glowed so brightly faded to monochrome. She reluctantly hung *Calypso*'s keys back on their hook, closed the office door and locked it behind her.

A few weekend tourists wandered past hand in hand, looking at the boats. One couple were animatedly discussing plans for their mini-break, which included renting a paddleboat and walking in the coastal park. Alice glanced down and her glossy, raspberry-red painted toes winked at her from her strappy sandals. She suddenly heard Meatloaf in her head—the soundtrack of her childhood courtesy of Peter playing it loud and often—all revved up and no place to go.

The thought of going straight home and enduring her parents' sympathy and concern, not to mention her mother's action plan—Karen's lifelong response to every situation that challenged Alice—made her head spin. She walked straight to the restaurant. Five minutes after taking her seat, her error of judgement hit her in a wave of heat. Dan van den Berg and his current squeeze were at the next table. Nick's second cousin was the sommelier. The wife of Libby's gardener was her waitress. Whoever the kitchen hand was, they were guaranteed to be no more than three handshakes away from Alice. It would take less than an hour for the erroneous news that she'd been stood up to flash around town.

Karen's text arrived fifteen minutes later.

On Monday morning, Alice hummed along to Ed Sheeran in her head phones, drowning out the noise of the upholstery cleaner as she removed dubious stains from the cruiser's seat cushions. She really didn't want to know what the weekenders had gotten up to but going by the number of bottles she'd hauled out to the recycling bin, it had been fueled by an unhealthy amount of alcohol. Had they had fun or had it led to a fracturing of friendships? Take ten people plus alcohol and the diminishing of inhibitions that scenario provided, add in the confines of a boat, and any simmering resentments generally surfaced. Some things could never be unsaid and Alice always knew when that had happened by the demeanor of the disembarking patrons.

Her phone buzzed as she propped the wet cushions in the sun to dry. She fished it out of her pocket, loving the zip of delight when she saw a message from Tim. It was a cartoon of an ear of corn asking, "Hot outside?" as an ear of popped corn walked into the picture. Tim had added, *Stinking today. Feel sorry for me and enjoy your sea breeze, Alice is wonderful.*

It was his first communication since the great broccolini disaster. She hadn't contacted him over the weekend, not wanting to add to his stress. Instead, she'd driven to Bairnsdale and bought new art supplies before inviting her father fishing. After her week hyped up on adrenaline, sketching Peter sitting beside the straight and smooth Tambo River had soothed the jangles. It had been almost three years since she'd drawn anything and she was woefully out of practice. It wasn't even close to her best work, but that hadn't stopped Karen from sticking it on the fridge next to Indi's finger painting. Alice had wanted to enjoy her mother's delight in the sketch, but she knew it was a mark of Karen's relief that she was back drawing again. Sometimes, the weight of her parents' concern for her made it hard to breathe.

Alice reclined on the boat's railing and took a photo of herself with the beauty of the creek behind her. She captioned it, *Not just a sea breeze; no broccolini in sight* and snapchatted it to Tim. As she slid the phone back into her pocket, movement caught her eye. She saw Nick standing on the jetty holding a cardboard tray with four bright blue travel coffee cups and a white bakery bag. It was a Monday morning tradition for the boss to buy coffee, although Alice had passed on an order this morning. Tim's texts were making her jittery enough without adding artificial stimulants. Nick was talking to someone who had their back to Alice, and while his face was in shadow, the tense square of his shoulders showed he wasn't the relaxed man who'd greeted her earlier.

At first, Alice assumed the woman must be a disgruntled customer. But when she turned and her profile came into view, Alice realized it was Jess. Libby's friend had her arms crossed tightly and was radiating taut displeasure. Alice was familiar with that look—back in the day it had been leveled at her often. Alice knew Libby was disappointed that Nick had hired Enza's niece, but Alice was secretly relieved. Having Jess in the office would have taken the shine off working for the Pirellis. Had Jess come down to berate Nick about the job? Alice wouldn't put it past her.

Miaow! Alice knew her catty thought was unjustified. As much as it pained her that she'd failed at being her twin's best friend, she couldn't fault Jess's loyalty to Libby or the support she'd given her since Dom's unexpected death. And Libby had told Alice that Jess was hesitant about working for Nick due to a conflict of interests between the two businesses. Right now, Jess's professionalism aced Alice's, given she'd just wasted ten minutes texting and staring down the jetty. Propelling herself back to work, she clambered down the stairs and tackled the filthy galley.

Three hours later, her back ached but the boat sparkled and she was full of the satisfaction of a job well done. She gathered her cleaning equipment and, buckets slung on her arms, walked along the jetty toward the office.

A young girl, who could have been late elementary or middle school age—Alice found it hard to tell—was sitting on the boards, legs dangling. A sketch pad lay in her lap and a tin of colored pencils sat next to her. She held a pink one and the tip of her tongue peeked out from between her lips as she concentrated on drawing a very realistic representation of a pelican that was perched regally on top of a pylon. As much as Alice hated it when strangers commented on her own work mid-flow, given the age of the kid and the skill of the art, she couldn't help herself.

"Wow! That's awesome."

The girl glanced up from under her hat. "I haven't got the beak right."

Alice studied the drawing then the pink-beaked pelican before returning her gaze to the drawing. She pointed. "Try shortening it here. Draw the line that's there and not the one your brain's telling you should be there."

"Like this?" The girl rubbed at her original line and redrew it.

"Exactly like that." Alice wondered why the girl wasn't at school. She was about to ask when she heard running feet behind her. A boy materialized by their sides, his face flushed and his body bouncing with excitement.

"Holly! Dad's bought chips! Hurry up, Dad!" he called down the jetty before spinning back and realizing Alice was there. "Hello. Who are you?"

Alice tried not to laugh as his energy crashed into her. "I'm Alice Hunter."

The boy's green eyes widened. "My name's Hunter too."

"It's a pretty cool name."

"Yeah. It was my grandpa's name and my mom—"

"Hunter! Stop lallygagging and let the lady get back to work." The male voice came from behind her as did the seductive aroma of salt and hot fat.

"She was helping me with my pelican. Look! I finally got the beak right." Holly scrambled to her feet, thrusting the sketch book at her father.

"And her name's Hunter too!" Hunter popped around to stand between Alice and his father. "How cool is that?"

The man's gaze swung to Alice, clearly confused as to why she'd have a male name.

Unable to offer her hand due to the buckets and mops, she introduced herself. "I'm Alice Hunter."

He nodded but didn't volunteer his name. "I hope the kids haven't been bothering you."

Something about the weary way he said it made her rush to reassure him. "Not at all. In fact it was me who stopped to chat. Your daughter's got an amazing eye."

"She really has." He smiled at Holly. "She didn't get it from me, though. I struggle with stick figures."

"Do you want some hot chips, Alice?" Hunter reached for the white paper parcel, clearly unable to wait any longer. "Dad bought heaps of chips, didn't you, Dad?"

"Dad" was looking distinctly uncomfortable about the idea of sharing his lunch with a stranger.

"Thanks for the lovely invitation, Hunter, but I've still got some work to do before I eat my lunch." She smiled at Holly. "Maybe when you've finished your pelican you might want to try drawing one of the seals that play under the pier. They're pretty cute with all those whiskers."

The girl smiled shyly. "Okay."

"Enjoy your chips!" As Alice walked away, she heard the children's father say, "Come on, you seagulls, let's eat these before they get cold."

Alice pushed open the office door and immediately heard yelling then took in the stricken face of Missy, the young receptionist. She realized the angry voice belonged to Nick. The closed door to Nick's office was doing little to dent the sound.

The shouting discombobulated her. The Pirellis' office could lurch from relaxed to frenetic in a short space of time, but the vibe was always upbeat. The only time Alice ever heard Nick raise his voice was during a race—captain's privilege—or to save someone from injuring themselves or a boat. He ran his business on the tenets of respect, responsibility and the expectation of high standards, and he always rewarded a job well done. His staff loved working for him and most went the extra mile every time, because they knew he worked as hard as they did. Brodie, the apprentice diesel mechanic, was a perfect example. He'd told Alice over a beer at one of the Friday staff barbecues, "If it wasn't for Nick, I'd still be doing shit or be locked up like my old man. I dunno why he ever trusted me that first day to wash a boat."

"He probably thought you were safer on the boat working than lurking around the marina unsupervised."

Brodie gave her a cheeky grin. "Yeah, Nick's not stupid. At first, I only rocked up every day for the boats. After a while he figured I liked engines. He kept banging on about me doing an apprenticeship and one day he drives me up to community college. I never knew playing with engines was a job."

But now this understanding man with the patience of a saint was yelling at someone.

"What's going on?"

"I don't know." Missy wrung her hands. "You saw him this morning. He was his usual happy self but when he came back with the coffees he was seriously pissed. I've been avoiding him, but poor Jannick's copping it. I mean, I know the dude's late with his visitor regional work form, but ..."

A subdued Jannick slunk out of the office clutching his 1263 form and exchanged a look with Missy that was both beleaguered and aggrieved. "What is his prob—Oh, hello, Alice."

"Hi, Jannick." She threw the backpacker what she hoped was a sympathetic smile before grabbing two cans of drink from the retail fridge. "I promise I'll pay for these before I leave." She walked into Nick's office.

Nick was staring out the window watching two swans diving for lunch among the weeds, their large black feet flapping wildly and working as a counterbalance. As he turned to face her, Alice saw deep lines carved around his eyes and mouth, and a slump to his shoulders that she hadn't seen since baby Dom's funeral. If Dom had been born at term, he'd be turning two soon. Was the absence of a happy little boy toddling around playing on Nick's mind?

By the time Alice had returned to the bay nursing her own grief for a relationship she hadn't known was dead, along with an abrupt stop it had brought to her career, both Libby and Nick had lost the haunted look of grieving parents. Working for Nick this summer, she hadn't noticed any overt signs of sorrow and, the other night, she'd been struck by how relaxed and happy he and Libby were together. Alice scuttled mourning as a reason for Nick's uncharacteristic outburst with Jannick.

A cell phone buzzed on his desk. He didn't move to answer it.

"You okay?"

He rubbed his face and sighed as if she was yet another problem on a very long list. "What can I do for you, Alice?"

She held up the cans and sat down without being invited. "It's hot and I've finished cleaning *Wanderer*. She needs a few minor repairs." Sipping her drink, she ran through the manifest, reading it upside down while Nick made some notes next to her own.

"Thanks. Customers, eh? Can't live without them but, jeez, sometimes ..."

Everyone moaned privately about difficult customers and there was a punching bag in one of the storage sheds so people could vent if required. But Nick believed most people only complained if their expectations weren't met and it was everyone's job to meet them. It was why Pirellis' won both state and national tourism awards each year. Alice knew Nick thrived on turning a difficult customer into a grateful one so it was unusual for him to allow anyone to ruffle him.

She recalled what Missy had said about Nick being out of sorts after his visit to the café and, matching the information with his body language on the jetty, she decided to wade right in. "Did a customer tick you off or was it Jess?"

Nick's open face shut down and his eyes narrowed warily as if Alice had just crossed a line. She held up her hands. "I'm not criticizing her. It's just when I was emptying the upholstery cleaner, I noticed the two of you talking and Jess didn't look happy."

For a few beats, the only sound in the room was the whoosh of carbon dioxide as Nick lifted the ring pull on his limonata. "Yeah. She's pissed off with me."

Alice wanted to ask why but something indefinable kept her silent.

Nick took a swig from his can, swallowed and then gave a tight laugh as he caught the look on her face. "No need to go all evil twin on me. It's not like it's a secret Jess is ticked off with me. But if it's okay with you, don't tell Libs you saw us arguing. She can be a bit ... touchy about Jess."

It was the first time Nick had ever mentioned her twin's protective instincts toward her friend, and just like that, they were coconspirators. "Tell me about it! None of us can say anything against her. And if we dare, we're instantly guilted about her difficult childhood and how hard she's worked to get where she is. Then we're told—" Alice raised her fingers in quotation signs, "—'instead of criticizing, you should admire how much Jess has achieved.'"

Nick returned her grin and an unexpected niggle of twin betrayal snagged her glee. Alice ignored it. "Don't worry. I won't say anything to Libs, but it's nice to know someone understands."

"Thanks. Don't get me wrong. I really appreciate the way Jess always has Libby's back, but—" The cell phone buzzed again and this time he glanced at the screen. A muscle close to his jaw twitched and he declined the call.

"But?" Alice prompted, hoping to hear more negative thoughts about Jess and knowing it was probably unhealthy to want it this much.

"Sometimes she goes too far and plonks herself into my marriage."

"Is that what she's done today?"

"Yeah. She's booked us a weekend at Dinner Plain."

Disappointment doused Alice. Given how much Libby and Nick

did for Jess, this didn't look anything like Jess inserting herself into their marriage—it looked like a token of appreciation. "And that's a bad thing how?"

"Hell, I don't know!" He flinched and rubbed his chest. "Just saying it out loud makes me sound stupid. I'm probably overreacting, right?"

Alice wasn't following. His words sounded reasonable but the tension in his body told a different story. "Overreacting's not something you're known for. I'm sure you've got your reasons."

He screwed up his mouth as if he was holding back words before huffing out a sigh. "It's just with the practice being one doctor down, it's a monumental effort for us to get away. I suppose it would be worth it. We've all gone away together before and I know the kids will love it."

"All of you?" Alice was confused. "I thought Jess was minding the girls so you and Libby can have a weekend away?" Nick shook his head and suddenly she understood where he was coming from. "If you're going to all that effort to make it happen, I think it's only fair and reasonable you'd rather go on a vacation with just your family. What does Libs think?"

"She doesn't know about it yet. Jess wants it to be a surprise. The thing is, she's insisting we go the day after Dom's birth—what should have been his birthday."

"That's—" Alice realized she needed a moment to process how she felt about this plan, not that she had any experience of giving birth to a baby, let alone a dead baby. But she was intimate with a level of pain and heartache when life dealt a stinging backhander. And for some reason, Libby had always found Dom's due date harder to bear than the day he'd been stillborn.

"I suppose it could be something nice after a tough day, although it might not be ..."

Nick threw her a grateful look. "Exactly! *Thank you* for understanding. If Libby was pregnant I wouldn't be so worried, but she tends to drop her bundle around—"

His phone buzzed again. "Jesus!" He flicked it onto silent, slid it into a drawer and slammed it shut.

His stress hit Alice in the chest, ratcheting up her concern. "Nick, tell Libby how you're feeling about this otherwise you're going to make yourself sick."

He barked out a laugh. "Yeah, right. Come on, Alice, think about it. Picture Libby's reaction when I reject what she'll consider Jess's thoughtful gift?"

"She might surprise you."

"And pigs might fly."

CHAPTER SIX

MARCH

Hilary van den Berg popped her head around the classroom door. Karen's long-time friend was now the chairperson at the University of the Third Age—or U3A as all the members called it. The moment Karen had retired, Hilary had roped her in as a volunteer tutor.

"Have you got a minute?"

Karen paused in clearing away the remnants of the wine and cheese her French conversation students had enjoyed. Recently, she'd been wondering if she should just give in and drop the word conversation from the course entirely and call it, "English Chat with French wine and cheese."

"*Bien sûr.*"

"I'll take that as a yes." Hilary plonked her behind on the table next to Karen. "How's Alice? I can't decide if that serve she gave the Chamber of Commerce in the *Gazette* about business putting tourism dollars ahead of the environment is a sign she's feeling more positive about life or the reverse?"

Karen stifled a sigh. She'd already been accosted by Henry Liu about the same article. "We do have a problem with the amount of cheap plastic that's sold in town and then dumped on the beach and in the lakes."

"At least she's channeling her disappointment and anger into something worthwhile."

Karen huffed. "I'd be happier if she was back in Melbourne. I'm furious with Lawrence and the Cahills. It was Alice who took their dingy art catalog from a small affair to a beautiful glossy magazine. It was the first time in her life she was leading not following. Now, she's lost her confidence and you know Alice ..."

Hilary nodded, understanding written all over her face. "I know you still worry about her, but look how far she's come since she was a little girl with a squint and a wobbly gait."

"Those were the easy fixes." Karen's mind slid to the terrifying months when Alice was fourteen, withdrawn and refusing to go to school. A time Karen watched her like a hawk, constantly fearful Alice might hurt herself.

"You've had a tough time recently with both twins having their hearts broken in different ways. It puts my worries about Dan *ever* meeting a nice girl in perspective. But dear Lord, I deserve grandchildren. I don't suppose we can match him up with Alice?"

"Unlikely. They've known each other since they were kids and Alice isn't really Dan's type," Karen said diplomatically. She was very fond of Dan but he wasn't right for Alice. He worked hard and played hard and charmed his way through life—usually with young willowy model types ten years his junior. "But Alice's started dating again, so I'm trying to take that as a good sign instead of another reason not to return to her life in Melbourne. I just wish she'd get a job that uses her talents."

"Actually, that's what I wanted to talk to you about. Summerhouse just called and they've got some funding. They're looking for someone to help a group of frail oldies—" Hilary consulted the note in her hand, "—'Scrapbooking as a way of connecting to the past and fostering memory and wellbeing.' Personally, I'd be worried they'd cut themselves with the Stanley knife! Anyway, it's arty and I immediately thought of Alice."

The jobs that matched Alice's skills, and provided the opportunities for her to reach her potential and achieve the sense of wellbeing she needed, only existed in big cities. That's why Alice had lived in Melbourne for a decade. That's why Karen wanted her to return. The longer Alice delayed, the more confidence she'd lose, and unlike Libby, Alice didn't have any reserves in that department.

Hilary was watching Karen expectantly. "Hil, it's really kind of you to think of Alice, but as I explained, her talents lie a long way from scrapbooking and the bay. It's really not her thing at all."

AFTER POPPING INTO THE CO-OP TO BUY SOME FLATHEAD TAILS for dinner and grabbing some groceries, Karen carried her reusable cloth bags into the kitchen. "I'm home."

"In here," Alice called from the living room.

Karen found her younger daughter on her hands and knees surrounded by photographs of every size, from tiny black and white prints to large color ones. Karen and Peter's wedding album, such as it was—a white and gold photo album from the discount store, which Karen had filled with photos taken by friends—was open on a picture of them standing on the steps of the old Royal Mint. She and Peter looked so young, yet Karen remembered feeling as if she'd already lived a lifetime by then.

Pragmatic, cash strapped and without any family of her own, Karen's idea was for a low-key wedding. She'd planned to be married in the dress she'd bought for her job interview at a prestigious school for girls, but the day before the wedding, Peter's mother, Dot had arrived unannounced at their apartment holding a large white box. Nestled inside sheets of pale blue tissue was a white, tea-length frock with a full skirt, a sweetheart neckline and a lace overlay. Feeling like Cinderella, Karen had lifted the dress clear of the box and pressed it up against herself.

"I know you're a very independent young woman and I admire you for it," Dot said, her words rushing out. "And there's nothing wrong with being financially prudent, but you only get married once. At least I hope you do. Anyway, I saw this and I thought it said, 'Karen.' But if you don't like it, I won't be at all offended. I'll just return it."

Karen loved the frock for its elegant simplicity and lack of froufrou, but she loved it more for what it represented—a welcome to Peter's family. The gift undid her carefully constructed lie that marrying Peter was just a necessary piece of paper so the bank would approve their home loan. Instead, the dress said love and acceptance. The contrast with her own family was stark and unforgiving, and it quickly exposed the ugly truth she tried so hard to bury. A home that was a prison. The baby sister she'd left behind. She doubled over at a twist of visceral pain and fell sobbing into Dot's arms.

The woman stroked her hair, clearly bewildered. "I'm sorry, dear. It was supposed to make you happy."

"I ... am ... h-happy."

Dot pressed a hanky into her hands. "I think we could both do with a sherry, don't you?"

A decade after Dot's death, Karen still missed her loving presence in their lives.

"Hi, Mom. Good class?"

Alice's question sent Karen's memories scattering and she got a flash of a much younger Alice creating chaos all over the house. Whenever Karen had complained, Alice defended her actions: "It's art, Mom, not mess."

Karen tried not to sigh at the disarray in front of her. "What are you doing?"

"Looking for photos."

"Why?"

Alice jumped to her feet, her face flushed with excitement. "Hilary called half an hour ago."

"Darling, we all like Dan but after your heartbreak over Lawrence, is he really the type of man you're looking for?"

Alice blinked, clearly confused. "What are you going on about? Why would Hilary call me about Dan?"

Damn it, Hil! Although she didn't think Alice dating Dan came close to a good idea, right now it seemed the lesser of two evils. "What did she want?" she tried to keep her voice casual.

"There's an art therapy job at Summerhouse. Hil gave me the details and I called the manager. She offered me the job on the spot! It's a great hourly rate, there's a decent budget and I've got total creative freedom to help the residents create life pages for a memories book. I'm so pumped!"

Karen pushed down her dismay and tried to infuse her voice with enthusiasm. "That's great news, darling."

"Isn't it? It's like the job's been tailor-made for me."

"I doubt that," Karen said crisply, unable to maintain her fake enthusiasm. "It's hardly working in fine art."

Alice grimaced. "You're forgetting I did some art therapy when I first graduated. Anyway ..." She waved her hand over the clutter of photographs. "I thought I'd make a couple of demo pages to show the residents and get their imaginations sparking."

Karen mustered up a faint, "Lovely," as she pictured glitter and glue and shavings of craft paper all over the carpet. "Just promise me you'll put everything away before dinner."

Alice didn't look up from flicking through a stack of photos she'd removed from an old yellow envelope. "No problem."

"I'll put the kettle on. Would you like a tea or coffee?" Given it was too early for a gin and tonic, Karen planned on nursing her disappointment with a cup of Earl Grey.

"Chai would be lovely."

Karen was almost at the door when Alice said, "Mom, where are our baby photos?"

An old frustration returned. Karen prided herself on being organized. Neat and tidy was her mantra, along with OHIO—only handle items once. But Alice and Peter had the "inability to file" gene and consequently they were always losing things and asking her where they were.

"They're where they've always been. Our favorites are in the pink album and you're holding the others in your hand."

"But the earliest ones here are labelled ten weeks. Where are the newborn ones?"

"They'll be there somewhere."

"Except I've been through them all and they're not here."

"Perhaps they got separated the last time you looked at them. That was probably the end of Senior Year when you needed a baby photo for graduation. You're not the best at putting things back in their rightful place, darling."

"But it just seems a bit weird that all of them are missing."

"Not really. Back then film was expensive and I think we only had twelve photos. They were out of focus and I probably threw them out."

Alice stared at her aghast. "Mom!"

"There's no point keeping fuzzy photos."

"I guess not. Oh!" Her eyes lit up. "Twins are always big news so the *Gazette* would have taken photos of us in the hospital, right? I wonder if the files are still around."

Karen's hand tightened on the door frame. "I doubt they archive baby photos. Anyway, there was a fire at The *Gazette* a year after you were born and they lost a lot of negatives. To be honest, Alice, that photo you're holding is my favorite. Before then, we'd been too worried about you to take photos, but you'd finally gained weight and smiled. I was so happy, I shocked your father by paying for a studio portrait."

Alice smiled dreamily at a photo of her and Libby in matching smocked gowns and matching gummy smiles, gazing up at the person behind the camera. "I know I was small but we were irresistibly cute. If we were babies today, you'd be bombarding Instagram with us."

Karen smiled weakly and left Alice looking at photos. Instead of returning to the kitchen, she walked directly to the dining room. With a shaking hand, she splashed brandy into a wine glass and gulped it down fast, welcoming the fiery burn that dominated the tangled mess of emotions rising fast from the past and threatening to choke her.

Libby smiled encouragingly at the mother sitting adjacent to her with her baby boy on her knee. Over the years, Libby had delivered and treated a lot of FLKs—funny-looking kids—but this baby was plump on the goodness of breast milk and utterly adorable. She had a crazy urge to grab him and kiss his rolls of baby fat. Was that a sign she was pregnant or was it just wishful thinking? Her period was due any day and she could easily find out now, but she was resisting the urge to ask Penny, her practice nurse, to draw blood. Libby didn't want to have to deal with the sympathy if the test came back negative.

Putting her own dreams aside, she switched her full attention to the mother and child. "Let's give this little dude his checkup."

The morning rolled along, dealing with everything from hypertension and associated erectile dysfunction to skin infections and referrals to specialists in Bairnsdale. Some days were more mundane than others, but since she had to drive to the Bairnsdale hospital for an afternoon seminar, she wasn't complaining if dull meant she could get away on time.

Her office phone rang just as she was checking some test results before meeting her next patient. "It's Lucy's school," her receptionist said.

The school had never phoned Libby before. Her gut tensed as she instantly ran through ten different scenarios, all of them featuring Lucy injured in some way. "Libby Hunter speaking."

"It's Cheryl from the school office. Lucy doesn't have her swimming gear and they're leaving for their lesson in half an hour."

Libby groaned. The last thing she'd said to Nick as she raced out the door this morning was, "Lucy's got swimming today." Normally when she micromanaged, he rolled his eyes, kissed her and said, "I've got this. Go save lives." But today he'd snapped at her, "Tell me something I don't know."

For some reason, he'd been irritable all week with her and the kids, and she was losing patience. If she hadn't been running late, she'd have called him on it.

"I've got back-to-back patients, Cheryl. Have you called Nick? His number's actually listed as first contact."

"Oh, sorry! I was on automatic pilot, phoning the mom first. I'll call him now."

"No, that's okay. I'll do it." Libby rang off and immediately pressed Nick's cell number. It rang and rang and she was about to hang up and try the office landline when he finally picked up.

"Yes. What?"

She flinched at his brusqueness, especially as the only reason she was interrupting him was because he'd stuffed up. "Hello to you too, darling."

"I don't have time for sarcasm."

"Fine." She heard the doctor in her voice—the tone that said, "Don't mess with me"—and she took a breath to banish it. She hated when they argued. "The school just called. Lucy doesn't have her togs and she needs them asap or she won't be allowed to go to swimming."

Nick swore. "I can't get down to the school."

There weren't many situations that kept Nick tied to the office. In fact, it was his work flexibility that made the juggle of their lives so much easier. He certainly hadn't mentioned anything important happening today. "How come?"

"Jeez, Libs. I just can't, okay. I'll call Mom."

"Your parents have gone to Paynesville to visit Leonora, remember?"

He swore again. "What about Alice or your mom?"

"It's Alice's morning at Summerhouse and Mom's teaching at U3A till noon." Magpies chortled loudly in the background. "Where are you?"

"I'll ask Jannick."

The idea of a backpacker wandering around their house looking for Lucy's swimming bag didn't thrill her. "I'll phone Jess. She said she was having a quiet morning at home and she's got a key. Hang on, I'll put you on hold while I call her."

"No!"

"No? To going on hold?"

"I mean, no, I'll call her." It sounded like he was sucking his breath in through his teeth. "I stuffed up so I'll fix it."

She should have been relieved he was being his usual obliging self, but the tension in his voice belied the sentiment. "Nick, what's going on with you today?"

"Nothing."

"Are you sure? It's just you've been—" *moody, snappy, grumpy, unreasonable,* "—a bit out of sorts this week. Are you thinking about Dom? Do you need to talk to someone?"

"Jesus, Libby! There's nothing wrong, okay? Look, I've got to go or Lucy will miss swimming."

He hung up before she could say goodbye. Was this delayed exhaustion after the frantic summer season? At this time of year, he was usually relaxed and happy, enjoying the slower pace but pleased there were still enough tourists around to keep things ticking over nicely so he didn't have to lay off any staff. Nick hated letting good staff go each winter and that was when he was likely to go quiet for a few days.

Libby was clueless as to what was bothering him, but something was and she made a mental note to get a babysitter for Friday. Nick needed a night off from work and daddy duties. He needed date night.

The intercom buzzed. "Need you in the treatment room," Penny said. "Sam Lukis is back. Asthma attack."

Libby handed Sam's care over to, Ramesh, her trainee, when he arrived at one o'clock and then she stepped out into the sunshine. Alice and Karen called her name from across the road and she looked around to see them waving white bakery bags and travel coffee cups.

"We've brought you lunch," Karen said. "And before you say you're too busy, you know you have to eat."

Libby laughed. "I'm starving, so I have no intention of saying no to a food ambush."

"It's Alice's idea. She ambushed me after my current affairs class finished."

"I bought our favorite." Alice sat at the picnic table and ripped open one of the bags to expose three rustic baguettes groaning with chicken and avocado.

"Oh, yum." Libby enthusiastically bit into one.

Her twin grinned at her. "You're welcome. There's also lemon tart and a chocolate one. And because I'm high on craft glue fumes, I'll even let you have first choice."

"Best twin ever."

"That's me."

Libby noticed Alice had glitter on her cheek and a bit of colorful Washi tape tangled in her hair—typical chaotic Alice. Libby realized with a jolt that this version of her twin had been absent during the Lawrence years. It was an equal shock to learn that she'd missed it. "So how are the oldies?"

"Fabulous! I could sit and listen to their stories all day. I'm a little bit in love with Martha Ingles."

"Me too. She's ninety-nine and sharp as a tack."

"Everyone thinks she's this sweet old lady who's lived an ordinary life on the land, married to Reg, raising seven kids and God knows how many calves. They think her only claim to fame is holding the record for winning the most Best Sponge Cake blue ribbons at the Bairnsdale Fair. But she was in Singapore when the Japanese invaded. She spent a year walking across Sumatra before finally being allowed to stay in a camp. A year! Can you believe it?"

"*A Town Like Alice*," Karen murmured. "There were thousands of women stranded in South-East Asia during the second world war."

"I had no idea," Alice said. "At school, we were taught about the men working and dying on the Burma Railway and at Sandakan, but no one talks about what the women went through. There's a photo of her brutally thin and emaciated, lying in a hospital in 1945. Her stories tear me apart. Now, after years of not talking about her experiences, Martha wants me to help her display the two photos she has of that time as part of her book. It's such an honor. I'm petrified I won't do it justice."

Karen sighed. "Alice, you put together two substantial art catalogs a year for three years and you won awards for your work. That's where your talent lies. It isn't getting anxious about an elderly woman's scrapbook."

Alice stiffened but instead of responding she filled her mouth with lunch.

A pregnant woman walked past them pushing a toddler in a stroller and Libby's gaze unconsciously dropped to her own belly. Was there a tiny new life beating inside her? Before now, she'd always conceived easily—once she'd thought too easily. The memory of her initial dismay when she learned she was pregnant with Dom morphed into rebuking guilt and shame. If she'd known what was coming, she'd never have taken anything for granted.

It was just over a year since she and Nick had been actively trying to conceive and a nagging question was gaining volume. "Mom, did you and Dad ever try and get pregnant again after having us?"

Her mother's finger toyed with some fallen lettuce. "We did."

A ribbon of disquiet unfurled. "And it didn't happen?"

"It did happen." Karen raised her head, memories clear in the depths of her eyes. "I fell pregnant three times, but none of them lasted for longer than eight weeks. After the third miscarriage, we decided that as we were already blessed with two beautiful daughters you were enough."

Alice looked stricken. "I didn't know that. Why didn't I know?"

Karen patted her hand. "There was no reason for you to know, darling. You were only little at the time."

"How old were you?" Alice asked softly.

Karen thought about it for a minute. "Much the same age you are now. Dr. Richards said my eggs were probably too old."

Alice flashed a look at Libby and she read her twin's distress for them both.

"Old Dr. Richards was talking through his hat, Mom," Libby said firmly, as much to reassure Alice as herself. "Back then the average age for a first baby was about twenty-two. Today, it's thirty and the highest fertility rate is among women aged thirty to thirty-four. There could have been any number of reasons why you miscarried. Pesticides and fertilizers were being used willy-nilly then."

Alice chewed her lip. "Libs, should I be thinking about freezing my eggs?"

Her heart ached for her twin. "Maybe. Does Tim want kids?"

"She needs to actually meet him first," Karen said snippily.

"I *have* met him, Mom," Alice said wearily.

"Texting and long phone calls is not meeting."

Alice hacked jerkily at the chocolate tart. "Can we please *not* have this conversation again?"

"What happened to meeting someone at a party or at the surf club or the yacht—"

"Times have changed, Mom." Libby moved to support Alice, despite part of her agreeing with their mother. "And let's face it, the dating pool in the bay's limited at best. Jess has just snapped up the last good guy."

"Are Will and Jess officially a couple now?" Karen asked, clearly skeptical.

"Pretty much. They're taking things slowly because of Leo, but from what Jess says, they're planning to move in together by July."

Karen's brows rose and despite trying hard to ignore her mother's look, Libby failed. "What?"

"It's just I saw Elsa Azzopardi at the U3A dine-out recently and she spent a long time talking about Will."

"So? She always does that."

"Yes, but she didn't mention Jess once."

"That's because they haven't told Will's parents yet. You know how overwhelming Elsa can be."

Karen leaned forward as if about to divulge some great secret. "The thing is, darling, Elsa said Will's dating a woman from Sale."

Libby laughed. "No need to panic, Mom. That's Will's decoy story to protect Jess. Right now, they're enjoying a honeymoon period before the Azzopardis and the town wade in. I fully support it. If I was them, I'd be putting off the full-on Italian mama scene with Elsa for as long as possible too."

Karen looked unconvinced. "I'm not sure that's the wisest thing—"

"Oh, God it's almost 2:00. I have to go." Libby still had time up her sleeve but she lacked the inclination to argue with her mother about all the reasons why Jess and Will were doing the right thing. Cutting the lemon tart in half, she scooped up her share and gave Alice and Karen a kiss goodbye. "Thanks for lunch."

The moment she turned on the car's ignition, her phone connected to Bluetooth and the podcast she was listening to filled the speakers. She'd just reached the highway when Jess called.

"Hey, Lib, crisis averted. Lucy-Goose has her swimming gear. I phoned the school and met them at the pool. Leo and I had a swim too, so it was win-win."

"Thank you! You're the best."

"I aim to please."

Libby laughed and suddenly wondered when Jess had gone from calling Lucy "Miss Lucy" to using Nick's pet name for their eldest daughter. "You've saved Nick from having a sad sack kid this evening."

"Talking about sad sacks, what's biting your husband on the bum? Talk about cranky."

"Oh no! Was he grumpy with you too? He should have been groveling. It's his fault Lucy didn't have her stuff. I'm so sorry. It's not personal though. He's been a pain at home too."

"Perhaps he needs a weekend away." Jess sighed. "I know I do. I'm totally over Leo teething."

"Poor you. Teething's the pits. Hey, I know. I'm off this weekend so we could have Leo and give you a break. Why not go somewhere?"

"Will's offshore and I don't want to go away on my own."

The petulant tone was reminiscent of teenage Jess when Libby was tied up with a family event, leaving her friend alone on a Saturday night. Unlike Alice, Jess was more than capable of holding her own socially, so it had taken years for Libby to realize that Jess wasn't upset about going stag to a party, but that she didn't have any family occasions herself. Now, Jess was godmother to the girls and Libby was godmother to Leo and Libby loved that Jess was officially part of her family.

"I've got a better idea than a weekend away." Libby smiled at the fast forming thought. "Ramesh has just agreed to work Easter so we can take four days."

"We as in you, Nick and the girls?"

The hesitancy in her friend's voice made her ache. "As in all of us. You and Leo too. You know I love it when we all go on vacation together."

"That sounds amazing!" All the petulance vanished and Jess's usual enthusiasm was back. "I'll do some research and see where we can get in. We can talk about it on Sunday night."

Jess's tongue clicked loudly in the speakers. Libby wasn't sure if her friend knew she did this whenever she wanted to change the subject. "I know you're in Bairnsdale until late tonight but Nick sounded strung out on the phone. I was wondering if I should organize dinner for him and the girls?"

Libby had a love-hate relationship with people adopting men for meals when the women in their lives were away. It never seemed to translate into an invitation when the opposite occurred so she was philosophically opposed to it. "That's kind, but you've already helped enough by bailing us out with the swimming gear."

"Very true! Thing is, I forgot we weren't doing dinner tonight so I've already made a massive pot of spaghetti Bolognese. I may as well bring it over like usual and Leo can play with the girls. That's if you're okay with it?"

Libby's resistance faded. This was Jess and although she certainly spent more time at Libby's house than Libby spent at Jess's, her friend did cook for them in Burrunan's kitchen most Thursdays. "Of course, I'm okay with it. It will be a nice treat for Nick."

"Great! I'll pick Indi up from daycare and grab Lucy from school. You always say she's exhausted on swimming days so this will save her going to after-school care."

Libby could hear Leo chattering in the background. He always got excited when he heard the girls' names. "Okay, thanks. I'll call daycare and school now and let them know. Listen, just before you go, Mom just told me Will's dating someone from Sale so the story's working."

Jess laughed. "Gotta love the bay's grapevine. And talking of the grapevine, I saw Sulli at the patisserie. He says he's selling and moving into town."

Sadness wafted through Libby. She loved her elderly neighbor, but she understood his decision. "It's the end of an era. He and Patty bought the block of land in 1972. But now she's gone and his eyesight's failing so life will be easier for him in town. He's trading in his car for a red mobility scooter."

"Of course he is. Everyone knows red goes faster. I wonder who'll buy his place?"

"Nick suggested we buy it to give us a buffer."

"From pesky neighbors?"

"Yes! Our road's getting so built up."

"You're such a princess," Jess teased then cleared her throat. "What if I bought it?"

Libby almost ran off the road. "Jess, the block is huge. Plus it's right on the water. Not to mention the size of Patti's garden."

"So?"

"So, the last block on the Arm went for $600,000 and it was empty."

"And your point is?"

Libby recognized the prickly confrontation slung over the words and she pictured the jut of Jess's chin. Libby tried skirting around the issue that was money. "It's just you said in January ... I thought you were still saving for a deposit? That you can't afford to buy right now."

Or ever afford to buy on the Arm. Why was Jess daydreaming about buying the Sullivan place?

Outside of the practice finances, Libby didn't discuss money with Jess, because why spotlight the fact that these days she earned considerably more than her friend? She knew Jess had earned good money in Sydney and had enjoyed many of the things that city had offered, but it was an expensive town that didn't facilitate saving. Although Jess's living costs in the bay were much less, she'd taken maternity leave and she was still only working part time. Her moderate savings had taken a dent when she'd decided to have Leo on her own.

"Costa's place is falling apart around me," Jess said. "The water in the ceiling was the final straw. Even Nick says I should move. I know Sulli's house is nothing to write home about, but at least the roof's sound. The good thing is, the market's finally falling so I've been crunching the numbers and I think I can do it. Just."

Libby's stomach sank at the bubble of excitement in Jess's voice. She'd had no idea Jess was so close to pulling together a deposit, let alone such a large one, and she hated she was about to pop her joy. "The thing is, Nick's not just thinking about buying. I'm sorry, but it's a done deal. He and Sulli have agreed on a price."

Silence oozed through the speakers long enough for Libby to wonder if she'd hit a cell phone dead zone. "Jess? You still there?"

"Yeah. I'm here." The words dripped with disappointment.

Libby opened her mouth to say sorry again when a brilliant idea struck. "I know! Why don't you and Will rent Sulli's place? Settlement's in June and that gives us time to paint and do any repairs. It would be amazing having you living next door."

Again, silence lingered for a few beats. "Thing is, Lib, I don't want to rent anymore."

"But we'd be much better landlords than the Giannopoulos

brothers." Libby was determined to make Jess see this was a great idea. "Think how much fun we can have choosing colors and—"

"Before you go renting out your new investment property, you should probably discuss it with your husband."

Libby snorted. "You're hilarious. Like Nick's going to object to having his best mate and my best friend next door. He'll be thrilled to have tenants we trust."

Leo squealed and Jess said, "I have to go. You call daycare and school and I'll call Nick now about dinner."

"Thanks. I hope he's better company for you tonight than he's been for me."

"If he's not, there's always wine!"

Text message from Jess Dekic to Nick Pirelli Thursday 4:40 PM

Surprise! I'm cooking dinner for us tonight

Text message from Nick Pirelli to Jess Dekic Thursday 4:41 PM

No need. I've got dinner sorted

Text message from Jess Dekic to Nick Pirelli Thursday 4:42 PM

Liar! I'm standing in your kitchen right now looking inside your fridge. You and Libby really need to shop. There's nothing here to eat although the bottle of Veuve is tempting

Jess smiled when her phone rang and Nick's name lit up on the screen. "Hi."

"What the hell are you doing alone in my house?"

His angry voice was so loud she instinctively held the phone away from her ear. "Take a chill pill, Nick. It's not like I'm boiling rabbits. Libby said you've been a bit tense and she thought it would be a treat for you if I picked up the kids and cooked dinner."

"I don't need your help. I've got everything sorted. I'm leaving work now to pick up the kids."

"Too late. Indi and Leo are playing happily and Lucy's practiced her spelling. We're about to jump in the pool and I promised we'd take them out for ice cream after tea."

"You shouldn't have done that without asking me." The words shot out tight and hard as if being forced through clenched teeth.

Jess sighed at his overreaction. Why did he always make everything harder than it needed to be? "It's ice cream, Nick, not a PG-rated movie."

"I'm not talking about the freaking ice cream!"

"You should be. It's a celebration."

He was silent for a moment and she imagined his hand tugging at a curl behind his ear. "What celebration?" he asked cautiously as if the answer might bite him.

"Your deal with Harry Sullivan."

The line went dead.

THE TWILIGHT SYMPOSIUM WAS LIVING UP TO LIBBY'S expectations. It not only kicked goals for medical content, it also gave her the freedom to only be a doctor for a few hours rather than juggling it with being a wife, mother, twin and daughter—or as she often joked, the director of Homeland Security. Jess, bless her, had sent a Snapchat of the girls and Leo splashing in the pool with the caption, *Homework sorted. Happy kids. All Good.*

Sometimes, Indi could be cranky and headstrong after daycare and Lucy always worried the night before a spelling test, but as expected, Jess had it all under control. Libby hoped Nick appreciated the unexpected treat of walking into a calm house.

During the dinner break she chatted with her colleagues, enjoying the opportunity to talk shop, although she noticed many of the blokes talked about their golf handicap or their upcoming vacation. Then again, unlike her, most of them worked in larger practices and had other doctors on site to discuss tricky cases.

The last presentation of the evening was a professor from Melbourne University. He was talking about his study on the SMOC1 protein and if it could play a role in treating type two diabetes, when her phone vibrated. She immediately recognized the practice's number and hit the decline button. Ramesh was on-call with Penny and whatever the issue, they could handle it. She'd just pulled her concentration back to how the protein responded to glucose and insulin, when her phone rang again. This time she didn't recognize the number and she let it go through to voicemail.

Then a text pinged in. *Please contact Bairnsdale Regional Health Services Emergency Department as soon as possible.*

Libby sighed. Perhaps Ramesh had sent one of her sickies to the hospital and they wanted to talk to her. She picked up her bag and, murmuring her apologies, shuffled past her colleagues before making her way to the emergency department. The place was buzzing, with at least a dozen people waiting in chairs, so that meant a lot was happening on the other side of the locked doors. Using her lanyard, she buzzed herself in.

She didn't recognize the nurse at the desk. "Hi, I'm Dr. Hunter. I just got a text. I think you've got a patient of mine here."

His fingers hovered over a keyboard. "What's the name?"

"I don't know."

"You've sent us a patient but you don't know their name?"

Libby ignored the man's incredulous tone and showed him her phone. "I just got this message."

He frowned as he peered at the screen. "Are you Libby Hunter?"

"Yes."

"Ah." He stood and gave her a rueful smile. "Sorry for the confusion. Come this way."

She was about to ask who'd been admitted but he was already striding away from her. She followed him past the cubicles to one of the monitored beds.

"Oh my God!"

Nick lay on a hospital gurney, his usually healthy, tanned face matching the color of the covering sheet. A pulse oximeter was fitted on his forefinger, an IV line ran into the back of his hand, oxygen prongs sat in his nostrils and leads protruded from behind his hospital gown. The EKG machine beeped rhythmically.

She grabbed his free hand, gripping it hard as if he might suddenly be pulled away from her. "What happened?"

"Your husband's experienced some chest pain," the nurse said matter-of-factly. "We've taken bloods and he's had a chest X-ray. We're just waiting for the results. His vitals are stable, although his BP's still a bit high. Dr. Naing will be in shortly to talk to you."

Libby's gaze swung to the EKG, frantically looking for signs of a heart attack. "Nick, how long have you had pain?"

"I dunno. A few hours."

A few hours! Panic skated through her. "Tell me everything."

"There isn't much to tell. I've felt lousy all day and then I got this pain ..." He rubbed his chest with his hand. "It got worse and then it got hard to breathe."

Her own breathing sped up when she thought of his briskness on the phone. Then her abiding love for him got tangled up with frustration. "Why didn't you tell me when I phoned you about Lucy?"

"I didn't have it then."

"When did it start?"

He blew out a long slow breath and closed his eyes, weariness emanating from him.

"Nick?"

He took a moment before opening his eyes and when he did, the swirl of confusion in their depths made her wonder if he'd been given morphine. "What?"

"When did the pain start?"

"I don't know. I didn't check my watch!"

"Okay," she soothed, horrified at the spike in his blood pressure. "Let's work it out. I called you at 11:00 and you usually have lunch at 1:00—" She suddenly remembered her conversation with Jess. "Jess would have phoned you soon after 2:00 about dinner and collecting the girls. Did you have pain then?"

"She didn't call."

"What?"

Libby had an appalling image of Nick arriving at after-school care and daycare and not finding either of his daughters where they should be. But before she could ask, her own phone started buzzing so incessantly, it bounced on the bed. Five texts tumbled in.

Missy just told me she called an ambulance for Nick! I'm with her and Jannick at the pub. They're stressing out. Call me! Or Mom! Please call! Alice x

Sent Nick by ambulance to Bairnsdale for tests. Ramesh

Hi, Libby, Nick's complaining of chest pain. We thought it best to send him to BRHS by ambulance Hopefully you're with him now. Call when you can. Best wishes, Penny

Hi, have you heard from Nick? He's not answering his phone and the girls are refusing to go to bed without him. I'm a bit worried. Jess xxx

Everyone's concerns piled in on top of her own and she sent up a vote of thanks that at least Rosa and Rick were out of town. If they'd known Nick was sick, they'd have tailgated the ambulance to the hospital and Libby would be talking them off the ledge while trying to keep a lid on her own anxieties.

Nick complaining of chest pain? Her entire body clenched as she tried to wrap her head around his symptoms. They made little sense. He was fit and healthy, didn't smoke, drank moderately and ate a Mediterranean diet. His grandparents had lived to a ripe old age and his parents were fit and well. His only risk factor was he was male. None of it reassured her enough to quieten her clawing terror that something was seriously wrong.

She heard someone clearing their throat and turned to see a man with a stethoscope slung around his neck. "Hello, I'm Dr. Naing."

"Dr. Hunter." Libby shot out her hand. "Nick's wife. Do you have his cardiac enzymes results?"

"I do. Good news, Mr. Pirelli. We're fairly confident you haven't had a heart attack, but we'll repeat the blood tests in another three hours so we're absolutely certain. Your white cell count is normal and your chest X-ray is clear with no sign of pneumonia—"

"And pulmonary embolism?" Libby asked, running through her own checklist.

"Yes." Dr. Naing gave a wry smile and concentrated on Nick. "I'm going to send you for a CT and echocardiogram so we can rule out a few other nasties." He glanced at the monitor. "Good to see your blood pressure's starting to come down. How are you feeling compared to when you first arrived?"

Nick fidgeted with the top sheet. "The pain's less but I feel like I could sleep for a week. It's stupid, because I haven't done anything to make me tired."

"Well, you're in the right place and we'll get to the bottom of it. The best thing for you is to get some rest. You're going to be here for a few hours yet."

Nick nodded and closed his eyes again.

"Will you admit him?" Libby asked the doctor, starting to think of the girls and logistics.

"We'll keep you informed."

Libby recognized the code for "it depends on his results." As the doctor walked away, she sat down again and slid her hand into Nick's. He didn't get sick often, but when he did, he was very capable of exhibiting all the symptoms of man-flu. Once, when he'd caught a heavy cold, he'd summoned her to their bedroom multiple times with requests for everything from Tylenol to new batteries for the remote. The ninth time he rang the bell, she'd confiscated it. But today, this quiet, exhausted and withdrawn—almost resigned—version of her husband scared her.

Her phone vibrated again and Jess's name lit up the screen. Technically, she wasn't allowed to have her phone turned on back here so she selected the offered text option, *Will call you back.*

She bent down under the gurney and pulled out the plastic bag containing Nick's clothes and other possessions. Placing it on her knee, she rummaged through it and the plastic crackled.

Nick's eyes flew open—the black of his pupils almost obliterating his irises—and he struggled to sit up. "What are you doing?"

"Looking for your phone."

"It's not there."

Nick never went anywhere without his phone—neither of them did. "Where is it then?"

"I dunno." His voice was agitated. "On my desk, maybe? I used it to order the diesel. No, that was the office phone ..."

The pressure cuff on his arm inflated, checking his blood pressure. The numbers on the monitor leaped.

"It's okay," Libby tried reassuring him, not wanting to see his blood pressure rise any higher. "It's no biggie. It will turn up. I just thought I'd check it to see if there were any urgent messages."

"Unlikely," he muttered, falling back on the pillow.

"My phone's full of urgent messages from family and friends. Everyone's worried about you, especially Jess. I better call her. Do you want to talk—"

"God, Libby! Why the fuck would I want to talk to Jess?"

Libby jerked back. In their nine and a half years together, Nick had never sworn at her—well once on *Freedom* during a race, but that didn't count. He'd never sworn at her on land. She realized with a grip in her heart that this must be what fear looked like on him. Nick hated hospitals and the fact he'd allowed Missy to call an ambulance meant he'd been terrified he was dying.

Reaching for calm, she stroked his hair off his clammy forehead and kissed him. "What I was about to say was, do you want to say goodnight to the girls? But I think you're a bit too stressed for that. We don't want to scare them."

Nick swallowed rapidly, as if he was trying hard to hold his emotions in check. He took her hand. "Sorry."

The apology came out in a husky whisper and she stroked his cheek. "Will you be okay if I go and make a few calls?"

He nodded. "Get Alice to stay the night with the girls."

Libby didn't want Nick worrying about the arrangements, so she nodded, even though she had no intention of asking Alice when Jess was already at the house. Alice coming over would just be another disruption and she wanted things to be as smooth as possible for their daughters.

"Libs, tell the girls I love them."

"Of course." She kissed him again. "Try and sleep while I'm gone. I won't be long."

He squeezed her hand hard and his voice caught. "I love you and the girls so much. You're my world, you know that, right?"

"Of course we know that. We love you right back."

CHAPTER SEVEN

"A panic attack?" Alice stared at her twin, unable to absorb the words. "That can't be right. Nick's so easygoing."

"I know! It makes no sense. But they've ruled out a chest infection, an MI, pericarditis, a dissecting aneurysm, cholelithiasis—"

"You know I don't understand any of that doctor talk."

"Sorry."

The blue water of the lake glowed a silvery pink in the dawn light and the twins watched the view from a bench in the Pelican House back yard. Libby had texted Alice earlier asking if they could talk—just the two of them—before she went home to the girls. The request had surprised Alice given Jess was sleeping at Libby's house and Libby usually debriefed with her best friend, but she hadn't second guessed it. Instead, she'd embraced a rare twin moment and met Libby at the gate with coffee and blankets. Even in the half-light, Alice could make out shadows under her twin's eyes that couldn't be confused with smudged mascara. Libby wore exhaustion like an ill-fitting coat.

"They've ruled out all the big things and it doesn't leave much else as the cause. They told me they still had some tests to run this morning, but I read the referral to the psychiatric intern."

"Just fell in front of your eyes, did it?" Alice couldn't believe Libby had read it—her twin was a stickler for confidentiality.

Libby grimaced. "Fine. I used my admitting rights to access Nick's history, but I'm desperate. I can't imagine what's upsetting him so much that it's making him sick. Or why he hasn't told me. We tell each other everything!" She suddenly gripped Alice's arm so tightly, Alice flinched. "Is anything going on at Pirellis'? Have you noticed anything strange at the office?"

"No. I mean, he was a bit grumpy the other week when J—" She tripped over her tongue, remembering her promise to Nick and quickly recovered. "When Jannick was late with his visa paperwork."

Libby make a dismissive sound as if the information was irrelevant. "Some of my patients are complaining that tourist numbers were down this summer. Do you think it could be the business?"

"The boats were booked solid, Libs. I know. I cleaned all of them. A lot."

"Then what can it be?" Libby's hands tore through her hair. "I mean, surely if he had an addiction, I'd know."

"An addiction? Libs, I really don't think Nick's doing drugs."

"Of course he's not. I know he's not. His behavior's not erratic ..." Libby's frantic gaze sought hers. "When I told Jess he was making himself sick, she asked me if I thought he might have a gambling problem."

"That's ridiculous!" Alice was both offended and furious on Nick's behalf. "I know you're grasping at straws, but gambling? Seriously? Rick's in and out of the office and he and Nick meet each week. It would be pretty hard to hide any large withdrawals."

"He hasn't been taking any large amounts out of our joint account. I checked at 3:00 this morning. Of course, we both have our own accounts too so I can't check his ... Oh, Alice, I'm going mad. Things have been so great between us lately. I can't imagine what's stressing him to the point of a panic attack."

"You both lost a baby," Alice said gently, hating raising the painful memory. "A few months after Dom died, you said you didn't think Nick was grieving properly. Could this be a delayed reaction?"

"Maybe."

"You don't sound certain."

"I thought we'd both found our way through it. He doesn't act like someone who's grieving. I mean, apart from this week, he's been happier and more content than he's been in months. I'm the one desperate for a baby."

Alice's heart cramped for herself and her twin. "Does Nick want it too?"

"Lately he's been saying the girls are enough and—Oh God!" Libby's hand flew to her mouth. "Is that it? He doesn't want another baby."

Alice shook her head, worried that her normally rational sister was jumping to conclusions based on fear and lack of sleep. "That's not what I'm suggesting at all."

"Except we've been trying to get pregnant for a year!" Libby wrung her hands. "I dropped my bundle just before Christmas and he suggested we stop trying so hard."

"Did you?"

"It wasn't easy but I was in such a state it made a sort of sense. The thing is, after we had sex on Valentine's night, I told him I was ovulating and I hoped I'd get pregnant. What if he's freaking out that I'm pregnant and he's too scared to tell me he doesn't want another child?"

Alice swallowed hope and regret before steeling herself. "Are you pregnant?"

"I don't know! I've been too scared to do the test." Libby sucked in her cheeks. "If it's negative, Al, it means there's a problem. Both of us would need to have tests. What if he says he doesn't want them?"

Alice shuddered, unable to shut out her mother's matter-of-fact words from the day before. "Oh, Libs. You have to talk to him."

"I need to read the psych report!"

"Libby!"

Her twin sighed and sank into her blanket. "I know. You're right. Nick and I need to have a long and frank conversation. Get ourselves back on the same page."

Alice remembered the last long and frank conversation she'd had with Lawrence and instantly reassured herself that Libby's conversation would be nothing like it. Nick loved her to pieces. He always had.

"Tell you what, how about the girls stay here tonight so you and Nick have some uninterrupted time on your own?"

"After the shock of neither of us coming home last night, the girls will be clingy. I know Jess had problems getting them to bed."

Alice tamped down her chagrin that Libby had rejected her offer to stay with her nieces the previous night, insisting that Jess remain at the house. "How about I look after Indi today and pick up Lucy from school. That way when they discharge Nick, there's no pressure to rush back. Talk in Bairnsdale and then you'll be home for the girls tonight."

"Nick will want to come straight home and if we're going to talk, I'm not having that sort of conversation in the Bean and Grind café."

"I'll look after them here until you call me to bring them to Burrunan."

"Jess will probably have Indi today."

"But I've already offered," Alice ground out. Years ago, she'd accepted that Libby's close friendship with Jess excluded her, but now it seemed to be shutting her out of her nieces' lives. "And I've got the day off, whereas Jess will have to juggle her work around two kids. Even if she does offer, is it fair to accept?"

Libby let out a low groan. "You're right. I'm sorry, I'm not thinking straight. I'll go home and have breakfast with the girls and talk to Jess. She was amazing last night. She sent me texts and called me every couple of hours to check I was okay and reassure me that the girls were settled and asleep."

Was the comment a shot at Alice and her parents? They'd deliberately hung back from barraging Libby with texts and calls, not wanting to bother her. They knew her energies would be focused on Nick and she'd contact them when she had news. It didn't mean they cared any less.

"Great," Alice finally managed, although it lacked conviction.

Libby's phone rang and she fished it out of her pocket. "Hi, Jess ... Good thanks. I'll be home soon. I'm not going back to Bairnsdale until ... Oh, okay, I'd forgotten. No, that's fine, please, don't stress. I totally understand. I just appreciate that you were ... Hang on, I'll ask Alice." She muted the phone. "Can you mind Indi and Leo today?"

Alice stopped herself from asking why Jess needed childcare at such short notice—did it really matter? "Sure. No problem. The more the merrier."

Libby blew her a kiss and returned to the call, firming up arrangements before hanging up. "I'll take Lucy to school, drop the kids off here, go and sort out the practice and then drive back to Nick."

"Sounds like a plan. I'll take the kids on a playground picnic."

"Thanks." Libby's fingers fiddled with a ragged bit of loose wool. "Listen, when you're in town and people ask how Nick is, can you tell them he's fine? The last thing he needs or wants is a fuss."

"Sure, but what are you going to tell Mom and Dad? Last night Mom was doing her "everything will be fine" thing and stress cleaning. Still, there are advantages."

"Besides a clean oven?"

"Absolutely. For a few hours her focus shifted far away from me and settled on Nick. I must thank him."

"You're exaggerating. Mom doesn't stress about you that much anymore."

Alice raised a brow. "Nice try, but we both know the truth. You cause her momentary concerns and I make up the other ninety-nine percent."

Libby looked like she was about to argue, but all she said was, "Tell Mom I'll call her this morning."

They fell silent, gazing across the lake and enjoying the spectacle of a flock of swans rising gracefully into the tangerine sky. Alice expected Libby to stand and leave, but she sat as if moving would take more energy than she could muster. The frigid early morning air was making sorties through any clothing gaps and Alice tugged the blanket more tightly around herself.

Eventually Libby spoke. "So, how *are* things with Tim?"

Alice sensed dangerous territory. "Don't you want to get home to the girls?"

"Don't you want to tell me?"

Alice thought about the recent 1:00 a.m. FaceTime session and pressed her thighs together against the delicious tingle. "There's not much to say."

Libby peered at her. "I think there is. You've just gone bright red!"

"No, I haven't." Except heat was rolling through Alice like molten lava, vanquishing her chill and ratcheting up her temperature. She dropped the blanket before she broke out in a sweat.

"Yes, you have! I can't believe you still blush like you did at sixteen when you were crushing on Tyler Hawkins." Libby's eyes lit up. "Did you see Tim last night?"

Alice knew the path the conversation would take if she told Libby the truth: that she and Tim were yet to meet in real life. Her twin would be outraged on her behalf but not understand that Tim made Alice laugh in ways Lawrence never had. How he gave a buzz to each day, which was something that had been missing from her life for a long time. Alice wasn't prepared to pressure Tim to commit to a date and risk losing all of that. It took her less than three seconds to decide to share a version of the truth.

"Tim knew I was upset about Nick—"

"He drove over?" Libby's voice filled with delight and she gently punched Alice on the arm. "Judging by that blush, he made you feel a lot better."

"Oh, yeah. He did that." At least on that front, she didn't have to lie.

Libby arrived home just before 7:00 to find Leo and the girls up, dressed and eating cereal in front of breakfast television. It wasn't a familiar scenario, because the girls were usually still in bed at this hour and they were never allowed to watch cartoons on a weekday morning, let alone picnic on the floor rug. They gave her a distracted hug and a kiss—very different from the teary girls they'd been on the phone the night before. Cartoons were obviously the panacea for all ills.

The surreal feeling continued when Jess greeted her in the kitchen with her curls blow dried into submission, a full face of perfectly applied makeup and wearing one of Libby's dresses, which fitted her perfectly.

"Wow! Look at you."

"It's the perfect interview dress. I thought I should look the part."

Libby loved how they still raided each other's closets. "I'm just envious that you look better in it than I do."

Jess snorted. "Hardly."

Libby recognized the glint in Jess's eyes—the one she got whenever she bought something new and shiny. A glint that had been largely absent this year as she adapted to a tighter budget. "Keep it as a thank you for last night."

"Lib, you don't have to thank me for that. Hell, what are best friends for if not to step in and hold the fort when your husband scares you to death by landing in the hospital?" Jess hugged her. "I'm just glad he's not about to have a heart attack or a stroke."

"Me too." Although a tiny part of her regretted that the cause of his chest pain wasn't an obvious physical condition. If it had been, the treatment would be straightforward instead of an unsettling question mark.

"Nick said you didn't phone him yesterday."

Jess frowned. "I called as soon as I got off the phone from you but his number was busy so I texted him. He phoned me back and said he'd be home for dinner. That's why I freaked out when he didn't arrive."

"I wish I knew what was going on with him." She pulled her attention back to Jess. "I can't believe I forgot about your job interview in Bairnsdale."

"Given the fright you got last night, you're lucky you can remember your name." Jess flipped a poached egg out of a saucepan and plonked it on buttered toast. "I cooked you your fave breakfast. You look like you need it."

Tears prickled Libby's eyes. "You're amazing. Please move in and wave your organizational wand here every morning. Do you have time for a coffee before you go?"

"Sorry. Gotta love you and leave you. The interview's early. Perhaps I could meet you for coffee at that new café in Bairnsdale and fill you in on how it went? What time are you picking up Nick?"

"Between 11:00 and 12:00."

"Oh!" Disappointment darkened her eyes. "That's not going to work. I'll already be back in the bay by then. I can't imagine Nick will want visitors tonight."

"Thanks for understanding and don't worry, we'll find a time to talk. Besides, with your smarts and in that dress, there's no way they won't hire you." Libby kissed her goodbye.

"Let's hope they share your confidence." Jess walked over to Leo and while he was distracted by the cartoons, she dropped a kiss on his head before slipping out the side door.

A few minutes later, just as Libby swallowed the last bite of her egg and toast, the cartoon finished. Leo wailed at his loss of enjoyment and then for his mother when he realized she was gone.

"Come on, you lot, let's go and give the hens their breakfast."

Libby turned off the television and swung Leo into her arms. The ache that had throbbed its pain through her whenever she'd held him as a baby had changed over time but it had never completely faded. As happy as Libby was for Jess, the hurt could still sneak in now and then that Leo was a little boy only a few months younger than Dom would have been if he'd lived. She fought the twinge of regret by thinking of holding another baby soon—hopefully a boy.

Her breath caught. What if she wasn't pregnant?
What if she was pregnant and Nick didn't want another child?
Both scenarios threatened to eviscerate her.

AFTER A HASTY CASE CONFERENCE ALLOCATING THE MORE
urgent cases to Ramesh and Penny, Libby wrote a dozen prescriptions,
checked pathology reports, and made yet another patient list for Penny
to schedule follow-up appointments. Glancing at the clock, she
groaned, realizing she was already fifteen minutes late. As she dropped
her phone and bag onto the passenger seat of her car, she noticed a
missed call. She immediately checked her voicemail.

"Hi, it's me," Nick's deep voice rumbled in her ear. "I'm about to
get into a cab. This way you don't need to reorganize your day. Love
you. Bye."

Not need to reorganize her day? Was he serious? She'd just spent
two hours doing exactly that. And it wasn't the eighty-dollar taxi fare
that shocked her the most, it was the fact the hospital had discharged
Nick into his own care, denying her the chance to speak to his doctor.
Argh! She immediately called Nick, but on the third ring she
remembered he didn't have his phone. Knowing him, he'd probably get
the taxi to drop him off at the office first so he could collect it.

He was probably planning to work today too. Over her dead body.
If she picked up his phone, he'd have no excuse to set foot in the office
and she could meet the taxi and drive him straight home. She pointed
the car in the direction of the marina.

Stopped at one of the two sets of traffic lights in the bay waiting to
turn right onto the esplanade, Libby was surprised to see Jess's car turn
into the main street. Her stomach dropped. Jess was back early, so did
that mean her interview hadn't gone well? The car pinged at her,
alerting her to the fact the car in front had moved. Libby pulled her
attention back to the road and turned onto the seafront.

Even though she'd grown up with the view of the fishing boats,
stacks of lobster pots and nets strung out to dry and the backdrop of the

ocean, she still experienced a momentary peace at the sight. After the stress of the last sixteen hours, the view centered her, reminding her that despite life not always going according to plan, she still had many blessings to count. She lived on a beautiful piece of the Victorian coast with Nick and the girls, she had the best friend anyone could wish for and a loving extended family. Even though she hated Lawrence for upending Alice's life, a selfish part of her appreciated having her twin back in town for a while.

As she parked under a Norfolk pine, she smiled—she already had her gratitudes for the day and it was only just 11:00.

The tinkling sound of metal halyards on masts filled the air and as Libby approached the office, she noticed that the sunny autumn morning had enticed fishermen onto the pier. Henry Liu waved a fish net at her and she returned the greeting.

"Mommy!"

She glanced around, expecting to see another woman, and realized the child calling out and running toward her, was Indi. Squinting into the distance, she looked for Alice and found her standing with a man who was holding a child. They both turned and waved. She blinked and lifted her sunglasses, not quite believing she was looking at Nick. Confusion tangled with surprise and delight and then her heart rolled. With his head bent close to Leo's and a smile on his face, Nick didn't look anything like a man who didn't want another child.

Indi threw herself at Libby's legs. She picked her up and kissed her. "Hello, sweetheart. This is a lovely surprise."

Indi nodded, her face pink with excitement. "Alice said we'd see boats. We found Daddy!"

"So I see." Libby closed the gap between her husband and her twin, wondering how on earth Nick had gotten back to the bay so quickly. "You're back early."

Nick kissed her. "Yeah. Taxi driver was a speed fiend."

"Were you going to call me?"

He had the grace to look sheepish. "I was about to but it looks like you knew where to find me."

"It's my fault," Alice apologized. "We ambushed him in the office and distracted him."

"Daddy!" Indi leaned out of Libby's arms and grabbed Nick's shoulder. "I want to see the seals."

"Okay." Nick transferred Indi onto his free hip. "Righto, you two, let's go."

"Giddy up, Daddy!"

"Go!" Leo squealed.

"Five minutes!" Libby called after him, annoyed that her plans to be alone with Nick were unravelling fast. She turned back to Alice, suddenly suspicious. "Hang on. I've only just got the message that Nick was coming back by taxi. How come you knew he was in the office?"

"Missy called me. She's still a bit wobbly."

"And that's connected how?"

"I think when Nick turned up wearing the same clothes as yesterday, she had visions of having to call another ambulance. We'd just arrived at the park so I walked down. Thought the kids would be good bait to get him away from the temptation of work."

"Yes, but why did she call you not me?"

Alice shrugged. "I work with her. She knows me."

Libby's aggravation spilled over. "She knows me!"

Alice inclined her head, the action loaded with sympathy. "Yeah, but she's twenty-one and you're the boss's wife and a doctor. Sometimes you can be a bit intimidating, Libs."

"Intimidating? I'm furious with all of you."

Alice brought her hands up in a gesture of resigned surrender. "Well, you're here now so we can return to the original plan. I'll take the kids back to the park and you take Nick home."

"Okay." Libby was slightly mollified. "Jess is back early so she'll probably pick up Leo soon."

"I don't think so. She just texted saying she'll pick him up at 3:00."

Had Jess told her that on the phone this morning? Probably. "God, I'm losing my mind."

Alice put her hands gently on her twin's shoulders, her gaze full of concern. "None of us think straight when we're worried. I've got the kids sorted. Take Nick home and find out what's bothering him, then weave your magic."

"My magic?"

"You make people better, Libs, that's your magic. That and the spell you cast on Nick years ago. If anything was going to test you both, it was losing Dom and you've come through that tighter than ever. He loves you. You love him. Everything else is background noise."

An intense rush of love for her sister filled her and Libby pulled Alice in for a hug. "Thank you."

Alice squeezed her back and for a moment they were twelve again, sharing a room, their secrets and their dreams. Then her twin released her and they were back to being two separate and very different individuals.

Libby watched Nick chase a piece of salad green around his plate. It was taking superhuman effort, but she was restraining herself from talking about anything to do with his hospital admission until after lunch. But Nick, whose appetite was legendary, had barely touched the chicken and tomato salad she'd thrown together.

"You finished?"

"Yeah." He pushed the plate away.

"Cup of tea? Coffee?"

"No, thanks."

Leaving the plates, Libby stood and tried to pull him to his feet. "Let's go for a walk."

Nick counter-tugged and brought her down onto his knee. "Or we could stay here. We've got the house to ourselves for a change."

She stroked his hair. "As much as I want to do that, we need to talk about what happened yesterday."

His gaze slid away. "There's not much to talk about. For a few hours, I felt like I had an elephant on my chest. Your mates at the hospital don't know why and a bloke in happy pants and a nose ring told me some BS about "focusing on the breath." I just need to get out on the water a few times a week."

"But you already do that."

He grinned. "I can add another day now it's doctor's orders."

Her frustration peaked and she concentrated on her own breath as she laid her palm over his heart. "Nick, you had a panic attack."

He pushed her hand away. "Don't be ridiculous!"

"I'm not. The reason the bloke in happy pants came to talk to you is because *nothing* showed up on your tests." Wearily, she dropped her forehead onto his. "What's going on inside there? Are you worried I might be pregnant?"

"No." It was devoid of any ambiguity. "Are you?"

"My period's due any day but I haven't done a test yet because—" She snagged her lip, not wanting to verbalize her fear.

"You don't want to see that you're not," he said gently.

His understanding buoyed her. This was her opportunity to find out how far he was prepared to go to have another child. "And if I'm not, I think we should both have tests to see if there's a reason we're not getting pregnant."

"You want me to jack off in a jar?" He winked at her. "I'm fine with that, especially if you help."

"I'm serious, Nick. If there's a problem, it might mean trying IVF. It's not an easy road, especially living down here."

"You really want another baby that much?"

"I really do." Her heart beat in her throat. "Do you?"

He stroked her face. "All I want is for you to be happy. If you want another child, then we'll do what we need to make it happen."

"Oh thank God. I thought you were going to tell me you didn't want any more children."

"Why? I love kids."

"I know." She kissed him, sinking into her relief and silencing her anxieties.

They sat together in companionable silence, listening to the whip-crack call of a bird, the only sound breaking the afternoon's torpor. Cuddled, safe and relaxed for the first time in hours, Libby's sleep debt exacted payment and her eyes fluttered closed.

" .... about Sulli's place."

The vibrato of Nick's baritone startled her and she dozily lifted her head. "Sorry. What?"

"I want to talk to you about Sulli's place. I'm about to get the papers drawn up, but I've been thinking ..."

"Hmm?" Libby's eyes started closing again.

Nick cleared his throat. "The thing is, now Jess is totally committed to staying in the bay for the long term, I thought we could help her out by—"

"Renting the house to her!" Libby was instantly reenergized, remembering her conversation with Jess the day before. "Absolutely! I was going to suggest that."

"Not rent it to her. Help her buy it."

"Buy it? As in, we give her a loan?"

"Not exactly. I was thinking more along the lines of a partnership. We buy Sulli's with her 50/50. That way she gets a leg up into the top end of Kurnai Bay real estate and you get your best friend living next door." He grinned at her. "Just think. We can pull down the fences and double the size of the yard. The kids can run wild."

The suggestion was so completely out of left field she grappled to make sense of it. Although Nick worked reasonably well with his father, over the years there'd been a couple of very cool Christmases when business issues had upended family harmony. Although those days were long gone now Rick was semi-retired and Nick ran the company, Libby still remembered the stress.

"I don't understand. At every big Pirelli family gathering, I hear you advising your cousins not to underwrite loans for family, let alone friends."

His mouth developed a sulky look. "I thought you'd love the idea."

Libby wondered at her own reticence given that she and Jess had been sharing things since they'd met. She cringed, remembering how they'd once shared boyfriends, but thankfully they'd grown up. The purchase of a house was a very different proposition than sharing clothes, perfume and jewelry. "I love the idea of Jess living next door but ..."

"What?"

"I can see problems."

"Really? Like what?"

"For starters, Sulli's house is old. It lacks character so it's not worth renovating. Jess will want to pull it down and build."

Nick shrugged. "I don't have a problem with that. A new house will add to the property's value."

"Yes, but we'd have to pay for half of the build. What if we couldn't agree? And if we did, we can only benefit financially if Jess decides to sell."

"I'm pretty sure the moment she's paid off her share of the mortgage, she'll get another loan and buy us out. Like I said, it's a leg up for her."

Pretty sure? That didn't sound like Nick. He might be relatively easygoing about many things but not vast amounts of money. "What happens if she defaults on her loan?"

"This is your best friend you're talking about. Jess might be many things but she's got a savvy business brain. Hell, you trust her with *your* business. You trust her with your children." He threw her a disbelieving look. "What's got into you?"

Libby didn't understand it either. All she knew was her gut was squirming, advising her this wasn't a good idea. "I think it's easier all round if she rents from us. It's not like we're ever going to kick her out."

"Jeez, Libby. I don't get it. We do just about everything with Jess, but I get a lecture when I suggest we have a family sail without her. You're constantly offering me up as her handyman even though I've told you I'm sick of it, but when I come up with a way of helping her get out of a decrepit house and the rental market so her money can work for her, you reject it. I can't bloody win."

Nick's arm fell away and Libby stood to avoid falling off his lap.

On one level his words made complete sense. On another, something felt off. She was still trying to work it out when her phone rang.

"Please don't answer it." Nick said wearily.

But he'd unsettled her and she needed a distraction—time to marshal her thoughts. "Hi, Jess. How'd the interview go?"

Nick grunted, spun on his heel and stalked outside.

"Who knows. It was over so fast my head spun. How's Nick?"

Acting weird. "Much better," Libby said too brightly.

"Great. I thought he sounded more like himself."

A whoosh of prickling goosebumps rose on Libby's skin and she closed the deck door against the cool breeze. "You've spoken to him?"

Jess laughed. "Of course I have. He phoned me with your amazing offer for Sulli's place. I'm still pinching myself that I'm a homeowner."

"Me too ..." Libby managed faintly. Disconnected pieces of information floated into her mind. It was like treading water amid flotsam and jetsam and trying to grab onto something—anything—that linked it all together to keep her afloat.

"Now I know why there's a bottle of Veuve in your fridge!" Jess squealed "I can't wait to crack it the moment we sign the papers next week."

Libby's heart kicked into overdrive and she suddenly wanted to end the call. "I've got another call."

"No worries. Call me back. Love you."

Jess hung up and Libby stared at the phone as if the device would make sense of the conversation. Nick walked back inside, cautiously holding a deep maroon rose. Its rich color and delicate fragrance belied the viciousness of its large and protruding thorns. It was a Mister Lincoln, her favorite rose, but right now she didn't care that Nick knew that or that he'd picked it for her.

Her arm shot out and her forefinger pointed accusingly. "You told Jess your idea about buying Sulli's place with her before you told me?"

He flinched at her shrewish tone. "Libby, I can explain."

"Good! Because right now I don't understand how you could have committed our money without discussing it with me."

He set the rose down on the table. "If you don't want to be financially involved, you don't have to be. I'll use my money."

"Your money?" What the hell was happening? "When we buy houses, we don't have your money and my money. We have *our* money."

"Yeah, okay." He ran his hand through his hair and his curls spiked. "The thing is, I'm looking for investments. If you don't want to be part of this one, then you have the equivalent amount to invest in something else. That's fair."

Her fingers pressed her temples as if the pressure would somehow clear the fog of his skewed logic. It didn't. "I don't get it. In the last few months there've been times when I've wondered if you still like Jess and now you're *buying a house* with her?"

Sweat beaded on his top lip. "Her place is falling apart around her. I ought to know, I've shored it up often enough. This way she gets out of the rental market and you get your best friend living next door. Jesus, Libby! I did it for you."

His face and neck were puce and he was heaving in breaths as if he'd run a marathon. She visualized his blood pressure and panicked. "I'm sorry. I didn't mean to yell and stress you out. It's just all of this is so ..." *Unlike you.* "Out of the blue."

"It wasn't supposed to be out of the blue." He fell onto the couch, his face haggard, looking like he'd aged ten years in twenty-four hours. "Jess shouldn't have told you."

The blame rankled and it swept her back to the source of her anger. Nick should have told her. Hell, Nick should not have committed to buying the house with Jess without first discussing it with her. "I know you did it for me and Jess, but as nothing's signed, I don't think we should go ahead."

His eyes shot open, their gaze frantic. "I can't break a promise."

And she knew he couldn't. His code of honor wouldn't allow him to and she loved him for it. "You don't have to. I haven't promised her anything, so I'll do it. I'll tell her we've re-crunched the numbers and we're sorry, but we can't manage it. She'll understand."

"She won't. For God's sake, she does the practice's books! She'll know you're lying." He grabbed her hand. "Think about it. Do you really want to risk your friendship with her?"

His fingers dug in so hard her hands hurt and she tugged them out of his grasp. "Then I'll tell her the truth. I'll say I'm worried about what this could do to our friendship. How it's too important for us to ever risk falling out over money."

"Please. Don't." The request was barely a whisper but the words roared with intent.

Her goosebumps rushed back so fast her skin hurt and then her entire body stilled. She scanned his face, searching for a sign, a clue, anything that would explain why she felt like she was teetering on the edge of a precipice.

His usually warm gaze was wide and filled with fear.

Her mouth dried. "Oh God. All of this is somehow connected to your panic attack, isn't it?"

Nick stared straight ahead.

Say no. Say, "Don't be ridiculous, Libs." Say something!

Nick dropped his face into his hands and his guttural moan chilled her down to her marrow. Something held her back from comforting him.

He finally raised his head, his face twisted in agony. "I'm sorry. So sorry."

Her blood thundered in her ears. Her tongue sat thick and ungainly in her mouth. "Sorry? Sorry for what?"

He swallowed, his Adam's apple bouncing erratically. "For everything."

"That's not an answer!" She was yelling now. "Tell me what's going on!"

He reached for her but she threw off his hands knowing whatever was coming, it was something so terrible it would pierce her clean through. Instinct told her he was having an affair with her best friend. Or worse than an affair—that he loved Jess.

"Tell me!" she screamed.

He licked his lips, opened them and then his breath shuddered out. "Leo is mine."

She heard the words but she didn't understand. "What?"

"Leo is my son."

If he'd stabbed her in the heart, it would have hurt less. "Leo?" Her voice sounded foreign and unfamiliar. "Jess's Leo is your son?"

He nodded slowly, tears spilling down his cheeks. "Libby, I'm so sorry. I never wanted to h—"

"Shut up! Shut up! Shut up!" Her hands flew to her ears as if they were barriers enough to stop the words from seeping into her heart and soul. But it was too late. Their terrible truth spread like indelible black ink, staining her. Nick was Leo's father. Nick had a son. Her best friend and her husband had a child.

"No. No. No, no, no!" Her gut cramped so swiftly she doubled over and then she felt the familiar thick dampness of blood oozing between her legs. Everything that defined her world and her place in it crumpled, crashing down around her like a building leveled in an earthquake.

"Libs?" Nick tried to hug her.

"Don't touch me!" Sudden repulsion for the only man she'd ever loved made her grip the solid red gum table. Normally, she struggled to move it an inch but she heard herself roar and then it was moving across the kitchen as if it weighed nothing. It sat between them, a blessed wall blocking him from touching her. "I don't want you anywhere near me!"

"But I want—"

"I don't care what you want! This isn't about you." Shaking, she grabbed her car keys.

"Please don't leave." His voice quavered like Indi's when she was about to burst into tears.

Libby ignored him and opened the door.

"Where are you going?"

She threw him a withering look. "Where do you think?"

CHAPTER EIGHT

JESS TURNED UP THE RADIO AND SANG LOUDLY TO QUEEN'S "WE Are The Champions" in a mixture of excitement and relief. She never wanted to relive the last twenty-four hours again. Nick's hospitalization had terrified her and her fear for him had been exacerbated by not being able to rush to Libby's side. Finding out in the early hours of the morning that Libby believed his chest pain was caused by stress had only added to her anxiety.

During her first year back in the bay, Nick had fallen over himself to be obliging and helpful and he'd done whatever she'd asked of him. But since the New Year, his behavior had been running hot and cold and she was never certain if irritable Nick or happy Nick was on the other side of her door. But despite his moodiness, he was generous with his financial support for Leo and he played with their son whenever Jess visited Burrunan. Since her insistence at Christmas that Leo needed more of his time, Nick had done a fair job at creating opportunities, but it was ad hoc and not enough. Leo needed the same access to Nick as his half-sisters. Living next door would expedite it.

To convince Nick to help her buy the Sullivan place, she'd drawn on his sense of duty —it was part of his ongoing commitment to Leo.

She'd emphasized that living next door was the easiest way for Nick to continue being closely involved in his son's life without drawing anyone's attention, and it would relieve the constant pressure on them both to contrive situations for him to spend time with their son. This was her trump card and she'd played it straight into Nick's desperate desire to keep his relationship to Leo a secret.

"Libby must *never* find out," had been the third sentence he'd spoken after she'd told him she was pregnant and keeping the baby. His first had been, "There's no way it's mine," and his second was far less of a sentence—more like a string of expletives. Over time, "Libby must never find out" had morphed into his mantra. It was almost as if he believed if he said it often enough, it would become true.

Since announcing her pregnancy, Jess had experienced a love–hate relationship with those five words. She oscillated between her need to protect her friendship with Libby and her desire to publicly declare that like Libby, she too had a claim on Nick. But in many ways Nick's mantra worked to Jess's advantage. Despite his occasional threats that he'd tell Libby about Leo, years of knowing Nick had taught her this would never happen. Jess also knew that Nick wasn't confident that she would keep the secret. That he thought this saddened her. Jess had no intention of telling Libby. Meanwhile, Nick's uncertainty gave her an edge and although she didn't employ it often, when the need arose, she took the threat out of its scabbard and waved it around. His lack of enthusiasm for the house plan was one of those times.

But the last twenty-four hours had rattled her. She reassured herself that despite Nick's recent unpredictable behavior, whenever she got him to sit down with her for a drink—tea, coffee, ideally alcohol —he eventually unwound. When that happened, the Nick she loved appeared and they talked and laughed together easily. It made perfect sense that if she lived next door and Nick could see her without the stress of having to create opportunities, then their rare moments of companionship would become an everyday event. Over time, they'd rebuild their closeness.

But life had taught her it wasn't a perfect world and timing was everything. It was going to take time to show Nick that his two families could coexist in harmony. Time for Nick to relax into that realization and the only way it could happen was with Jess living next door.

She'd mulled over the best way to achieve this and had eventually decided to go through Nick, rather than Libby. Despite Libby owning the medical practice, she preferred being a doctor and deferred to Nick and Jess for business advice. It had taken Jess weeks of reasoning and demanding, along with some pouty pleading, to get Nick to agree to the three of them buying the Sullivan place together. He'd finally conceded that Leo deserved to grow up in a better house and have the security home ownership offered her. She suggested she sow the joint ownership seed with Libby, but for reasons she still couldn't fathom, Nick had been unusually adamant that he do it. As much as Jess wanted to override him, she wasn't stupid. She heeded the tension in his warning and waited for the excited phone call from Libby telling her the good news. Or better yet, anticipated arriving at Burrunan for one of their twice-weekly dinners to find her friend greeting her with a bottle of Veuve.

Neither of those things happened so after two weeks of silence on the topic, Jess tested the waters. Libby's bald statement that Sulli had accepted Nick's offer and her suggestion Jess rent the place had not only devastated Jess, it had lit a bonfire of fury inside her. In a rare moment of unguarded anger, she'd allowed it to burn Nick. Oh, how she regretted the texts and the phone call. It was why she'd faked a job interview so she could drive to the hospital, apologize and rescue everything with Nick on the drive home.

At first, the overwrought man sitting beside her reminded her of the Nick she'd found when she'd first returned to the bay. On her second day back in town, she'd asked Libby if Nick could bring around a ladder so she could clean the light fixtures. It was the first time they'd been alone together in months and his hands shook so much she'd lifted the ladder and set it up herself.

"You promised me no matter how much Libby begged, you'd stay in Sydney. Why are you back?"

"This is why." Jess laid Leo into his arms.

He threw her an agitated look. "You living here is too much of a risk!"

"Relax, Nick." She smiled reassuringly while she stroked Leo's dark curls, so much like his father's. "Everything's going to work out fine."

And for a year, everything went according to plan until Nick fell apart and landed himself in the hospital. During their precious hour alone in the car, Jess had carefully and calmly reminded him of all the positive reasons why her name needed to be on the title deeds.

"Nick, you've made yourself ill for no reason and worried us sick. Libby loves you. She loves me. She'll love this idea."

His fingers drummed on the dashboard. "What if she doesn't?"

"Come on, Nick. You know that's as likely as the tide not changing." Jess plucked at the dress she was wearing. "I asked to borrow this and she gave it to me on the spot."

"Sulli's place is hardly a dress!"

"This dress cost $350 on sale and she gifted it to me without blinking." Jess shook her head indulgently. "Think about it, Nick. There's no way Libby's going to say no. She already knows I was thinking of buying somewhere. Tell her you've crunched the numbers and discussed it with me to check I can afford my share. Tell her it's a concrete way the two of you can help me get a foot in the market. You know she prides herself on helping. In fact, I bet you a Mars Bar that in a year's time, she'll have reinvented history and be telling us it was her idea."

"Yeah." Nick's shoulders fell and he managed a small smile. "You're probably right."

"Finally, the man believes me," she'd joked. "I promise you, this is the perfect solution for everyone." But after the previous day's events, she was no longer prepared to let Nick run things. When she dropped him off a street away from the marina, she'd said, "I'll call Libby this afternoon."

Now at home in her kitchen, Jess belted out the final chorus to

"We Are The Champions" and hugged herself. Not only was she finally entering the property market, she was staking a legal claim in the Hunter-Pirellis' lives—a partnership. It would give her and Leo one type of security she craved and the rest would follow.

Excited, she grabbed some paper and doodled house plans. Unlike this small 1930's clapboard with its tiny windows and dark rooms, she sketched a large, light-filled open-plan living space that would face the water. It wasn't dissimilar in design to Burrunan but Jess planned an outdoor kitchen and a dedicated office. Lucy and Indi would need their own rooms too so they could come and go freely between the two houses like their father and their brother.

Lost in a daydream of creating her utopia in a modern, sprawling home devoid of cockroaches and black mold, Jess startled at the sound of a car braking hard on gravel. She rose to look out the window and saw an ashen-faced Libby getting out of the car. It wasn't the first time Libby had arrived on her doorstep looking like this and it meant only one thing.

Genuine disappointment filled her and she opened the door and her arms. "Oh, shit. You've got your period. I'm sorry, Lib."

Libby brought her elbows up, knocking Jess's arms aside. "I don't think you're sorry one little bit."

The action and accusation stung. Jess had spent hours listening to Libby's pain and sadness over losing Dom and her failure to conceive again. "Of course I am. I know how gutted you are every time you get your period. Sit down and I'll make tea."

"I don't want a bloody cup of tea."

It didn't happen often, but occasionally Libby's practical and scientific mind went into full-on drama queen mode. It was usually connected to the girls and to a lesser extent Nick when he'd dropped the ball and wasn't world's best husband, but today it was the disappointment she wasn't pregnant. When this version of Libby appeared, experience had taught Jess it was best just to let her vent.

"Coffee then? It's a bit early for a drink. Don't want to be the stereotypical single mother who has her kid in the car and gets nailed for being over the legal limit," she said.

"Nothing about you comes close to being a stereotype."

Normally, Jess would have basked in her friend's admiration, but today there was no way Libby's words could be construed as a compliment. A niggle of unease made Jess examine their earlier phone call, searching for clues, but the only thing she came up with was Libby had sounded slightly distracted. For the previous year, Libby had been obsessed with having another baby. Once, when Nick had been replacing faucet washers, Jess had managed to draw him out on his feelings about another child.

"I think we should accept it's not going to happen and move on."

Jess had almost cried in relief. As much as she understood Libby's desire for a son of her own, Jess didn't want another baby drawing Nick's attention away from her and Leo. As it was, it took all her energy to keep hold of the small share of him she'd managed to carve out.

Jess flicked on the kettle and lifted two mugs from their hooks.

Libby's hands gripped the back of a kitchen chair. "Nick told me Leo is his."

Like an Arctic chill, a tingle swooped Jess from head to toe. The mugs slipped from her numb fingers, hitting the floor and shattering. A tiny part of her brain prompted her to pick up the scattered shards but her body refused to move a muscle. Her mind scrambled frantically to the early days after Leo's birth, when Libby had flown up to Sydney on her own for a quick visit. In anticipation, Jess had written a script just in case Libby caught on to Nick being Leo's father. But when Libby had gazed down at Jess's son, all she'd said was, "He's got your nose! He's utterly perfect. I'm so happy for you."

When Jess had moved to the bay, the script was still on hand, but as the weeks and months passed, she'd discarded it as obsolete. Libby didn't suspect a thing and Jess had done everything she could to keep it that way and protect their friendship.

But now her best friend's face was contorted in vicious hatred and rage.

"You lying, cheating bitch! You told me you used donor sperm to have Leo."

"I did."

"Nick's not a sperm donor."

"We share each other's stuff all the time. I just borrowed a part of him."

"He's my husband!" Libby screamed and Jess's heart galloped. She scrambled to remember the words and phrases she'd worked so hard to develop in case this situation ever eventuated. Words that would make Libby understand that this was just another facet of their very close friendship.

"I know it's a shock, but you have to know I'd never deliberately hurt you."

"Are you freaking kidding me?" Libby's hand hit the table. "You've been having sex with my husband!"

"That's no—"

"What would you call it then? An accident? His dick just happened to slide inside you and knock you up?"

"I'm just trying to give you some context—"

"There is no context! There's no possible excuse for my best friend to sleep with my husband."

Jess's calm snapped. "This isn't all on me, Libby. Nick's involved too."

Libby made a strangled sound—half cry, half scream. "But you didn't say no. You were supposed to say no. Take the moral high ground. Tell him that friends don't betray each other."

The beat of an old betrayal resumed its tempo. "I'd already slept with you so I was just evening the score."

"Oh my God! How can you possibly think that a drunken experiment at twenty equates to this—this—treachery. You had sex with *my husband!*"

Libby's constant use of "my husband," as if she owned Nick,

slithered along Jess's veins like a snake ready to strike. "I had sex with *my friend*. A man I've known a lot longer than you."

"That doesn't give you the right to sleep with him!"

"Why not? It's called friends with benefits. We'd been having sex long before you and Nick ever did."

The shock on Libby's face told her that Nick hadn't disclosed that bit of information. Jess wished she knew exactly what he'd shared and what he'd withheld. More importantly, she wished she knew why he'd broken his own rule and told Libby at all. And why today, when they were so close to making their lives easier and securing Leo's future? Frigid fury formed an icy ball in her gut. How could Nick have betrayed her by telling Libby about their son without her being in the room?

"You've never told me about you and Nick," Libby finally spluttered.

"Well, we both have our secrets about Nick, don't we?"

"Not me! I'm an open book. The secrets are all yours. All I've ever done is love you. God! My family's looked after you."

Jess sloughed away a pang of remorse. "Growing up, your mother was forever telling me to go for what I want. I wanted a baby."

Libby's hand flew up into the air. "She didn't mean steal my husband in the process! You've abused my friendship in the worst possible way. I don't know how you can sleep at night knowing that. All I've ever done is love and support you, especially this last year—" Libby's body suddenly flinched violently as if she'd been electrocuted. "You must have been laughing at me every time I sent Nick around to fix something."

"No!" The need to clarify was suddenly important. "It's not like that. It was never like that."

"How dare you do this to me after everything I've done for you!"

"Everything you've done for me? From the moment we met, Libby Hunter, you haven't done anything for me that didn't serve you too. You loved the excitement and exhilaration of spicing up your vanilla life with a bit of my working-class smut. But it made you feel uncomfortable so you eased your guilty conscience by offering me entry into your clean and tidy life."

Libby's cheeks burned red. "If it was so abhorrent to you, why didn't you reject the gifts and the holiday trips? My friendship? My love? My support?"

Jess swallowed around an uncomfortable lump. "I didn't say I didn't get anything out of it. I'm just painting this friendship in its true colors. We love each other but we're both guilty of taking advantage when we need to."

"I've *never* used or abused our friendship. I've only ever been a true friend, unlike you, you lying, backstabbing witch!"

The tempo of betrayal increased, throbbing like a pulse deep inside Jess. "You've peddled the story of our perfect friendship for so long you believe every word. Get real, Lib. Ours is great, but nothing's perfect."

Libby stared at her from eyes filled with loathing. "Especially when one friend's screwing the other one's husband. You don't even know the meaning of the word friendship. I'm looking at a stranger."

"No, you're not. I've been a good friend to you. I am a good friend to you. Nothing's changed."

Libby's eyes dilated, their serene blue suddenly wild and unpredictable. "You're insane if you believe that. You have a child with my husband. How could you do this to me?"

Jess wanted to scream at Libby's blindness. "I wanted a child."

"That's not an excuse! I want a child too, but I'm not sleeping with someone else's husband to make it happen." Libby's tone was the self-righteous one of a woman who'd only ever known love. She had no idea what it meant to be forced into the trenches and fight for what you want and deserve.

"Sometimes the means justifies the end. Leo is proof of that."

"Oh my God!" Libby's hands tore so hard at her hair, strands came away in them. "You're not even sorry!"

There was no point disagreeing with her. It was impossible to be sorry when Leo was the perfect gift.

CHAPTER NINE

"Oh thank God. I wasn't sure you'd come home."

Libby heard the concern in Nick's voice. She tried looking at his warm brown eyes, his open and familiar face and his friendly mouth, but all she saw was him in bed with Jess. Her stomach lurched and she dry retched.

"Are you okay?"

"Are you fucking kidding me?" She never swore and he flinched, but she didn't care. She wanted to hurt him. She wanted to upend his world like he'd upended hers. She wanted to destroy him. She threw her handbag and keys on the counter and marched to the fridge. The only bottle of alcohol was French Champagne. If she opened it, did it mean she was celebrating the end of her marriage?

"I'm sorry," Nick said. "That was a stupid thing to say."

Her hands trembled on the slippery bottle as she fumbled with the foil. "It's not stupid. Stupid is fucking my best friend!"

"I know, I know. I should have told you earlier."

The cork popped, the sound as hollow as she felt inside. She poured the liquid into the glass and it fizzed up the sides before spilling over like her emotions. "What you should have done is not had an affair with her."

"She told you it was an affair?" He poured himself a drink and took a big gulp. "It so wasn't an affair."

"What then?" She forced herself to ask the question she feared the most. "True love?"

"God, no! Did she say that? It was nothing like that. *Tesoro mio*, you're my one true love."

He reached for her but she side-stepped him. The thought of Nick touching her made her skin crawl.

"How can you say I'm your true love and mean it? You slept with her! You have a *child* with her. You wanted to move *her* and *that child* next door to us so you could keep sleeping with her."

"Libby, no. I don't want her anywhere near us."

"Then why are you buying Sulli's place with her?"

Nick's head dropped and his curls drooped. Libby got a flash of Leo and the air rushed out of her lungs so fast and sharp, she almost cried out.

When Nick looked at her again the only emotion she could detect in his Tuscan eyes—oh God, Leo's eyes—was anguished exhaustion.

"I thought I owed it to Leo," he said quietly.

Libby thought she'd experienced every possible emotion from shock and betrayal to an all-encompassing fury that had driven her to claw and rip her dress off Jess's shoulders. But none of those feelings had prepared her for the savage grasp of jealousy that tightened around her like a vice.

"You thought you owed it to Leo?" she said quietly and then lost control of her restraint. "What about what you owe me? Your daughters?"

"I'm sorry." He wrung his hands. "I'm just trying to do the right thing by everyone in a very difficult situation."

"A situation you created because you can't keep your dick in your pants!"

He stiffened at her shrewish tone. "I know you're upset, and you have every right to be, but I haven't been screwing around on you. It only happened once."

Libby desperately wanted to believe him, but how could she? He'd hidden an affair *and* a child from her, which meant he was hiding a lot more. "That's not what Jess told me. She says you've always been friends with benefits."

"Well, she's lying," he said quickly. "She does a lot of that, Libs. We just didn't realize."

We? One small word that used to represent love, marriage and teamwork now flayed her like a whip. "So you're saying you never had sex with her before you dated me?"

"That's right."

The words felt like rods of cold steel sliding into every bone of her body. "So you'd stand up in a court of law and swear to that?"

He hesitated, guilt flashing white and bright in his eyes. "Mostly."

"So, she didn't lie. *You're* lying. Again."

"I'm not. This is semantics, Libby. I was eighteen and she gave me a BJ in the dunes behind the surf club."

Which meant she and Jess had been fifteen. Back then Libby hadn't even seen an adult penis but Jess had been running wild and Libby had soaked up every salacious story. "And?"

"And I was inexperienced. I shot my load in about a minute and a half."

"And?"

Tiny beads of sweat broke out along Nick's hairline. "Jesus, Libby. It was years ago. It's not important."

"Of course it's important! You had sex with her before you met me, but you've never told me. She's never told me. There's a reason both of you hid it from me and now you have a child together! What else aren't you telling me?"

Agitated, he swilled more champagne. It was surreal knowing Nick was upset and she didn't want to do a single thing to ease his distress.

"It's only going to upset you."

She snorted. "That horse has well and truly bolted. Just tell me."

He was quiet for a moment and then he sighed. "It happened a few other times."

"How many?"

"I don't know."

"How. Many. Times?"

He shrugged. "Three or four, I dunno. Maybe five."

His evasiveness only exacerbated her suspicions he was withholding information. "Where did these three, four, maybe ten times take place?"

"It wasn't ten!"

"The fact you can't remember isn't doing anything to reassure me."

"I'm doing my best."

She snorted. "Not even close."

His hand snagged in his curls. "Okay, fine. I can't remember the exact number. But I promise you it only ever happened at parties when I was filthy drunk."

Detecting another lie, she squinted at him. "You never drink until you're drunk."

"I did between sixteen and twenty-four." He gave her a wry smile. "By the time I met you, I'd grown up."

She ignored his pleading expression urging her to understand the foolishness of youth. Perhaps if that was all this had been, she'd have forgiven him. But Nick was too far removed from young and stupid for it to be an excuse. When she coupled that with the fact he'd never once hinted that he and *that woman* had a teenage sexual history, it drove her belief down deep that there was so much more to this situation than either of them were telling her.

Despite his answers hitting her like shot, she needed to know everything—even if it explained nothing. "Was it always a just blow job?"

He closed his eyes and sighed. "No."

"When did that change?"

"Um ... After the second time."

"So you sought her out to have sex?"

"No!" It was the first time he'd sounded decisive. "It was nothing like that. She always initiated things."

"And you never said no."

"Like I said, I was young and stupid. Libs, it didn't mean anything. Not like you ..."

She gripped her arms and started pacing. "But you'd stopped with her before you met me?"

"Yes! Ages before I met you. I grew up and stopped writing myself off." He opened his hands in supplication. "Please believe me. When I'm sober, I don't have a problem resisting Jess."

"Hah! If that's true, then how the hell did you end up fucking her two years ago?"

Shame pinked his face. "Jess and I shared a bottle of Bundy."

"You don't even drink rum!"

He sighed again. "I did when I was eighteen. So did Jess. Every country kid did."

"I didn't!"

"Your childhood was a little more sheltered and cultured than most of the bay. I drank it to rebel against my parents' homemade vino. Jess probably drank it because her mother always had bottles in the house."

A memory shot into Libby's mind of the week she started working as an intern. She was lifting a bottle of rum out of Jess's hand and replacing it with a wine glass of chardonnay. "Sophisticated city women drink wine."

"We're sophisticated now, are we, Dr. Hunter?"

"Absolutely."

Jess had laughed, or at least that's how Libby had always remembered it. But in today's memory, Jess's pink bow mouth was pressed tight and the laugh more of a "humph."

Libby shook away the irrelevant detour into the past, recognizing it as a delaying tactic. Her need to know exactly what had happened between her ex-best friend and her husband was matched by an equal desire not to know. Once she heard the story, she couldn't unhear it. But she couldn't go through life not knowing either.

"So, when you screwed her and knocked her up, where was I?"

He grimaced at her vernacular and she got a dart of pleasure at his discomfort. "You'd taken the girls to Melbourne to see Disney on Ice."

His tone of voice took her straight back to that dark week and some of her volcanic anger momentarily cooled under the onslaught of misery. Instead of welcoming her baby boy, she'd kept herself frantically busy—anything to keep her grief from felling her.

Her anger reignited like lava erupting. "You went to Sydney?"

"Hell, no. Why would you think that?"

"I don't know what to think anymore."

"Jess flew down here to surprise *you*," Nick said with an edge. "Remember?"

Libby gagged on the gratitude she always experienced whenever she thought about Jess's generous gesture that weekend. Even though Libby had been out of town and had missed her, she'd always considered it a hallmark of what made their friendship special: unconditional love and support.

Her mind raced. "So, while I was in Melbourne, the two of you drank rum and relived your sordid, drunken trysts."

He stiffened as if she'd offended him. "It wasn't anything like that."

"What was it then?"

He remained silent, his gaze fixed on his feet.

"Tell me!"

"I was sad and upset. I wasn't thinking straight."

The urge to scream and pound her fists into his chest was so strong she gripped the edge of the counter to steady herself. "Are you saying that instead of telling me you were sad, you had sex with her?"

For the first time, his eyes darkened in anger. "Jesus, Libby. I shouldn't have had to tell you. I did try, but you weren't exactly reachable then."

The black web of grief wrapped its sticky strands around her. "My baby died!"

"*Our* baby died!" His voice cracked. "My arms ached too, you know. But that week, when we should have been together as a family, you took off to Melbourne without me."

Libby blew away the guilt that tried to settle. "You'd have hated Disney on Ice."

"You didn't give me the option. I'd have come just to be with you and the girls."

His grief struck hers and a spark ignited. "Don't you dare pin this on me. You're an adult. It's not my fault you slept with her."

"I thought you wanted to know everything? Or do you only want to hear how badly I've let you down and not the other way around?"

"I'm *not* responsible for your behavior."

"Do you truly believe I'd have let this happen if my head had been on straight that night?"

For the first time, tears threatened. "I don't know what to believe. I don't even know who you are anymore. Or her. You're both strangers."

"If you believe one thing, believe me that Jess tricked me that night," he said bitterly. "It's why we're in this mess."

Libby desperately wanted to believe that the woman she'd considered a sister up until this afternoon was truly evil. That Nick was completely innocent. But even in the fog of her shock and distress and her need to lay blame, she recognized it would never be that simple.

"Do you hear yourself? Poor sad Nick was incapable of saying no. He just lay back and let Jess service him. Give me a break!"

"I'm trying to."

"No, you're not. You're withholding information."

He rubbed his haggard face. "I'm protecting you."

She heard her laugh and it scared her. "You're protecting yourself. You've been protecting yourself and her for years!"

"That's not true. I've been protecting us. You and me!"

"That's just another lie you're telling yourself."

Nick spun around. She opened her mouth to order him to stay but he turned back and his mouth was a hard, white line. The veins in his neck bulged.

"This is what happened," he said, his voice low and ragged. "Your best friend turned up at the door with booze and sympathy, but you weren't here and I stupidly let her in. I drank, I talked. She listened and I staggered off to bed. I don't know how long I slept but I woke up groggy from a skinful and with a warm body spooned in next to me. I thought you'd come home."

He lifted his gaze to her. "It was over before I realized what was going on. She promised me she was on the pill. She showed me the condom. You're the doctor, so you tell me. How the hell did she get pregnant?"

But Libby barely heard the question over the roar in her head. Images of Jess and Nick bombarded her. Nick and Jess in their house. In their bed. Two naked bodies moving as one and creating a baby. Something she hadn't been able to achieve in that bed in over twelve months.

Every part of her told her to run from the house. To leave Nick and never see his traitorous face again.

"You've destroyed us."

He shook his head, the action infused with deep despair. "Dom's death did that."

"No! We were battered and bruised but not smashed into irreparable pieces."

Sunlight dazzled her, bouncing off the edge of the silver frame containing a photo of the girls and Nick. She'd taken it this summer on *Freedom* when she'd had no reason to doubt she understood her world and everyone in it. All three of them were happy and laughing at the camera, and Nick's face was alight with the pride and joy of a doting father.

The girls. Pain ricocheted through her. She hated Nick for what he'd done to their trust, their marriage and their family. For the chaos his bombshell was raining down on them now, tomorrow, next week and for all the years to come. She wanted to stop thinking and questioning. Stop feeling. More than anything, she wanted to shut down and block out this nightmare. The thought of running away—leaving this house—reached out its hand, tempting her. All she had to do was grasp it and let it pull her far far away.

Think!

But thinking was almost impossible.

More than anything, she wanted to leave but fleeing Nick and the house would only rescue her for tonight. Even then, it wouldn't really rescue her. There was no way she was leaving the girls with him and if she took them to Pelican House, they'd be confused as to why the three of them were having a sleepover at Glamma and Da's when Daddy was at home. When she woke up tomorrow, all this mess would still exist, She'd have to return to Burrunan, face Nick and deal with a thousand arrangements.

It was all too awful. All too hard. Too much.

A flicker of cogent thought penetrated her overwhelming urge to flee. *Go slowly.*

"I hate you for doing this to us."

"I hate myself." Nick tried again to touch her. She slapped away his hands. "Libby, can you forgive me?"

"I don't know."

"Are you leaving me?"

"I don't know." The only thing she was certain of was that she would never sleep in their bed again.

"I'll do anything to fix this," Nick pleaded.

"Fix?" It came out on a shriek. "You can't fix anything. You have a child with her!"

"I love you, *tesoro mio.* I've always loved you. Nothing's changed that. Nothing ever will."

Words she'd once treasured and held close to her heart—words she'd believed to be the absolute truth—rolled over her like mercury, without a trace of residue. "Everything's changed, Nick. Absolutely everything."

CHAPTER TEN

Karen slammed the meat tenderizer into the steak, visualizing Nick's testicles. "I want to do this to our bastard son-in-law!"

Peter gave her a worried glance. "Do I need to hide the cooking knives?"

"How can you be so calm about it?" She whacked the steak again. "He's betrayed our daughter in the worst possible way."

"And he regrets it."

"So that's it? He regrets it, so he's forgiven?"

"I didn't say that." Peter spun some washed lettuce. "I feel sorry for him."

Her disbelief at the statement almost matched her fury at Nick. "How is that even possible?"

"If you'd come with me to see him, you'd feel the same way. He doesn't look like Nick. I swear he's shrunk."

"Good!" She slammed the meat again. "I want him to suffer!"

"And I don't want pulverized porterhouse." Peter lifted the mallet out of her hand. "He made a mistake, Karen. An error of judgement."

"Having sex with his wife's best friend, getting her pregnant and bringing the child into his marriage is not an error of judgement! It's duplicity and treachery."

Peter tossed the diced salad ingredients into the bowl. "I'm not defending what he did. I hate what he did, but calling it treachery's a bit rough. I think Nick's been trying to do the best he can in an untenable situation. Surely the fact it's made him sick must count for something."

"Nonsense! He wasn't being made ill by anything honorable or noble. It was fear of Libby finding out."

"I don't know." Peter sounded doubtful. "He seems genuinely remorseful."

"Well, bully for Nick!"

Throughout their marriage, Karen and Peter often found themselves on opposite sides of a debate. Sometimes Peter genuinely disagreed with her, but mostly he played devil's advocate. He knew she needed it to reassure her that, unlike her father, robust discussion with him was safe. She loved him for it, but right now she was furious.

"This situation demands far more than just an 'Oops, I'm sorry.' If I were Libby, I wouldn't accept an apology as being anywhere near good enough. In fact, if I was her, I'd—"

"We're parents of two adult daughters, Karen. The days where you get to call the shots and make all their decisions for them are long gone."

"You make it sound like it was a bad thing. You know I was only keeping them safe. All I've ever wanted is to keep them safe."

Peter sighed, the sound old and taut. "Whether we like it or not, we're going to have to respect and live with whatever Libby decides. And not just for her, but for the little girls too. We can't badmouth Nick. He's their father and they love him."

"I concede no such thing. More than anyone, I know that not every father deserves the love of their child! I never want to see Nick Pirelli again."

"You can hear how irrational that sounds, right?"

"He's cut our daughter clean through and destroyed everything she's ever believed about their life together. You're her father. Instead of standing there rationally intellectualizing the situation, you should want to call him out."

"You've been reading too many historical novels. Besides, dueling's not my style." Peter laughed but when Karen didn't crack a smile he sobered. "Come on, Kaz. You've always said you fell in love with me because I offered you the calm oasis you needed."

And during all their years together, that's exactly what he'd given her. Karen never had any intentions of entangling herself in a relationship—why give a man an opportunity to control her life when she'd fought so hard to get out and away from her father's vicious dominance? But Peter had walked unexpectedly into the life she'd built herself.

They'd met at a tiny, inner-city art gallery in Melbourne. The art teacher at her school had invited her to an exhibition there, and since Karen was still making up for a childhood devoid of any culture, she'd accepted. Jittery with nerves, she'd planned to wait for Sylvia outside but rain drove her indoors. Her friend never arrived and Karen found out later that her car had broken down in the wet weather.

Utterly out of her depth, Karen had stared at the major canvas of the exhibition, trying hard to match the artist's story of the work with the image in front of her. People around her murmured affirmations about the use of light, color and texture and how brave the artist was to expose his soul in such a harrowing work. As they drifted away, Peter walked up and scratched his head.

"Looks like ..." he peered at the artist's name, "... Dukes had an accident in the garage with a can of blue paint and he didn't want to waste an expensive canvas."

She laughed. Peter grinned. They strolled around the rest of the exhibition together and as they studied each work, he drew her out, seeking her opinions. He didn't always agree, but his equable responses were always delivered with polite regard. When the gallery owner flashed the lights at eight o'clock to hurry out the lingerers, Peter said, "If you're hungry, there's a cheap Greek around the corner."

Perhaps it was the casual invitation and the way it gave her control, or the fact that a noisy BYO restaurant full of Greek families was devoid of any of the ritual signatures associated with a date, but whatever the reason, Karen found herself sitting opposite a man for dinner for the first time in years. Over taramasalata, baba ganoush and gyros—foods she'd never tasted before—she became increasingly drawn to Peter's intellect and his quiet and relaxed manner. It scared her, so she deliberately made some outrageous statements to elicit a strong response, telling herself that the moment he yelled at her or called her a stupid woman, the attraction would be cut off at the knees. Her busy single life would once again be safe. But nothing ruffled Peter. He smiled and gently but evenly argued, either deconstructing her statements or firming them up. It was a new and heady experience.

Within six months, they'd rented an apartment together—a calm oasis—and for the first time in her life Karen not only knew she was safe, she was loved.

But over this past week, calm had deserted Pelican House. "That was thirty-seven years ago! I'm allowed to change my mind."

Peter poured them each a glass of mineral water and added a slice of lemon. "Why are you angrier with Nick than with Jess?"

"I'm not."

"I think you are."

"Don't be ridiculous."

He lifted a brow. "You've always had a soft spot for Jess and it makes sense. In some ways, she reminds you of Lisa and you wanted to—"

"Nonsense." Hating her husband's astuteness, Karen furiously whisked balsamic vinegar into olive oil. Brown flecks appeared on the countertop. "I never got the chance to know teenage Lisa."

"Exactly. Anyway, it's not a crime to like Jess."

"You're only saying that because you're defending Nick. Jess's crime is she broke a friendship. Nick's broken Libby's trust, her heart and his marriage. Not to mention the security and wellbeing of our granddaughters."

"Jess broke Libby's heart too."

"It's not the same!" Karen shoved silver servers into the salad bowl.

"From Libby's perspective, I think it might be worse. If Nick's to be believed, Jess orchestrated the whole thing."

"Given their antics, I doubt either of them are a reliable source of the truth."

"There is that." Peter picked up the steaks for the barbecue. "But if Nick's right, it begs the question, is Jess's calculated betrayal worse than Nick's stupid mistake?"

ALICE PULLED HER KNITTED CAP DOWN AS LOW AS IT COULD GO without interfering with her vision and then shoved her gloved hands into the pockets of her puffer jacket. Although she'd prepared for the 3:00 a.m. chill, the cloudless autumn night had a crisp bite to it and not even brisk walking was keeping the nip away. It was the Relay for Life fundraising weekend. Kurnai Bay had managed to field six teams, including the medical practice, the parents and friends of the school and the bushwalking club. Bright white light flooded the sports ground, mimicking mid-afternoon sunshine and Alice always got a surprise when she glanced up to see a pitch black sky.

Dan van den Berg, Kurnai Bay's outdoor education teacher, summer surfing instructor and unabashed player, passed her before swinging around to face her. His shirt declared him to be part of the bushwalkers' team and he grinned at her, walking backwards with ease. Like Libby, Dan only ever did things with a confidence Alice envied. She'd grown up with him and although they'd never hung out in the same group at school, their parents' friendship meant they knew bits and pieces of each other's adult lives.

"Slacking off there, Twin Two," Dan said, using his childhood name for her. "At this rate, I'll lap you."

She resisted an eye roll. "Totally what I intended, Danny Boy. I wouldn't want to upset your need to be faster or fitter."

"You look pretty fit to me. You should come on our next walk."

Her body gave an involuntary shudder. "Does it involve me carrying my bed on my back?"

"Only if you want to."

"I will never want to," she said emphatically then laughed despite the memory of driving rain, mud and a pack that had almost toppled her off the side of a mountain when she was sixteen. "I'm surprised you'd want to invite me."

"Who can forget the Alice Hunter Hoadley Hide hike meltdown?" He laughed at the memory, but then his face became almost serious—for Dan. "Back then your pack was too big for you. The right gear makes all the difference."

"Exactly and my camera, lunch, water bottle and a light rain jacket constitutes the right gear."

"It's a day walk at Cape Conran so it's a perfect match. I'm hoping to see sea eagles."

Dan treated life as a competition and she could just imagine the pace he'd set, practically jogging through the bush. "Are there some slow walkers in the group?"

"Youngest is twenty and oldest is eighty so we cover all speeds."

The idea of walking in the bush appealed and for all Dan's faults, he was good company. "I'll think about it."

Fergus McLean called out from the side lines, "Change over, Dan."

"Gotta go, Twin Two. Call me if you're coming and I'll get you a seat in the car pool." With a grin and a wave, Dan was off and Alice had no doubt that by 7:00 a.m., he'd have invited another ten women.

When Alice passed the medical practice's team tent, Penny called out, "All good, Alice?"

She gave a double thumbs-up and kept walking. Alice was filling in for Libby and she was happy to do so but that didn't stop the anxiety for her twin grinding in her gut. Her usually confident and indomitable sister had placed herself in voluntary isolation from the town. Alice tried reassuring herself that it was only a week since all hell had broken loose and perhaps Libby was wise to avoid the gossip burning around the bay like a firestorm. Not that Alice expected it to die down anytime soon.

The situation had all the elements of a solid-gold scandal: a betrayed and devastated wife, a well-respected man's massive fall from grace, the *other* woman, illicit sex and a child. It had been years since something this sensational had electrified the town and it would grease the rumor mill for months until someone else made a spectacular mess of their life worthy of frantic feasting by the gossip vultures. Libby and Nick had each taken a week's leave from their jobs, but their return to work on Monday would give fresh oxygen to the fire of chatter.

When Libby had phoned distraught and almost incoherent the previous Friday, Alice's first response was, "Come home."

"I am home!" Libby sobbed.

"I'll come to you then."

"Bring the girls."

Alice had glanced at Indi and Lucy playing happily, oblivious to the fact their parents' lives, and therefore theirs, had just changed irrevocably. "Are you sure?"

"I'm not sure of anything anymore," Libby said, sounding unrecognizable. Libby's lack of certainty upset Alice more than her tears.

Alice had been at Burrunan for eight nights so far. Her nieces needed her, Libby needed her and in a way, so did Nick. For years she'd loved the house on the water, but she didn't at the moment. Although it looked the same with its relaxed seaside décor and eclectic knickknacks that told the story of love and laughter and a life shared, now it was rigid with tension. It held the putrid air of a torture chamber—pungent with unmitigated pain and torment.

Each morning, Libby would clutch her coffee cup and say brightly, "I'll be okay today," but by the afternoon it was obvious to Alice that her twin was far from okay. Glassy eyed and barely able to string a sentence together, Libby had shut down, retreating to a place where

Alice couldn't reach her. It scared Alice so much she'd called Ramesh. He'd prescribed medication that Libby was refusing to take.

Nick wasn't doing much better. Round shouldered and slumped, his aura simmered with shame and remorse. He veered between racing around the house cooking, cleaning, working in the yard and playing with the girls to staring vacantly out at the water as if it could offer him a solution to the nightmare. Alice had expected him to go sailing but, like Libby, he hadn't left the house.

Part of Alice wanted to scream at him and ask, "How could you have betrayed Libby?" *How could you have betrayed me?* Her own level of hurt stunned her. She loved Nick like the brother she'd never had and she respected him—had respected him. Still did in all ways except this. Nick hadn't offered Alice an excuse for his behavior, nor had he asked her to see things from his perspective or asked her to speak to Libby on his behalf. Although he wasn't wearing sackcloth, Alice got a strong sense of a man doing penance.

One night, as they tidied up the kitchen together, Alice asked, "You kept it a secret for so long. Why did you decide to tell her now and ruin her life?"

"The guilt was killing me."

Alice glimpsed the lapsed Catholic who'd been raised to go to confession and a flash of anger hit. "If you'd wanted absolution for your sins, you should have protected Libby and told a priest!"

He dipped his head. "I wanted Libby's forgiveness."

"Yeah, well. Good luck with that."

When Lucy had asked Alice why she was living at Burrunan, both girls had accepted her explanation that, "Mommy and Daddy are sick." It wasn't a lie, it just wasn't the sort of illness the girls understood.

At night, Alice lay awake for hours, filled with fury at Jess and Nick for destroying her twin's sense of self, and when she slept, her dreams were filled with her dragging Jess along the beach by the hair. They forced her to admit that she hated the woman more. She wanted to hate Nick just as much, but she'd had years to build up her antipathy to Jess and as hard as she tried, she struggled to wrap her head around her brother-in-law actively setting out to wound Libby. Not that she'd ever anticipated Jess slicing Libby down to her heart and soul either. Alice's dislike of Jess stemmed from being cut out of Libby's life. Not once had she ever doubted Jess's loyalty to her twin.

Alice had seen that loyalty in action and not just back in the day, but in the last year—a period she now knew Jess had already betrayed Libby. Was that still friendship or was it guilt? Judging by what Libby had said about her conversation with Jess, the woman displayed no signs of guilt or regret for her actions. So why had Jess continued to invest in the friendship?

"Alice! Slow down, I want to talk to you." Genevieve Lawry power-walked up to her, puffing slightly. "We're all worried about Libby. How is she?"

Bereft. Heartbroken. Enraged. "Surviving."

"Oh my God, it's just so awful. You know, I always thought that Nick Pirelli was too good to be true. I mean, what man is ever that helpful around the house or with the kids, right? If Jake did anything like that to me, I'd castrate him. Then I'd take the boys and leave him."

Initially, Alice and Karen had believed that Libby should do exactly that. Now, after a week living at Burrunan and talking with Libby and Nick, Alice wasn't close to certain what she'd do in the same situation.

"It's easy to say what you'll do when it's not happening to you."

Genevieve's mouth pursed in disapproval. "So, it really is true then? Libby's still living at Burrunan with that scumbag?"

Alice's hands fisted in her pockets. "Libby's not in a fit state to make any important decisions just now."

"Then Nick should do the decent thing and move out," Gen huffed. "He and Jess deserve each other."

The thought of Nick leaving his daughters and moving in with Jess and their son sent furnace-hot rage tearing through Alice, banishing the chill she'd battled for two laps. She unzipped her puffer with a jerk. "*Nothing* in life is black and white, Genevieve."

"Murder and adultery are," Genevieve muttered before crossing her arms. "I'm surprised at you, Alice. You, of all people, should want the best for your twin."

"Of course I want the best thing for her!"

"Then encourage her to kick him out. Believe me, staying married to a prick like that's the worst possible thing she can do to herself."

Alice's teeth locked. "Only Libby can make that decision."

"Let's hope she does it then."

The urge to slap the self-righteous woman's face was so strong that Alice picked up her speed, putting distance between them. When Alice had arrived at the team tent earlier, all of Libby's staff had expressed their concerns. She'd texted her twin, *Please come down. The team misses you.* But Libby had texted back, *Can't.* After Genevieve's brutal interpretation of the situation, Alice was glad Libby had stayed away. Her twin wasn't up to dealing with well-meaning work colleagues, let alone judgmental acquaintances.

As she rounded the turn, her phone buzzed and she read a text from Libby. *Is she there?*

Alice examined the small crowd, scanning it for Jess. Surely Jess wouldn't walk into the heart of Libby's loyal team? It would be the equivalent of self-flagellation and that really wasn't Jess's style. Then again, given what she'd done to Libby, who could predict her thought processes and behavior?

The original plan had been for Libby and Jess to walk the graveyard hours together. Alice remembered the sense of isolation that had jabbed her when she'd heard them organizing it. Although they'd told her they'd taken the time slot to give the other team members a break during the difficult hours, she'd known it was also because it gave them uninterrupted time together. Theirs had always been an intense friendship—one that didn't require anyone else and it came complete with its own set of gestures and words. Their friendship not only bruised Alice, it often filled her with envy. But now Libby was cleaved in half by the double betrayal of her best friend and her husband, and the once intimate friendship lay shattered. Destroyed. Alice didn't have to guess how Libby was feeling—it was there in front of her every minute of the day. In a way, it was part of her own self.

But no matter which way Alice came at it, she couldn't fathom what Jess was experiencing. Was she hoping Nick would leave Libby for her? As soon as the thought percolated, Alice discarded it. Surely if Jess had wanted that, she'd have told Libby about Leo months earlier. Was Jess angry that Nick had spilled the secret and jettisoned her friendship with Libby? Was she grieving too? Or had she known for a long time that she'd sacrificed the friendship the moment she'd slept with Nick and decided to have his child?

Alice understood Jess's desire for a baby. How one day the intense need appeared out of the blue and burrowed in with fierce determination before spreading its thickening branches into muscle, bone, fiber and cell. How it consumed mind, body and soul with a gnawing need that hollowed a woman from the inside out. Alice was living this—she had been for a couple of years. But despite the all-encompassing yearning, would she squander love and support by hurting the person closest to her to get it?

No.

But what if the choice was having a child with a friend's husband or no child at all?

Alice felt a sharp tug on her values and hastily reminded herself that Jess could have chosen far more ethical options to conceive. She could have entered a committed relationship or used donor sperm. Those choices wouldn't have upended Libby's world. Of course, Nick wasn't innocent in all of this either, but it was so much easier, and almost enjoyable, to blame the other woman.

Alice's phone emitted a sound like a frog and delicious delight—an almost Pavlovian response—throbbed through her. Tim. She immediately plunged into a pool of lust, remembering their video session. Reality jolted her—that had been well over a week ago. She'd been so caught up with Libby, Nick and the girls, she hadn't had time to text or daydream about Tim. Or notice that he hadn't been in touch either.

I know it's late, or maybe it's early, Alice my Wonderland, but if you're there ...

Her fingers flew. *I'm very much here&k!zd9*

Alice hit something, stumbled backwards and her finger accidentally tapped send. Glancing up, she realized she'd just walked into the back of someone.

"Oh, God, I'm so sorry! I didn't see you." Trying to hide the reason for her distraction, she shoved her phone into her pocket, but not before the bloke turned around and caught her.

"Problems with your night vision? Or a phone addiction?"

It took Alice a moment to register that he was the father of the artistic girl she'd met on the pier a few weeks earlier. It wasn't so much that she remembered his face—although in this light his eyes were an arresting emerald—it was his vibe of world-weary acceptance that nothing in life could surprise him, that rang a bell.

"Dad! You found Alice! Hi, Alice." Despite the very early hour, Hunter bounced on the balls of his feet.

"She found me, mate."

"Hello, Hunter." Alice's phone buzzed again in her pocket but despite every part of her wanting to swoop on it, she ignored it. "Is Holly here too?"

"She's over there." Hunter pointed to the coffee stall.

The first time Alice met Hunter, he and Holly had been on the pier during school hours. Now, when most kids their age were in bed, they were up in the middle of the night. Alice considered herself fairly easygoing but a tween drinking coffee at any hour crossed her boundaries.

"She's buying hot chocolate," the man said, clearly reading Alice's disapproval.

"They're yum. Do you want one?" Hunter asked.

"Thanks, Hunter. That would be great." She reached into her pocket for some coins, but he was already haring off, running toward his sister.

"Does he ever stop?" Alice asked as they resumed walking.

"When he's asleep. Mind you, he thrashes about a lot. It's dangerous sharing a bed with him."

"My nieces are the same. They either edge me out or give me bruises." Alice realized she still didn't know his name. "So, Holly and Hunter's dad—"

"Harry."

"Holly, Harry and Hunter?" She laughed. "Does alliteration run in the family?"

"It was their mother's idea. Helene. She called us the 4H club." He must have seen Alice's confusion, because he added, "She was American. It's a club for kids."

Was? "Helene's not here?"

"No. That's why we are. She died fourteen months ago. Brain tumor."

"Oh God." Her heart ached for Hunter and Holly. "I'm sorry. Cancer's such an invasion."

"You're not wrong."

Alice waited for Harry to expand but he didn't offer anything else. She was about to ask him how long he'd lived in the bay when she noticed he was staring straight ahead, his body rigid. Grief was a bastard. Alice knew that despite the awkwardness, sometimes it was better to ride out a silence.

As they entered the straight, Harry shoved his hands under his armpits. "H loved this coast. Every opportunity she could, she'd drag us down here from Melbourne to walk and sail. We spent a crazy amount of time daydreaming about buying a yacht or a beach shack somewhere between Golden Beach and Lake Tyers. A year to the day she died, the house we used to rent down here came on the market."

"You took it as a sign?"

"Thought the move might help the kids."

"And?"

"Too early to tell. Some days it's all good ..."

Alice thought about what had precipitated her return to the bay and the difficult early months. "And others are crap."

"I see you're familiar with my life." He gave her a half-smile and it softened his face, stripping away years. "Some days, like that day on the pier, we take a sick day from this new routine we're still trying to fit into. Holly draws and Hunter gets a day off from having to sit still."

"We all need a day off now and then. My mother's all about routine but Dad's a bit more flexible. We sneak off together sometimes. He fishes and I draw."

"Holly's always drawing, but she's getting frustrated with herself. She's started saying she's useless at it."

"She's not," Alice said emphatically.

"I know. Thing is, I'm useless at it and I don't know how to help her."

Alice thought about her father. "Take an interest and encourage her."

"I've always done that, but it's not enough anymore. Now when I compliment her, she rolls her eyes and says, 'You're just saying that, Dad.' I talked to the art teacher at the school. She's good, but she's got nineteen other students in the class so she suggested I get Holly a tutor."

"That's a good idea."

"It would be if there was someone in town." He shoved his hands into his pockets. "That day on the pier, you helped her get the line of the pelican's beak. Are you an art teacher?"

"God, no. It's just a hobby."

"I doubt that."

"Why? You don't even know me."

"True, but Holly's mentioned you more than once since then and this afternoon at the fundraiser, I was the successful bidder for the pen and wash sketch of the old Clarendon homestead. Nothing about the drawing says hobby and the signature says 'Alice Hunter.'"

She wanted to fully bask in his compliment but she couldn't. "Thanks, but I drew it four years ago. I haven't done much art since and I'm pretty rusty."

"You'd still know more than my twelve-year-old." His mouth

tweaked again into a half-smile. "I'm only asking for an hour a week. What do you say?"

"An hour? Art isn't like a piano lesson, Harry."

"Two sessions a week then? I dunno. I really want to give Hol this opportunity. Whatever works for you and we'll work it in around your commitments."

As much as Alice admired his commitment to his daughter, drawing was her sanctuary. She didn't want to formalize it into yet another job. "I don't know ..."

Harry looked straight at her then and in place of the grieving man, she clearly saw the steely determination of a father who wanted the best for his child. "What if I played the motherless child card?"

Alice railed at the pressure. "I think you just did."

"Did it work?"

"Does it often?"

He glanced at his feet, suddenly sheepish. "I dunno. It's the first time I've ever tried it."

Vague memories of Lawrence working to get his own way flittered through her mind, along with the way it had made her feel. Months earlier, in the midst of her shock and grief when she was glorifying in what she'd thought was a perfect relationship, she'd forgotten these instances. Now they hissed and spat like hot oil, bolstering her newly developed determination to live life her way.

"Don't *ever* try it on me again, okay?"

"Fair enough." He looked up, chastened. "I'm sorry, Alice. I was completely out of line. Thing is, I'm desperate. I don't know if it's hormones or missing her mom or what, but Holly's struggling. I'm terrified she's about to give up on something that gives her pleasure."

He sighed. "I get you're not keen and I've just made things worse. Sorry. Forget about the tutoring, but if you can suggest anyone who might be interested, I'd be grateful. I promise I won't guilt them into it."

His love and concern for his daughter got tangled up with Alice's own memories of a time when hormones had thrown her into a confusing and bewildering place full of dark and scary corners. Combined, they took the edge off Alice's displeasure at Harry's hamfisted attempt to convince her to help Holly. "I'm not making any promises, but how about Holly and I draw together one afternoon this week? If we click, then you and I can discuss terms."

His entire body relaxed and he shot out his hand. "Thanks, Alice."

She slid hers into his and returned the firm shake. "Don't thank me too soon. You might not be able to afford me."

His smile reached his eyes. "I'll give up top shelf red wine if I have to, Alice. Now, before you change your mind, can we swap numbers?"

"Sure."

She pulled out her phone for him to type in his digits but as she handed it over she saw a photo that Tim had sent for her eyes only. Flashing hot and cold, her fingers fumbled, trying to shut down the screen and in her panic, she increased the size of the photo. And the size of Tim's penis.

"I can see why you were distracted enough to walk into me," Harry said drily.

Embarrassment burned her. She wished she could magic herself away from this excruciating moment. "I—he—we—"

"I can see that."

"I doubt you'll want me to help Holly now."

"Hey, you're not getting out of it that easily. Just hold off teaching her nudes for a while, eh?"

She managed a weak laugh. "Deal."

Jess pushed Leo in his stroller, bumping her way across the grass to the team tents at Relay For Life. It was seven o'clock and the smell of onions wafted on the early Sunday morning air as people huddled together drinking coffee and scarfing down egg and bacon rolls. It was easy to pick the fresh walkers from those who'd done the nightshift, but despite the difference in the fatigue factor, the esprit de corps was high, with people cheering each lap.

Jess had spent months enthusiastically fundraising for the Anti-Cancer Council. She'd organized a champagne, popcorn and choc-top ice-cream movie night at the local cinema, raffled herself as a cook for a dinner party for twelve and baked and sold more chocolate chip cookies than she ever wanted to see again. On top of all that, she'd also secured $500 of sponsorship money if she completed her laps this weekend. She'd wanted to honor her commitment to her sponsors by walking the night-time hours, just as she and Libby had planned, but when Nick had failed to arrive to collect Leo as arranged before everything had gone to shit, it left her with no time to organize a babysitter. Given Libby's borderline psychotic behavior when she'd torn the dress from Jess's shoulders eight days earlier, she wasn't risking taking Leo to Burrunan just yet.

Faced with deathly silence from both Libby and Nick, Jess had spent Friday through Tuesday on tenterhooks. When Nick's weekly support payment tumbled into her bank account, she'd relaxed. She was still desperate to talk to him, but for the sake of fruitful discussion, Leo's wellbeing and all their futures, she was biding her time. Waiting for the dust to settle and giving everyone a chance to find some calm and gain perspective. She included herself in that plan.

Jess was battling some residual anger toward Nick for breaking the news to Libby without involving her in either the decision or the telling. But the fact he'd done it mostly heartened her—she was taking it as a breakthrough. It meant he wanted to be known publicly as Leo's father. That's why she needed to talk to Nick and Libby. For Leo's sake, as well as Lucy's and Indi's, they needed to control how and when the information was released into the wider Kurnai Bay community. It was vital they protected the children from the inevitable gossip and the way to do that was presenting a united front—a family committed to one another.

Jess passed a row of portapotties and a plastic door at the end of the row banged open. Penny, the practice nurse at the medical center, stepped out, turned, then stopped abruptly.

"Hi, Penny. You look like you could curl up and nap right now."

"What are you doing here?"

The growl in the woman's voice caught Jess by surprise. Then again, Penny had been up all night. "You really must be tired, Pen, if you're asking me that. I'm here to walk."

"You missed your time slot so you can't walk."

"Nowhere in the rules does it say that."

"It's in *my* rules. I don't want you to walk."

A warning knot tied low in Jess's belly but she reassured herself this was just Penny being her usual pedantic self. She plucked at her team polo shirt. "There's no I in team, Pen. Besides, would you really be that petty and deny the Anti-Cancer Council $500 just because I've tweaked your roster?"

Leo squawked loudly, protesting at being ignored by Penny, but the nurse didn't bend down and talk to him. Instead she crossed her arms and glared at Jess.

"You've always thought the rules don't apply and that bending them makes you better than everyone else. But you're wrong. All it does is make you a bitch."

Jess flinched. "*Don't* swear in front of my son."

Penny spun on the heels of her cross-trainers and stalked away.

Had Libby said something to the practice nurse?

Jess instantly discarded the thought as ridiculous. Since "the big reveal," as she'd taken to calling it, and Libby's associated meltdown, Jess had spoken to the practice manager about the payroll as well as to the receptionist. Both had been their usual friendly selves. It reassured her that despite Libby's unhinged behavior and her subsequent refusal to talk, her friend was sticking to their long-held commitment of holding each other's secrets safe and protecting those they love. There was no way Libby would ever share the news that Nick was Leo's father with her practice staff.

Penny was just being a pain. Usually Jess wouldn't let anyone's opinion of her change her plans, but she had Leo to consider and she wasn't convinced Penny wouldn't have another go at her if she went into the team tent. Did it really matter who she walked with? Wasn't the important thing the fact she walked and earned the money people had pledged to her in good faith?

Decision made, Jess headed for the school tent. She knew some of the parents through their younger children and their association with the toy library and story time.

"Jess!" Lexie Patric waved. "Look at you, yummy mommy! How do you manage to look so fantastic this early in the morning?"

Jess laughed. "Leo woke me up at five thirty so I've had plenty of time." She didn't mention how clingy he'd been and how she'd put him in the backpack and hoisted him onto her shoulders just so she could apply her makeup.

"Five thirty's a sleep in."

"You live in a crazy world." Jess liked the Swan Reach woman, but as Lexie ran a dairy farm with her husband, she wasn't often in town. "I haven't seen you in ages. How are those cows of yours?"

"Ruling our lives. I've snuck away for a few hours and Ian's coming after milking. His dad's just had surgery for bowel cancer so we're walking for Walt."

"Is he okay?"

"The surgeon thinks she got it all, but he has to have radiotherapy just in case." Lexie glanced at the growing crowd. "Coming to something like this makes you realize how many people have been brushed by cancer either personally or through family and friends. Didn't your mom die of cancer?"

"Yep."

Telling people Linda died of liver cancer was easier than revealing the truth: that the liver failure that killed her was self-induced by her alcoholism. Cancer generated understanding and sympathy, whereas alcoholism brought out judgement and criticism. The latter had been the ever-present backdrop of her childhood.

The terse disapproval of Linda's lifestyle by doctors, teachers, social workers, neighbors—let's face it, by most middle-class adults—had circled Jess and her mother like a high wall of condemnation. Few people had differentiated between Linda's many failures and Jess's childhood naiveté. She'd hated them for it, but she'd hated Linda more for putting her in the position to be censured as "the drunk's daughter." Thinking about Linda wasn't something Jess allowed herself to do very often, because it always dampened her mood.

Shaking away the memories, she said, "Want to walk with Leo and me until Ian comes?"

"I'd love to! I thought you'd be walking with Libby?"

"That was the plan. But when your best friend's a doctor, you get used to last minute changes."

"Libby's loss is my gain then." Lexie grinned at her with a mix of delight and gratitude before sliding her arm through Jess's. "It feels like ages since I got off the farm. Let's walk and talk and you can fill me in on all the town gossip."

"You're in good hands, Lexie," Tenika said, joining them. "Not only is Jess always up to speed with the gossip, she tells it in such an entertaining way."

Jess smiled, enjoying the praise. "Sadly, I'm going to have to let you down today. Apart from the public exchange of insults in the Buckets and Bouquets section of the *Gazette*, the town's pretty quiet."

"Surely you can do better than that." Genevieve stepped in, flanking Jess.

"I'll try and do better next time."

"Why don't you tell Lexie how you've been screwing your best friend's husband," Tenika said.

Lexie's feet stalled and her pupils dilated so fast that black obliterated most of the hazel. "Tenika! That's a terrible thing to say."

Shock whipped through Jess, racing her heart and loosening her gut. They knew about Leo? No! Not possible. Even if the senior Hunters and Pirellis or Alice had broken rank out of spite and spread a rumor she was having an affair with Nick, they would have protected the children.

Come on! Get it together. Show no fear. Jess schooled her face into what she hoped was an impassive mask of disinterest. "Language, Tenika. There are lots of little ears flapping."

"Including the product of your affair," Genevieve snapped. "After what you've done to Libby Hunter, you've lost all rights to be the moral compass."

Holy Mother. How did they know? But right now, "how" wasn't important. They knew and the implications pummeled her like the jagged spikes of an ice storm. A tremor in her toes quickly gained momentum and as she tried to keep her legs steady, a second wave of horror caught her. If these women knew Nick was Leo's father, then all the members of the toy library, toddler gym, daycare, playgroup and the wine and whine club knew too. Her entire social network! Her throat threatened to close.

Years of well-honed survival skills fought their way through her thick fog of shock. "Genevieve, you don't get to use unsubstantiated gossip to denigrate my character or inaccurately broadcast my private life at a public event."

"I do when it's the truth."

"You wouldn't know the truth if it bit you."

"I think it's you who's been bitten." Genevieve gave a triumphant humph. "Libby told me what you've done to her."

Betrayal slammed so violently into Jess that it almost knocked her off her feet. The denigrating soundbites from her childhood escaped their soundproof box, screaming at her. Her best friend was so driven to hurt her that she'd just broken their long-held secrets pact and exposed innocent little people to the vicious gossip of the town. Jess had a momentary desire to inflict pain.

A white-faced Lexie dropped her arm away from Jess's and glanced between Genevieve and Tenika. "Nick Pirelli's Leo's father?"

Tenika nodded vigorously, her eyes glinting with glee. "It's disgusting, isn't it?"

The growl of a lioness filled Jess's ears and then a red hue blurred her vision. "My son is not disgusting!"

"He might not be yet, but give him time. He's tainted by you and your mother."

Years of fury poured out of her. "Leave my mother out of this!"

"I don't think so. According to my mother, yours was a drunk and a ho." Genevieve smirked. "You might have gone to university, had some high-flying job and worn designer clothes, but on the inside, you're exactly the same as Linda. You're white trash. You've got the morals of an alley cat and you'll screw over anyone to get what you want."

The muscles in Jess's legs quivered like jelly and she gripped the handle of the stroller so hard her hands ached. "You're talking BS like usual, Genevieve."

"You're not welcome here, Jess," Tenika said. "It's time you left."

"This is a public event. I have as much right to be here as any of you."

"Enjoy walking on your own then, because you stink so bad no one will come anywhere near you. Come on, Lexie," Genevieve said.

The women turned as one and walked away.

Jess stood, aware only of her thundering heart and the sound of her blood in her ears. As if registering the sudden silence after all the vitriol and yelling, Leo's eyes filled with tears and then he was screaming, his little chest heaving with great hulking sobs. With shaking hands, Jess unbuckled him and lifted him into her arms, kissing his damp curls.

"Shh, my darling boy. It's okay. Those horrible nasty women have gone."

Only Jess wasn't certain who she was reassuring more—her son or herself.

CHAPTER ELEVEN

"Journal your feelings. It helps," Alice suggested a week after Libby's world imploded.

Libby doubted it. Besides, her feelings weren't complex, they were glaringly simple: rage and despair. She'd spent the week being flung back and forth between the two and the energy required rendered her inert. The sensations battered her—pain, anger, heartache and hopelessness—and brought her as close to a premonition of death as she'd ever been before. Sleep was impossible, but constantly wondering why this had happened to her, how could they have done this to her and what else wasn't she being told, made it agonizing to be awake.

Thank God for Alice. She was the unexpected blessing in this nightmare. Her twin, who so often hesitated and doubted herself, had walked unflinchingly into this house of pain. She'd surprised everyone by quietly taking charge. Although Alice did things in very different ways from Libby, the results were the same. The children were bathed and fed, cuddled and read to, and taken to all their activities. If the pictures in Libby's room were anything to go by, the girls had been allowed unfettered access to the craft box, including free and liberal use of the glitter.

When they were children, Alice had been the physically weaker twin, struggling to execute tasks Libby had taken for granted, and she'd never been any good with bodily fluids. But she'd held Libby while she sobbed until she vomited and then she'd changed the bedsheets when Libby's faithless uterus had added insult to her pain and distress by flooding and staining the bed with blood clots. Alice even cooked her their favorite childhood comfort food of soft boiled eggs with bread and Vegemite 'soldiers', coaxing her to eat after she'd spent days gagging on the thought of food and existing on milk and coffee.

Karen had provided practical help too, filling the cookie jars with baking, taking the girls on outings and scrubbing the bathrooms with potent rage. Karen's anger at Nick was a licking ball of fire that heated every room she entered. It surprised Libby that her mother's outrage hadn't melded with hers and comforted. Instead it had buffeted and hustled, demanding answers Libby didn't have.

"Libby, think of the girls!"

"I am! It's why I'm still here."

"Then put yourself first. God knows, if you don't, no one else will."

The comment smacked Libby like the sting from an open palm. This from the woman who'd raised her to always consider how her actions would affect other people. "Apparently, you gave that selfish and useless advice to Jess years ago. It's her and Nick putting themselves first that's got us into this mess!"

Alice had come into the room then and asked Karen for a hand with the girls. When she'd shut the door behind them, Libby had fallen back on her pillows and cried with relief.

When Rosa and Rick had arrived at Burrunan asking to talk to her, it was Alice who came and found her. Libby braced herself for an argument. "I can't do it, Al."

But all Alice said was, "I get it. Leave it with me."

For half an hour, Libby lay listening to the rise and fall of voices, knowing her twin, who once would have devolved into tears at a partially raised voice, was taking a bullet for her.

"They send their love," Alice reported later, sitting on the bed in the guest room nursing a cup of tea.

"For what a Pirelli's word is worth."

Libby's in-laws had only ever been welcoming and loving toward her, but then again, she'd always thought that of Nick too. Apparently it meant squat.

"They're really upset, Libs. They almost got me to sign a promise that I'd tell you they love you like a daughter. They're absolutely furious with Nick."

"Good! Did you tell them to take a number?"

"Put it this way. If Nick dares to go into Rosa's kitchen, I wouldn't be surprised if she takes the wooden spoon to him. And Rick, well, I learned a couple of new Italian swear words."

"And Jess? Are they going to burn her at the stake?"

"Mmm-hmm." Alice's nose was buried in her mug of tea.

Libby knew her twin only did that when she was avoiding an issue. "What?"

"Nothing." Alice kept her gaze fixed inside the mug as if tea was the most fascinating thing on the planet. "Like I said, they're furious with Nick so of course they're not happy with Jess."

Libby sat up and pinned her twin with something the two of them had labelled years earlier the "truth stare." "There's something you're not telling me."

Alice shook her head.

"It's something about Jess, isn't it? You have to tell me!"

"No, I don't."

"You do. I'm the first twin!"

Alice rolled her eyes. "We're not kids and you're not the boss of me anymore."

"God, I wish we were twelve again."

Alice's face, almost a mirror image of her own, creased in lines of disagreement. "I'm not telling you because it will only upset you. I don't want you hurt again."

"Hah!" The sound cracked the air like a whip. "After what Nick and Jess did to me, believe me, I'm fully immune. And you not telling me is just as bad as them not telling me. If it affects me, I deserve to know."

Anguish filled her twin's eyes. "Okay ... They've asked Nick to arrange—they want to spend time with Leo."

Libby's chest tightened so fast the pain shot clear through to her spine and she stifled a cry. As she pressed a fist against the burn under her sternum, she made her first real decision since the apocalypse.

That night Libby sat at the kitchen table opposite Nick with the red leather-bound notebook Alice had given her for another purpose entirely. The children were asleep and on Libby's insistence, Alice had returned to Pelican House. It was the first time she'd been alone with her husband in nine days.

Libby had spent most of that time in the guest room and the study, only coming into the main living areas when she knew Nick was out of the house. Now, looking at the stubble on his face and the deep lines carved around his mouth and eyes, she took pleasure in the fact he looked as drawn and haggard as she did. He'd caused this chaos—he deserved to suffer.

During her self-imposed isolation, he'd knocked on her door a few times each day, but she'd limited their infrequent conversations to issues regarding the children. She'd ignored his pleas of, "Please, Libby. We need to talk."

Now she broke the silence. "You're still here."

His brow furrowed and his eyes scanned her face, looking for clues as to what she meant. "Yes."

"I thought you might have gone to live with her and your son."

His hangdog look was reminiscent of their terrier, Monty. "I told you. I don't love her. I love you."

And do you love your son? It was beyond her to ask the question—she feared the answer too much. "You say you love me—"

"I say it because it's true." He stretched his arm across the table, his fingers stopping just short of touching hers. "Thank you for still being here."

She pulled her hand into her lap and shook her head. "I'm not here for you, Nick. Right now, I'm here for the girls. Unlike you, I'm not thoughtlessly destroying their world. I'm trying to limit the carnage. I refuse to make any life-changing decisions until I've found my footing in this nightmare you've pitched us into. We're both going back to work tomorrow, which means facing the town. There are things we need to discuss."

"I'm just glad you're open to discussing things." He tried a smile.

Once she would have smiled back, appreciating him and her good fortune. Now she could hardly bear to look at him. "Is Leo your son?"

His bewilderment returned. "You know he is."

"No. I don't."

"Libby," he said patiently as if he was talking to a child. "He's got my eyes and my hair. Mom says—"

"His mother has brown eyes and dark curly hair too," she interrupted, not wanting to hear Rosa's opinion that Leo looked exactly like Nick as a child. "It's not definitive proof."

"He was born nine months after—"

Libby gripped onto hatred, fighting the image of Nick and Jess locked together that always undid her. "You told me she lied to you about using contraception so she's likely lying to you about Leo being yours. I want a paternity test."

He looked skeptical. "She won't agree. I asked her when she was pregnant and she said it was too dangerous. I asked again when he was born. She said she wasn't subjecting Leo to the pain of a needle."

God, how gullible was he? "She lied to you about that too. It's not a blood test. It's just a swab inside his mouth and yours. Simple and painless." Libby pulled the lid off her heavy silver pen and made a note beside item one on her list. "Are you paying her any maintenance?"

He looked affronted. "Of course, I am."

"It stops until we get the results of the paternity test."

"Libby, that's not very fair to—"

"*Fair?*" She lost control of her barely restrained fury. "If life was fair, you wouldn't have put us here. I know her and she'll dig her heels in about the paternity test just because she can. But as from tomorrow, when I cease contracting the financial side of the practice to Dekic Accounting Services, she's going to be chasing money."

"Okay. I'll ask her."

"No! You won't ask her anything. That's our next discussion point. All direct communication with her stops. I don't want you talking to that woman again."

He plowed a hand through his hair. "That's going to be bit tricky because of—"

"You say you love me." She speared him with a look loaded with the daggers she wished she could plunge into his heart.

"I do. So very much."

His sincerity didn't touch her like it had once. His actions had tainted it so badly she no longer believed it. "The night you broke me, you told me you'd do anything. Well, words are easy, Nick. Now you need to prove they're true. If you want a snowflake's chance in hell of staying married to me, then we're doing things my way."

"I do want to stay married to you," he said firmly. "What else is on that list?"

"Have you been unfaithful to me with anyone else?"

"Jesus, Libby! No!"

"You need to have tests for sexually transmitted diseases."

He recoiled. "But I just told you, she showed me ... Why?"

She ground her teeth. "Because I haven't been able to get pregnant since you had sex with her. An infection could be the reason."

He paled. "I'll have the tests."

She ticked off item three and took a steadying breath. "Tomorrow you're getting a new phone number and I'll have access to all your texts, apps, emails, bank account, the lot. That woman will be blocked from my phone, my personal and work emails and yours. I'm creating a Gmail account solely for contacting her and it will *only* be used when both of us are sitting in front of the computer together."

The initial burning heat of her anger had changed to a cold and determined chill. Now it iced her heart. "And Nick, if you *ever* try and contact her or see that child, we're over. Do you understand me?"

Misery pulled hard at his mouth and anguish flared in his eyes. For a moment, she thought he was going to object. Finally, he nodded. "I understand."

Libby replaced the cap on her pen, closed the red notebook on her first list and waited for the anticipated sense of relief and reassurance to wash through her. It didn't come.

April

"*Au revoir, les étudiants,*" Karen said.

The school had called her in for some emergency substitute teaching after the French teacher broke her leg water skiing during the Easter break. Karen was always happy to take a mini hiatus from retirement—a state she still hadn't fully accepted despite almost a year of living it. It was discombobulating to feel twenty-three but inhabit a post-menopausal body that thickened despite exercise and healthy eating, and ached in places she didn't know it could.

"*Au revoir, Madame,*" the small senior year class chanted back, their minds already on the imminent bell and a weekend of freedom.

"*Soyez sage le weekend ou ne vous faites pas prendre.*"

Most of the class laughed but a couple of the boys gave her a quizzical look. "Be good on the weekend or what?"

"Be good or don't get caught."

"Respect, Mrs. H."

She laughed. "Perhaps I should have said write your dialogue ready for me on Monday."

They groaned good-naturedly and walked out into the pale autumn sunshine. As Karen slid her computer into the padded section of her backpack, she ran through her mental check list of the things she needed to do before meeting Peter at the RSL for dinner. The first job was to pick up Indi from daycare. Libby had telephoned at 7:00 this morning with the request—or to be more accurate—the command. Given Karen's unexpected teaching load, she'd asked Libby if there was a reason why Nick couldn't do it.

"Leo is at childcare today."

"And you don't want to risk him running into Jess?"

"That too."

The bitterness in her daughter's voice both shocked and rattled Karen. It triggered memories of her father—memories she'd buried long ago—and their unexpected and unwelcome intrusion left her shaky. "I understand why you don't want Nick anywhere near Jess, but, sweetheart, Leo is just a little boy."

"Just?" Libby's voice cracked on a screech. "I really don't understand you, Mom. You told me to leave Nick. You said he didn't deserve me and I should protect myself. Well, I'm trying to protect myself and the girls while I work out if my marriage is over. But you're so focused on punishing Nick, you don't care that me leaving him means it rocks your granddaughters' world to its core and slashes time with their father. Yet, you're saying he should see *that* child? None of this is helpful, Mom. None of it!"

Libby's rancor burned Karen's ear. "Darling, I only want what's best for you."

"Then be like Dad. Support my decisions! And if you can't do that, then give me space, because right now, I don't need any more enemies."

Apprehension jittered in Karen's belly. Even when Libby was a teen and establishing her place in the world, she'd never spoken to her this way. From the start, Libby had always known her own mind and been goal oriented, and Karen appreciated the strength those traits gave her elder daughter. More than once she'd wished Alice had been blessed with similar mental fortitude. But as much as Karen appreciated Libby's strength of purpose, her own childhood experiences were never too far away, so she'd been almost obsessive about teaching both girls to be kind and considerate, thoughtful and loving. Exactly like their paternal grandparents. Nothing like her own parents.

Apart from the occasional and very normal moments of teenage self-centeredness, Karen had never had any cause for concern that Libby wasn't kind and caring—her choice of career reinforced it. But now there was a sharp and biting hardness to her and an uncompromising stance on people being either for her or against her; an almost brutal insistence that family and friends choose a side.

Karen opened her mouth to tell her daughter that unlike Nick, she was on her side and that was possible even if she didn't completely agree with her. But the past suddenly rushed at her in vivid flashes of memory. Soundbites of her parents' rancor. Hunger chomping through her stomach lining. Being faced with impossible choices. Cuddling Lisa and making promises to her baby sister that she never got to fulfill because her father—

Her stomach cramped so tightly she doubled over. This acrimonious version of Libby was devastatingly familiar—a female version of Karen's father. This Libby wouldn't hesitate to cut Karen out of her and her granddaughters' lives. Karen refused to make the same mistake a second time. The little girls needed her. Libby needed her, even if she couldn't see that through the red haze of her current paranoia.

"I'll pick up Indi."

"Thank you."

But there was no gratitude attached to the word, only critical expectation. Karen rarely cried, but tears pooled behind her eyes. What if Libby's new hardness and intractability weren't temporary? Karen gave herself a jolly good shake. Of course they were temporary. Anything else was too awful to contemplate.

THE BRIGHT MURALS GREETED KAREN AT THE DAYCARE CENTER as she punched in the security code and signed the book. Instead of having a specific baby room, toddler room and preschool room, the center operated on a family model that mixed ages. Karen walked into the Wombat Room and scanned the various activity stations for Indi. She spotted Leo in story corner with his thumb in his mouth, cuddling a board book.

"Hi, Mrs. Hunter!" Jaci, the daycare worker, greeted her and then blushed. "I mean Karen."

Karen had taught Jaci a couple of years earlier, without much success. Fortunately, the young woman's grasp of the needs of the under-fives far exceeded her French language skills. Indi adored her.

"Hello, Jaci. Is Indi outside?"

"Sorry, Mrs.—Karen. She's in the Rosella Room now."

Karen felt disappointed for Indi. "I bet she's missing you."

"We're all missing her." Jaci inclined her head toward story corner. "Especially Leo. He's been really clingy."

"Was there a reason for the reshuffle?" But as she asked, Karen realized she recognized all the other children.

Jaci looked uncomfortable. "Dr. Hunter insisted."

Karen sighed. "I see. I better zip off to the Rosella Room then. Thanks, Jaci."

She returned to the corridor and immediately came face-to-face with Jess. The younger woman's face fell momentarily and then she lifted her chin, the action identical to the one she'd often used as a wary and defensive teen.

"Hello, Karen."

"Hello, Jess."

Jess blinked as if she'd expected Karen to ignore her. "The last two weeks Alice has been on Indi duty. I don't suppose I'm ever going to see Libby or Nick here, am I?"

Something about the way Jess said the words, and her accompanying tight face, scuttled sadness and regret through Karen. "Did you really expect that?"

Jess's eyes flashed. "I didn't expect the intensity of her savagery and spite. Not after years of sharing everything."

Neither had Karen, although surely Jess must have known Libby would push back? She ached for the young girl inside Jess, whose dysfunctional mother had failed to teach her the unspoken laws of family. In the early years of her marriage, Karen had shared some of the same bewilderment when, like a soldier returning from active duty, her highly tuned survival instincts collided with normal family life. If it hadn't been for Dot and Peter, Karen might have found herself in a similar situation to Jess.

"You didn't ask to borrow Nick."

Jess's shoulders squared. "*Mi casa es su casa.* Remember?"

Oh, yes. Karen did remember.

Libby and Jess's friendship had started much like a love affair— heady and intense and without need of other people. Until recently, it hadn't changed all that much. Right from the start, they'd made *mi casa es su casa* a pact and they'd shared everything. It had taken Karen many months to realize there was a constant flow of Libby's possessions out of the house as, initially, Libby had been obstructively vague about their whereabouts. It was Alice's tears of fury and betrayal when Libby gave Jess their copy of *Harry Potter and The Goblet of Fire* —a shared gift for the twins from Peter's sister—that brought the extensive sharing into focus.

Even though none of the things Libby had lent or given away to Jess had belonged to Karen, their loss had raised hives on her skin and invited flashes of unwanted images. Her father purging the house of all the items he'd determined were the devil's handiwork. The pungent smell of books burning. The shattering of the glass dome mingling with Lisa's sobs as a snow globe hit the flagstones. The crack of her father's axe breaking into the walnut case of the piano and the tear of wood splintering along with her heart. When Karen finally got the chance to construct a life without her birth family in it, she'd put all her energies into buying a house. Over time, as she'd surrounded herself with precious things that made her feel safe and secure, she'd turned the house into a home. When she dusted and polished the piano, a daily ritual, the girls would tease her that she cared more for the instrument than for them. She'd always laughed to keep the unmitigated horrors from surfacing.

Although she'd told Peter the bare bones of her childhood, she'd only done it during periods of duress, revealing just enough to make him understand why, in that particular instance, she needed his help. The girls knew nothing about her family and Karen was determined their lives would never be tainted by stories or association. This had put her at great disadvantage when she'd tried talking to fifteen-year-old Libby about her excessive sharing with Jess.

"Daddy and I work too hard for you to just give away your things."

Libby's mouth had formed a mulish line. "I'm not giving stuff away."

"Then why aren't some of these things coming back? Sharing means something far more equal than what's happening here."

"You're so middle class, Mom! And it's such a double standard. You're always telling me to think of others and that's exactly what I'm doing. I'm sharing what I have with my best friend, no strings attached."

As altruistic as Libby sounded, Karen had long suspected that Jess was giving Libby items in return—things Karen didn't want her to have. But as those items never made their way to Pelican House, it was an impossible suspicion to prove. Once Libby and Jess were no longer teens, Karen had expected the communal sharing to stop, but it hadn't. Jess was right, they'd shared a house, clothes, makeup, music, meals and vacations. More recently they'd shared child-minding and, apparently, Nick. Karen had never fully understood the sharing or approved of it. Now it seemed neither Jess nor Libby understood it either.

"You struck at the heart of her family," Karen said gently.

"I *am* part of that family."

"Oh, Jess ..." Karen recognized a grain of truth in the statement, but it was buried in such skewed logic that she had no idea how or where to even start to try and understand it.

"It occurs to me, Alice," said Bert Lascelles, "you're hearing all our stories but you're suspiciously quiet about your own young man."

"I don't have a young man.'

"Would you like an old one?"

A titter went around the table and Alice glanced up from Tansy Donovan's memory page. She met the rheumy gaze of the wily nonagenarian. In Bert's heyday, he'd have been described as a ladies' man and Alice was certain he'd be flirting until he took his last breath.

"I couldn't keep up with you, Bert."

He grinned at her. "You're not wrong there."

Alice was always surprised by the banter and the direct questions the Summerhouse residents asked her. She supposed they'd dispensed with some of the social niceties and went straight to the heart of any issue since they were now short on time.

"Ignore him, Alice, love," Tansy said. "He's all talk. What he won't tell you is he was faithful to Ivy for fifty-nine years."

"My Ivy always said, 'You can dance with any girl at all as long as you come home with me.' I just did what I was told."

"What's it like to be married for so many years?" Alice asked Tansy.

The woman considered the question. "Swings and roundabouts. Bad times, good times and a lot of ordinary times in between. "What sort of man are you looking for? Or is it a woman? Back in my day, you had to hide that sort of thing but thank goodness not anymore."

"I like blokes with a sense of humor and who can hold a conversation."

Someone like Tim. Except, after his random dick pic, Tim had gone silent. The photo had shocked Alice. It wasn't so much the content, more its out-of-the-blue appearance and complete lack of context. When she'd told Tim it had put her in an excruciatingly embarrassing position, he hadn't exactly apologized.

He'd mumbled something about the lateness of the hour, as if that excused the fact he'd sent it. When she'd explained that it would have made more sense if they'd been sexting at the time, he hadn't said anything that implied he understood the subtle difference. Both of his reactions annoyed her. Not that she'd told him that—she was keen to give him the benefit of the doubt. After all, it was only one mistake after weeks of fun. Almost everyone deserved a second chance.

She'd given him a few days to absorb her point about context, photos and timing before texting him again with a breezy, *How's it going?* She followed it up with *R U OK?* a day later. He didn't respond to either text. It was one thing not to meet in person because he was frantic at work, but it was another thing entirely to ignore her after one perfectly reasonable request. Her annoyance had been simmering now for a few weeks. How could he have walked away from such a great connection? And they had connected—she hadn't imagined it. They'd shared a lot of great conversations before they'd moved on to sexting.

Partly out of low-grade anger but mostly out of a need to take back control of her dating life, Alice had returned to the dating app. Initially Finn had seemed like a great guy, funny and interesting, but when she'd insisted they set a date for coffee, he'd texted, *Wow, I didn't realize you were a control freak.* The follow up text—*Kidding!*—hadn't eased the discomfort, which had stayed with her for days, making her constantly question, whether she was a control freak. She eventually realized that whenever she deviated from banter and asked Finn a direct question, not only did he avoid answering it, he managed to insult her. She'd been in the Pirellis' office when his next text pinged onto her phone.

You look pretty good for someone your age.

She'd audibly huffed.

"What's up?" Missy asked.

Knowing she couldn't bother Libby with any of this stuff, she'd told the young backpacker about Finn.

"That's negging, Alice. Ghost the prick."

"Do what now?"

What followed was an entertaining and enlightening, if sometimes worrying, explanation of dating terms. After three more negging texts from Finn, Alice blocked him without a moment's thought, which, for someone raised to be polite and considerate, was a huge breakthrough.

Missy gave her a high-five. "You've graduated to the next level of online dating—take no crap."

Two more weeks of lackluster conversations with five other matches followed before Alice faced up to the reality that there wasn't a single spark between her and any of these men. The only person benefiting was the owner of the dating site and Alice could ill afford to throw good money after bad. It was time to reassess and strategize— free dating apps. She'd gotten as far as downloading Tinder and Bumble, but she was yet to activate her account.

And why is that Alice?

Shut up.

"Would you like me to read your tea leaves, Alice, love? See who's in your future?" Tansy's question interrupted Alice's thoughts.

"Oh, I don't think—"

"She's good," Bert said. "Told my Ivy we were having a baby before we knew."

Tansy had already grabbed Alice's almost empty cup and was upending the dregs on the saucer. Peering at the leaves, she turned the saucer and viewed them from different angles. "There's a lover in your future."

"Soon, I hope," Alice joked and immediately changed the subject. "Let's get back to your story, Tansy. What do you think of using this photo of you with the Landcare group next to the article from—" She glanced at the woman, who'd taken a sharp breath. "Everything okay?"

Tansy was frowning now and even though Alice knew she

shouldn't take any notice of an old lady and tea leaves, it didn't stop unease skating through her. "What?"

"Nothing, dear." She exchanged a look with Bert, who immediately said, "I've changed my mind, Alice. I do want this photo of me and the shark."

"Hang on, Tansy. You can't look upset and then say that."

"Don't take any notice of me. I'm just a silly old woman."

"Is it something to do with the lover?"

"No." Tansy knotted her arthritic fingers. "I can see an owl."

"Great! Owls are wise and I could do with some wisdom."

Tansy shook her head. "In the leaves, they mean sickness or poverty."

Alice laughed. "Relax, Tansy. There's nothing to worry about. I'm as fit as a flea, but the poverty part is close to accurate. I'm not earning as much as I used to when I worked in Melbourne."

"So, you feel well?"

Lately, Alice had been sleeping fitfully from midnight and by 4:00 a.m. she was wide awake again, her head full of her worry for Libby and Nick and the girls. Not to mention the weight of her mother's fretfulness at her current life choices. After Alice lay in the dark examining the entire mess, she'd crash back into a deep sleep somewhere between five thirty and six o'clock only for the alarm to drag her unhappily back to consciousness at 7:00. Most days she was foggy-headed and desperate for a nap by 3:00 in the afternoon.

"Nothing that a good night's sleep won't fix," she told Tansy.

The elderly woman patted her hand.

ALICE ARRIVED HOME TO AN EMPTY HOUSE. SHE DUMPED HER tote bag on the kitchen table and a notepad, two gel pens, tampons, loose change and her drawing hat spilled out. She lacked the energy to scoop them back. All she really wanted to do was slouch on the couch, but she had a 5:00 till 8:00 shift behind the bar at the RSL and she needed to eat something first.

The fridge yielded leftover chicken curry and while she ate, she thought about what Tansy had said. If she had a lover in her future, she'd better set about finding him. Opening the Bumble app, she read, "In our hive, ladies make the first move." Okay then. How did she feel about that? Apart from Tim, the hit rate for suitable men contacting her on the other app hadn't been a big success.

You can't call Tim a success when he's not talking to you.

Overruling the tiny part of her that still held out hope Tim would contact her again, she channeled Missy's words, reassuring herself she was a modern independent woman who knew what she wanted and deserved to take it with both hands. It was unexpectedly exhilarating and a very different approach from her years before and with Lawrence.

Scrolling through her phone, she uploaded a photo Libby had taken of her on *Freedom* a couple of months earlier. She was laughing and the wind had caught her hair, throwing it out like a golden halo. She looked tanned, content and relaxed—a version of herself she wished her mother could see when she looked at her.

Filling in the Bumble profile was a walk in the park compared with the monster questionnaire from her first dating site, and she whizzed through questions, laughing at the place to fill in her star sign. Why not? After all, she'd just had her tea leaves read. Typing in "Cancer," she quickly answered yes to the question about wanting children, linked her Spotify playlists, but declined to link her Instagram account.

She clicked on the verification code and was told she was good to go. Anticipation thrummed and she was busy scrolling through a cornucopia of men when her mother walked into the kitchen. Alice laid her phone face down on the table. Karen immediately frowned at the mess.

"Sorry." Alice shoved the contents back into the voluminous bag and put it under her chair. As much as Alice appreciated the cheap board her parents offered, she and her mother didn't have the same definition of tidy and they never had.

Karen set down the stack of magazines she was holding. "It looks like you need to clean out that bag." Since Nick's bombshell, irritable was her mother's default setting. She glanced toward a small counter in the corner of the kitchen. "Did you go to the post office?"

Alice face palmed. "Sorry, I forgot, but funny story! Tansy Donovan read my tea leaves and—"

"Honestly, Alice! What's wrong with you? Lately, you're forgetting everything."

"Sorry. I'm not sleeping very well. My head's full of Libby." *And Tim. And four jobs. And the fact you told me you couldn't get pregnant again after thirty-three.*

"It doesn't leave room for much else. I'm going back into town for work tonight so I'll pick up the mail then. Promise."

"I'm sorry." Karen gave herself a shake. "My head's full of Libby too. I feel like I'm treading on egg shells every time I talk to her." She pushed the magazines toward Alice. "Hilary's had a clear out. She insisted I bring these home for you, but I only accepted because I thought they might be useful for Summerhouse. *Please* don't leave them scattered all over the house."

"Thanks." Alice appreciated how hard Karen found overriding her decluttering setting so it was a big deal that her mother had brought the stack home. She immediately leafed through them to see if she could use anything with the nursing home set. There was a mixture of *Australian Geographic, Women's Weekly*, car and four-wheel drive magazines and a few health-related ones. The headline, "Fertility preservation for women over thirty," caught her eye and she thumbed the pages until she found the article. Scanning the horrifying statistics of falling fertility from age thirty-five, she slammed the magazine shut.

"Alice, you've still got time to meet someone and have a baby," her mother said gently.

"I don't think anyone can say that with any accuracy."

"And it's just as inaccurate to say it won't happen." A familiar glint entered Karen's eyes and Alice recognized it. It was the same determined light that had burned brightly when she was a child and Karen had taken her to the many appointments with doctors, physiotherapists, speech therapists and tutors. What the family called Alice's catch-up years.

"You say you want a career and a family, yet you're languishing down here."

"I'm not languishing!"

"Darling, you're hardly thriving. Perhaps you should go back to Melbourne and talk to that counselor you used to see?"

Anger slashed Alice along with a splash of guilt. It had been years since she'd seen a counselor and even then, she'd only gone to placate Karen, who'd freaked out when she'd refused to share a house with Libby and Jess. Alice loved her mother, but dear God, was she ever going to see her as an adult? Or was she always going to view her as someone who needed fixing?

"I have to go to work." Without waiting for a reply, Alice hoisted her bag onto her shoulder and left the room.

THE WEATHER HAD CLOSED IN AND WIND AND RAIN BUFFETED the bay. As a result, the regulars were absent making it a very quiet night at the RSL. Dan van den Berg had signed in solo—the third time since Alice had gone on the Cape Conran bushwalk with the Bay Bushwhackers—and he'd taken a seat at the bar. Usually, Alice was happy to chat and banter with him, but after the conversation with Karen, she was out of sorts.

"So, Twin Two ..." Dan spun a coaster through his fingers.

"So, Dan the man ... Can I interest you in a raffle ticket for the meat platter?"

"Maybe. What's it for this week?"

"A swing for children with disabilities. Basically, you'll look like a prick if you say no."

"That's a bit harsh."

"Harsh would be not buying any tickets."

He shot her his trademark grin. "Are you sure I'm not talking to Libby? I don't remember Alice ever being this confrontational."

She poured him another beer and rang it up. Dan was right. Libby was the twin who called a spade a spade and held people accountable. Not Alice. She'd spent her life turning herself inside out to be accommodating and avoiding confrontation. But had it served her well? It was a question she'd been asking herself a lot recently.

"Tell you what, Alice. I'll take ten dollars' worth of raffle tickets if you have dinner with me one night soon." Dan's blue eyes dazzled and he was looking at her as if she was the only woman in the world.

Having watched from the sidelines for years, Alice was used to Dan's modus operandi. "I'm a bit old for you."

"What do you mean? We're the same age."

"I've been back in the bay six months, Dan. I haven't seen you out and about with anyone over twenty-three."

"Perhaps you can convert me."

Leaning her elbows on the bar, she looked straight at the man who'd been a player from the moment puberty took him from a scrawny kid to a tall, blond, broad-shouldered and sun-kissed adult. "We both know that's a lie."

He laughed. "I like this new you, Alice. It's incredibly sexy."

She wasn't sure if she liked the edge that had recently sharpened inside her, but either way, she was in no mood for nonsense. "What are you really proposing, Dan?"

"What are you up for, Alice?"

His voice—deep and rich, smooth as vintage port—rumbled around her and something shifted inside her. "I'm up for honesty."

"That's unexpected, but doable." Dan sipped his beer thoughtfully. "This is me being brutally honest. I'm not interested in commitment or kids. I'm single, you're single, I like you, we get along well and we've known each other since the cradle."

"That's a series of facts."

He smiled. "Can't get anything past you, can I? Okay, winter and spring are the tourist doldrums in the bay. I'm proposing a friends-with-benefits arrangement to while away May to November."

She straightened up. "I'm not interested in 2:00 a.m. booty calls, Dan."

"Jeez, Alice." He pressed his hand to his heart. "Give me some credit. That's not what I'm suggesting. There will always be food and conversation. Always the three Cs."

"What are they?"

"Consent, clean bedsheets and condoms."

An unexpected tingle shot through her. "You've actually thought this through."

"I'll take that as a compliment. So, what do you reckon?"

"What do I reckon?" Alice couldn't believe they were even having this discussion or that she hadn't shut him down yet, let alone the fact she was considering his outrageous suggestion. But weeks of flirting with Tim had not only kickstarted her libido, its growing need to be sated was wearing her down.

Growing up, Karen's advice had been, "Sex is an extension of a loving relationship." Unlike Libby, who'd apparently done way more experimenting growing up, Alice had only ever had sex inside a relationship. Even the virtual sex with Tim had occurred after hours of conversation. Friends with benefits was something utterly foreign to her, but then again, up until a few weeks ago online dating had fallen under that banner too.

Dan was correct—they'd known each other all their lives, although they were hardly close friends. Every year when she'd come home for a vacation, they invariably ran into each other and enjoyed a quick catch-up. One Christmas, she'd enrolled Lawrence in Dan's "Learn to Surf" classes. As it turned out, it hadn't been her best gift. Her ex had complained bitterly that Dan spent more time flirting with her than teaching him. At the time, she'd rejected Lawrence's accusation, but it had been true. Alice knew that flirting was as natural as breathing for Dan and it meant nothing, so she'd allowed herself to enjoy his compliments. Plus, Dan had always been easy on the eyes—if the sun-bronzed surfer look was your catnip.

It had never been hers. Historically, Alice, like Libby, had been attracted to dark-eyed, dark-haired men, and both had been betrayed. But she'd just asked blond-headed Dan for honesty and surprisingly he'd delivered. Still, did she really want to go down this rabbit hole just to scratch an itch?

You haven't had sex in over six months. Dan's athletic, experienced and you know him. He's much safer than meeting a random guy online.

"If we do this, we'd need rules."

Dan immediately grabbed a napkin, wrote Rules of Engagement and underlined it.

"Don't you think we should have sex first before we worry about rules? We might not be compatible."

"The fact you're considering this means we're compatible." He clicked his pen and wrote, 1. No strings. 2. CCC.

"No dick pics."

"Crikey, Alice. You're lucky I'm here to save you from dating apps."

She stifled a bubble of laughter, protecting her attempt at a business-like manner. "Yeah, right. Just write it down."

As he wrote down the number four he said, "No sleepovers."

It was code for no cuddling or spooning—no ambiguity. Was she really prepared to give up intimacy for sex? "Sure. But as I'm currently living at home due to financial constraints, we'll need to use your place. I promise to get up and go as soon as the job's done."

"Job?" He gave her a pitying look. "And to think I pegged you as a romantic."

"We both know this has nothing to do with romance."

"Sure, but it doesn't mean we can't have fun. Just tell me what you like and don't like, and I'll do the same."

During her one attempt with Lawrence to ask for what she wanted, he'd accused her of giving him stage directions. "That's one of those things that sounds good in theory but never actually works without someone's feelings getting hurt."

"Alice," he said gently. "The whole point of this is there's no relationship bullshit getting in the way. That leaves us free to enjoy ourselves."

What Dan considered relationship bullshit was everything Alice missed about being part of a couple. Still, she couldn't fault his honesty. "Thursdays are good for me."

"Thursdays could work." He tapped his pen against his lips. "What else?"

"You said food and conversation, but we can't be seen eating in town every Thursday or we'll be tagged as a couple after week two."

"Too easy. We'll get takeaway or we can cook. I make a pretty mean risotto. Hilary's even complimented me on it."

The thought of Dan's mother sent a geyser of stomach acid splashing and burning. "No one can know about this. Especially our mothers!"

This time his look was loaded with gratitude. "Excellent point. If Hilary got wind of this, she'd jump straight to weddings and babies."

Alice's thoughts were never far from babies and they immediately drifted there in a delicious daydream. Like the pointed tip of a knife, her mother's words about miscarriages and the black and white statements of the magazine article jabbed sharply. The dream vanished, leaving her anxious. Alice didn't have plenty of time. To have any hope of meeting someone who not only shared her interests but her life plan, it was imperative she play a numbers game on the dating apps. She must commit to talking to five men a week and if she sensed a connection with any of them, run their photo through reverse image, do a social media and google check and then insist they meet for coffee. If any of them fobbed her off, they'd be immediately struck off the list. But looking for a life partner was going to take time and, according to the graph she'd looked at earlier, her biological clock was fast ticking down to an inevitable end point. If she wanted a baby, just focusing on meeting someone wasn't enough—she needed to buy some time. She decided to make an appointment with a doctor and discuss freezing her eggs.

Dan put down the pen. "I think we've covered everything."

Alice considered Dan. If their arrangement survived their first attempt at sex—and they were both clear it would only ever be about sex—and if it continued as a pleasant way to pass the long winter months, there was one more thing that needed to be crystal clear.

"Not quite." Alice tapped the napkin. "Write this down. The moment we start dating someone, we stop being friends with benefits."

"The moment?"

"Yes, *the moment.*" Alice got a sharp pain thinking about Libby. "I refuse to unwittingly cause another woman pain. And if I find out that you're seeing someone and still sleeping with me, your tackle will be in grave danger from my very blunt palette knife."

Dan instinctively crossed his legs. "Noted."

"Good."

Alice had never been particularly forward when it came to sex, but perhaps Dan had a point—there was nothing at stake here, nothing to complicate things. She picked up the napkin and folded it in half before shoving it into her pocket. Then she pushed the raffle ticket book in front of Dan.

"Buy the meat raffle tickets and we have a deal."

"Excellent." Dan took out his wallet. "When do you finish?"

"In five minutes."

"Any chance you're free for dinner?"

"You know, I'm not that hungry for food. Are you?"

"I like the way you think, Alice."

His smile was long and slow—pure seduction— and she gave herself over to its delicious effects. A dart of desire made her press her legs together and she laughed. This idea might just work.

CHAPTER TWELVE

MAY

Libby saw Florence Jeffers out, but instead of calling in her next patient, she popped back into her office and punched in the now familiar numbers. With each ring, her heart beat faster, pumping adrenaline to all points.

"Hi, you've called Nick Pirelli." The recording of her husband's deep and friendly voice came down the line. "Sorry I can't come to the phone right now. Please leave a message or call Pirellis' Boat Hire and Fishing on ..."

At breakfast, Nick had told her that apart from lunch with his parents, he'd be in the office all day. It was 10:40—far too early for lunch. She disconnected the call and called the office. "Hi, Missy."

"Hi, Libby."

Before the apocalypse, if Libby ever had a reason to the boat office, the backpacker had always said, "How can I help?" Now Libby phones six times a day, Missy just said, "I'll put you through to Nick."

The breath Libby had been holding released a little. The phone rang a couple of times, then her husband picked up.

"Hi." The greeting was imbued with caution—so much of Nick's conversations were these days.

"Hi. You're at the office."

"Yes. I said I'd be here all day except for lunch and the coffee run."

"You didn't mention the coffee run."

His sharp intake of breath whistled down the line. "Surely, I don't have to tell you that? I've been doing the coffee run on Mondays, Wednesdays and Fridays for years."

Yes, but that was when I trusted you implicitly—before you did something so hurtful it changed everything. Before you turned me from a stable, functioning woman into the doubting and suspicious one I hardly recognize.

"Where were you two minutes ago?"

"What?"

"You didn't answer your cell."

"Jesus, Libby. I was taking a piss after drinking the coffee. Why don't you just attach a camera to me and be done with it."

Her anger, constantly simmering just under the surface these days, flared. "Don't you dare try and pin this on me. You brought it all down on yourself. If you want a hope in hell of me ever trusting you again, then this is part of it."

For a moment Nick was silent. Then he sighed. "Libby, I haven't met her. I haven't spoken to her, texted or emailed her. I've had no contact with her since I told you about Leo. You know it's the truth, because you've read her email sprays that include both of us. And none of your spies—"

"I don't have spies!"

"Yes, you do! I see them in the street, at the school gate, the pub, everywhere. They look at me and scope out who I'm talking to."

"I have *friends* who have my back."

He grunted. "And none of them have reported anything back to you, have they, because there's nothing to report. But despite all that, you're still checking up on me half-a-dozen times a day. I hate living like this. It's been two months, Libby! How much longer is it going to take?"

A combination of stewed rage and impotence battered her. She had no idea how long before the obsessive thoughts, the nightmares and the flashbacks would stop. Or when her hair-trigger responses to so many things would cease whipping her from fulminating anger to the depths of despair. How long before she could look at Nick without pain, loathing and misery and once again see the man she fell in love with at Bunga Arm? Did that man even exist anymore? And how long until Nick could look at her without shame, guilt and regret shining off him like a beacon?

Maybe it was impossible. Maybe their marriage had been in its death throes two years earlier, when Nick had turned away from her. Perhaps holding it all together was not only too hard, it was pointless. Was walking away easier than this half-life they were living?

Recently, Lucy had asked, "Mommy, why are you sleeping in this bed?"

The question had caught her off guard and she'd fought back the words, "Because your father's hurt me in the worst possible way and I feel worthless and unlovable." But it was her job to protect Lucy and Indi from the mess that was her and Nick.

"Daddy's snoring keeps me awake."

But going by the concerned phone call from Lucy's teacher, her elder daughter was picking up on the anguished vibes in Burrunan and acting out in the classroom. Would it be better for the girls if she ended this agonizing impasse with a clean break?

Who was she kidding? She and Nick were forever connected by the girls. They had a lifetime of birthdays and Christmases, graduations, future weddings and grandchildren ahead of them. In the immediate future, they had years of school runs, dance recitals, swimming and soccer to juggle, not to mention a million shared parenting decisions. Their lives were inextricably joined and the only end to it was death.

As it was, it felt like part of her had already died.

JESS WAS WORKING AT THE PATISSERIE DOING THE ACCOUNTS. Sitting in the back room and enjoying the spicy scents of baking and the aroma of good coffee was a welcome sanctuary from all the other parts of her life.

"*Café et gateau, cherie.*" Patrice put down a tray as she always did at 11:00.

Jess patted her belly, which was more rounded than it had been since her pregnancy. Not only was she comfort eating, her exercise routine of walking, running and surfing with Libby, had come to an abrupt stop. "Thanks, Patrice, but as amazing as it looks, I think I better pass on the cake."

Patrice gave a Gallic shrug and returned to the kitchen.

It had been a rough few weeks but Patrice was one of a handful of people who only judged Jess by her ability as an accountant. Jess wondered if it was because the woman was French, but she hadn't asked, because she wasn't about to open herself up to unwanted comments. She got enough of those from the rest of the town.

Having finished with Patrice's ledgers, Jess logged into her own bank account. While she waited for the page to load, she sipped her latte. The balance finally appeared, lower than expected, and she set down her mug and clicked on the recent transactions. Double-checking everything, she swore and automatically reached for her phone to text Nick. She dropped her hand and swore again.

In moments of high stress, she forgot she no longer had his number. Not that it was from lack of trying. The first time she'd heard the disconnected message, she'd phoned the boat hire office. Missy confirmed Nick had a new number but instead of giving it to her, she'd only offered to pass on a message. After the sixth unanswered message, Jess called Will.

"Sorry, Jess. I don't have his new number."

"That's BS!"

"It's not. Libby's got him on a pretty tight leash. Not many people have it."

"So, she's not only stopping Nick from seeing me and his son, she's blocking you too?"

There was a long silence. "Will?"

"What?"

"You're his best friend."

"Yeah."

"So how do you contact him?"

"I call him at the office."

"I've tried that but he's not calling back. You need to tell him to call me. He's Leo's father. He's got responsibilities!"

Will sighed, the sound soft and loaded. "Maybe it's time to accept Nick's not calling you back because he doesn't want to."

"He's not calling me back because he's a pussy!" As she'd slammed down the phone, Jess didn't know who she hated more—Will, Nick, Libby or the town.

She'd tried asking numerous other people but everyone claimed they didn't have Nick's number, or if they did, they weren't prepared to share it with her. Not even the individuals who happily bad-mouthed Nick in public over what Kurnai Bay was calling "babygate." The town that had welcomed her return as a successful and community-minded adult, instead of the wild daughter of an alcoholic, had now mostly turned its back on her.

Rationally, she knew this was no different from the censure she'd endured from many for being Linda's child. She should be used to it and not care. But in the early hours of each morning when her resistance was at its lowest ebb, it was always a shock how much worse it was to have known approval and lost it, than never to have known it at all. She ached for the loss of respect, the sense of belonging and purpose, and for the friendships she'd forged.

She grieved for Leo.

Fortunately, when the dawn light came it replaced those unwelcome feelings with the more familiar and far more palatable fury. She raged at the petty-mindedness of most of the Kurnai Bay residents. This situation wasn't all on her. Other people were involved —people who the town had elevated to virtuous and above reproach. The unfairness of it flared and roared inside her like a chained dragon.

Now, weeks after the name of Leo's father had been leaked to the town, the curt email informing her that Kurnai Bay Medical Center no longer required the services of Dekic Accounting, the blocking of all calls, the brutal demand for a paternity test, and the cessation of her support payments, Jess was in no doubt who she hated the most.

Libby's cruel act of telling everyone that Leo was Nick's son and exposing Jess's little boy to malicious gossip drove her as far as the Burrunan gates with abuse screaming in her head. Only thoughts of protecting Leo and his sisters had forced her to return home without making a scene. But the abrupt halving of Jess's income and the loss of Leo's support payments did not apply the same brake. Locking onto outrage about the unnecessary paternity test—clearly Leo was Nick's son—she'd driven to the marina, demanding to see Nick. The staff at Pirellis' blocked each of her attempts. She'd barely been allowed inside the reception area, let alone Nick's office. Short of accosting him in public, which would only create more meat for the gossips to feast on and open Leo up to more harm, she'd had little option but to dip into her savings to pay her bills.

It was at that point she'd conceded for Leo's sake and agreed to the paternity test.

She'd recently received a copy of the results. The original had gone direct to the medical practice. Jess eyed her bank balance again then logged into her email account and clicked on the message with the subject line, Paternity Test. Her fingers hovered and then frustration rushed in.

"Stuff this!" Logging out, she grabbed her bag and car keys, called a quick goodbye to Patrice and drove to the medical center.

"Tell Libby I'm here and I'm not leaving until I see her," she informed the receptionist.

"Dr. Hunter's fully booked today," Trina said snippily.

Penny appeared from the office just behind reception. "And for the rest of the week. Actually, for you, she's fully booked forever."

"I'm not leaving until I see her." Jess glanced at the full waiting room. "I'll happily wait and talk to these good people. I'm sure they'll be interested in hearing all the questionable things the good doctor got up to when she was younger."

"You're a truly awful person, you know that?"

Jess shrugged—she'd been called worse. She silently watched Penny pick up the phone and murmur into it.

When the nurse hung up, she said, "Follow me."

Jess felt the eyes of the waiting room bore into her as she walked down the corridor and into Libby's consulting room. Libby sat at her desk, dark shadows under her eyes and her arms crossed. She didn't turn her chair to face Jess or rise to greet her.

"What do you want?"

Despite wanting to slap Libby for being such a princess, Jess strove for the high ground. For Leo's sake, they needed to find a way to resolve this bitter impasse. "How are you?"

"What. Do. You. Want?"

Jess sat, partly to annoy Libby, but mostly because seeing her friend again after all these weeks had unexpectedly affected her legs. "I want to talk to Nick about his support payments.'

Libby's eyes chilled to Antarctic blue. "That is *never* going to happen."

"Talking or support payments?"

"Both."

Jess took in a couple of deep breaths and tried to stay calm. "I did what you asked. You've had the results of the paternity test for a week. You now have the unequivocal scientific evidence you wanted, proving what we already knew. Leo is Nick's son. I want the support payments reinstated and back pay for the weeks you've ..." she swallowed the word *spitefully*, "... withheld it."

"I don't care what you want."

The statement stung with the same bite of lime juice in a cut. "This isn't between me and you. It's between me and Nick."

"Like hell it is. Nick's *my* husband, not yours."

Jess's control frayed around the edges. "But I wonder for how much longer? With you controlling where he can go and who he can talk to, life with you must be so much fun for him."

Libby jerked in her chair. "I hate you so much."

"I think you established that weeks ago. I'm here to remind you that Nick's Leo's father and the law states he must provide financial support."

"So, you're suddenly citing the law now it suits you? You don't have that right when you've broken every social more in the book! Nick never wanted *that child*, you did. You tricked him to get what you wanted."

"I didn't trick him." She ground out the words between clenched teeth. "But I imagine it's convenient for Nick to tell you that."

Libby stood so fast her chair skated back and hit the wall. "Get out."

Jess stayed seated. "You know what? For a caring professional and a friend who insisted we share everything until it suddenly wasn't convenient to you, you have a filthy malevolent streak."

"You're deluded if you thought sharing included Nick!"

It was tempting to tell Libby she was reinventing history but Jess stayed focused on Leo. "Punish me and punish Nick all you like, but don't punish Leo. He's an innocent child."

"He's absolutely nothing to do with me. And if you come here again, I'll take out a restraining order against you."

"Empty words, Lib."

"I don't think so. Pip Beyers is a good friend of mine."

The circuit court magistrate was good friends with them both. "Your memory's conveniently faulty."

"Not really. I introduced you to Pip, remember? Just like I sponsored you at the yacht club and book group and the lawn tennis club. The only reason you've ever had any social standing in this town is because of me. I took your white trash ass out of the muck you grew up in, but when you screwed my husband, you screwed yourself."

Libby's smug face said checkmate and the dragon inside Jess roared, railing against privilege that was never questioned and never required to prove itself. Whereas no matter what she did, be it good or bad, it was held up against all previous misdemeanors dating back twenty years.

"The whole town doesn't love you, Libby."

"The people with power do. You might want to take that bastard child of yours and leave town."

Jess slapped Libby's face so hard her palm stung. Then she opened the door and walked away.

⚓

ALICE AND HOLLY SAT ON THE PIER, TAKING ADVANTAGE OF THE last of the late autumn sunshine before it dropped too low and the chill struck, reminding everyone winter was coming. Alice had lost her initial reservations about tutoring Holly during their first session a few weeks earlier, when she realized that teaching was a loose term. The reality was, Harry was paying her to draw while she gave some tips and encouragement to his daughter.

Knowing that she was taking his money to indulge herself in something she loved made her squirm a little. When those moments of guilt struck, she reminded herself that she did put time and effort into each session. She was already planning for when the weather got too cold to be outside and was excited about exploring some different mediums with Holly. With her work at Summerhouse, her opinion pieces for the *Gazette,* her occasional bar and boat jobs and tutoring Holly, her bank balance was finally edging forward.

"Aren't you drawing the seal too?" Holly asked.

Alice's own experience of having her work compared with others meant she never drew the same thing as Holly. Alice didn't want to give her student any excuse to say, "Yours is better," or "I'm not good enough."

"I've drawn Salty lots of times already. Today I'm fascinated by the way the sun's dancing around that bollard."

"You should draw that bird too. It's cool how it hangs its wings out like that."

"It's a cormorant drying its wings. Also, I'm not great at drawing birds."

Holly's pencil stalled on her sketch pad. "Dad says the only way to get better is to practice."

Holly even said it the way Alice imagined Harry did—serious and solemn—like a lot of his conversation. It wasn't that Alice disagreed with the advice—so much of what she'd conquered as a kid came from dogged practice. But she was close to thirty-four and the reality was, she really didn't enjoy drawing birds. "Your dad makes a good point."

"So, you should practice."

"You know, I did practice for a long time, but birds are not my thing. You're already way better at drawing them than me."

Holly gave a dismissive shrug. "You're just saying that."

"I'm not."

On the receiving end of Holly's glare, Alice gave an exaggerated sigh. "Okay, I'll give it my best shot. But you do realize you're asking me to ruin my lovely bollard by drawing that shag."

She sketched the white beak, the long black neck and the bottle-shaped body before feathering out the wings, but, as usual, her perspective was off. She laughed. "Now do you believe me? Your pelican's so much better than this."

Holly flashed her a shy smile. "I like drawing them."

"I can tell."

"Pelicans remind me of my mom."

It was the first time Holly had volunteered any information about her mother and as Harry admitted to having no artistic ability, Alice wondered if Helene had passed on the gene. Then again, neither Karen or Peter drew either, so Holly's mother might have been equally as stumped by stick figures as Harry. "Did your mom like pelicans?"

"She sculpted them in clay."

"Wow!"

"And she took her best one to some place in Brisbane. They made a mold and filled it with bronze," Holly said, clearly proud of her mother's achievement.

The "mold" would have been wax, the "place" a forge and the molten metal poured into it under intense heat. The cost would have been in the thousands. "That's very impressive."

Holly nodded enthusiastically. "We've got one in our living room. Would you like to see it?"

"I'd love to." Alice was surprised when Holly immediately placed her pencil into her tin and hurriedly closed her sketch book. "Hang on, Holly, I didn't mean right now. Besides, your dad's picking you up from here."

The young girl's face fell. "Oh, okay."

Holly's disappointment rode into Alice, taking the shine off what had been a very happy fifty minutes. She supposed she could take Holly home and see the bronze pelican, but she felt uncomfortable rocking up unannounced. She and Harry had an employer–employee relationship and he always delivered Holly to her. He'd never suggested that Alice come to the house and pick up Holly. Not that Harry wasn't polite, but from the first time they'd met on the pier, Alice had sensed a reserve and a need for privacy. The only time it had wavered was at Relay for Life when his obvious concern for Holly had made him fight for her.

"It's not that I don't want to come, Holly. I'd love to see the pelican. It's just you should probably ask your dad first."

"Ask me what?"

Harry's voice startled Alice so much she almost dropped her pencil into the bay.

"Daddy!" Holly scrambled to her feet. "I want to show Alice Mom's pelican."

Surprise lit up his eyes, immediately followed by hesitation, giving Holly the opportunity to add, "You said I could invite a friend home anytime I wanted."

Alice stood and gave Harry the out he obviously wanted. "I was just explaining to Holly that today might not be convenient."

"Please, Dad," Holly begged. "Alice sucks at drawing birds. Seeing Mom's pelican might help her."

Harry's face morphed from being cornered to horrified. "Holly! Manners! That's a very rude thing to say."

"I was trying to help!" Holly's voice was thick with impending tears.

Alice gave the girl's shoulder a gentle squeeze. "Actually, Harry, she's right on the money. I totally suck at drawing birds."

"See, Dad!"

Harry shoved his hands into his pockets and studied the toes of his boots, reluctance rising off him like steam. "I suppose as long as you don't mind that the breakfast dishes are still in the sink and there's a mountain of unsorted clean clothes on the couch and—"

"I'm coming to see the pelican, Harry, not to rate your housekeeping."

He gave her a rueful smile. "I'll hold you to that."

"So, you'll come?" Holly asked eagerly.

"Sure, but I can't stay for long." It was a Dan night and he'd promised to cook if she bought the ingredients for mushroom risotto.

"Yay!" Holly started stowing their gear into her backpack and Alice's giant tote.

"Alice!"

She turned and saw Nick standing a yard away, holding his hand up in a stationary wave.

"Have you got a minute?"

It wasn't the first time her brother-in-law had come and found her, wanting to talk. Usually it was on the one day a week she still worked for him—a job Libby thought she'd given up, but a twin had to eat—but this was the first time Nick had approached her outside of those hours.

The conversation always followed a familiar pattern—she listened to his regrets and then suggested he find an impartial professional to talk to. Although he nodded his agreement, he kept seeking her out and she doubted he'd spoken to anyone. Experienced marriage counselors were thin on the ground in the bay. Ones with expertise in dealing with the complication of a child whose mother was the wife's best friend were non-existent. Even in Melbourne they weren't exactly easy to find.

These conversations with Nick tore Alice in half. Her allegiance lay with Libby—most of it anyway—but she loved Nick and it was clear he was floundering. She worried about his mental health and that's why she always gave him her time. The only person who understood her dilemma was her father. She'd discussed it with him and he'd told her not to tell Karen or Libby, but the advice was unnecessary. Alice's gut instincts warned her it would be unwise, but she hated that the secret existed. If Libby and Nick's situation had taught her anything, it was that when secrets came out, it was the betrayal of the hiding that wrought pain and suffering.

Knowing all of that didn't help—saying no to Nick wasn't an option in case he went and did something stupid.

"Give me five minutes, Nick. Okay?"

Nick nodded and walked back toward his office.

"Is he okay?" Harry asked, clearly concerned. "He's got the look."

"What look?"

"The quiet desperation of someone grieving." Harry shrugged at her double-take. "I'm familiar with it. Saw it in the mirror every morning for a long time."

His matter-of-fact tone made her ask, "What about now?"

"It comes and goes." He cleared his throat and moved them both away from Holly. "So that bloke. Is he the one sending you photos?"

"God, no!" Intense embarrassment crashed through her and she felt the flush rise up her neck and keep going until it hit her hairline. Indignation followed. "And even if he was, it's none of your business."

"True. Sorry." Harry ran his hand through his hair. "It's just ..."

"What?"

"It's the way he looked at you. Like he was apologizing for something big, like a dick move—or picture."

Alice smiled. "I'm learning in the war of modern dating, men don't apologize for random photos of their junk."

"Sounds tough out there."

You have no idea. "Hmm."

"So who is he?"

"My brother-in-law, Nick. He's married to my twin and things between them aren't great right now. He says it helps to talk."

"Are you identical twins?"

"Similar but different," she said automatically as she'd been saying for years. Her brain suddenly kicked in. "Are you saying you think he wants to talk to me because I look like Libby?"

"I have no idea. But he's not happy."

It was an odd comment for a man to make about a stranger to a woman he barely knew. "Are you a counselor?"

Harry's face broke into a wide and unexpected smile and then he was belly laughing as if she'd cracked the biggest joke. "That's classic. I wish Helene was here to hear you ask me that. She was a typical Californian, always banging on about me needing to get in touch with my feelings."

"Sounds like you have."

He shook his head and his face sobered. "Nah. I've just learned to recognize compatriots in the misery trenches."

Holly appeared at their sides clutching the bags. "Can we go now?"

"Sure." Harry looked at Alice. "We have to pick up Hunter from soccer practice, so we'll be home in twenty. Also, we've got a greyhound. Please don't terrify Brutus by ringing the doorbell."

"Seriously?"

"Absolutely. Even that scarf you're wearing could push him over the edge."

Alice fingered the length of her bright blue, pink and green hand-dyed silk tied around her neck, trying to work out if Harry was being his usual serious self or uncharacteristically deadpanning her. She checked with Holly. "He's kidding, right?"

"No. Brutus is scared of lots of things. He loves cuddles though."

Alice couldn't get a picture. "How do you cuddle a greyhound? Aren't they too big and bony for that?"

Harry laughed. "It's a skill. Best if you just come round the back."

"The back of where exactly?"

"Seventeen Seaspray or as the locals say—"

"Two doors down from where Joe's garage used to be."

His eyes crinkled in another rare smile. "That's the one."

CHAPTER THIRTEEN

IT WAS LIBBY'S HALF DAY AND, SOMEHOW, SHE'D MANAGED TO GET away on time, although she had a strong suspicion that Penny and Ramesh were still taking the lion's share of the workload. She appreciated they were trying to protect her. Or perhaps they were protecting the patients.

For years, Libby had been well versed on the results of published research focused on the effects of grief and trauma on the body. How the brain releases a cocktail of chemicals that make clear thinking not only difficult, but skews normal thought processes. Someone had coined the phrase "magical thinking" to describe it. Libby had experienced it after losing Dom and now it was back, although in some ways this grief was far more catastrophic.

The loss of her son had been devastating, but her emotional house, with Nick at its center, was still standing. Now the house had been washed away in a flood of faithlessness and lies. Some days, it was almost too hard to get out of bed, let alone turn up to work and be the doctor her patients depended upon to treat them correctly. So many times in the previous weeks, she'd felt the papery touch of an elderly hand on hers, bringing her attention back with a start. It was always followed by the question, "Are you okay, dear?"

At least she'd only broken down in front of a patient once.

Libby tracked Alice down in the *Gazette's* office and her twin glanced up, blinking, as the bell over the door tinkled. Libby's heart rolled at the familiar sight—a reassuring salve in the turmoil that was her life.

"You're drawing again!"

Alice grimaced. "Trying to. I have an idea for a sketch to accompany my article about tree vandals, but between my uncooperative fingers and this expletive deleted desktop publishing program, I'm going nowhere fast."

"I thought Jim did the layout?"

"He does, but it's Lillian's birthday and he's taken her to Canberra for a couple of days. Heaven help him, but I'm in charge of getting this edition sorted." Alice stood up and kissed Libby. "It's great to see you."

Libby unloaded her shopping bag. "I brought lunch."

"Bad morning?"

"Does it have to be a bad morning for me to have lunch with my sister?"

Alice paused mid-rip of a salad dressing sachet. "I want to say no."

Guilt spiraled on a continuous helix. Since her ex-friend's heartless betrayal, Libby knew she was relying on Alice in ways she'd never done before. It wasn't only for support either, but for much needed friendship. Unfortunately, it threw up in stark relief how many years she'd put *that woman* ahead of her twin.

"If you're too busy ..."

"Don't be silly. Besides, I can't afford to say no to a free lunch." Alice grinned and forked spinach, roasted squash, pine nuts and goat's cheese into her mouth. "Mmm, yum!"

"The paternity test came back," Libby blurted out. That was one thing she'd noticed about herself since the apocalypse—she no longer had the ability to make polite chit-chat.

"And it's conclusive that Nick's Leo's father."

The fact Alice hadn't framed it as a question pressed down on Libby like lead weights. "Oh, Al! I didn't want to believe them. I've babysat him, I've changed his diaper and played with him." Her voice cracked. "What does it say about me that I didn't notice he looks so much like Nick?"

Alice's eyes filled with sympathy. "You trusted them so you never had a reason to look."

"Fat lot of good that did me. I feel so stupid!"

"You're not stupid or foolish or any other of those words you keep using. And you're not alone. Mom and Dad and I didn't notice, and neither did Rosa or Rick. I doubt anyone in the bay noticed. And let's be honest, if any of the hardcore muckrakers suspected, we'd have heard about it ages ago."

Libby's mouth dried and she took a slug of water. "I keep going over and over twenty years of friendship. It can't have been fake for all those years, can it?"

Alice chased a stray pine nut around her bowl. "I suppose not. Then again, if she loved you, how could she do that to you?"

"Nick says he loves me but he did it to me!"

"He does love you," Alice said quietly.

"What makes you so sure?"

"I've googled. Most men leave their wives when their mistress gets pregnant. Nick didn't do that."

"He says it was never an affair. He says it only happened once."

"Do you believe him?"

Libby sighed. "Sometimes. Other days I'm convinced he's lying. I mean, I know if the timing's right, it only takes once for a woman to conceive, but the fact he lied to me about it for two years drives me crazy! It makes me think he's hiding information."

"It's hard, but doesn't it help that he truly hates himself for causing all this pain? I mean he's done everything you've asked so far. Did the counselor have any suggestions?"

Libby shuddered as she recalled the two sessions she'd attended by herself. "None that were useful. She said that for this to have happened, I must have 'given away my power' to Jess and Nick and 'lost myself.' I told her she'd lost me."

"That sucks. But well done you. Bad help's worse than no help."

"Exactly. That's why I'm reading self-help books." Libby stabbed at the chicken breast in her Caesar salad. "It's the double whammy that undoes me. Two people who supposedly love me hurt me."

"She hurt Nick too."

Libby was finding that hard to acknowledge. "You should be on my side."

"I'm on both your sides," Alice said sadly. "But not hers."

"You know I've always believed that underneath her 'don't give a damn' layer, she was a kind and decent human being. Hell, dogs love her! She's always been generous to me, but it turns out I've been deluding myself about that too. I mean, God! Not only did she do what she did, she can't see anything wrong with it! She hasn't even hinted at being sorry. She's acting as if she's been wronged."

"And that surprises you?"

"Yes!" Libby realized Alice had stopped eating. "What?"

Her twin shook her head. "It doesn't matter."

"It does. What were you going to say?"

Alice took a moment to raise her eyes from their intense examination of a piece of cheese. "In all the years I've known her, I've never heard J—her apologize for anything."

Libby opened her mouth to say "That's not true" but quickly closed it. Her automatic habit of defending that woman was now well and truly broken. Alice's quietly spoken words brought old memories bubbling to the surface and many of them involved Alice being upset at something Jess had said or done. All of them showed Libby telling her twin not to be so sensitive, to learn how to take a joke and not be a wet blanket. Yet again, guilt pinched and her appetite vanished as it often did these days.

She pushed away the rest of her lunch. "I've been reading about toxic friendships, but there are no clues there either. She was fun and she made me laugh, although now I realize it was often at the expense of someone else. But she never put me down. She was amazing after Dom—None of it makes any sense! Have I been wearing blinders for years?"

"Maybe." The look on Alice's face matched Libby's bafflement. "Or not. She was always nicer to you. Less mean girl and more selfless. And when you met her, you were ready for a change from me."

"Alice!"

Her twin gave her a long and unflinching stare. "Come on, be honest. We'd started high school and you'd gone through puberty but Mom was still insisting we do everything together as if we were ten. Looking back, I'm not sure that was a good idea. I was trying so hard to keep up with you even though I never could and you felt I was holding you back. You were ready for some excitement and Jess had that in spades. I think you had a girl crush."

Libby squirmed at the accurate tag, and again questioned her maturity. "But surely if it was a crush, I'd have grown out of it?"

"I dunno. Friendship's really complicated. And I think she had a crush on you too. She got me out of the way pretty fast so she could have you to herself."

Libby thought back to those few months when they were fourteen and Alice had retreated into herself. How her parents had looked worn and gray with worry. How she'd been so caught up with her new friendship with Jess, she'd spent little time with her twin. Old guilt stabbed her.

"Was our friendship why you stopped going to school?"

Alice thought about it. "If you'd asked me back then I'd have said yes to make you feel bad. But it's never one thing, Libs, you know that. It was the culmination of years of wanting to be you instead of me. I was sick of being the dorky twin, the slow twin, the one who wore glasses, couldn't run far and got picked last for T-ball. I'd worked so hard trying to be like you and I was still different and sick of it. Chuck in puberty hormones and, kaboom! Chaos."

"God, Al, I'm sorry."

"None of it's your fault."

"You sure?"

"Well ..." Alice grinned. "I'm sure you owe me something for stealing all my food in the womb."

Libby wanted to laugh and enjoy her twin's forgiveness, but instead she felt the sting of tears. "I'm sorry for being selfish and thoughtless. I don't deserve you, but I'm so thankful you're here now. I couldn't get through this without you." She hugged Alice and took an almighty sniff, trying to head off a messy cry. "I'm sick of me and I'm sure you're sick of me too. Let's talk about you. How are things with Tim?"

Alice stood and turned the cardboard clock on the door to two o'clock. "Let's go for a walk along the beach."

"Okay, but you're still going to tell me about Tim, right?"

"Just Tim?" Alice jogged toward the bridge and crossed the inlet.

Libby ran to catch up, realizing how badly out of shape she was after not having exercised for weeks. Panting, she caught Alice just as she got to the beach. "There's someone else? What happened to Tim?"

Alice twirled on the hard sand, arms out wide and scattering seagulls, just like she'd done as a kid. "He vanished without a word. Then there was Finn, but I realized he was full of back-handed compliments ..."

For years, Libby had smugly congratulated herself for being able to recognize the qualities that constituted a good man—someone who loved, respected and supported her—and she'd never accepted anything less. Alice, on the other hand, always seemed to give away a part of herself in every romantic relationship. Libby no longer felt smug—more chastened, humbled and embarrassed by the supercilious advice she'd dished out to her twin.

"Back-handed compliments sound like Lawrence."

Alice grimaced at the mention of her ex. "Sadly, yes, but I'm learning. This time I recognized it so much earlier and I ditched him before we even met."

"Good for you!"

"And I've stopped paying to meet men who don't come close to being ideal. I've joined Bumble and Tinder."

"The swiping apps?"

"Well, two of them, anyway. There are heaps out there, Libs. I'm currently in conversation with Kurt, Lachlan, Spencer, Luca and Ben, and I'm meeting Todd and Andrew for coffee on the weekend. And you'll be proud of me." Alice winked. "I have it all color coded on Google Calendar."

Libby laughed. "You either take ages to decide something or you jump right in."

"Oh, and I'm also having sex with Dan van den Berg. But twin blood promise, you can't tell anyone and that includes Mom and Dad."

"Oh my God!" Libby stared at her, openmouthed. "You and Dan the man? Alice, you know he's more likely to give you an STD than a marriage proposal. Not that I'm recommending marriage at the moment, but he's not even a medium-term proposition."

Alice's head tilted and she pursed her lips. "Give me some credit. It's the off- season in a small town so we've struck a deal, including all the healthy precautions. Sex and fun until one of us meets someone."

Libby was trying to wrap her head around this information. "I—um —you ... Is it fun?"

"So much fun! And believe me, Dan knows what he's doing. It's pretty good."

A complicated feeling that lurched between happiness for Alice and envy for herself unsettled Libby. "Only pretty good?"

Alice's cheeks pinked. "The thing is, I've been a bit um, tender down there."

"It sounds like too much sex or not enough foreplay."

"No, it's neither of those things. Like I said, Dan knows what he's doing and we usually only get together once a week, occasionally twice. We're using condoms and plenty of lube but ... I dunno, I can't explain it."

"Maybe it's because you're not a couple and there's no future in it. Your body's telling you that."

Alice's brows shot up. "I can't believe the scientist just said that. Lust is lust and me and my body definitely enjoy most of it."

"Sorry. What I mean is, what's your mind saying?"

"It's saying I deserve to have some fun while I'm searching for The One. Dan's great about making sure I come and he's a much better lover than Lawrence or Geoff ever were and I never had this issue with them. Right now, we're limited to one position, because all the others are uncomfortable. You're the doctor. What do you think's causing it?"

Libby ran through the usual suspects. "If you're sure you're aroused and well lubricated then it could be any number of things, including low level yeast infection. How about I write you a referral to Lacey Chu? She's my OBGYN and she's great."

"Any tips while I'm waiting to get an appointment?"

"No waiting for my twin. I'll call her and she'll happily squeeze you in."

"Thanks, Libs."

"My pleasure."

In the rough seas of her own confusion and pain, it felt good to be able to do something for Alice.

Karen bid farewell to her senior year French class and wished Alice or Peter was at home so she could share the buzz. Since none of her students had been to France, they were struggling with some of the conversation topics that were part of their oral exam, so Karen had obtained permission to bring them back to Pelican House. She'd cooked them coq au vin and tarte tatin and finished with a platter of French cheeses. As they'd sat around the table set with Provençal-style crockery and linen, she'd discussed the food, its origins and their reactions to it in French, helping them construct conversations about the importance of cuisine in French culture.

It had been a golden teaching moment and she'd loved every minute of it. The only thing that marred the experience was the impending return of the permanent French teacher, which meant Karen's return to retirement. Over her long career many of her colleagues had often said in bewildered tones, "It's a vocation for you, isn't it? You really love it."

"I really do," was always her response. Not once had she confessed to any of them that the joy she got from teaching had been a surprise, or that her decision to enter the profession had been a pragmatic one, far removed from any altruism. At the time, the government had been offering scholarships to boost teaching numbers and that money, combined with a part-time job, allowed her to leave home. Or to be more accurate: escape.

Thoughts of Lisa drifted into her mind. For some unknown reason, Karen had been thinking about her sister more and more lately. Was it age? Did the dull ache of regret start to sharpen again when the years ahead added up to less than the years lived?

Karen gave herself a shake. Sixty is not old! But it wasn't enough to disperse her melancholy thoughts. She went into the laundry and dragged out the step ladder before climbing it and opening the top cabinet. Pushing aside vacuum-sealed summer duvet and blankets, she pulled out an old box and carried it into the living room. The photo album was on the top and she lifted it out, rifling through the meager pages.

Lisa wearing a blue and white toweling dress with her hair in tightly permed curls. Lisa leaning against a Toyota Celica with the top down, licking an ice-cream. Lisa in a bikini standing in the shallows. Time had changed some of the colors on the Polaroid photos to purple and brown, starkly stating how many years had passed since the long hot summer when they'd been taken. Karen snapped the album shut, not wanting to follow those memories any further. Yet when she went to drop the album back in the box and seal it up again, the bundles of letters made her fingers itch. They were tied with ribbon in neat stacks of ten. Two bundles were clearly marked *return to sender*. The third was addressed to her and she held it close to her nose, breathing in deeply and hoping for the faint scent of cheap perfume. All she got was the stale and musky smell of old paper. She carefully stacked the letters on top of the album and that's when she saw the copy of *Anne of Green Gables*. Her eyes filled with tears.

I'm sorry, Lisa. I should have tried harder. Done so much more.

"Hi, Mom. You okay?"

Startled from her memories, Karen turned to see Alice looking at her with a quizzical look. If she swiped at the tears that teetered heavily on her bottom lids, Alice's next question would be "What's wrong?" Karen would do almost anything to avoid the question so she blinked rapidly, glad for once that her glasses hid the finer details.

"I'm on a bit of a high!" she babbled. "It was an excellent class and it's got me thinking. I'm going to talk to the school about the possibility of leading a trip to New Caledonia next year. The students would really benefit from soaking up some French culture."

"Sounds like a plan." Alice spotted the copy of *Anne of Green Gables* and her face lit up. "Remember how much I loved the Anne books? My favorite was *Anne of the Island* when Gilbert finally proposes. I remember sobbing my way through *Anne's House of Dreams* when she lost the baby."

"I read you the first one."

"When I had the chicken pox and was quarantined. You read it to make up for Libby and Dad going to the Tina Arena concert without me. I've got the complete set, so where did this one come from?"

Before Karen could reply, Alice picked up the book and flipped it open. "'To Lisa. Happy birthday, thinking of you. With lots of love from Karen xx.' Who's Lisa?"

Hot and cold chills raced across Karen's skin. She'd kept her family a secret for longer than Alice had been alive and she wasn't about to falter now. "A friend."

"So why do you have the copy you gave her?"

At least Karen didn't have to lie about the acquisition. "When Lisa died, it was returned to me."

"I'm sorry."

"Oh, Alice, it was a long time ago," Karen said briskly, fighting more tears. "I'd forgotten all about it until now. I only came across it because I was cleaning out some boxes."

Alice laughed. "That has to be a first."

"What?"

"You not knowing what's in every storage box. What else is in here?"

Karen deftly slid the lid into place. "Just some old lesson plans I'm going to throw out. I'll do it now while you make tea."

After the box was safely stowed in the back of the laundry cupboard and Karen had repaired her makeup, she joined Alice in the kitchen. Steam curled from a mug of Earl Grey tea, the bergamot scenting the air. It wasn't Alice's favorite tea and Karen appreciated her thoughtfulness.

"Thanks, darling. How was the group?"

"Really good. But hearing all the oldies' stories about their lives and families has made me realize I don't know much about our family."

"Of course you do. You've met the cousins in Adelaide and southwest Queensland. And Grandpa did the family tree before he died. I think he traced the Hunters back to Germany and Scotland. Dad's got a copy of it in the office somewhere."

"I meant your family."

The tea washed back into Karen's throat, making her cough. "My parents died when I was seventeen and—"

"Then there was one." Alice completed the sentence in the same tone Karen had always used when the twins had asked the question as little girls. "Surely you've got distant cousins out there who are still alive? Wouldn't it be cool to find them? Ancestry.com has a huge data base so if you got your DNA tested—"

"No!"

Alice flinched and Karen immediately regretted her sharp tone. "Sweetheart, I've got you, Libby and your father, not to mention the little girls. That's enough family for me."

The disappointment dragging on Alice's mouth told her she didn't agree. Karen held her breath, trying to predict her daughter's next question.

Alice sighed. "I guess I'll ask Dad to look out the Hunter family tree."

Karen relaxed. "Good idea. There are some great stories in there, including the failed gold miner who made his fortune selling provisions to other miners." Determined to change the subject, she asked, "Are you in for dinner tonight?"

Alice shook her head. "No. I'm cooking with Holly and Hunter."

"Why are you doing that?"

"Harry's got an evening meeting at the school."

Karen hadn't met the Waxmans so she only knew what Alice had told her—widower with two kids. It was one thing for Alice to be tutoring the girl, it was another thing entirely to be the domestic help. "He better be paying you!"

"Mom!"

"Don't 'Mom' me, Alice. Your time is valuable. Put a monetary value on it."

"You never say that when I mind the girls."

"That's different. It's family."

"This from the woman who got an award for service to the bay community?" Alice laughed. "What happened to giving a helping hand?"

"I've seen too many of my friends become convenient cooks and cleaners for men who take the path of least resistance. Besides, I thought you said he was grumpy?"

"He is. That's why I'm cooking with the kids while he's out of the house."

The corrosive worry that had been a part of Karen since Alice's unexpected arrival into her arms all those years ago dug in. Her younger daughter was too kind. Too giving. Too open to be hurt. "Promise me you'll be careful."

"Of what?"

"Of being used."

Alice shot to her feet. "What's wrong with you? You raised us to think of others and be involved in our community. Now you're saying be selfish?"

"Sometimes it's important to put yourself first."

"And sometimes—No! Make that all times, you have to accept that your daughters are adults and capable of making their own decisions." Alice jerkily pushed the chair under the table. "I think it's time I moved out."

Karen didn't know if it was the tone of Alice's voice or the way her eyes glittered, but the past rose in a rush, bringing with it a geyser of panic. "If you had a real job instead of these stop-gap ones, then you could afford to move out."

"How I live my life is not your concern!"

Only Alice had it wrong. From day one, she'd always been Karen's beautiful, ethereal concern.

CHAPTER FOURTEEN

JUNE

Thursdays were Libby's long days, but tonight she'd managed to leave the practice just after 7:00. She arrived home to find the girls bathed, fed and cuddled up on the couch with Nick. The rich aroma of oregano, wine and nutmeg permeated the kitchen, there was a bottle of merlot open and breathing on the counter and a huge bunch of purple irises were arranged majestically in a vase. Nick, who'd usually only ever bought her flowers on her birthday, had been buying her a bunch each week. She couldn't deny he was working hard at showing he was committed to her and the girls, but an unbridgeable chasm continued to exist between them. It was keeping her in the guest room.

"Mommy!" Indi jumped up and ran to her. "Read me a story!"

"Give Mommy time to put her bags down." Nick rose from the couch and kissed her on the cheek.

Libby automatically stiffened and his lips barely brushed her skin before he stepped back. Loss settled over her. Why couldn't she control this instinct to recoil?

Nick lifted her computer bag from her shoulder. "Normal day?"

What was normal anymore? "Pretty much. No emergencies, but I had to give a patient the bad news that his cancer has spread and all we can do is keep him comfortable. That never gets any easier."

"Sorry to hear that." His sympathy was genuine and he swept his arm out toward the open bottle. "I thought we'd eat after the girls are in bed, but would you like a glass of wine now?"

"Sure." She forced herself to add, "Thanks."

Seating herself on the couch between her daughters, she picked up the story where Nick had left off. It was an evening identical to so many they'd shared before the apocalypse, but now tension ringed the normalcy, making everything unfamiliar. For years, she'd never questioned or even considered their easy camaraderie, she just took its existence for granted and now it was gone. Would they ever get to a point where they were relaxed around each other again? Could they?

Nick brought her wine and settled on the couch leaving a respectful gap between them.

Lucy scrambled into his lap. "Daddy, you be the dragon voice."

Nick raised his brows at Libby in query—something he did a lot these days. She nodded and he moved closer to read the text. His warmth enticed her to relax into him. It was what she wanted to do, because in so many ways she was tired of fighting, but giving in seemed like an easy out for him. She moved slightly, creating space between them. He didn't shift to close it again.

When the nighttime routine of stories, teeth brushing and tucking in was over and the girls were snuggled into bed, Nick served up the cannelloni and the salad he'd made. As they ate, he told her about his plan to expand the fleet.

"Some city slickers love the idea of owning a yacht, but they don't have the time to sail her more than a few times a year."

"This sounds like those investment apartments in Queensland."

"That's exactly it. We hire out the yacht and take a cut and the owners get some money to cover the marina fees. They block out the times during the year they want to sail her."

"How will you find investors?"

"Boat brokers, word of mouth, the internet and some old-school ads in sailing magazines."

"It sounds like a good idea."

"Thanks."

He shot her a grin and she realized she'd missed seeing that smile. She returned it, enjoying the sensation until she remembered the reason neither of them had been smiling for so long. While they ate the tiramisu Rosa had brought over, probably to help Nick's cause, their conversation drifted to logistics planning for Lucy, who was doing a soccer camp during school vacation.

"Do you want to have coffee on the couch?" Nick asked.

"Okay."

"This is nice," he said, sitting down next to her.

"You've always made good coffee."

"Thanks." He stroked the back of her hand.

This time his warmth trickled through her and the ice around her heart softened. This was the caring man she'd fallen in love with.

"But I wasn't talking about the coffee. I meant this evening's been nice. Normal. Like it used to be." He kissed her hand. "I've missed us."

The memory of his betrayal kicked in and suddenly the man kissing her wasn't her Nick. Her desire flatlined. "That's not my fault."

Nick sucked in his lips. "I didn't say it was."

Libby remembered Alice's comment that Nick was doing everything she'd asked of him to prove himself. She heard her twin saying, "cheap shot, Libs," but it wasn't enough to halt the march of her indignation.

"Do you miss sex?" she asked.

"Of course I do."

Accept his words. But the next question was already burning the back of her throat and leaping across her lips. "With her or with me?"

His eyes widened in confusion. "What? With you. Of course with you."

But there was no of course about it. "Was the sex with her good?"

"Jesus, Libby!" His coffee cup clattered onto the table.

"Is that a yes or a no?"

"How many times do I have to answer that question?"

"As many times as I need to hear the answer!"

"But we've been over and over it for *three months*. There's nothing left to say."

"Humor me."

The veins in his neck throbbed. "The sex I had with her before we started dating was nothing to write home about. Nothing like what we've shared."

"Yet it happened quite a few times. You must have liked it the night she got pregnant."

Nick jerked to his feet and started pacing, his gaze fixed on a point on the wall. "I was tanked and miserable. I can barely remember it."

Her heart thumped. *Why are you doing this to yourself? Why not just order a whip and flagellate yourself?* She wanted to stop quizzing him and protect herself from thinking about him having sex with that woman in their bed, but all the books and websites told her the betrayer never tells the full story straight off the bat. Betrayers continue to lie. And parts of Nick's story didn't make sense to her. She needed to keep probing until Nick's answers were consistent. Otherwise, how could she ever trust him again?

"If you were tanked, how did you get it up?"

He paled. "Libby, how does this help? Talking about it only upsets you."

"Not knowing upsets me! If you were so drunk, how did you get it up?"

He swallowed. "She gave me head."

It was like a knife plunged deep into her heart. Despite the risk of even more pain, she grabbed hold of the information, determined not to let go until she exposed the real story. "You keep insisting you thought it was me in bed with you even though I was in Melbourne."

"I did."

"You're lying."

"I'm not."

Rage kept her upright. "Want to know how I know you are? I don't give you blow jobs!"

"I was drunk! Hell, I was more asleep than awake. My blood was in my dick, not my brain."

"That's not an excuse."

"What do you want me to say then?"

"I want to know why you did it?"

He sighed and rubbed his face, his three-day stubble reddening his palms. "I don't know why. All I know is that I'd been feeling like shit for weeks and suddenly I was having this dream where for the first time in ages I felt warm and safe and the pain was fading. I'd have followed that feeling anywhere ..."

He raised his eyes to hers, guilt and shame shining bright. "I dunno. I just remember coming to and wanting to keep feeling like that. I didn't think too hard about who was in bed with me. I just concentrated on how it was making me feel ..."

It was the first time Nick had admitted that he wasn't the victim and that woman hadn't taken total advantage of him.

"And Libs, you know what I'm like when I'm half asleep. Sex is instinct. You know it is. It's not like you've never crawled on top of me and woken me up slowly."

When Nick's half asleep, he lets me do just about anything to him. A conversation she'd once had with Jess about sex went off in her head like the pop and scream of fire crackers. Her mouth dried. Jess had always been interested in her marriage and the girls, happily listening to her prattle on about everything, including her sex life. Had she given Jess the tools to seduce him? The thought brought her dinner rising fast to the back of her throat.

Nick misunderstood her distress and wrapped his arms around her. For the first time, she allowed it, letting her head sink onto his chest and welcoming the soft lub-dub of his heart. In his safe cocoon, she tried to unravel yet again how a friendship she'd valued so much had gone so horribly wrong.

"*Tesoro mio,* I'd do anything to turn back the clock. I wish I'd never invited her inside that night. Wish I'd never gotten drunk. Hell, I wish she'd never been your friend."

Suddenly it was *her* fault? The insatiable demons of distrust leaped inside her, brandishing pitchforks. She pulled back fast. "This is on you, Nick. Not me! You chose feeling good for a few minutes over our marriage. You took something wonderful, turned it inside out and ripped it to shreds so it's no longer recognizable. I wish you'd never told me!"

"Believe me, ignorance isn't bliss," he said bitterly. "I owed you the truth about Leo."

"A truth you hid for so long I don't know how to trust you anymore."

"I'm sorry!" His entire body pleaded with her. "I'm so, so sorry. I promise you, I've told you everything now. There's nothing else. *Please* trust me."

"Never lie to someone who trusts you and never trust someone who lies to you," she muttered the quote she'd found on the internet.

Bewilderment spun around him. "But I've given you access to my phone and email. I've put up with being treated like a child, reporting in and meeting curfew. I've done everything you've asked and more. I don't know what else I can do to make you understand that I love you. That I love the girls and our family. I know I hurt you, but honest to God, Libby, it's time to let it go. We have to get on with our lives."

Her heart beat so hard she heard the echo in her ears. "Let it go? Our lives aren't a Disney song!"

His shoulders slumped and his chin fell into his chest. "Then what more do you want me to do to prove that I love you?"

"Do you miss her?"

His jaw worked as if he was grinding his teeth. "I don't miss her at all."

"Really? You saw a lot of her."

"Not by choice." His rich brown eyes sought hers, their gaze wary. "I'd be happy if I never saw her again."

"Good."

"But that isn't going to be possible, is it?"

The softness of his tone sent a whoosh of prickling sensation streaking through her. "Why?"

"Because of Leo."

A silent scream filled her head as it did whenever she thought about the child and her hands clenched. "What about Leo?"

"He's the innocent in all of this mess."

"You're meeting your financial responsibilities."

"That's not enough. I'm his father. Despite what his mother did and how he came into existence, he deserves to know me."

"No!"

Nick's mouth tightened. "I get that you're hell-bent on punishing me, but you can't punish Leo."

"You've lost the right to tell me what I can and cannot do. Let's get our priorities straight and make things perfectly clear: the girls and I are your family. That child is hers. He's *nothing* to do with us."

"Libby, that's not fair."

Was he serious? "What's not fair is being reminded every time I see him that my son died and you screwed my best friend."

"And I'm sorry! Dear God, am I sorry. I hate myself for creating this nightmare and hurting the people I love most in the world. I know it hurts like hell that Dom died and Leo is here, but I can't change either of those things."

The ice around her heart that had begun to thaw hardened. "You can control it."

"How?"

"By not seeing him. That also solves our problem about not seeing her."

"That's not a solution!"

"It is if you want to stay married to me!"

Nick's dark eyes blazed and he studied her face for a long moment. For the first time since he'd dropped the bomb that had exploded their lives, she could see his apology and remorse waver. Guilt still spun around him, but so did a new iron clad resolve.

"That's an ultimatum I'm going to have to think about."

An unexpected chill settled over Libby.

THE KURNAI BAY WINTER SOLSTICE CELEBRATION WAS underway. Unlike the previous year, when the event had been rained out, there wasn't a cloud in the inky black sky, only a carpet of shining white stars. The organizers had decorated the park with lanterns and light danced across the paths while shadows leaped between the trees, giving life to the giant and colorful art installations. Excited children ran around while families and friends clustered on picnic blankets, drinking hot chocolate and listening to the live music, which ranged from Brian Baker's Bush Band to the high school's rock bands along with some classical violin and piano recitals.

Jess had arranged to meet Patrice and her family, but as she arrived at the park a text pinged onto her phone informing her that the Marceaus were running fifteen minutes late. Not wanting to set up on her own and wait like a sitting duck, giving people the opportunity to make insulting comments as they passed, she pushed Leo's stroller over to the children's tent. It was full, but unexpectedly quiet. Kids concentrated intently on their artwork, the tips of their tongues peeking out between their lips. Alice was twirling and flittering about wearing a multicolored top, a green and blue tutu, navy leggings and ballet flats. She sported a royal blue headband that sprouted glitter balls that wobbled back and forth on their wires, and on her back was a beautiful pair of intricately decorated wings. The dorky twin was in her element and Alice positively glowed, although she momentarily paled when she saw Jess. Unlike Libby, Alice didn't deliberately shun her, but then again, she didn't greet her either.

A young girl wearing wings that were almost as much of a work of art as Alice's came over to her. "Hi, I'm Holly. Would your little boy like some wings?"

"What do you think, Leo? Do you want to be a butterfly?" Leo had already spied the felt pens on the table and was reaching for them from the stroller. "I think that's a yes."

"Awesome. When he's finished coloring, Alice will hot glue any ribbons, sequins or pom-poms he wants."

"He's a boy!" a voice declared. A sandy-haired kid with the same nose and smattering of freckles as Holly slid into the chair next to Leo. "He won't want pom-poms!"

"Boys can like pom-poms. It's important that he decides what he wants, not us," Jess said, smiling at the boy. "Your design's pretty cool."

"It's not a butterfly," he said firmly. "It's a redback spider."

Leo, who was scrawling green all over the material that was stretched over wire, picked up a red felt pen and handed it to the boy. "Wed."

"Do you want me to help?" Hunter looked at Jess. "Can I? I'm Hunter."

"Sure." She sat back and relaxed.

Jess loved watching Leo play. She got pleasure from his total absorption in the activity and seeing the world through his eyes. His joyful delight was hers and she cheered for him whenever he achieved his goal, whether it was building a tower, driving a truck through sand or running around in a sequined cape. Lately, she'd been playing with him a lot more, because apart from his time at daycare, these days the two of them were pretty much on their own. She'd tried to continue with playgroup, but she'd stopped going when she realized the other women were actively removing their children from Leo's orbit and he was essentially playing on his own.

The clusters of people in the tent modeled the bay's response to her. The mothers sitting at the craft tables with their children studiously ignored her. The dads said "G'day" or nodded hello before being silenced by their wives. Right now, her only social contact was Patrice and Jess was trying hard not to lean too heavily on her. She was also working hard on channeling patience.

History had taught her that eventually some of the town would thaw and that would provide an opening to establish new friendships.

When the softening came, it wouldn't include the friends she'd shared with Libby. Those women took their cues from the doctor and Libby's antipathy was now set like concrete.

Holly joined Hunter in helping Leo, suggesting color combinations. The three of them worked together, filling in the wide wing span. Leo beamed under the attention of the older children, lurching between instructing them on where to color and doing whatever they asked. It was the same behavior he'd shown with his half-sisters. Sisters he hadn't seen in months because their mother was denying him access.

The thought sent oxygen blowing across the embers of Jess's anger and flames licked. Libby had no right to break family bonds by preventing Leo from having a relationship with his sisters. Jess had expected better from Nick. Sure, he'd back paid the child support payments he'd withheld during the paternity test impasse and each week his money dropped regularly into her account, but that was the extent of his support. Instead of fighting for his son, Nick was rolling over on every single demand from his dictator wife.

The child-sized chair Jess was sitting on pushed her belly up against her breasts, making her feel full and uncomfortable. She rose and stretched but it didn't totally rid her of the sensation, which had been coming and going recently. She did a quick calculation of her cycle. Day twelve. She shouldn't be bloated this early in the game.

"Daddy, I want to be a fairy!" a little girl's voice said behind her.

Jess stilled, her heart almost skipping a beat.

Leo dropped his felt pen and jumped up, running straight to the girl. "Di! Di!"

Adult conversation in the tent ceased and all heads swiveled toward her before swinging back the other way. Jess turned slowly and for the first time in months, came face-to-face with Nick. She smiled, soaking him in.

"Hello, Nick. It's good to see you."

His dark eyes didn't sparkle and his usually friendly mouth flattened. "Jess."

The dislike that clung to her name loosened her gut with a sharp and jagged pain. During all their months apart, she'd believed it wasn't Nick's choice not to contact her and that Libby was the problem. Now she wasn't so sure.

Nick squatted to speak to Leo. "Hey, buddy."

"Deer," Leo said hopefully.

Nick grinned and sat on the chair Jess had just vacated. He sang softly as he jiggled Leo on his knee.

Indi tugged on Jess's hand. "I want to make fairy wings."

"Here you go, Indi." Alice appeared holding a set of undecorated wings and inserted herself between Indi and Jess. "Do you want me to help?"

Indi shook her head. "I want Jess."

Jess almost cried. She'd desperately missed her goddaughters. Despite the look Alice and Nick exchanged, neither of them voiced an objection, so Jess swallowed against a tight throat and took control. "I'd love to help, Indi. What colors do you want?"

"Purple and pink."

Alice hovered, clearly torn between leaving Jess alone with Indi and Nick and returning to her glue gun duties at the other tables. Nick studiously kept his back to Jess—his message loud and clear. As much as his rejection hurt, she was soothed in part by the sight of Leo sitting on his father's knee and squealing in delight. While Jess lost herself in coloring, her world moved closer toward normal than it had been in months. Something resembling peace flowed.

As they filled in the big flowers Alice had sketched, Indi chatted easily about all sorts of things, from her favorite TV show to swings in the park with Karen, so Jess wasn't prepared when the little girl lobbed her grenade.

"Why don't you visit me anymore?"

Nick's head shot around, his gaze flinty with warning. Like the slicing sting of a paper-cut, Jess realized that he and Libby hadn't told the girls about their brother.

Anger roared, stomping over the new and fragile peace and

crushing it into dust. So, Libby thought it was fine to betray her and Leo to the town by revealing the truth about his father, but she hadn't told his sisters? Had she banked on Lucy not hearing anything at school? Jess supposed that was likely, given Leo wasn't at school and Indi was too little to understand if anything was said at daycare.

She wanted to hit something. No, someone. Her fury raged like wildfire at Libby and her disregard for Leo when she was clearly protecting her daughters. Indi and Lucy deserved to know they have a half-brother. If Nick and Libby wouldn't do the job, then she would.

"I wanted to visit you, but—"

"Indi! Nick!" Libby's emergency-doctor-in-control voice filled the tent. "It's time to go."

The chatter in the tent died instantly and the slightly off-key singing drifting from the music stage became loud. Some people kept their heads down but most sat back on their too-small chairs with as much anticipation as a blockbuster movie audience. All that was missing was the popcorn.

"Look, Mommy!" Indi called out. "Jess is here."

Libby's eyes glittered with the blue chill of glacial ice. "So I see."

"And we made wings."

Libby picked up the wings and held out her hand to her daughter. "It's time to go."

Indi stamped her foot. "But Leo got pom-poms. I want pom-poms!"

Alice, who'd been helping another child, shot back to her niece's side clutching the glue gun. "You can never have too many pom-poms."

Libby's gaze roved between her husband, her twin and Jess before settling on Alice. "How could you let this happen?"

Alice winced. "I'm running the craft tent, Libs, not policing it."

"This wasn't planned," Nick said quickly. Leo zoomed around his legs, playing at being a butterfly.

"I don't believe you."

"Of course you don't," he said wearily. "But it's the truth."

Jess read the distance between husband and wife, seeing the wide cracks in the united front that the Hunter-Pirellis had been displaying for months. It was an unexpected gift and it gave her room to maneuver. Despite Nick's frosty response and his refusal to engage with her, she hadn't imagined his delight at seeing Leo. Nor Leo's happy response to Nick. This was her chance for her son.

"Leo has access rights."

"Not here, Jess," Nick muttered.

As if sensing tension, Indi protectively grabbed Leo's hand.

"When then?"

Libby's lips whitened at the edges. "Never."

Jess didn't want to discuss access arrangements in front of an audience of gossips and interested bystanders, but if this was her only opportunity to secure Leo's rights, then so be it. It wasn't like she had anything left to lose. "Then we discuss it here."

"We'll set up a time," Nick said hurriedly. "We'll email you."

Jess remembered the Mexican standoff over the support payments and the paternity request. No way was she giving away her power again. She looked straight at Libby. "By ten o'clock tonight or I'll betray you to your daughters like you betrayed Leo to the town."

"Come on, Nick, we're leaving." Libby separated Indi from Leo and gripped her hand hard.

"Ouch, Mommy!" Indi pulled her hand away. "Don't want to go."

Nick picked her up and swooped her around like a plane. "Come on, let's go and find your sister and Nonna."

"Me! Me!" Leo called out, tears filling his eyes.

"I want Leo to come too," Indi said.

"Out of the mouths of babes," Jess said.

"He has to stay with Jess. It's where he belongs," Libby said tightly.

"But—"

"Do. What. You're. Told. Indi."

"Look, Indi." Alice held out the wings now heavy with sequins, ribbons and pom-poms. "Your fairy wings are ready just in time for you to dance on stage with the fairy queen."

Nick threw an appreciative look at his sister-in-law as Indi demanded her wings. She ran happily from the tent, calling for Lucy.

Nick and Libby followed their daughter without a backwards glance, leaving Jess and a crying Leo behind.

Jess heard a muttered, "When is that bitch going to realize she has no rights?" She sat down hard before pulling her son onto her lap. "Shh, it's okay, sweetie. Let's draw something."

"You look sad," Hunter said kindly. "Maybe you should make yourself some wings."

IF LIBBY THOUGHT LEARNING ABOUT LEO'S EXISTENCE WAS THE worst thing to have happened to her, it had nothing on dealing with it.

They only stayed for the Fairy Queen's concert to avoid Lucy and Indi melting down. Such a scene would have added even more glory to her and Nick's status of being the bay's most scrutinized couple. But as Libby watched the performance, instead of seeing Chrissie Templar and her dance students moving around the stage in sequins and tulle, all she saw was the constant replay of Nick smiling and happy and playing with *that child*. The moment the Fairy Queen and her handmaidens exited the stage, Libby and Nick bundled two excited girls into the car.

Libby was so incandescent with rage she could have powered the bay and the surrounding district. The target of her fury encompassed many. Nick for not walking out of the tent the moment he'd seen that woman. The bitch, who'd not only used her husband as a sperm donor, but was now demanding access rights for the child. That request had brought back every ravaging emotion that had pummeled Libby in the early days of the nightmare. It had cracked her wide open again, raising the devastating question: How could I have believed that woman was closer to me than my own twin?

And then there was Alice. How could her sister have allowed the meeting to happen? It was yet another betrayal from someone who professed to love her.

Libby deliberately turned up the girls' favorite song before saying quietly to Nick. "Drop me off at Mom's."

"What about the bedtime routine?"

"That's on you tonight."

"I've told you multiple times, I didn't know she was there."

"And I've told you to drop me off at Mom's."

He swore under his breath and took the next left. When the car came to a stop outside the Pelican House gates, Libby turned and blew kisses to the girls. "Daddy's taking you home and I'll be there soon."

"But want to see Glamma," Indi demanded.

"Not tonight, it's bedtime." Libby slammed the door against Indi's cries of disappointment and Nick's dark glare. She jogged along the winding drive to the house.

"Mom?"

"In the TV room, darling," her mother's voice floated down the hall. "I thought you'd be at the park?"

Libby found her mother on the couch and threw herself down next to her, tears threatening. "You won't believe what just happened."

Karen listened and offered tissues. "That must have been hard."

"It was awful. Alice should—"

"I think Alice did her best in a difficult situation," Karen said unusually firmly.

"How? She didn't even text me!"

"Has it occurred to you that perhaps she was trying to protect you?"

"I don't need protecting! I need honesty and the truth and no one's giving it to me."

"Sweetheart." Karen sighed. "Alice, Dad and I only have your best interests at heart. If, in your eyes, we get it wrong occasionally, it might be worth trying to look at it from our point of view."

Indignation rankled. "So—what? I'm the problem now?"

Karen bit her lip. "Come into the kitchen and I'll make you a hot chocolate."

"Swiss Miss not going to fix this." Whenever Libby was upset or couldn't sleep as a child, her mother had made her a soothing hot chocolate.

"Probably not, but it will give you time to calm down before going home."

As Libby watched her mother prepare the drinks, she focused on trying to still her swirling thoughts and empty her mind. By the time Karen slid the mug toward her, she was feeling a little calmer.

"I've been thinking." Karen wrapped her hands around the warm mug. "Would it make things easier if Alice or I picked Leo up for access visits? That way you don't have to see Jess and Nick is never alone with her."

The viscous milk clogged Libby's throat and she coughed. "There won't be any access visits."

Karen's eyes dimmed with something Libby refused to interpret as disappointment. "I really wish you'd change your mind."

I won't. Libby gripped her mug, welcoming the burn on her palms. It hurt a hell of a lot less than everything else in her life.

Despite the winter chill, Libby walked home from Pelican House, embracing the salt-infused night and its soothing qualities. Nick met her the moment she walked inside.

"You're cutting things fine," he said accusingly. "We need to choose a date, time and place to meet Jess and email her the details before 10:00."

A red haze blurred her vision, stealing every soothing effect of her walk. "We are *not* negotiating with that woman."

Nick's jaw tightened and he poured himself a shot of grappa. The guilt and contrition that had ringed him for months had faded recently, along with his eagerness to please. It had been replaced by muted anger.

"You can't ignore Leo."

"Yes, I can. He's got nothing to do with me."

"Of course he's got something to do with you! He's connected to you and the girls through me. He's family."

"He's not part of my family!"

"I want him to be part of our family."

He said it so quietly, Libby tried to pretend she hadn't heard the words. Unfortunately, the nausea spinning her stomach was confirmation. "And I don't."

Nick downed the grappa and then the glass clinked on the counter. "I'm trying hard here, Libby, but you're not making it easy."

"Given the circumstances, that's not my job."

"Fine! But you're not making sense either. As the local doctor, you champion children's rights all the time. Hell, for years you ranted long and hard about how much Jess suffered at the hands of this town, yet you're inflicting the same thing on Leo."

"I'm not!"

"You are!"

"There's no comparison. Leo is loved by his mother. You're providing for him financially. He's well fed and safe from harm."

Nick sucked in a deep breath, the sound sharp and taut. "I'm his father. He deserves to know me."

His words ripped her apart. "Why not go ahead and say it? Just get it over and done with."

"I've got no idea what you're talking about."

"The girls and I aren't enough for you. You want to know *him*. You want a son!"

His body shook and he flung out his arms, looking as Mediterranean as his grandfather. "It wouldn't matter if Leo was a girl. I'm trying to right a wrong, Libby. To find my integrity and be the honorable man you fell in love with. I'm owning my responsibilities."

"What about your responsibilities to *me*?"

"Whatever I do, it's never going to be enough, is it? I've tried reading those bloody self-help books you keep giving me about healing marriages after an affair, but none of them fit our situation. I didn't have a long-standing affair. Hell, it wasn't even an affair! It was a stupid mistake I regret every single day. But I'm not an island, Libby. When it happened, neither of us were capable of supporting each other."

"That sounds like you're parroting something a counselor said to you."

"Doesn't make it any less true."

"*None* of this is my fault."

"For fuck's sake! When you say things like that it makes me think you really don't want our marriage to survive."

Although there'd been moments when Libby had wondered if they could ever come back from the world of pain, hurt and betrayal, Nick had constantly reiterated his desire to stay. At least he had until recently—but lately that reassurance was absent. She forced out words from a tight throat. "Do you want it to survive?"

"Yes! How many times do I need to say that before you hear me and believe me?" Misery pulled at his mouth. "But, Libby, if this living hell we're enduring is as good as things are ever going to get between us, then no. I don't want to live this way."

The bald words lanced her and the empty spaces inside her, created by months of desperate loneliness, throbbed with a dull ache. Still mired in the fallout of the apocalypse, there were only two things she was certain about—Jess was dead to her and she missed the man she'd always believed her husband to be. Her love for Nick still had more moments of intense fury than it had of forgiveness. It was these volcanic emotions that kept her sleeping in the guest room.

"Is this about us not having sex?"

"No," Nick said, far too defensively, and she snorted.

"Maybe. A bit, but as you still flinch when I kiss you, we're not ready for sex. This is more about you being lily white and above reproach while I'm stuck in the muck being blamed for everything that's wrong between us. You're too angry to give an inch and I'm sick of being the only bad guy—bad *person* in this relationship when it's not strictly true." He rubbed his face. "How long are you going to be angry for, Libs?"

Tears stung her eyes—she hated the anger almost as much as she needed it. "I don't know."

"I love you, *tesoro mio*, but our marriage is like sailing through a never-ending storm. I'm stuck in the troughs with the constant threat of being rolled by massive waves. I don't know how much longer I can stick it out."

Something her mother had said tonight forced its way into her head. *Does Nick have a point?* Had she been nursing her anger and pain for so long it was now her default position no matter what? Hurt him so he didn't hurt her again?

"Libs," he pleaded. "We need better help than those bloody books."

"But we've tried three counselors. All of them have been clueless. The last one straight out goggled at us when we told him."

"Yeah." Nick pulled out his phone and handed it to her open on a web page. "I found this. It's a workshop in Melbourne. I dunno if the reviews are fake or not, but it's a combination of individual, couple and group therapy. It comes with ongoing support."

She read the blurb, cringing at the idea of sharing their messy story with strangers. "You're not serious."

"Why not?"

"Because—because even at the best of times you hate discussing your feelings, let alone admitting what you've done in front of people we don't know."

He laughed, the sound harsh and unsettling. "Half the town knows what I've done to the people I love and respect. Telling a group of strangers whose marriages are floundering and who might just understand what we're going through will be a walk in the park. Telling anyone is easy compared with telling you."

A part of her hated him for having told her the truth that day and fracturing her belief that their life together was rock solid. For plunging them into this black vortex of anger, grief and shame. But for the first time since that day, she heard the torment in his voice. Something in her softened.

"I never thought I'd say this, but hearing it from you was better than hearing it from anyone else."

"Thank you." Gratitude played in the hollows of his cheeks. "Libs, when we lost Dom, we both fell apart. I don't think either of us had anything left over to help the other. I want us to learn how to do that so we're never lost in this hell hole again."

Panic joined the flood of emotions rolling around inside her. If they went to this workshop, her thoughts and actions would be exposed, examined and judged. "I bought a new book yest—"

"No more books! Right now, we're treading water. Something has to change or we may as well call it a day."

Her mouth dried. "You really want to spend a weekend with strangers?"

"No. But I'm desperate and I think we should try. It says we'll be taught ways to bring back the trust. That sounds pretty bloody good to me."

"And if it doesn't work?"

He sighed. "Can we focus on now instead of trying to predict the future?"

She couldn't argue with that—it was the same approach she'd been operating on for weeks. "I guess."

"Please." He reached his hands toward her. "We owe it to ourselves and the kids to do something that will help us live happy lives again."

The kids, not the girls. And just like that, they were back to where they'd started. Leo was never going away. "And your interpretation of us being happy involves you seeing Leo?"

"*Us* seeing Leo."

"I can't do that."

Anguish creased his face. "You just said you wanted to try."

"I do. I want us to be happy again, but don't push me too fast, Nick. I need more time. Can't we concentrate on fixing us first?"

"I want to say yes, but if we don't agree to some sort of access arrangement, I don't trust Jess not to carry out her threat and tell the girls. I don't want that to happen. I want them to hear it from us."

The thought of telling the girls made her gag. "I hate that she has the power!"

"So we take it back."

"How? I don't particularly want to explain to Lucy that you had sex with that woman."

He blanched. "She's six. Can't we just say I'm Leo's daddy too? I mean, you and Jess were always saying Leo was their little brother so I doubt we need to be any more explicit unless Lucy straight up asks how babies are made."

"That still doesn't solve the access issue."

Nick screwed up his face. "To use counselor-speak, 'I hear that you're not ready to accept Leo.'"

Optimism flickered. "Thank you."

"I've got an idea. Promise you won't freak out."

If he was asking her that, she probably would. She steeled herself. "I'll try."

"What if the girls and I spend time with him?"

No! Categorically, no. But Indi's cry of "I want Leo" in the craft tent tonight was booming in her head. In the ongoing fog of her own grief, she hadn't considered that the sudden severing of ties with Jess and Leo would negatively affect the girls. Karen's offer came back to her, along with her mother's obvious disappointment of her rejection of it. Libby tried hard to silence Nick's accusation that her attitude toward Leo went against everything she'd ever believed in and she was punishing an innocent child, but the weight of the claim crushed her. Despite the abhorrence that scuttled through her every time she thought of what that child represented, she could no longer withstand the tide of disapproval.

"I'll agree to you and the girls spending time with him *only* if you never see her. Mom will do the pick-up and drop-off."

Appreciation lit up his eyes. "That's a great solution. What about Alice?"

"I'm not asking Alice."

"Okay ..." By the look on his face, he clearly wanted to ask her why, but he didn't. "My parents will happily help out too."

Her heart tore at how much Rick and Rosa wanted to see that

child. "They have to understand the rules. They can't be emissaries for her."

"They won't be. Believe me, I wear their disappointment in me almost as much as yours. How about we sit down with Karen and Peter and Mama and Papa and discuss how we want this to be handled?"

Libby knew she should feel some relief that they were managing to cooperate, but access was an unwanted obligation pressing in on her from all sides.

Nick rubbed his jaw—a clear sign he was wrestling with something. "Um ... can Leo come here or is that too much?"

It was too much. She'd just made a huge concession by allowing him to see the child. How many more compromises would she be forced to make? And where did she draw the line? *Just say no.*

But despite the heartache pulsating through her, she surprised herself by not going straight to punishment. Nick could certainly entertain a toddler elsewhere, but did that leave him open to Jess intercepting him? Libby had the girls to consider too. They needed to be protected and she could already hear them pleading for Leo to come and play at Burrunan like he'd so often done in the past.

Tension stiffened her spine. "Thursday afternoons and no sleepovers."

"Your long day?"

"Yes."

"Thank you."

But she didn't want his thanks. She wanted his acknowledgement that he understood her position. "Let me be absolutely clear, Nick. He's one hundred per cent your responsibility, not mine. I'll come home after he's left."

Despite the dismay on Nick's face, he didn't argue. "I get it."

"Good."

"And I'll book us into the next available course." He kissed her cheek. "I love you, *tesoro mio.*"

But as much as she wanted to say it back, something about the unevenness of the compromise stopped her.

CHAPTER FIFTEEN

JULY

"You're gorgeous."

"Um, thank you." Alice withdrew her hand from the table in the corner of the coffee shop and placed it in her lap as Killian tried to grab it.

"As soon as you've finished that coffee, let's take a selfie by the river. Together, we'll make an amazing photo."

Alice kicked herself. She'd seen Killian's Instagram feed—handsome guy in stunning places—but she'd allowed herself to be seduced by his banter, convincing herself there was more to him than just looking beautiful. Wrong again, Alice! A selfie of them together would be the equivalent of the old notch on a belt. Although Alice wasn't against sex, she already had that base covered with Dan. Dating was supposed to be all about meeting a life partner, not attaching herself to a self-obsessed man.

"Actually, Killian, I think I'll pass on the photo." And the rest of this coffee date.

A wrinkle creased his brow. "Never pass up the perfect photo op, Alice."

She could see he was struggling to absorb her message. "That's the thing, Killian. There's more to my life than a photo op."

He shrugged and to Alice's relief he stood and left, saving her from having to say, "This isn't going to work." Sadly, she was becoming very good at that statement.

"Another dud?" Zadie, the waitress, cleared the table.

"It's a numbers game."

Zadie glanced at the door. "Oh, is this your next one? He's cute in a shaggy dog sort of a way. He could be a project."

"I don't want a project! I want a fully functional man."

Alice's next date wasn't due for ten minutes, but she peered around Zadie anyway just in case Devon, whose photo declared him to be well groomed, had arrived early. It wouldn't be the first time a man had used an out-of-date profile pic or even someone else's photo.

"Hi Zadie. Can I have a latte, please? Oh, hello, Alice. What are you doing over this side of the river?"

Alice was suddenly battling a ridiculous flash that was racing heat across her skin. It couldn't possibly be because of Harry. Zadie must have the heater up too high.

"Speed dating." Zadie filled in the blank.

"Really?" Harry glanced around the almost empty café.

"I'm on a ten-minute break." Alice downed the glass of water she would have loved to pour over her head.

"How's it going?"

"Yeah, good," she lied.

"So good that you're six miles out of town?"

"Neutral territory."

Harry looked bemused. "I've only seen this sort of stuff on sitcoms. Do you have a friend who calls you after half an hour?"

She gave a wry smile. "Ten minutes."

"Crikey! A bloke has to make a fast impression."

"It's not like I'm meeting anyone cold. I trade a few texts before I decide to either ditch or meet." Watching Harry standing while she was sitting reluctantly brought out the manners her parents had drilled into her. "Is your coffee to go or do you want to sit for eight minutes?"

"With an invitation like that, I can hardly refuse."

Zadie handed him his coffee and he slid into the empty chair. "So, Alice, do you like long walks along the beach at sunset and reading books by an open fire?"

"If it's not blowing a gale or a hundred-degree day."

"Ah, pragmatic."

She laughed. "No one who knows me well would ever call me that."

"What would they say?"

Her mother's words played in her head. "Worrying, vague, disorganized, wafting through life without any direction ..."

"Your approach to dating sounds pragmatic."

"That's a recent phenomenon. It was forced on me by the reality of being dumped after a three-year relationship and the constant ticking of my biological clock."

"These days you don't need a man to have a baby."

"Your sole parenting isn't by choice, is it?"

"Point taken." Harry stirred half a sachet of sugar into his coffee. "Doesn't talking about wanting kids on the first date put blokes off?"

"You've never done digital dating, have you?"

"That obvious, eh?"

"On the site or the app you say if you've got children, are interested in having children, or not. So it's already out there before you make contact."

"Unless they lie."

Alice thought of Todd. "Well, there is that."

"Is there a spot to say vasectomy? Just asking for a friend."

"I think that's covered by has kids, doesn't want any more. How are your pre-vasectomy kids?"

"Not bad. Hunter's soccer team won on the weekend and he got MVP for the match."

"He'd be pumped about that."

"Bouncing more than usual you mean?" Harry's lips quirked into his elusive smile. "By the way, I should have called and thanked you for involving Holly in the winter solstice thing. She loved it."

Alice shuddered involuntarily.

"What?" Harry's smile vanished. Suddenly he was the concerned parent again. "Was there a problem? Did the kids do something? Misbehave? Get upset? You should have told me!"

"Breathe, Harry." Alice was now used to his warrior parenting style. "I would have told you if there was a problem. Holly was a huge help and Hunter was surprisingly good with the little kids."

He frowned. "Then why do you look like someone just kicked you?"

Twin loyalty made her deflect. "You're what, mid-forties? Sounds like it's time to get your eyes tested."

"Even if I was half blind, I'd have noticed. You wear your emotions on full display."

"I do not!"

"Yeah, you do." He sipped his coffee. "If you want to talk, I'm happy to listen."

With her family divided over what had happened at the winter solstice celebrations, Alice found herself wanting an impartial opinion, even if it was from Harry, whose mood she could never quite predict. "There was a bit of an incident with the woman who had the baby with my brother-in-law."

His emerald eyes widened. "That's the reason for the marriage problems? Jeez, no wonder he looked like hell that day on the pier."

"Oh yeah." Alice sighed. "Jess brought her son into the butterfly tent and that was fine. I mean, I don't choose to socialize with her, but she has a right to take part in a publicly funded community event. Anyway, Nick arrived with Indi—"

Harry quirked a brow.

"—one of his daughters. He and Libby have two girls. Nick maintains he had no idea Jess was at the event or in the tent and I saw his face drain of color when he laid eyes on her. I totally believe him. Apart from responding to her hello, he virtually ignored her."

Harry's shoulders squared. "What about the kid?"

"Leo? He was excited to see Nick. Then Libby found out and made a beeline for the tent."

"Let me guess. A good KB citizen texted or called her."

"Goes without saying. Anyway, Libby stormed in and now she's pissed off and refusing to talk to me."

"Why's she angry at you?"

"Apparently, I should have prevented the meeting."

"That's crazy thinking."

"Sure, but it's *her* thinking. When it comes to Jess, Leo and Nick, seeing reason isn't something she's capable of right now."

"I get that. Had a bit of the crazy thinking stuff for a while after H died." He leaned forward, his gaze intense. "But you know you're not to blame, right? You were there in an artistic capacity, not crowd control."

"On one level, I know that. I had kids who'd come to have a good time and my job was to make everyone happy. I needed to head off a scene that would upset all the children, not just Indi and Leo. But whenever I think about how much Libby is hurting, remembering my noble aim doesn't really help."

"You did a good job, Alice."

She fiddled with the spoon on her saucer. She was familiar with grumpy Harry and warrior-parent Harry, but he rarely showed this side of himself. When he did, she never knew quite what to do with the compliment. "You don't need to be kind."

"I'm not. I'm going on facts. Holly hasn't stopped talking about how much fun she had helping you and the littlies, and Hunter enjoyed himself too. He's hung his redback spider from the ceiling. I keep walking into it and getting a hell of a fright."

"It is pretty terrifying."

"You're telling me." He smiled and this time it was free of the reserve that often clung to him.

It was the most natural thing in the world for her to smile back. "Thanks for telling me that."

"Too easy." He checked his watch and stood. "I better get out of your hair before your next victim shows up."

"Why do you do that?"

He looked genuinely bewildered. "Do what?"

"Be a nice guy then a bit of a dick."

"It was a joke, Alice."

"Would you say that to a bloke? I'm not lying to these men or deceiving them in any way. I—"

"Sorry. It was a cheap shot."

Alice was in full flight—indignant words rushing out of her—and it took her a second to realize he'd apologized. She checked his face—he looked sheepish and repentant.

"Truth is, Alice, I'm in awe of you for taking the bull by the horns and making things happen. I'm not sure I'd have the guts."

She was still speechless when he walked away, pausing at the door for Devon, who walked in.

"Alice?" Devon half leaned in for a kiss and half shot out a hand.

Dazed, she took his hand, although she wasn't sure if her dumbfounded state related to Harry or the fact that the pony-tailed Devon, whose profile read part-time surfer, part-time philosopher, full-time consumer of life, was a man well into his sixties.

⛵

"'DATING DILEMMAS? ASK ALICE! EMAIL HER HERE AT THE *Gazette*.'"

Dan brandished a copy of the paper at Alice as she arrived at his place with the ingredients for their weekly dinner. It was her turn to cook. "You're an agony aunt, now?"

"Why so skeptical? I'm getting enough dud dating experience to write a book."

"Then do that instead of this. Kurnai Bay's too small for the promise of anonymity this sort of column needs to work."

Alice moved confidently around the familiar kitchen, grabbing a chopping board and a cook's knife before dicing the vegetables for the stir-fry. "I disagree. The *Gazette* covers a pretty big area and I only need one question a week. I thought I'd get the ball rolling using our awesome ground rules as a template for how to do friends with benefits well."

A horrified look filled his face. "I don't think so."

"Why not? It could help others."

"I'm not interested in helping others. This is the bay. Think about it. People won't read it for advice, they'll read it as a challenge to work out who the couple is. It will replace trivia night at the pub!"

"Instead of name that tune, they can play name that couple." Alice laughed at her own joke. "You never know, it might cheer everyone up after the disappointment of not getting the funding for the women's football change rooms."

"It's not funny."

"I know. They've waited patiently for three years."

"I'm not talking about the community development grant." Dan rarely looked serious, but right now he was glowering as darkly as a blond man could.

It surprised her he was still talking about the column. "No one is going to connect us."

"You don't know that."

"I know that the information I'm actively dating's not a secret. It doesn't matter if I go to a pub or a café in Bairnsdale, Marlo or anywhere else in between I run into people from the bay." She bumped him playfully with her hip, wanting fun-loving Dan back. "The only reason you're worried about word getting out is that winter's reduced you to sleeping with someone your own age."

"I'm serious, Alice. Don't write about FWB in the column."

"Fine." His reaction confused her. He'd suggested their "friends with benefits" arrangement and been totally up front with her about not wanting a long-term relationship or kids. Or was he only open about that with her? Like Alice, Dan had grown up in a tight and loving family and he too had a mother who was not backward with her point of view.

"Is this about Hilary?"

Dan opened the fridge and handed her a cider before twisting the top off a beer for himself. "If there's a biological clock dictating a woman's desire to have a kid, then there's definitely one for a menopausal woman wanting grandchildren. Mom's fixated on becoming a grandmother and she's on the warpath."

"Hasn't that been happening for the last year?"

"Yep. But she's moved on from making casual suggestions and stepped up to full-on matchmaking. Invitations are being issued as we speak."

Alice scraped the onions into the hot pan, considering how this news affected them. She'd hoped to keep their arrangement going until the summer as originally planned, especially if the cream Lacey Chu had prescribed meant they could explore more than one position. She planned to test drive it tonight. But sex aside, it was Dan's undemanding friendship she valued most. It made a refreshing change from the current problems in her family.

"Who's she got in mind?"

"You."

"Me?" Her voice hit an unappealing pitch.

"Why so surprised? You're attractive, well-educated, funny and you want kids. That's catnip for my mother."

"But it's not catnip for you so—"

"Three out of four is catnip for me."

Dan propped a hip on the counter next to the stove. The stance was casual but it showcased his toned body to perfection and his eyes sparkled at her. A flash of desire shot through her and she wondered about abandoning dinner for sex. Then her stomach grumbled, reminding her she was starving. If they didn't eat first, she'd miss out on dinner, because sharing a meal after sex moved into couple territory. Neither of them wanted that.

She reduced the heat under the onions and between them. "Why don't you tell Hilary you're not interested in commitment or children?"

For a moment he looked like the sandy-haired little boy who'd once clung to his mother's hand at kinder drop-off. "I don't want to disappoint her."

"But she's already disappointed."

"No. She's hopefully frustrated."

"What's the difference?"

He lifted the spatula out of her hand and added the other ingredients to the wok. "There's a lot of pressure being the first born. Something you wouldn't understand, Twin Two."

Being the slower second twin came with its own pressures, but Alice didn't enlighten him. "But I thought your parents were okay with Bram coming out."

"They are. But the way Mom sees it, Bram has to jump through a lot more hoops to have a kid so it's easier for me to give her the grandchild she craves. Plus, I live here and Bram's in Melbourne. I've been hoping time would do the job and she'd eventually just give up on the idea, but now you're back in town and she's hell bent on getting us together. That's why, when you get around to checking your email, there'll be an invitation for Sunday lunch."

"I—"

"Before you suggest that politely declining will solve the problem, Hil will keep at it until you capitulate. We may as well get it over with sooner than later. It should be easy enough to have a decent argument about politics. You can call me a few choice names and that will let her down gently."

"That's not really my style."

"I know. You retreat from conflict. But this is your chance to stand up for yourself in a safe and controlled environment." He winked at her. "So really, I'm looking after both you and Mom. I promise I'll bring good wine."

Alice felt unexpected sympathy for Hilary. "Sorry, Dan, but I've got plans this Sunday."

He pressed his hand over his heart. "You can't put some random bloke you barely know ahead of a good mate."

She laughed, mostly immune to the repertoire of actions and phrases he used to get what he wanted. "I'm not standing you up for a random bloke. I'm keeping a promise to Holly Waxman. We're experimenting with clay."

Dan sighed and dished up the meal. "And this is exactly my point. Kids get in the way of everything."

Alice appreciated it when Dan said things like this. It kept her grounded on the few occasions her post-sex hormones built castles in the air. "We could argue about that in front of your mother on Saturday night if you like."

"You're hilarious." He twirled some noodles onto his fork. "Let's workshop your first column so it kicks ass and encourages people to send in questions."

Her heart gave an odd kick. No! She reminded herself this wasn't Dan being supportive. This was self-interest—he was making sure she didn't use their experience in the column. She was not going to be one of those women who let herself fall for a man who couldn't offer her what she wanted. This was fun, pure and simple and right now she needed it.

"How about we eat fast and have sex instead?"

He shot her his best smile. "You're on."

An hour later, Alice rolled off him, grinning like an idiot as relief consumed her. The cream Lacey had prescribed worked like a charm.

"Thank God. I thought you might have traded me in by now for a newer model."

"You're safe until summer," Dan teased before giving her a long and considered look. "You know I've got no complaints, Twin Two, and surely the most important thing is that you're more comfortable?"

She knew she should agree but she felt herself prevaricate.

"Alice, Alice, Alice." Dan shook his head as if she'd just failed a test. "You've gotta demand your rights in and out of bed."

"I'm getting better at it."

He kissed her lightly on the forehead. "Keep practicing."

Jess shivered and checked on Leo. Thankfully, he was fast asleep, his cheeks flushed pink. She'd dressed him in a fleecy onesie and tucked him into a sleeping bag, because he was a restless sleeper and she didn't want him to wake up cold. Maybe she'd overcompensated for the lack of heat? Deciding not to wake him, she returned to the living room and her gaze immediately strayed to the bottle of rum. Three days earlier, born out of the fear of becoming her mother, she'd drawn a line on the label indicating how much she could drink in a week. The level of the tawny brown liquid already matched the line.

"That was before we risked freezing to death." She poured herself another rum and Coke and wrapped herself in a blanket. Sitting on the couch, she sipped the drink, soaking up the heat of the alcohol streaming through her veins and warming her from the inside out. According to KB Radio, today was the coldest day Kurnai Bay had experienced in a decade. Not the day for the heater to fail. She'd left the house at seven thirty that morning and returned eleven hours later, hungry, tired and with a toddler exhausted from hours in daycare, to find the house was an ice box. The automatic ignition on the heater had never worked so Jess had tried to light the pilot using a taper just like Nick always did—had done—whenever it blew out. It refused to light for her and with the realtor closed for the day, she had little choice but to wait until eight thirty the following morning. Even then, the landlord always dragged his feet.

Meanwhile, she was alone and chilled to the bone in an old clapboard house without insulation. This wasn't the life she'd envisaged for herself. Or for Leo. Six months earlier, she'd have picked up the phone and called Libby, who'd have sent Nick over with his tool box. He'd have fixed the problem then stayed for conversation and cake. Stayed to see Leo.

The rum in her blood soared high on indignation and for the first time in weeks, Jess gave in to temptation. She tapped out a furious email on her phone.

Dr. Hunter, the heater's on the fritz and Nick's son is freezing. If Leo gets sick, you'll have child abuse on your conscience. Do the right thing and send Nick around to fix it.

The moment the email vanished into the ether, her mood dropped like a stone. The Hunter-Pirellis might have created an email account exclusively for her to contact them, but it didn't mean they responded instantly. Or even by the end of the day. There was a minimum two-day turnaround and it drove her insane. How dare they treat family like this!

Her eyes strayed to the email she'd received over a week ago, the subject title, Access. The email she was yet to answer. Her anger surged as it did every time she thought about its contents. Nothing about it was conciliatory or cooperative. Nothing about it resembled the love and care that Libby had promised her when she'd begged her to leave Sydney and return to the bay. The love she and Leo had known during their first year. It had been the love Leo deserved and Jess desperately wanted him to know, because it was the opposite of her own childhood.

No, this email was a list of demands. Jess Dekic would do A, B and C, and Nick Pirelli would do D, E and F. Legal action would be taken if Jess did G, H, I or J. Third parties would be involved. Negotiation was off the table. It was Libby's way or no way.

On top of Libby exposing Leo's parentage to the town's scrutiny, actively encouraging their friends to exclude Jess, and the vitriolic letter stripping her of the title and role of godmother to Indi and Lucy —who she loved like daughters—did she think Jess would just roll over and agree to the limited and unsatisfactory access arrangements? Did her former best friend think that because she decreed it, everyone would fall into line?

"Stuff this." She dialed Libby's number. She might have been blocked, meaning her texts were never delivered or her calls answered, but she could still leave voicemail.

"You told me you don't want to have anything to do with Nick's son. That means you gave up your right to dictate terms. Nick and I decide what's best for Leo."

Nick and I ...

Jess's twenty-second summer had been a watershed. Libby was in Peru doing an elective as part of her medical degree. Without her company in the bay, Jess had planned to stay in Melbourne during her enforced work break between Christmas and New Year. Her mother had other ideas.

"I'm the only family you've got. You'd be a cruel bitch if you let your mother spend Christmas on her own." Linda's sharp words burned down the line before changing to wheedling. "I've already got the fruit soaking for the plum pudding."

It was an annual tradition for Linda to soak the fruit in a cup of brandy and herself in the rest of the bottle. Over the years, Jess had thrown the fruit out after Christmas more times than a pudding had ever been made. As she listened to her mother, Jess glanced at the tiny live Christmas tree in a pot and the beautifully wrapped gift Libby had left underneath it with the instructions, "Don't open it until Christmas morning." The house suddenly seemed quiet and empty, as it would be on December 25th.

"Come home," Linda said. "It'll be nice. I miss you."

And just like that, Jess made the long drive back to Kurnai Bay.

Her mother managed to excel herself that year. She was sozzled by noon and incapable of eating the lunch Jess had prepared. Furious at Linda, and at herself for believing things might be different this year, Jess avoided her mother as much as possible for the rest of the vacation, spending her days on the beach and her nights at the usual shack parties. While she waited for Nick to show, she fended off the usual suspects of drunk blokes, some of whom had more reason to hope than others. Nick didn't turn up to any of the parties.

When New Year's Eve tipped into New Year's Day—an assignation they'd shared enough times for her to consider it a tradition —and Nick still hadn't made an appearance, she finally cracked and asked Trent Fallon, "Where's Pirelli these days?"

"He was only ever playing at slumming it with us. These days he's drinking the good stuff with the other rich kids at the yacht club."

The next day, Jess visited the pier at various times until she ran into Nick. Dressed in the Pirelli summer uniform of navy polo shirt, white shorts and boat shoes, nothing about him showed even a hint of the good-time boy she'd known and enjoyed. His stance stated he owned the pier, the fleet and the respect of the town. His g'day was polite but restrained, his gaze just off-center. Clearly, he was uncomfortable talking to her.

Memories assaulted her. The two of them laughing together. Her sitting on his lap at parties, his arm flung casually around her waist. The time he said it was her "no bullshit, take-charge attitude" he found as sexy as hell.

Now he couldn't bear to look at her, but it was his embarrassment that slashed and scarred her heart. Made her feel dirty. That night she got drunk for the first time in a long time. It was Will Azzopardi who took her home, held back her hair while she puked, then plied her with water. It was her reflection in the mirror the following morning—a young version of Linda before the ravages of alcohol had wrought their worst—and her mother's tart comment about being a drunk slut that had shocked her out of her pity party.

She realized Nick was returning to his roots and answering the call of the preceding generations of Pirellis, who lived by the rules of society—hard-working, law-abiding, honorable citizens who put family first. Everything Linda had failed at. Now Nick associated Jess with partying hard, recreational drugs and questionable choices. Not only did he want to leave all that far behind him, he wanted to forget.

The devastating irony was that, in so many ways, Jess had left her white trash life far behind, qualifying as an accountant and securing a well-paying job. She only dropped into the old crowd and the parties when she visited the bay so she could see Nick. But if Jess wanted him, she needed to show him she'd left that life far behind too and that she belonged in his world. But how? Linda's legacy of being thrown out of almost every venue in town meant Jess never received a warm welcome unless she attended with Libby.

Her gut churned at the idea of involving Libby and her WASP respectability to get close to Nick. Every survival instinct told her not to introduce them. No, there had to be another way to ooze into Nick's world.

When Will called in later that morning to see how she was feeling, his visit and solicitude took her completely by surprise. She'd only met him a couple of times—he'd moved to the bay since she'd left—but if his actions were anything to go by he was a decent enough bloke. Embarrassed that he'd seen her heave her stomach contents into the toilet, she offered to buy him a burger and a beer as a thank you. He accepted the burger but declined the beer, drinking sparkling mineral water instead. They sat by the estuary, each with a Kurnai Bay burger with the lot, watching pelicans and cormorants diving for their lunch.

"Do you sail?" Will asked.

"I'd love the opportunity." It was a phrase she used to show her interest and mask a childhood that had prevented her from taking advantage of activities many took for granted.

"Can you follow instructions and wind a winch?"

"Possibly to the first and yes to the second."

He grinned, his smile endearingly crooked. "Great. We're short-handed for tonight's twilight race, if you're up for it."

"Who's we?"

"Nick Pirelli and me."

"I'd love to come."

For the first time in her life, Jess truly believed the universe was smiling on her.

Now Jess pulled the blanket more tightly around her, trying to ward off not only the chill, but the loneliness that had been walking alongside her for months. She considered eating dinner, but she wasn't hungry. That was probably a good thing. Lately, no matter if she ate healthy food or binged on junk, everything seemed to go straight to her belly. Was that part of being thirty-four? She must get back to regular exercise, but the thought of walking and running reminded her of Libby and the loneliness intensified. No, she needed to do some exercise that didn't remind her of Libby. Yoga? A strong core helped, so maybe she should start with some sit-ups right now.

Jess unwrapped herself and spread the blanket on the floor to cushion the hard boards and lay on her back. She stretched her arms up toward her knees but her stomach felt in the way. She sucked it in and focused on her core. Lifting her shoulders off the floor, she started counting. "One, two, three. Sweet mother—!"

A sharp and twisting spasm started just above her pubic bone and ricocheted with lightning speed into her groin before blasting out of her into the floor. It immobilized her, stealing her breath and sending stars dancing across her vision. When it finally faded, she blew out a long, slow breath, gingerly rolled onto all fours and gradually stood up. She poured herself another drink, rationalizing it was medicinal. Still tender—it felt as if someone had punched her—she snuggled back on the couch and gave herself over to the delicious rum haze. It was like drifting with Will in an inner tube on a warm current.

I love you just the way you are. Will's words made her smile. Whenever she obsessed about a few extra kilos, he always said soppy stuff like that. With his shaved head and weight-toned muscles from staving off boredom at the drilling platform's gym, he might look like a tough nut, but he was far more puppy than wolf. With everything that had been going on, Jess hadn't spoken to him recently. Was this an offshore two-week stint or an onshore one? She sent him a message—*I need some Will*—and watched for the three wiggly dots, anticipating his reply.

Her phone rang, vibrating in her hand and making her jump. "Hi, Will." Her voice sounded loud in her ears.

"Hey, Jess. You okay?"

"I'm freezing. Come over and warm me up."

"I thought we'd stopped doing drunk booty calls."

She wound hair around her fingers. "I'm not drunk. I just miss you. It's been ages."

"Whose fault's that?"

Her rum buzz told her he was just being playful. "My bad."

He sighed. "You're calling me because of all this shit with Nick and Libby, aren't you?"

"No! And it's not like I haven't spoken to you since—" *Everything went to hell.* "—I'm calling because I miss you."

He gave a long sigh. "Come on, Jess. After everything that's happened, can't you at least be honest with me?"

"I am being honest. I miss my mate."

"And that's always been the problem." The loaded silence was filled with his hurt and disappointment. Eventually, he cleared his throat. "Remember that woman I told you about?"

The rum had reached her brain, fuddling her thoughts. "Remind me again."

"Casey."

"Have I met her?" Over the years, whenever she and Will were on one of their many breaks, he would introduce her to his girlfriends. She found it reassuring. "She's not the one obsessed with cats, is she?"

"That was Jasmine and two cats is hardly an obsession."

"If you say so."

"The important thing is, Casey and I are serious."

Jess had heard Will tell her "it's serious" half-a-dozen times. The statement was always followed by a "but" and then came the detailed explanation of his concerns. The conversation always ended with her telling him that when he met The One, they wouldn't be having this conversation. Invariably, they ended up in bed. Her fingers tingled with the tell-tale sign of chilblains—a sensation she hadn't experienced since she was a kid.

"... best. I'm moving to Sale."

Jess had been so busy trying to stay warm that she'd missed hearing Will's problem with Casey. She grasped at something to cover. "Um, but you've got a beautiful house here."

"It's being listed at the end of the week."

"But you hate Sale."

"I don't hate Sale. I was born there." Will's voice was unusually firm.

"Why would you move and give up that gorgeous view? It sounds like Casey's putting a lot of pressure on you. Don't rush things you might regret, especially when all your friends are here."

"Jess." His sigh reverberated down the line. "Are you really going to make me spell it out?"

The first ripples of unease fluttered in the pit of her stomach. "Is it because Sale's closer to Longford?"

"No. It's because it's two hours away from you."

The words walloped her like the burning sting of one of Linda's lover's belts. Her thoughts staggered under the assault. "Will—"

"I want to give this thing with Casey my best shot. I can't do that with you in my life."

"Of course you can. We're friends!"

"We're not."

"Don't be ridiculous—"

"I'm not. You only ever dated me because I'm Nick's mate."

"That's not true and you know it."

"I know I've been blind for years, but since I found out Nick is Leo's father, it's pretty clear you've accepted my love as a way to stay close to him. When Libby married him, you took off to Sydney without a second thought for me, but you didn't let me go. I was too convenient, especially when Libby was hell bent on us becoming the ying couple to their yang."

"What do you mean I didn't let you go? You kept coming back to me."

His voice cracked. "Did you laugh when I wanted to be your husband and Leo's father?"

"No, of course not!"

"Yeah, right. I've been so stupid. Since you came back, you've virtually been living with the Pirellis, so you didn't need me or any other bloke, did you? Jesus! I even defended you when Nick complained you'd moved into their marriage. Our friendship took a big hit over that. It's still not back to what it was."

Fear raced through her. Will had never been this blunt with her before. "I don't know why you're talking like this. None of it's close to true. We're friends. We've been close friends for years."

"Maybe once, but not anymore. Casey's right. The last few years have been toxic and damaging."

"That's an outright lie!" Her brain whirled, seeking examples. "When your father died, I took a week's leave and flew down from Sydney. I did the same thing after the explosion on the platform and when—"

"We're done, Jess. It's over."

"Don't be stu—" The line went dead, leaving the sounds of silence buzzing loud in her ear. The rum and Coke turned rancid in her stomach, then rose to burn the back of her throat. She determinedly pushed it back down.

"He doesn't mean it," she said to the wall.

Except, even after their worst ever argument when she'd fled to Sydney after Libby's wedding, he'd never called her toxic. She wasn't toxic! She'd been a good and faithful friend to him for all the reasons she'd just told him, and then some. Back in the days when she had money, she'd even given him a short-term loan when he was buying his house to avoid a costly double mortgage. God!

It wasn't her fault she'd fallen in love with Nick, any more than it was Will's for falling in love with her. Hell, he should be grateful she'd been a true friend and protected him by refusing his proposal. Where did he get off calling her toxic?

You don't know the meaning of the word friendship. Libby's accusation played faintly in the back of her mind. Before Jess met Libby, Linda had moved them so often that she'd never invested in friendships. If Linda's relationships with her friends were anything to go by, friendship involved drinking, acrimony, verbal abuse, stolen PIN numbers and the occasional punch. Jess had enough of that going on inside the house with Linda and her boyfriends so why open herself to more heartache and hurt?

But Libby had been determined to be friends. At first it was Libby's physical generosity Jess found attractive, but it was her emotional generosity that tempted Jess to let her in. It opened her to a form of friendship she'd never known before and she cautiously gave some of herself, waiting for it to come back to bite her. It didn't. It was a shock to realize that being open actually made her feel better about herself. For the first time in her life, she'd thought beyond herself. She'd been generous and giving in her friendships with Libby and Will, caring for them both and going the extra mile every time.

And now, after years of them happily accepting her love, support and loyalty, they said it counted for nothing?

What the hell did people expect from her?

CHAPTER SIXTEEN

Karen scanned the park, wondering if Jess would show up as arranged. According to Libby, getting to this point had been rocky.

"The bitch isn't happy about it," Libby had said when she'd outlined the terms and conditions of Karen's offer to be Leo's conduit.

Karen flinched. "Sweetheart, don't you think that term demeans you?"

"If you knew the BS that woman's been pulling over the last few weeks, you'd be calling her a bitch too! She's leaving vitriolic voicemails at 2:00 a.m. Her emails are horrible. You won't believe this, but she thinks she should be able to drop him off at Burrunan!"

Of course Jess was railing at having all the access arrangements for her son taken out of her hands. If Libby was in a similar situation, she'd be fighting tooth and nail too, but the red haze of her daughter's anger clouded everything.

"What if Jess dropped Leo off at Pelican House?" Karen suggested, looking for a work-around that might diminish Jess's blocking behavior without raising Libby's hackles.

"No. Nick and I agreed it has to be somewhere neutral. The park works because if it's wet, the library's next door. Not that she agrees. When we wouldn't budge on the drop-off, she started trying to change the day and time."

"Sometimes things come up."

"Mom! We've talked about this. She doesn't get to set the boundaries. The only reason she's trying to change everything is because she wants access to Nick. That's *never* going to happen. She's deluded if she thinks she can be part of the visit and play happy families."

"Darling, I'm sure if Jess felt more involved she'd be less antagonistic. Perhaps if you compromised on some of the arrangements, things would be a lot less fraught for all of you."

Libby's eyes flashed. "Whose side are you on? You know I've made the biggest compromise in allowing the access visits."

Talking to Libby these days took more diplomacy than the Middle East peace talks. It was a constant battle to steer the conversation toward reason without risking Libby getting upset. As Alice was currently persona non grata with her twin, Karen was desperately trying to effect change without upsetting Libby.

"I'm worried you're making things harder for yourself." *I'm worried you're pushing everyone who loves you away.*

"Harder? I'm taking back control of my life." Once, it had been rare to see such a look of granite on her elder daughter's happy face, but now it appeared whenever Libby talked about Jess and Leo. This raging hatred stole Libby's humanity and looked worryingly familiar. It was reminiscent of everything in Karen's childhood she'd kept hidden from the twins. She'd been determined to shelter them from the uglier parts of life and she'd fought hard to shower them with unconditional love—something she'd had to learn from Peter and his family. But for the first time as a mother, she was questioning if she'd made the right choice. Perhaps if she'd carefully chosen one or two stories to use as examples when the twins were growing up instead of hiding everything, it might have prevented Libby changing into this controlling and vindictive woman.

She tried again. "Don't you think that by choosing not to be involved with Leo, you're opening up an opportunity for Jess to gate crash a visit?"

"If she does that, all visits are off."

"And Nick agreed to that?"

But Libby was called to an emergency and Karen had left the clinic.

Now she squinted into the weak winter sunshine and finally picked out Leo standing at the bottom of the slide on the opposite side of the park.

Halfway over Karen called out, "Hello, Jess."

The younger woman turned and for a split second Karen didn't recognize her. Jess's usually well made-up face was puffy and devoid of makeup and her shiny chestnut curls hung dull and limp around her pale face. Her trim waist had thickened and instead of wearing tailored pants or her signature tight jeans, she was clad in cheap and shapeless track pants.

The hairs on Karen's arms raised in a jolt of sensation. Jess looked exactly like Linda the first time Karen had met her. Was Jess drinking like Linda? Karen's heart ached at the thought.

"Hi, Leo."

The little boy's big brown eyes, so much like Nick's, gave her a long and solemn stare. Then he suddenly got shy and hid his face against his mother's legs.

Not the best start. Karen bobbed down so she was at his level. "Would you like a swing?"

He tilted his head, considering the offer.

"I can push you and Mommy can watch."

Leo let go of Jess's leg and ran to the swing. Jess strode after him and Karen noticed she flinched as she lowered him into the bucket seat.

"Sore back? Lifting a toddler up and down all day is like hefting sacks of potatoes."

Jess didn't reply so Karen turned her attention to Leo. "Here we go." She pushed him gently.

Leo squealed in delight. "More."

"I thought Libby would have instructed you to grab him and run," Jess said bitterly.

"I thought you wanted him to spend time with his father."

"I do. It's not an unreasonable request that his father pick him up."

Karen didn't want this first pick-up to devolve into an argument over Jess's inability to understand that her action of conceiving with Nick meant she was no longer welcomed into Libby's family the way she'd once been. She focused on Leo instead.

"I want Leo to trust me, not fear me. I want him to associate me with fun not dread. A bit of a play here before we leave will help." Karen lightly touched Jess's arm. "So will him seeing you happy with me."

Jess sighed and unfolded her arms. "It's a shame your daughter doesn't think the same way as you."

"Well, we're not in the same situation, are we?"

"Leo is your grandson."

Technically, he wasn't. But as Karen had often been a stand-in mother to teenage Jess, she didn't have the heart to say it. "I want us to make this transfer a positive experience for the three of us."

Jess stared into the middle distance. "I didn't think it would be this hard."

Having a married man's child? Losing your best friend? Being ostracized by half the town? Sole parenting? "What would be this hard?"

"Leo spending time with Nick without me. Me not knowing what they're doing. And Leo's not old enough to tell me!"

Oh, Jess. Karen's heart bled for the confused and lonely woman who reminded her of herself before she'd met Peter. Although Karen understood Jess was accountable for her actions, the memories of her own parents' zealotry could still lance her with pain. She had a sudden and violent urge to bring Linda back from the dead and scream, "How could you have let her down so badly?"

The professionals, with their middle-class life experience and privileges, might dole out advice such as "Every parent does the best job they can given their circumstances", but that didn't make up for the massive damage some parents inflicted upon their children. Linda had not only let down Jess by failing to provide her with safety and security, but also by randomly giving and taking away her love and affection. Had it left Jess floundering in a moral and ethical morass when it came to the responsibilities inside friendships and intimate relationships? All Karen knew was her own parents had inflicted their warped religion and love on her but thankfully, she'd found Peter and Dot to love and guide her.

And Lisa?

Guilt screwed down so hard and fast, Karen almost cried out. She'd failed her sister. Had she failed Jess too? When Jess was a teen, Karen had tried to help and guide her, but Jess had never lived with them and seen the daily negotiations and choices that go hand in hand with a functioning relationship. Once, when Libby was seventeen, Karen had tried to point out to her daughter some of the problems that can arise from such an exclusive friendship. It had not gone down well.

"How would you know, Mom? It's not like you even have a best friend!"

And she didn't have a best friend. Her shuttered childhood had precluded making friends and she'd never really learned how. As an adult, she had plenty of female acquaintances, but not a best friend. Karen wanted to use Alice as an example of someone who had a few different friends, but immediately saw the flaw in that argument— Alice craved from Libby the same friendship Libby had with Jess.

As the years ticked over and the friendship flourished, Karen had thankfully concluded that unlike many women, Libby and Jess knew how to maintain their friendship. So, when Jess had returned to Kurnai Bay, Karen believed she loved Libby to the best of her ability. She just hadn't realized Jess loved Nick too—none of them had twigged to that. Yet now, it was glaringly obvious to anyone who looked that Jess had loved both Libby and Nick for years.

"And what the hell is wrong with Libby?" Jess said. "One minute I'm family and we're loving and mothering each other's children and the next she's treating Leo like he doesn't exist. How can she turn her love on and off like that and hurt my gorgeous boy? Hurt her daughters? I know they miss Leo and me."

Karen agreed with Jess that Libby was putting her own needs ahead of the children—it was the driving force behind her offer to do the transfers. But loyalty stopped her from saying so. She focused on the job at hand. "This afternoon will go quickly. It's only three hours. Have you got something nice planned?"

"Oh, yeah. I'm getting my eyes tested."

"Good idea. I used to split up the trinity."

Jess looked confused.

"All the check-ups. Doctor, dentist and optometrist. It's important to look after yourself."

"I need to find a new doctor," Jess said pointedly. "Your caring daughter is insisting Leo comes home at 6:oo. By then it's cold and dark. Can you bring him home to me instead of doing this BS transfer in the park?"

She doesn't get to set the boundaries. Libby's voice rang loud and clear. Karen opened her mouth to say, "I'm sorry," but she noticed the fine lines of strain and the black shadows under Jess's eyes. Images of Linda's alcohol-ravaged face were followed by Lisa's deathly pallor. A weight pressed on her chest. This situation was already difficult enough without it spiraling further out of control. At least if she returned Leo to the house she could look for tell-tale signs of Jess's drinking. Karen owed Jess that care and concern. Owed it to Leo.

"I can do that."

Jess's eyes widened in surprise. "I didn't think you'd agree."

"It's my one concession. Please don't ask for any more." Karen lifted Leo out of the swing.

"I never told Libby about your mother," Jess said abruptly.

Karen wondered at the fact Jess felt honor bound to keep that secret for all these years yet she justified sleeping with Nick to have Leo.

Jess kissed Leo's head. "I won't tell Libby about this either."

"Thank you."

Karen added yet another secret to a lifelong pile.

⚓

ALICE PULLED UP OUTSIDE THE WAXMANS'. USUALLY, HARRY dropped Holly off at Pelican House, giving Alice a cursory wave from the car as Holly jumped out. Now the weather was improving, Alice wanted to take Holly to the silt jetties. It didn't make sense for Harry to schlep all the way out there so she'd offered to collect her. As Alice turned off the ignition, her phone beeped.

She checked the message and her heart swooped into overdrive, racing heat all over her.

Hi, Alice, I know your first reaction will be to delete this but I'd love it if we could talk and I could explain.

Months had passed since Tim went silent on her, but she still remembered the heady excitement she'd gotten just from anticipating his calls, let alone the electrifying connection they'd shared. The conversations that lasted hours. The way his voice made her go weak at the knees and took her a good way down the path toward an orgasm. Despite all the men she'd spoken to and met since, none had come close to generating the same feelings Tim could create with one text.

But it had been such a long time since he'd last made contact. What would she reply to someone who wrote to her column: *Dear Alice, this guy I really like behaved like a total dick. Now he wants to reconnect. What should I do? Confused.*

Dear Confused, perhaps he wants to apologize and start over. Everyone deserves a second chance. Alice.

Alice was already typing her reply to Tim when a completely new internal voice chimed in. *Sure, give him a second chance but don't be needy. Do it on your terms. Let him stew for a bit.*

Her fingers slowed but it took real effort to completely stop. She closed the message app and shoved her phone deep into her bag where she wouldn't be tempted to look at it. Turning her mind to Holly, she got out of the car and crossed the road. As she opened the Waxmans' side gate, she pulled a dog treat out of her pocket.

"Hey, Brutus," she said softly, approaching slowly. "I bought you a Schmackos."

The lanky greyhound backed up, his body shaking all over. Alice sighed and put the treat back into her pocket.

A smiling Harry appeared at the back door. "Nice idea, Alice, but he has a complicated relationship with food."

"He has a complicated relationship with everything."

Today was Alice's third visit to the house and each time, without success, she tried something different to lessen the neurotic dog's fear of her. She thought of McDougall, her parents' enthusiastically friendly border collie, and of Libby's mutt, Monty. Both dogs were great with people.

"Exactly why is Brutus a good pet?"

"He makes us look and feel emotionally healthy."

Alice laughed. She was learning Harry had a wicked sense of humor when he chose to unleash it. "The superiority effect?"

"Pretty much. Come in."

The house was in a much neater state than previous visits and the scent of melted sugar and chocolate wafted on the air. She noticed jars of daffodils, freesias and jonquils scattered around the living area—the sirens of spring. "I see Holly's been busy decorating."

"Sorry?"

"The flowers."

"No, I picked those. The garden's exploding with color. Take some."

Her mother's garden was mostly natives these days and although Alice knew that was best for the local fauna and water consumption, she missed the bulbs. "Thank you! I'd love to. I'll pick them up when I drop Holly back at 6:oo."

"Do you have a hot date tonight?"

"No, that's Thursdays," she said absently.

Harry's brows rose. "Lucky for us it's Wednesday then. When you get back from the jetties, why don't you stay for dinner?"

The invitation was as unexpected as Harry's cheerful and upbeat manner. *What about Tim?* Even if she'd replied to his text, they wouldn't be meeting for dinner. And Harry was suggesting family dinner on a school night. She'd be home by 9:00 at the latest, which left plenty of time for a long conversation with Tim.

"Sure, why not? Sounds great."

"Excellent. The kids have been pestering me for ages to invite you. So, how are things?"

The last time she'd said more than "hi" and "bye" to Harry had been at the coffee shop. "Things with Libby are still a bit rocky, but otherwise, all good."

Judging by Harry's face, he didn't believe her. "What?"

"I've been following your Dear Alice column. If those scenarios are what you're dealing with, I'm surprised dating hasn't reduced you to a dribbling mess."

"Those questions are from readers!"

"I wouldn't have thought the bay was big enough."

He sounded just like Dan. "Okay, fine. You got me. There's been the occasional quiet week when I've mined my own experience to create a question."

"Please tell me the one about dating the separated guy who's still living with his wife wasn't one of yours."

Her irritation spiked. "I'm not an idiot, Harry. How about you stick to fathering your own kids, not me, okay?"

"I didn't mean—" His hands rose in supplication. "Sorry. How about a peace offering? A cuppa?"

Alice's surprise spurt of anger had faded as fast as it had arrived, leaving her feeling foolish. "Sounds great. And I'm sorry. I didn't realize I was quite so sensitive about that particular Q&A. I got hate mail."

"Why? Your answer was spot on. That woman's deluding herself if she thinks he's separated and putting her first."

"She didn't agree. And she told me using a lot of four-letter words."

"Ouch. That's never pleasant, but it says more about her than you."

"Thanks." Alice sat down and realized the house was far too quiet. "Where are the kids?"

"Hunter's got Bike Ed so we've been riding to and from school all week. This morning, my children announced I was *not* to come and pick them up."

"A strike at independence?"

"It's terrifying. I've spent the afternoon trying not to think about it." He indicated the tidy house, the crockpot and the cooling brownies on the rack. "I haven't been able to concentrate on work and if you weren't here, I'd be waiting at the end of the road."

"You can still do that if it makes you feel better."

"And bring the wrath of my kids down upon my head?" His mouth tweaked up on one side and she caught a hint of a dimple. "No, thanks. I did get them to promise on pain of never being allowed to leave the house again that they meet up and ride home together. I also got a blood pact from Hunter that he'll do what his sister tells him."

Alice thought about Hunter's impetuous enthusiasm and suppressed a shudder. "Do you want me to go and follow them home?"

"Good to know my terror's not completely unfounded. Then again, you're not exactly reassuring me."

"Sorry."

"No need. I appreciate your perspective. I keep telling myself that apart from the last hundred yards, they're using the bike trail."

"They'd be lucky to see a car."

"Now you're getting the hang of it."

"Hang of what?"

"Reassuring a neurotic father."

She laughed and he gave a wry smile. For the first time in all the months she'd known him, his face looked less careworn. The rest of him did not. Harry struck her as one of those blokes who had little interest in fashion and had let his wife buy his clothes. Alice's artistic eye scanned his generalized scruffy state and detected in the faded chinos and the worn collar on his shirt that Helene had been a fan of the designer casual look. Alice bet she'd bought those clothes before she'd gotten sick and that Harry hadn't bought any since.

"How do you take your tea?"

"White, no sugar." Her gaze landed on the stunning life-size bronze pelican that commanded the room. With its long beak facing the window and its wings slightly extended, it looked ready to commence a sea bound flight. It awed her every time she saw it.

"Your Helene was incredibly talented. Each time I look at the pelican I see some new detail."

"Yeah." Harry set down mugs of tea along with a plate of enormous chocolate brownies. "That pelican was her best work. I'm surprised she's not haunting me for keeping it."

"What do you mean?"

"She was negotiating to sell it to an art collector in Western Australia, but they hadn't agreed on a price. When she died, I pulled the pin on the sale. I think the kids need its presence in the house."

"Just the kids?"

"Mostly. I've got a lot more years of H memories to draw on than they have." He pointed to the pot-bellied statue. "See the gold on the wing? That's from them stroking it whenever they pass."

"Polished with love." Sorrow jabbed her and was instantly overtaken by delight. Granted, art had the ability to shock and question, but the art that gave Alice the most were works that filled her and other people with joy and love. "Surely, Helene would be thrilled her pelican's in the heart of your home and working hard?"

"She'd prefer it to be working for cold, hard cash. H was what you'd call a creative capitalist. She loved the process, but once the work was complete, she didn't attach any sentimentality to it. She expected it to find its way in the world and earn her a decent amount of coin." Harry laughed. "I was the sappy one in the relationship. While H was out celebrating a sale, I'd be crating up the work and having a quiet cry that it was leaving the studio, never to be seen again."

As much as Alice tried, she couldn't imagine the often-taciturn Harry wearing his heart on his sleeve, but she understood his sentiment about art. "Not that I've sold a heap of paintings, but the few I've parted with have left me equally exhilarated and bereft."

"Talking of your work, I got your Clarendon homestead pen and wash framed. It's come up really well. I've hung it in the office."

Alice got a little shiver of delight that her painting had found a home. "Is it working hard?"

"It reminds me what will happen if I don't keep on top of the house maintenance and the gardening."

Her shiver flatlined. So much for her work having meaning. "That's something I suppose," she said morosely.

"Better than nothing." His teasing faded and his face settled into worn lines. "When H died, our home collapsed around us. Grief grew as rampantly as the garden you've painted invading the homestead. For a while, it was tempting to stay lost in the vines and weeds."

"And now?"

"We've pretty much got the grief garden under control. Finally having the kids settled helps. We still need to get the Roundup out occasionally for the weeds, but not as often." His voice deepened. "Every day your sketch shows me how far we've come."

A bucket of emotions tipped over inside Alice. She wasn't sure if it was sympathy for Harry that led the spill or gratitude for him giving thoughts and feelings to her work. "I'm really glad it's helping."

"Yeah." Harry cleared his throat. "You told me at Relay for Life that you hadn't drawn for a while. "You're too talented not to use that gift."

She thought about talent and her mother's push for her to return to the type of work she'd done for the Cahills. "Should we always do what we're good at, even if it doesn't fulfill us?"

"You don't enjoy sketching?"

"No, I do."

"I don't understand ..."

"Me neither. I've spent the last few years doing something people thought I should do. Something I'm talented at and generated some kudos in the industry, as well as paying the bills. Something my mother is very vocal about me returning to."

"Something that stopped you drawing?"

"Something or someone. A bit of both I think."

"Ah." He nodded slowly, as if joining the dots. "The three-year relationship."

Alice stared at him—part stunned, part horrified. "God, why haven't I made that connection before? I always said I was too busy with work and Lawrence to draw, but really, I stopped because it became too hard."

Harry's mouth tightened. "He didn't like you drawing?"

"I think it was more he didn't like who I become when I draw. I tend to disappear into my own world where time doesn't exist. Lawrence preferred me present in real time. I have a horrible feeling I let drawing slip away for an easier life."

"I hope you start again."

She smiled at him. "Already happening and it's all down to you. Working with Holly's helped me rediscover the joy, so thank you."

"Does that mean you've forgiven me for the unfair way I asked you to tutor her?"

She paused, needing a moment to work out what he was talking about. "Oh, that? I've got many faults but holding a grudge isn't one of them."

"Phew! That's good to know."

"All this time you thought I was still pissed off?"

He shrugged. "I was just checking. You're very good at letting me know when you're not happy."

"Am I?" Astonishment sat her back in the chair. "Generally, I suck at it. I wish I'd been better at it with Lawrence."

"If it helps, I think it's safe to say you've improved. A lot."

Embarrassment heated her face. "Sorry. Recently, D—a friend's been telling me to demand my rights. I didn't realize I was practicing on you."

"Happy to help. I think."

She smiled at his dry humor, but at the same time wondered what it was about Harry that made her stand up for herself. He was a grieving widower so surely that meant she should be kinder to him, not confrontational. Was she more direct with him because he had an uncanny knack of noticing things about her she thought she'd hidden? That him giving voice to them made her acutely uncomfortable? Or was it the fact there was no chemistry between them so she didn't censor herself for fear he'd walk away?

Her stomach dropped. Oh God. Was she one of those women who never asked for anything for fear of being abandoned? And yet she'd been abandoned anyway ...

"Alice?" Harry's voice sounded a long way away. "You okay?"

She nodded and bit into the brownie, desperate for the feel-good qualities of chocolate. It was a relief when Hunter and Holly tumbled through the door, chattering with the excitement of having ridden home alone.

⚓

THE HOTEL EVENTS ROOM WITH ITS WHITE CLOTH–COVERED tables, fresh flowers and luxury afternoon tea stand looked like many of the medical conferences Libby had attended over the years. The irony wasn't lost on her, given this weekend's live-in workshop was called Heal Your Marriage.

"Nervous?" Nick's hand shook slightly as he relieved her of an empty cup and saucer.

"Yep. You?"

"Same."

"We shouldn't be. It's not like we haven't sat down with a counselor before."

But they both knew far more was at stake this time.

It was day two of the weekend workshop and just like the day before, they'd spent the morning with the group, learning and practicing communication skills. They felt clunky and odd to Libby and when she and Nick had tried using them in a conversation, they'd both dissolved into laughter. Although laughing wasn't the aim, it had been the closest thing to normal she'd experienced with her husband in months. When they'd apologized to their mentor couple for cracking up, Liz and Jason had been sanguine, reassuring them that with practice, the tools would become second nature.

Now that the break was over, she and Nick were about to have a couple's session with the facilitators, Teresa and Chris. If it was anything like Libby's earlier individual session with Teresa, she'd need another fast swim in the hotel pool to exorcise the parade of emotions marching through her.

Nick held out his hand. "Ready?"

Libby looked at his wide hand, studying its familiar scatter of white scars—the legacy of a lifetime spent on boats. She thought about how once she'd never needed to think twice about holding it and accepting the love it represented. Teresa's voice from another session reminded her that for some couples being intimate after an affair took good will and practice. Libby had lacked both in recent months, including this weekend. She'd insisted on a hotel room with two separate beds.

But Libby prided herself on keeping her word. She'd promised Nick she wanted to try and save their marriage, although sometimes she wondered if that took more effort than walking away. Whenever she considered that, she focused on the girls, who loved their father. Her love for Nick still existed, although under her anger and despair, it had changed its shape and form to be almost unrecognizable.

Forcing herself to act, she slid her hand into Nick's. It was sweaty and, in an odd way, that was reassuring. "Ready."

During the session, Libby wondered if Nick regretted his insistence they spend $3,500 only to have more pain heaped upon him. Despite the room being on the cool side, circles of sweat stained his shirt.

"I want her to forgive me," Nick said.

"Can you forgive yourself?" Chris asked.

"It feels wrong to do that before Libby's forgiven me."

Libby silently agreed. Nick had hurt her and she decided when he was forgiven.

"It's not wrong," Chris said. "One mistake doesn't define a person and your mistake doesn't define you. From what you've told me individually and as a couple, you've made amends and committed to Libby and your children."

"I have."

"So why can't you forgive yourself?"

Nick's eyes were fixed on the intricate pattern woven into the plush carpet. His voice was soft. "Because when Libby looks at me, I see how much I've hurt her."

"Do you think there's more you could be doing?"

Nick threw a beseeching glance at Libby. "I'd do more if I knew what you wanted." He faced Chris. "Thing is, I'm out of ideas, so I just keep doing the same things over and over."

"And what are they?"

"Libby works long hours so I do a lot of the cooking and after-school activities with the girls. I've been trying hard to make home a pleasant place to be. I cook her favorite meals, buy her flowers, buy her books she might enjoy, give her time alone ..."

Chris turned to Libby, his features benign. "Do you feel this shows Nick's commitment to you and the marriage?"

"He's always done that stuff. He was doing it during the two years he knew he'd fathered a child with another woman!"

Chris didn't react to her outburst. "What more do you need Nick to do?"

Libby's fingers dug into the arms of the chair. "I don't know. I just wish he'd never done what he did."

Nick tugged at his hair. "So do I. You know I do. I keep telling you it's the biggest regret of my life. It's why I'm putting up with you punishing me by wanting to know where I am every minute of the day, and you asking me over and over what happened that night."

"It's very normal for a betrayed spouse to need those reassurances, Nick," Chris said smoothly. "Accepting it with grace is part of your commitment to Libby."

"Thank you!" Libby felt vindicated. "He needed to hear that."

"We've talked about anger and punishment, Libby," Chris said. "How it's normal to feel all those emotions at the time. But what we do with the anger is the important part. There comes a point when holding onto anger and pain causes more damage than the initial betrayal."

Libby thought of Leo. "That's not possible."

"Think of it like constantly picking at a scab. It prevents the wound from fully healing. That's counterproductive if you want the marriage to change, heal and grow." Chris leaned forward slightly. "And it's exhausting. Have you felt that?"

Libby hesitated, uncertain if she wanted to answer. She glanced at Nick, taking in his mix of contrition and sadness, but she couldn't miss the slither of aggravated discontent that ran through it. She sighed. "My anger's volcanic and it wrings me out. Sometimes I don't even recognize myself. I hate how it's controlling me."

"Learning how to control it takes time. If you try the different techniques we talked about yesterday, you'll work out which ones suit you and which don't. That way you can build up a repertoire. I strongly recommend your list includes meditation."

"I've already tried swimming. I was a lot calmer after twenty laps."

"That's great to hear," Teresa said. "There are always stressors in a marriage, but yours has borne the cyclonic gale of the two biggest traumas a relationship can experience. The death of a child and the arrival of an affair child—"

"It wasn't an affair!"

"Nick," Teresa said firmly, unfazed by his protest. "Does calling it something else lessen the impact on your marriage?"

He sat back in his chair, shame circling him. "No. But can we please refer to Leo by name?"

"Affair child works for me," Libby muttered.

"You sound angry, Libby," Teresa said.

"You think!" She heard herself and blew out a long breath, seeking calm. "Sorry. It's just ... right now, it's taking everything I've got to work on our relationship. I can't deal with the child too."

"But he—"

"Nick, can you hear Libby?" Teresa interrupted.

"Yes."

"Sometimes couples try to rush to fix everything all at once. It inevitably sinks them. Right now, you need to respect Libby's feelings regarding Leo just as she's respected yours with your current access arrangements. Does that sound fair?"

Nick's leg jiggled up and down, a clear sign he was reluctant to reply. "I s'pose."

"Libby, do you commit to revisiting this when you're stronger as a couple?"

Faced with the force of the question, Libby understood Nick's reluctance. "I suppose."

"Good." Teresa smiled. "Okay, so back to what I was saying before. Based on what you've told us both individually and as a couple, the months after Dom's death were understandably the most difficult you've ever faced as a couple. Grief changes our brain chemistry and can alter our thinking. When two people are hurting at the same time, often neither is in a position to help the other."

"Libby's the strongest and most together person I know," Nick said. "She's never needed help before and I didn't know what to do to help me cope, let alone help her. Whatever I tried, it felt like it wasn't enough and I watched her moving away from me. We'd lost our baby, but it was a double whammy, because I felt I was losing my best friend too."

His words bumped against Libby like gentle waves on *Freedom*'s hull. They didn't accuse or blame, they merely existed. Just as Nick's feelings existed. She didn't know what to do with them.

"Would you like to speak to any of this, Libby?" Teresa asked.

Her fingers twiddled with the bracelet Nick had given her on their fifth anniversary—a happy time when thoughts of being mired deep in a marriage crisis were so unimaginable, it would have been laughable to think it possible. Yet here they both were, hurt and bleeding.

I watched her moving away from me.

It jolted Libby to realize that some of her rage at Nick might be redirected anger from that time of darkness when her world had caved in for the first time. "I didn't just lose a baby, I lost the son we wanted." She turned to Nick. "For weeks, every time I looked at you, all I could think of was how badly I'd let you down."

"God, Libby, no." He grabbed her hand. "It was never your fault. I never said it was. I never even thought it. Why would you think that? I mean, you explained the autopsy report to me ..." He trailed off, clearly perplexed.

"I don't know." Pain struck her like a blunt knife. "I'd never failed at anything before and—"

"You didn't fail. We had an unexplained stillbirth."

The official term didn't offer any solace. "Our baby died inside me! That feels like failure. I blamed myself so it seemed reasonable you'd blame me too." She sighed. "Teresa's right. I wasn't thinking straight. If I had been, I'd have known you were the last person to place any blame. Instead, when we needed each other the most, I pushed you away."

She heaved in a breath, forcing it into a tight chest. "I haven't wanted to admit it, Nick, but I've got some responsibility in all of this nightmare too."

"Thank you." Relief filled his face and he blinked rapidly. "I'm sorry I didn't cope better. I'm sorry my stupidity added to our pain. I'll always regret it. Always be sorry for it."

She touched her forehead to his. "I'm sorry too."

They stayed there, tears mingling, until Libby shuddered in a very loud and snorty breath. Nick laughed. Teresa passed a box of tissues and offered water.

"This sort of conversation can be a reset button for your marriage," Teresa said when Libby finished blowing her nose. "When we own our mistakes, it empowers us to make changes. This is your time to strengthen and improve your relationship into the future. I know you found the communication workshop difficult, but both of you have just demonstrated open listening, empathy and gratitude."

"Who knew," Libby joked weakly.

"We realize you've got some extra challenges, because of the affair ch—because of Leo. Leo means the other woman will remain in your lives until he's an adult. But, and this is very important, if you're committed to each other and you're prepared to put in the hard yards and work as a team, there'll come a point when you'll look back and realize you're not only over the hump and on the other side, you're both happier for it." Teresa smiled warmly. "And remember, you're not alone. Use your support network."

"And have more sessions with you," Nick said emphatically.

Teresa and Chris rose, signaling the end of the session. "We'll see you at dinner."

Still slightly dazed, Libby held Nick's hand as they left the room. Deep in thought, they didn't say much as they rode the elevator to their room. Once inside, Nick fell on the bed, rubbing his eyes. "I'm knackered."

"Do you want a drink?"

"Nah. I think I'll have a quick nap so I can cope with dinner. This talking about your feelings stuff wears a bloke out."

She looked at his long form stretched on the bed, his drawn and exhausted face and the new strands of silver peppering his hair. It had been an emotionally challenging weekend, but then again, it had been an emotionally challenging couple of years. Yet they were at this workshop because Nick had insisted. He'd admitted his mistake to the group. He'd talked about how one poor decision made him feel less of a man and how much he regretted it every time he saw the impact of it on her and the girls.

The truth hit her and she took a sharp breath. Despite what she'd thrown at Nick over the last six months, he'd been working hard at living the best version of himself. While she'd been clinging to anger, allowing it to blind her, he'd been in the trenches, fighting for himself, for their marriage and for a happy family life for the girls.

Only an honorable man admitted his mistakes and worked that hard for redemption. Another lump of anger dissolved, exposing a bridge she wanted to cross. "Can I nap with you?"

He opened his arms to her and she lay down, rolling into him and resting her head on his chest.

He wrapped an arm around her and kissed her hair. "*Tesoro mio. I've missed you so much.*"

"I've missed you too." She slid a leg between his and rose on her elbow. Brushing a curl from his eyes, she lowered her mouth to his. She savored his familiar taste, yet was slightly discombobulated by the city scent of cologne instead of his usual tang of the sea with a frisson of engine oil. "Do you really need a nap?"

"What did you have in mind?"

"Something that always helps you sleep."

"Sex in a single bed?"

"Well, we've pushed the reset button on our marriage so it seems appropriate to have sex in a single bed like we did in the early days."

Nick laughed. "At least this one's a bit wider than the bunk on *Andiamo.*"

She traced his jawline with her finger. "And then we can fast forward to a new future by getting housekeeping to convert the beds into a king while we're at dinner."

"As much as having sex again will be amazing, I think I'm more turned on by the idea of having you sleeping in my arms all night."

Her heart rolled in a combination of joy and aversion. She instantly sobered. "Nick, when we get home, I don't think I can move back into the master bedroom."

A shadow crossed his face. "Fair enough. But can I move into the guest room with you?"

"Yes, please."

CHAPTER SEVENTEEN

September

Hey, Alice my wonderland. Not getting much work done today and who slowed the clocks? Can't stop thinking about us. Can't wait to hold you IRL. xx

"Squee!" Alice spun around in delight on the Bairnsdale street.

A little girl asked, "Why are you dancing?"

"Because I'm happy. Do you dance when you're happy?"

"I dance to the Wiggles."

"Maeve! Come here." A woman gave Alice a wary look. The little girl trotted back to her mother and Alice heard her say, "You shouldn't be talking to strangers, especially ones that squeal on the street."

But not even the woman's inference that Alice was crazy could dent her euphoria. In less than two hours, she and Tim were meeting in real life. They'd video chatted every night for close to two weeks. During their first conversation, Tim had apologized for vanishing without a trace. "I wasn't ghosting you, Alice, I swear. At least not intentionally. It's just life went unexpectedly off the rails."

Alice was no stranger to that concept. Tim had explained that his father had been hospitalized with emphysema and his deteriorating health meant he needed more of Tim's time. On top of that, his brother-in-law had walked out and he'd found himself supporting his sister, Sasha, and being a surrogate dad to his confused and angry nephews.

"Why didn't you tell me?" Alice squinted at the computer screen, watching Tim's face carefully, looking for clues that might support or disprove his words. "I would have understood."

"It wasn't a conscious decision not to tell you. Dad was rushed to the hospital and after that I went into crisis mode. Work, Dad and Sasha took up my time and you and me, well, we were so new. It wasn't fair to ask you to hang around waiting when I knew I'd be tied up for weeks."

"Months," she said, appreciating his thoughtfulness. "And now?"

"Now we set a date and a time and we meet no matter what. In between, we talk."

"I like the sound of that."

Alice had almost stood Dan up on Thursday, but she'd been so wired on lust she'd gone anyway and imagined Dan was Tim. She wasn't proud of it. To be honest, she felt a little queasy whenever she thought about it. She promised herself she'd never do it again.

Now, she hugged herself. After tonight, she wouldn't need to do it again. After tonight, she'd tell Dan their time together had been fabulous, but it was over. Online dating was over. She had Tim. She was part of a couple again and the world sparkled around her. Just thinking about Tim made her giddy and she couldn't resist another twirl.

"Ouch." She collided with someone, her shoulder crashing bone on bone.

"Whoa!" Hands gripped her upper arms, steadying her. "Alice?"

For a second she thought the deep and familiar voice was Dan's, but Dan had blue eyes and right now green ones full of questions were looking at her. Her mind finally caught up—Dan was at work in the bay. This man was wearing a suit and tie. She blinked and checked again. "Harry?"

"I didn't realize that, on top of your many skills, you were also a whirling dervish."

"Sorry. I had an overwhelming urge to twirl."

Bemusement filled his smile. "In the main street?"

"Why not? When you're happy you should celebrate. I did a twirl check and the coast was clear until you stepped out of nowhere and out of context."

"The bookshop is hardly nowhere and you're as out of context as me."

"This is the second time I've bumped into you outside of the bay. I wonder what the odds are?"

He grinned and his eyes sparkled. "Probability's my catnip."

"Really? Numbers are so not my thing." She didn't know a lot about what Harry did for a living, other than he was "in IT" and did contract work from home. "What brings you into Bairnsdale?"

"I had a prospective client meeting earlier. And I was just looking for a fun science book for Hunter. You?"

"Doctor's appointment," she said without thinking.

"Everything okay?"

His smile had faded and Alice kicked herself, realizing he was remembering doctors' visits with Helene. She waved her hand airily trying to compensate. "All good. Just an oil check."

"I guess seeing a doctor at your twin's practice might be problematic."

"Only if I want to see a woman."

"Let me buy you coffee and you can fill me in on your good news." Harry indicated a café across the road. "It hasn't been taken over by tree-change hipsters yet and you can still get a good, old-fashioned jam lamington."

Even though Harry knew she was actively dating, Alice felt awkward telling a widower that she'd met someone—hopefully The One—when he was alone and still grieving. "Thanks, but you're already cutting it fine if you want to get back in time for school pick-up."

He shot her a quizzical look as if he was surprised she knew about school pick-up, then checked his watch. "Damn, you're right. Sorry. I better get going and leave you to your twirling."

"Say hi to Holly and Hunter for me."

"Will do." He turned away then turned back. "Alice?"

"Hmm?"

"Hunter's joined Scouts and he wants to practice lighting and cooking on a campfire. I was thinking, seeing as Holly's current thing is drawing flowers and she's getting close to exhausting the bulbs—"

"The wild flowers are just coming out in the river reserve. You want to kill two birds with one stone?"

He smiled and it lit up his eyes. "That's the plan. Are you up for a burned sausage after school on Monday or Tuesday?"

"A burned sausage?" She laughed. "Hunter knows the way to a girl's heart."

"I've taught him well."

Alice had enjoyed the chaotic dinner she'd shared with the Waxmans. She'd ended up staying later than planned as she'd gotten involved helping Hunter with his papier-mâché blue-ringed octopus for his school project on the ecosystem of rock pools. There was something remarkably soothing about sitting around a table talking about nothing much, tearing newspapers into shreds and getting all sticky with glue. Afterwards, she'd gone home, feigned exhaustion to her parents, locked her bedroom door and phoned Tim. He'd apologized, told her he'd missed her and how desperate he was to make up for lost time. It had been one of her best days in months.

"It sounds like fun." *Hello? Tim!* "Oh wait, sorry, Harry. I've just remembered some tentative plans."

Harry shoved his hands into his pockets. "Judging by that blush, I reckon they're connected with your overwhelming need to twirl."

"Not at all." Why did he always notice this sort of stuff about her? Why couldn't he be oblivious like Dan?

"Let me know if the plans fall over."

"They're not going to," she mumbled pettishly to Harry's

retreating back.

Her phone rang and she didn't recognize the number.

"Hello?"

"Alice, it's Flis Carter."

Her heart leaped into her mouth not certain if this call was good news or bad. Three weeks earlier, after spending hours crafting a submission, she'd been interviewed by a panel led by Flis.

"Hi." It came out as a squeak.

"Alice, the arts council is excited to offer you this year's position of artist in residence."

Yes! "Thank you."

"No, thank you. Your submission was very professional and we love your idea for a mural. There'll be an official announcement next month with drinks, but meanwhile I'll email your contract. If you can sign it and get it back to me by the end of next week, that would be fantastic. Congratulations again, Alice. Talk soon."

Artist in residence! Alice hugged herself. Could this day get any better?

She crossed the road and walked into the gynecologist's rooms for her long overdue follow-up appointment. Alice took a seat in the waiting room and bypassed the magazines, preferring to read a copy of the *Bairnsdale Advertiser*. As she read the articles, she thought her writing for the *Gazette* held up against that of the professional journalists. She was skimming the social pages when her eyes landed on a photo. Suddenly she was looking straight at Tim. He had one arm slung casually across an attractive woman's shoulder and the other resting across the top of the heads of two young boys. Tim's sister and his nephews.

Her gaze drifted to the caption. "Tim Classen, his wife Sasha and their children Joel and Rufus enjoying all the fun of the elementary school spring fair."

Her skin caught on fire. Her lunch lurched in her stomach. *No! No! No!* She swallowed and closed her eyes. She'd misread the words is all. They really said, "Tim Classen, his sister Sasha and his nephews

Joel and Rufus enjoying all the fun of the elementary school spring fair."

She opened her eyes and the print shot into focus. Not a single word had changed. This was Tim with his wife and sons.

"You bastard!"

The receptionist's head jerked up. "I beg your pardon."

Alice wanted to shred the paper, but her hands were shaking so much she couldn't get her fingers to work. "Why are men such cheating, lying bastards?"

"That's the million-dollar question, isn't it?" The woman poured Alice a glass of water from the cooler and handed it to her. "Read something that triggered you?"

I've been sexting with a married man! But no way was she admitting that to a stranger so she covered. "I just get so angry when I read stuff like that article about the bloke who conned that woman out of her savings." Alice felt a kindred connection to the duped woman. Not that Tim was after her money, but she had trusted him implicitly. She'd shared her deepest thoughts and feelings with him. Felt and believed their friendship was real.

What the hell was his game? What did he want from her? Why had he bothered reconnecting after all those months? He was married! Why was he even on the dating site in the first place?

She wanted to move—run, hit—do something, anything that would release the fulminating rage inside her that was as much directed to herself as it was to the lying, cheating and conniving Tim. How could she have been so stupid? Why had she broken her new rules for this guy and committed to him without meeting him in real life? But she knew why.

He was the first man who'd reached out and right from the start, she'd fallen for him. She'd wanted him, so she'd convinced herself that their video calls were the same as sitting at a table across from each other. Their virtual sex had been so hot his words alone tipped her over the edge without much push from her fingers or her vibrator. All day today her body had been awash with lust from the anticipation of spending the night with him in the Airbnb she'd booked and paid for. Stupid!

Tim had a wife.

Her brain flailed, trying to wrap itself around this new and unwanted information. Thoughts of Libby filled Alice with another surge of rage. How could Tim look at Sasha with love in his eyes while betraying her by having an emotional affair with Alice? An emotional affair he certainly planned to make physical. Who was she kidding? Given what they'd said to each other, shown each other, the things they'd done on camera, "physical" was purely semantics. He'd actively sought her out and chosen her to cheat with on his wife.

Alice suddenly wanted a shower.

Was what Tim had done and planned to do worse than what Nick had done? Was Tim the Jess in this situation, using Alice? Had Tim dumped her months earlier for someone closer to home and now that had fizzled, he'd reappeared like the undead?

Worse than that, she'd been so desperate she'd fallen for it.

Humiliation joined nausea. For months, she'd been congratulating herself on taking control of her life when all she'd really been was a stupid and trusting idiot! Again! Only this time, she wasn't the only person being cheated on. Sasha Classen deserved to know that her witty, charming, intelligent husband, the father of her two children, was a cheater.

A chance to regain her power flickered. Alice made a decision. She would find Tim's wife and tell her.

I wish he hadn't told me. The memory of Libby's desolation turned the sweet taste of revenge sour in Alice's mouth. Yet, didn't Sasha Classen deserve to know? Or did she know already? Did she and Tim have an open marriage? Were they polyamorous? If that was the case, though, Tim would have told her. Put it on his dating profile. Mentioned his children! A thousand possible and confusing scenarios trickled through her mind, fogging her initial clarity of purpose and leaving her ashamed and ill-used.

Outrage roared. How dare Tim make her the other woman!

"... see you now."

Alice realized the receptionist was talking to her. "Sorry?"

"Dr. Chu will see you now."

Still dazed, Alice managed to get her legs to walk her into the consulting room. She took a seat, nodding at Lacey's greeting and got out a "Good, thanks" in return.

"Before we start, Alice, I just need to check if you want me to send a copy of your results to Libby?"

"I'd prefer it if you didn't."

"I understand. Okay, down to business. How's the cream working?"

All day she'd been thinking of sex with Tim but now her thoughts veered fast away from him and straight to Dan. Dan who was a generous and understanding lover no matter what. "It's great. You saved my sex life."

"Excellent. I'll write you some refills. In associated news, your cervical screening test is fine. Repeat in five years."

"Wow! That's great! I like this new test." The all clear focused her, bringing her mind back to one of the reasons she'd originally come to see Lacey. A plan she'd been fixated on until Tim had reconnected and she'd allowed pie-in-the-sky daydreams to take over. Well, timing was everything—at least she'd discovered the truth about the rat bastard before this appointment so she could get her ducks back in a row.

"Since I saw you, I've found out I can withdraw money from my retirement fund to pay for egg harvesting and freezing. I think you said last time that Monash was the closest IVF facility?"

"Before we get to that, I want to discuss the results of your blood tests."

At the first appointment, Lacey had insisted on a full raft of tests before she wrote the referral. Alice had a history of erratic periods, which were either super light or running like a red river in flood. Sometimes she needed to up her red meat consumption.

"Am I anemic?"

"Your hemoglobin's a bit low, but your estrogen levels are more concerning." Lacey clicked her pen. "They indicate premature ovarian insufficiency."

"What's that?" Alice asked worried about the word, *insufficiency.*

"Early menopause."

Menopause? Every part of her recoiled. "That's not possible. I'm thirty-four."

"Even so," Lacey said evenly, "your hormone levels indicate that you're menopausal."

Alice's mind scrabbled for purchase. "But—how? I get periods."

"They're very irregular, Alice."

"But—but—Mom only got the change a few years ago."

"Does she have any sisters who went through early menopause?"

"She's an only child."

"On your father's side?"

"Dad's sister is still having periods at fifty-five. I can't possibly be going through the change!"

Lacey clicked her mouse and quickly read something on her computer screen. "Besides painful intercourse and erratic periods have you had any other symptoms?"

"No!"

Something about Lacey's expression made her ask, "Like what?"

"Fatigue, irritability, depression?"

Alice laughed and heard the manic edge. "I've had all of those things, because of a major relationship breakdown, online dating that makes me feel like a piece of meat and working four jobs to pay my bills. *Not* because I'm menopausal!"

"Have there been any occasions you've flown off the handle without warning and been surprised by your reaction?" Lacey asked, her tone worryingly sympathetic.

"My mother's driving me nuts about my current life choices so those explosions are totally warranted."

I'm not an idiot, Harry! Stick to fathering your own kids. She swallowed, not able to as easily dismiss her reaction to Harry's comment about her Dear Alice column.

Lacey continued gently, "Do you suddenly get hot for no particular reason?"

It was like standing on an empty stage in a pool of light with nowhere to hide. On and off for months, she'd woken with her skin on fire, frantically kicking off the blankets and blaming her parents for overheating Pelican House. She'd taken to wearing light clothing at Summerhouse, because she thought they kept the building super hot so the oldies stayed warm. How she'd dripped sweat a few minutes earlier when she'd seen Tim in the paper.

"Oh God." She dropped her head into her hands as the group of symptoms laid down one on top of the other like planks of wood, making a high stack. "I never made the connection."

"And there's no reason why you would. No one expects to go through menopause in their thirties."

Alice looked up and tried to corral all the chaos into some sort of order. "When you say "early menopause" you mean perimenopause, right?" She had no idea where the word had come from—probably from the magazines Hilary gave her. "Thank God, I came to see you now while there's still time to harvest some eggs."

Lacey's pen clicked. "I'm sorry, Alice."

The stark apology knocked Alice's world out from under her and then she was falling. Her hand flew to her mouth, trying to stifle the agonizing cry that rose, seeking an exit. Brutal despair ripped and tore, and tentacles of pain spread their way through her, leaving no cell untouched. They found the images of her longed-for babies—pictures she'd created in her mind years ago. Babies she loved. Children she'd woven hopes and dreams around as much for them as for herself. Children she loved so deeply she'd navigated the app-driven dating scene, sifting through every type of man, optimistically searching for the one she loved, who loved her and who wanted children too.

Meeting Tim whose online persona hid the liar within.

Her heart broke and the images of her little boy and girl pixelated slowly, square by square, disintegrating in front of her eyes then falling like a shattered pane of glass. Irreparable. Irreversible. Gone forever.

CHAPTER EIGHTEEN

JESS CHECKED HER EMAIL, HER EYES SEARCHING FOR A REPLY from Libby. Nothing. Again.

It was four days since Jess had sent her email. After corresponding with Libby this way for seven months, Jess knew the drill. Libby's fastest response was forty-eight hours and her longest was seventy-two. Now she was agonizing over the best next step. If she re-sent the email, would Libby reset the clock and make her wait another two or more days? Would sending it weaken her already vulnerable position in this triad? But what if the first email was circling, lost in the ether of cyberspace and Libby had never received it?

Not knowing was doing Jess's head in.

During all the years she'd known Libby, not once had she ever considered her capable of behaving without empathy. Of knowingly inflicting pain. But this was a side of her friend she'd never glimpsed before, let alone seen. A parade of words teenage Jess had once reserved for her mother, her mother's friends and half the women in the town—mean and thoughtless bitches one and all—played in her head, every one of them directed at Libby. They demanded to be screamed until her throat burned and her voice was hoarse. The only thing stopping her was that Leo was in the house. She didn't want to scare him.

Jess's gaze moved hungrily to the tawny liquid in the rum bottle. She was already imagining the fiercely hot flames burning in her chest, before they dimmed to cozy warmth and snuggled around her like a soft baby blanket. She was in no doubt the rum would take the edge off her sorrow and disappointment that, yet again, Libby was refusing to meet and talk. It would deaden the pain that although Nick loved Leo, she could no longer hide from the fact he didn't love her. Although in this instance, the rum was a catch twenty-two. It reminded her of a younger Nick who'd enjoyed her company and her body as much as she'd enjoyed his. A drink would soften the ongoing disappointment that when it came to Libby, Nick was a weak and controlled man. Why else wasn't he fighting harder for Leo?

It would numb the pain that she was the only person in her son's corner.

And God help her, she wanted the oblivion the alcohol promised— she craved its anesthetizing reassurance.

"Screw it." She reached for the bottle.

"Mommy." Leo held out a plastic plate. "Num, now?"

Shame drenched her. Dear God, it was only lunchtime and she was contemplating her first drink. She made Leo a peanut butter sandwich, but she didn't bother making herself anything. Her appetite had vanished a while ago—stress making her nauseous both with and without food. Given her unwanted weight gain, she was working on the theory that her body could use that fat as fuel instead of food. She cut up some fruit. Once he was safe and happy in his highchair, she grabbed the step ladder and the bottle of rum, climbed up and shoved the alcohol into the far recesses of the cupboard over the fridge. Stepping down, she folded the ladder and took it outside to the shed. The more obstacles she put between herself and a drink, the better for Leo.

"I am not Linda. I am not Linda. I refuse to be Linda," she chanted under her breath.

Only right now she knew she'd come as close to following Linda down that self-destructive path as she'd ever come before. By the time Jess turned sixteen, her mother was specializing in day drinking. That Jess was even considering it terrified her. Should she go to a meeting? She shuddered at the thought. This town was too bloody small and if she was seen coming out of the old community center on a Friday night, it would only reinforce the long-held prejudices of narrow-minded people.

"Talk to someone" was the advice Al-Anon had given her as a teen. But who? Patrice? Jess rejected the thought the moment it landed. She didn't know the woman well enough and she couldn't afford to lose her job. The hot oil of anger spat all over her fear. This was Libby's fault. How dare she put Leo at risk like this when she knew what Jess had been through as a kid!

Libby was a doctor, for God's sake. Libby knew that children of alcoholics likely had a predisposition to addiction and yet, it wasn't stopping her from treating Jess like she had no rights in this situation. The easiest day of the week not to drink was Thursdays. Access day for Leo and exclusion day for Jess. It should have been the hardest day to stay sober, but it was the knowledge that Karen was visiting that kept Jess far away from the bottle. She didn't want to read disappointment in Karen's eyes. It was hard enough knowing she was failing Leo.

Each time Jess watched her son toddle off with Karen to spend the afternoon with Nick, another bit of her heart crumbled. She'd anticipated Leo's access visits with his father would include herself and that the three of them would continue to have short but undeniable family time together. During the long nights on the couch with her good friend Bundy rum, she dreamed up ways of seeing Nick. In the light of day, she knew Libby was just waiting for her to turn up at Burrunan or anywhere else Nick took Leo and the girls and use it as an excuse to revoke Leo's already limited access to his father.

So much for Libby's oft-repeated phrase "It takes a village to raise a child." The six of them were supposed to be that village—one big, happy extended family living on a sprawling property. Leo deserved to have his father and sisters in his life every day. She wanted him to be surrounded by Nick's love and grow up learning how to be a good and decent man, living his life with his family at its heart, not be a once-a-week visitor. But Libby was not only blocking it, she was making *everyone's* life a living hell.

The town chatter about Nick and Libby had never completely gone away, having moments of resurgence when the gossip mill was particularly quiet. Lately it had started up again.

"Have you seen Nick Pirelli? He looks like shit."

"You would too, if your missus had you by the balls."

"He deserves everything that's coming to him."

"He didn't murder anyone."

"Women are evil. You watch. She's put him through months of shit and then she'll up and leave and expect him to pay for the lot."

"If he wasn't so whipped he'd have left months ago."

"She should have left him. A clean break's better."

"I heard that Jess and Libby are bi and they shared Nick."

"Yeah? Lucky bugger."

"Wonder if Jess is looking to be part of another threesome?"

"I feel sorry for the kids."

Wherever Jess went, she heard hundreds of variations on a theme, because despite her being within earshot, the fact she was the "other woman" meant her feelings didn't matter. That and the urge to gossip was greater than people's restraint. As hard as it was to listen to the talk, she craved it as a way of staying connected to Libby and Nick.

What the hell was wrong with Libby? Was she going to blow up her marriage? If she was stupid enough to do that, then Jess would grab the chance she hadn't had in years and change that look in Nick's eyes. She'd be there for him in ways she'd never been allowed to be before. She and Leo. They'd be the three musketeers. That hope had kept her going for months.

At least it had done until four days earlier.

Jess left the bakery as usual to pick up Leo from daycare but as she turned left onto the esplanade, she'd stopped short. Libby and Nick were walking toward her. Unlike the previous months when she'd glimpsed them from a distance and seen the vibrating wall of Libby's antipathy separating them, this time they were holding hands.

Her unfulfilled hopes for Leo and herself detonated around her and she swayed.

When Nick saw her, he radiated discomfort, but at that moment, Jess only had eyes for Libby. "How can you forgive him and not me?"

"The fact you need to ask answers your question."

Jess had stumbled home. Knowing Libby had forgiven Nick changed everything. The only gains Jess had managed to get for Leo had been by mining the fault lines between Libby and Nick. Now all the fissures had sealed shut and she was firmly locked out. Was access to Nick even worth it if Leo bore the brunt of Libby's antipathy? If he became aware he was treated differently from his sisters? Less valued. Less loved.

Not loved.

Jess was all too familiar with the effects that sort of insidious harm inflicted. The hoop- jumping involved to get any scraps of attention. The self-blame and loathing that inevitably followed. She didn't want any of that for her beautiful little boy. But her not wanting it for her son wouldn't stop Libby's savage rejection inflicting thick and livid scars on Leo's pure soul.

Her rage blew as hot and as dangerous as the outback wind on parched grass. She wanted to throw Libby to the ground and punch and scratch her in the same way she'd once fought Tegan Drinkwater when she'd called her a slut. Like Linda fought when a woman stole her wallet. But street fighting didn't belong in Libby's world.

As much as Jess hated the idea, the time had arrived. She had to play the game Libby's way and use the polite guidelines for conflict resolution. It had taken Jess five drafts but she'd finally sent a carefully worded email requesting a meeting with the presence of a mediator. It was exactly the sort of thing she knew Libby suggested to patients who were dealing with challenging health issues.

An email Libby had failed to respond to so far.

Jess hit refresh on her mail app again, willing the dots on her phone to stop spinning and for the mail to load. Eventually, two emails tumbled in. The second was from Libby.

"About freaking time!" It didn't take long to read the brief correspondence that was devoid of both a greeting and a sign off. It was barely two lines in length.

With or without a mediator, there will never be an occasion or a reason that will induce me to meet with you. You're dead to me.

Jess screamed at her phone.

Leo squealed in fright.

Then her stomach heaved and she vomited onto her feet.

"Knock, knock."

Alice spun around from her computer and saw her father standing in the doorway of her bedroom.

"Dad?"

Unlike her mother, Peter didn't comment on the chaos in her room. Or the fact that Alice had retreated to it on the weekend. Or that she was hiding from her life. "What are you doing home?"

"It's perfect fishing weather so I took off early. Thought you and I might head out?"

After this morning's one-sided argument at breakfast, where Karen had vented, "It's like you're avoiding us," and Alice had remained mute, because in this instance her mother was correct, Alice knew Karen would have insisted Peter take the afternoon off to "talk to Alice." This fishing trip was more to do with fishing for information than about landing bream.

But Alice wasn't up to telling anyone that her body was defective, let alone her parents. It would be yet another area of her life where she'd given them cause to worry. It was easier to lie.

"Lovely idea, Dad, but I've got a *Gazette* deadline."

He nodded, disappointment clear on his face. "Well, if you change your mind ..."

"Thanks."

He walked away. Alice shoved down her guilt and returned to her digital spring cleaning. The only positive thing about being told her body was useless was how it put Tim's betrayal into perspective. Although she hadn't deliberately planned to ghost him, she'd been so shattered by Lacey's shocking news, she'd lacked the emotional energy to do anything, let alone verbally abuse him or track down his wife.

At first his texts had been romantic, counting down the minutes until they met. Then worried, then angry. She didn't care and as each one had hit her phone, she'd deleted them, just like she'd cut off his calls. The deleting now extended to all his texts, emails, photos and the treasured poem he'd written her earlier in the year. She'd turned up the volume on her computer, taking pleasure in the loud scrunching noise as it all disappeared into the virtual trash.

Her four dating apps faded as her phone did an update, prompting Alice to question their place on her device. Her approach to dating had been all about finding The One—the father of her children. A sob clogged her throat. No point now. She set about trying to delete the apps, but in the end, after being asked so many times if she was absolutely certain, it was easier to switch them to offline. When the apps asked why, she chose the ridiculous option of *I'm prioritizing me,* when really, she wanted there to be an option of *Men on dating apps are lying pricks.*

An hour later she was officially off the dating scene. It felt—she'd hoped for great, freeing, redemptive, wonderful. All she felt was empty.

For only the second time outside of their standard Thursday arrangement, she texted Dan.

Fancy a spur of the moment benefit? Like right now?

Aw, Twin Two! Lousy timing. Relief teaching then training. Tonight?

Tonight was hours away. Alice needed something right now. Anything to stop this awful nothingness churning inside her.

Harry's open-ended invitation popped into her mind. If anyone could take her mind off her own misery, it was Hunter. Just keeping up with the kid's rapid thought processes blocked all thoughts of her own and today that sounded damn near perfect.

She started texting then stopped. Harry didn't text. He either emailed well in advance or he called. She brought up his number and hit the phone icon.

"Alice!"

"Hi, Harry. Does today work for Holly's wildflower drawing class and Hunter's fire?"

Five minutes later, she was heading out the door to the butcher.

According to Harry, Brutus responded to modulated tones so, despite feeling ridiculous, Alice walked into the Waxmans' back yard attempting to emulate the TV weather woman.

"There's a slight chance of precipitation this evening, Brutus, clearing overnight for a fine and mild spring day."

The greyhound stood stock still, staring at her. At least he wasn't trembling violently.

Harry appeared at the back door with a smile and a wave. Excited by her progress with the neurotic dog, Alice called out, "Hey, Harry! It worked!"

Brutus took off like a shot, diving under some bushes.

"Oh God. Sorry!"

Harry laughed. "Don't worry. Expecting a twirler to be quiet and sedate is a lot to ask."

Alice almost said, "I'm so not in a twirling mood," but Harry would pick up on that and then he'd ask questions she didn't want to answer. Besides, the whole point of going out with the family was to forget the last few days. "Yes, but life with a twirler is never boring," she quipped instead, faking upbeat until she felt it. She suddenly noticed Harry looked different. Neater? "Have you got new glasses?"

He took them off and looked at them in surprise. "No. Why?"

"You look different."

"I got my hair cut. Holly told me it wasn't surfer dude cool just dad messy."

She laughed. "That's harsh."

"Was she right?"

"You need to ask? We both know she has an aesthetic eye."

"Now who's being harsh? Anyway, she insisted I go to that new unisex salon. I'm still in shock at the price. It's the most expensive haircut I've had in my life. What do you reckon? Was it worth it?"

Alice tilted her head and studied him. Without the shaggy mess, his salt and pepper hair sat thick and neat, giving him a distinguished yet casual look. Alice wondered if this was closer to the hairstyle he'd sported before grief settled over him. It suited him and he looked good.

"You never know, it might just earn you a casserole or two from the mothers at school," she teased.

He gave a dismissive wave. "I've been getting those since I arrived in the bay."

Really? "Well, in that case, now you're neat and presentable, you'll be fending off invitations to the school trivia night."

"Been doing that since well before the haircut."

Women were asking Harry out? Alice didn't know why it surprised her other than she'd never thought about him in terms of dating. But she supposed for divorced women in their forties, Harry was probably a catch. Except, Harry had clearly given her the impression he wasn't ready for another relationship.

"So, you're dating?"

"God, no. Just eating a lot of casseroles and enduring some long evenings at community fundraisers."

"You could always say no."

"That's not as easy as swiping left, Alice."

He walked inside and she followed him, trying not to take his comment as a criticism. The house was back to its usual state of clean clutter—a lot like Alice's bedroom—but the kitchen was a little more chaotic. A trail of cocoa spilled across the counter and the sink was full of dirty baking implements. Lopsided cupcakes cooled on a rack and a cooler and picnic basket sat on the floor.

Alice handed Harry the large butcher's. "I didn't know what everyone liked so I got a mixture of plain, herb and garlic and a couple of chili sausages."

"Sounds perfect, thanks." He pulled out his wallet. "How much do I owe you?"

"My treat."

"Don't feel you need to pay for them just because you collected them."

"I can afford to buy a few sausages, Harry!" The quick rise of irritation came out of nowhere, blasting furnace heat across her skin. She jerkily pulled at her jacket, ripping it off, desperate to cool down. Sweat pooled beneath her eyes. Sweat or tears? She didn't know.

Harry lifted her jacket out of her hands and hung it on a chair, then he opened the freezer. He offered an icepack. "Stick that on the back of your neck."

Alice wished the floor would open and snatch her away. When she didn't move, Harry put the cold pack in place for her. The instant chill killed the fulminating heat almost as fast as it had flamed her, but its presence meant Harry knew exactly what was going on. His kindness had exposed her mortifying and devastating secret.

Don't cry. Don't cry. Do. Not. Cry. "Thanks." Her voice wobbled on the word.

Harry shrugged as if it was no big deal to be handing an icepack to a woman in his kitchen. "H used to get hot flashes."

"Yes, but I don't have cancer!"

"Which is wonderful," he said gently.

But this was her personal nightmare and she didn't want him lessening it. "What I mean is, I shouldn't be getting hot flashes at thirty-four. They should be twenty years away."

"HRT will help, won't it?"

"*Nothing* will help me have a baby."

His face fell into sad, well-worn lines. "Shit. Alice. That was thoughtless. I'm so cancer focused, I—Sorry. I know how much you wanted kids."

His remorse and her grief pulled her forward and she almost moved in for a hug. At the last moment, she realized what she was doing and spun around, tugging open the freezer. What was she thinking? This was Harry. They couldn't get through a single conversation without one of them feeling the need to apologize.

"As soon as the kids get home we'll head out," Harry said to her back.

She appreciated his change of topic and turned to the thump of sausages being dropped into the cooler. "Just to be clear, I'm hopeless at getting fires going. I'll stick to drawing with Holly and leave the campfire to you and Hunter."

"I've been using firelighters for years so I may not be much better."

"Should we make sandwiches just in case?"

"Jeez, Alice. You're tough on a bloke. Have some faith."

She laughed. "It's nothing to do with faith and everything to do with not going hungry."

The side gate banged and Hunter's greetings to Brutus floated into the kitchen.

"Hi, mate, how was your day?" Harry said as his son rushed inside.

"You made chocolate cupcakes? Cool. Oh, hi, Alice. So that's why there's cake. Dad never makes it for us." Hunter dropped his bag where he stood and reached for a chocolate delight.

"Hands! And bag." Harry caught Hunter by the back of the shirt, returned his backpack to him, kissed him on the top of the head and turned him in the direction of the bathroom.

"You better be quick, Hunter," Alice teased. "I hold the record in my family for eating the most cupcakes in the shortest time."

"Don't eat them all!" Hunter bolted to the bathroom.

The screen door squeaked and Brutus snuck in, head low, followed by Holly.

"How was your day?" Harry asked.

But Holly kept her head down and pushed straight past him, disappearing into the hall. A moment later, a door slammed.

Hunter reappeared, holding his hands up for inspection. "Can I have some milk?"

"Did something happen on the ride home to upset your sister?" Harry asked.

Hunter shrugged.

"Did you do or say something to upset her?"

"Nup. She was sad before we left school."

"Back in a sec, Alice." Frowning, Harry left the room.

Seemingly unperturbed by his sister's meltdown, Hunter poured himself a glass of milk and sat at the table with his drink and cake. Brutus gave Alice a leery glance and settled like a bag of bones on the other side of Hunter's chair, using him as a shield from scary Alice.

"Alice, do you know chocolate makes dogs really sick?"

"Does it?" Alice asked, knowing full well that it did, but happy to chat.

"Yep. Cos of the theo-something in the cocoa. The vet told me."

"Theobromide."

"Theobromide," Hunter repeated before stuffing his mouth with cake. He asked Alice something else, but the question was muffled by the food.

"How about you finish that mouthful first, then ask me."

"Um, Alice." Harry reappeared in the kitchen. "Can I have a word?"

"Sure." She followed him into the other room. "Is it Holly?"

"She's crying a river and she won't tell me what's wrong. All I've managed to get out of her is that it isn't me, Hunter, or her mom ..." He blew out a breath. "I don't know what to do next. She hasn't been this distraught in a long time. Even when H died ... Can you have a word with her? Find out what the hell's going on?"

Harry's distress and worry ringed her, hooking onto her own concern for Holly. "I can try. But, Harry, if she didn't tell you, she probably won't tell me."

He shrugged. "You chat a couple of times a week when you do art. I reckon it's worth a shot."

Alice knocked on Holly's door then opened it and walked into the room. The girl was lying face down on her bed, her dark hair splayed out like a cape. A memory rolled back of herself at a similar age, lying spread-eagled and crying on her childhood bed. What had Karen done then?

"Hi, Holly. It's Alice." She sat on the bed and placed her hand gently on Holly's back. "Rough day?"

A muffled sobbing sound squeezed up from around the pillow.

Alice rubbed the girl's back until her crying eased and her breathing was no longer labored. "I'm sorry you're so upset."

Holly rolled onto her side, her luminous green eyes red-rimmed and watery. "It was horrible."

"Was it?"

Holly nodded. "I hate school!" She flung herself over, hiding her face, and the tears started afresh.

Alice waited until the crying ebbed. Holly loved school so something big must have happened to make her say that. Then again, she was thirteen. Alice remembered those tumultuous teenage years when all it took was one girl saying, "You can't sit with us," or your twin announcing, "You're a wet blanket," and everything changed from sunshine to darkness.

"Are you sure you hate school?"

"Yes."

"Even Mrs. Main?"

"Yes."

"Wow. Poor Mrs. Main. Hated for giving you an A+ for your clay vase."

Holly moved her head until Alice spied one green eye.

"Do you hate school or do you hate someone at school?"

"Someone at school."

It was said so quietly Alice almost missed it. "Mean girl or mean boy?"

Holly mumbled something unintelligible into her pillow.

"How about you sit up and tell me?"

Holly hiccuped and eventually sat up, her entire body slumped and dejected. "It was Olivia Grayson."

"How did she upset you?"

Holly's face flushed pink.

Alice thought of all the things teenage girls found embarrassing and decided it was unwise to try and guess. "You can tell me, because I bet whatever Olivia said or did probably happened to me when I was at school."

Holly looked doubtful so Alice leaned in conspiratorially. "You might not have guessed it by looking at me now, especially with me wearing these elephant print pants, but I was pretty dorky when I was at school."

Holly smiled weakly. "You're still a bit dorky, Alice. But in the best way," she quickly added.

"That's kind, but would Olivia appreciate my dorky super powers?"

Holly shook her head. "She's one of the cool girls."

"Ah." Alice recalled the cool girls and their snarky comments. "And?"

"I got my—" her voice dropped, "—period."

Something about the way she said the word made Alice wonder if this was Holly's first period. It was like a knife to her own heart. Holly had no real sense that periods meant everything was working well and one day, if she wished, she could have a baby. Alice, on the other hand, had endured years of sometimes painful and often irregular periods and now, when she was more than ready to have a baby, her body had failed her, drying up like a wrinkled prune and old before its time.

She blinked back her own tears. "Have you had a period before?"

Holly shook her head. "Mom told me about them. She gave me some stuff and said I'd get it in fifth or sixth grade, but I didn't. I threw them out cos they were old."

Alice ached to hug her. "So you didn't have anything with you?"

Again, the head shake. "Olivia was in the toilets when I ... so I asked her for a pad. She told me—" Holly's voice broke and tears splashed her cheek.

Even though Alice had no idea what Oliva Grayson had said, she already knew she wanted to thump her. This time she gave in to instinct and pulled Holly in close. "I bet whatever she said to you, it was wrong."

Holly's head thrashed against Alice's chest.

"I bet you a Mars Bar she's wrong. But the only way to win the bet is to tell me what she said."

Holly mumbled something into Alice's sweater.

She dropped her arms and lifted Holly's chin with her fingers. "Say it again, this time for chocolate."

Holly's lips quivered and her voice was soft. "'Only dirty trash wear pads and sit in their own blood.'"

Spare us from treasures like Olivia. "Well that's wrong for a start. Did she say anything else?"

"That I have to use tampons or I'll smell and everyone will know."

"Well, I've got some good news for you. Olivia Grayson knows squat. Despite what everyone thinks, more women use pads than tampons."

"Really?"

"Really. And tampons take practice. A lot of practice, so I bet Olivia used pads for her first period too." Alice kept an arm around Holly. "And I promise, as long as you change your pad every two to three hours, the blood won't smell. Today's pads are pretty amazing. They trap the blood in little cells and they have wings so you don't leak. They're nothing like the pads my mom had to use. She said they were like wearing a canoe between her legs and she had to wear a special belt to tie hold them on."

"Gross."

"Exactly. We're lucky."

"But what if Olivia and the other girls at school see I'm using pads?"

"How are they going to see? Think about all the women you see every day who are over fourteen and under fifty-five. They all get periods. Have you ever noticed any of them wearing a pad?"

Holly considered the question. "No."

Alice thought about the brown sludge that had greeted her this morning, staining her pajamas and taunting her with the fact that even though her eggs were pretty much dead, she was still forced to wear a pad. She bit her lip and honored Holly's painful disclosure with one of her own. "Can you tell I'm wearing one?"

"Are you?" Holly asked breathlessly.

"Sort of. It's called a panty liner. It's like a mini pad. I've got a spare in my bag I can give you."

"Thank you." Holly gave a giant sniff of relief and wiped her face on her sleeve.

"Gross!" Alice fished out a tissue from her pocket along with a dog treat.

"That's more gross."

"This from the girl who lets Brutus lick her face. It's clean and it comes with the added scent of chicken. Brutus will adore it."

Holly laughed and accepted the tissue.

"You and your dad need to go on a shopping trip for supplies."

Holly's eyes widened. "He won't know what to buy."

"What won't I know what to buy?" Harry appeared in the open doorway, obviously drawn in by the sound of laughter.

"Dad! Go away. I'm talking to Alice."

"Holly's got some news, Harry."

"Alice!"

"It's all good. Holly. Your dad knows all about periods and pads, don't you Harry?"

Harry threw Alice a look that combined "kill me now" with "how dumb am I?" A dart of sympathy hit her. Harry was a loving and caring parent who was working really hard at being both father and mother to his kids, but he didn't seem to recognize the great job he was doing. Without thinking, she gave his arm a quick squeeze.

Harry rallied and sat on the other side of Holly. "Your old dad knows a thing or two about feminine hygiene products. I only made the mistake of buying no name pads once and your mom had my guts for garters. She was a Libra girl all the way."

"Libra makes funky pads in awesome colors," Alice added, trying to give Harry some street cred. "They're perfect for arty girls."

"Congratulations, on becoming a woman, Holly," Harry said clumsily, raising his hand for a high five.

It was awkward and full of love—Hallmark would have bottled it if they could. Alice's chest filled with a rush of emotions and she didn't know if she wanted to laugh, cry or sigh.

"It's not something to celebrate!" Holly yelled, clearly incensed by the idea.

So much for Hallmark. "Actually, Holly, your dad's right."

Holly glared at Alice, clearly skeptical. Harry blinked, equally surprised.

"It *is* something to celebrate," Alice reiterated. "Lots of cultures have special ceremonies for girls that can last for days. I remember when my twin got her period first, I was so jealous she got to go out for a special celebration without me. I had to wait another year and a half."

"What did you do when you got yours?"

"My mom took me out to lunch and then we went shopping and I got a Roxy T-shirt. After that, she bought me a sparkly makeup bag for the pads so no mean girls or stupid boys teased me."

"Your mom sounds really nice," Holly said sadly.

Hating that she'd inadvertently added to Holly's pain, Alice glanced at Harry for some guidance. But he was no use—he just nodded encouragingly, as though saying, "Good job, keep going." It reminded her of her own father. "My dad was great too. He gave me a "Girl Power" badge and bought me some new paints."

Holly visibly brightened. "Hear that, Dad?"

Harry laughed. "We can go to Bairnsdale on Saturday if you like."

"You and Holly should go shopping for supplies now and then go out for dinner," Alice suggested. "Hunter and I can hang out here."

"But I thought we were doing the campfire ..." Harry's voice trailed off as Alice shook her head fast over the top of Holly's. "How about we all go to the Thai place for dinner instead?"

"Awesome!" Holly squealed, her distress vanquished by the offer of dinner out. "I *love* the Thai place."

Was Harry utterly clueless? This was supposed to be a father–daughter outing not a family dinner. "Holly, can you please go and grab my handbag for me?"

"Sure." Holly slid off the bed and left the room.

"Thank you. You were amazing." Harry's heartfelt appreciation filled the room. "I hope it wasn't too hard for you, given what you're going through ..."

Alice glared at him, picturing pearl-handled daggers flying out of her eyes and pinning him to the wall, as she tried to counter her rising tide of shame and embarrassment. She hated Harry's empathy and intensity—it was too much, too revealing. She had a sudden appreciation for Dan's easygoing, no-drama personality and their lack of deep and meaningful conversations.

"Can we *not* talk about me right now?"

"Right. Yeah. Of course." He took his glasses off and cleaned them on the hem of his shirt before sliding the dark frames back into place. "I thought Holly was all prepared for periods. H gave her the talk and some pads before she died."

"That was over two years ago. Holly thinks sanitary products expire so she threw them out."

Harry blanched. "So, that's why she's upset? She doesn't have anything?"

"That, but mostly because a girl at school upset her telling her she had to use tampons."

"She's far too young for tampons," he said emphatically before adding, "isn't she?"

Alice felt sorry for him. "Using tampons is more about feeling comfortable and relaxed using them than age."

"Bloody hell. Parenting takes you to places you never expected to go and then it abandons you in the mud without a map or a compass."

"I'm not a parent, but I can say I never expected to be discussing tampons with you." *Or hot flashes and my failed menstrual cycle.*

"My point exactly. It's a perfect example of going places you never expected to go."

Alice knew she didn't want any more sympathy from Harry and decided not to give him any. "Now you're just being dramatic. There's both a road map and a compass for puberty. There's heaps of information either online or in books. The first step is opening the conversation and the best way to do that is take her shopping. Show her that buying pads is a perfectly normal and everyday thing to do."

He gave a rueful grin. "You're right. But it's been years since I bought any of that stuff and all the packaging will have changed. I've already let Holly down once by not checking she was sorted. I don't want to stuff up again."

Alice thought about the array of pads on the market for the needs of women across their reproductive lives. She took his point. Whatever Holly's mother had used might not be what Holly needed. "These days they make smaller pads for young girls. Buy those, but get the ones with wings."

"Wings?"

"They fold over the crotch of the panties to hold the pad in place."

He tapped on his phone. "Right, what else?"

"They make longer pads for overnight—"

Holly returned with Alice's bag. "Here you are."

"Thanks." Alice pulled out a makeup bag decorated with Monet's water lilies.

"That's so pretty."

For the first time in a long time, Alice really looked at the little bag. She'd bought it at the Musée de l'Orangerie when she and Lawrence had spent two idyllic weeks in Paris visiting galleries big and small, famous and unknown. Back then, she thought she needed Lawrence to live a full and rounded life. She'd since realized he'd stifled her creativity and trampled her self-confidence. Now, she was proud of not only surviving without him, but of creating her own job opportunities in art, like winning the artist-in-residence gig. That she didn't need Lawrence hurt a lot less than no longer needing this little water lily bag.

She handed it to Holly. "This is yours now, unless you'd prefer something sparkly for your pads?"

"No, I love it. Thank you!" Holly unzipped the bag and pulled out a liner, turning the small rectangle over in her hand. "So, I put this in my panties?"

"You peel off the wrapper and press the sticky side down. When your dad buys you your proper pads, the heart goes at the top and the wings—"

"Can you buy them?" Holly asked at the same time Harry said, "I could do with some help." Both sounded equally desperate.

"I bet if you help, Dad will buy you the satay chicken for dinner," Holly added.

"And I won't make you share it either," Harry said, laughter reaching his eyes.

The heady delight of being valued filled Alice, but her mother's comment about being convenient rose unbidden into her mind. She banished it. Over many months, she'd eaten with the Waxmans, played with them and done art with them. Hell, today she'd admitted to Harry she was menopausal—something she was yet to tell her own family. No, this request had nothing to do with convenience and everything to do with friendship.

Even so, she thought she better lay down some ground rules. "Tell you what. I'll come and help as long as I'm teaching you to fish."

Holly glanced up at Harry, clearly confused.

"She means she'll come shopping with us and explain stuff, but next time we shop on our own."

"You better listen, Dad."

Alice laughed. "You too, Holly."

"I'm not buying them! That's Dad's job."

It was classic teen horror, but Harry didn't bat an eye. "How about you go and get yourself sorted and then we'll head out."

"Okay." Holly stopped at the doorway. "You're coming to dinner too, right, Alice?"

"You bet I am. I've been promised satay."

The moment Holly left the room, Harry said, "I can't thank you enough."

"Happy to help," she said lightly, trying to counter his serious tone.

"You help in more ways than you realize," he said softly.

Something deep inside Alice stirred, tingling faintly. She didn't know whether to laugh or cry that her body was so hormonally screwed up it couldn't manage to mature an ova, but it suddenly thought Harry Waxman was attractive. She remembered Harry when she'd first met him: grumpy, disheveled and monosyllabic. The errant and deluded tingle vanished.

"It's easy. Holly and Hunter are great kids."

"Yeah." Harry pulled out his wallet, peeled off some bills and pressed them into her hand. "Thanks again, Alice."

She stared at the money. It was more than he'd ever paid her for tutoring Holly. "What's this for?"

"Your time. You shouldn't be disadvantaged just because Holly's period came and changed our plans."

"But I didn't earn it." Alice pushed the bills back at him, anger and offense dueling inside her.

Harry folded her fingers over the money. "You've earned it ten times over."

Alice didn't know whether to feel happy that her mother was completely wrong about Harry expecting something for nothing, or unhappy that she'd misinterpreted her role in today's family drama and upcoming celebration. It appeared that she wasn't attending dinner as a family friend, but as a valued employee.

That she felt the distinction keenly made it worse.

CHAPTER NINETEEN

KAREN WALKED INTO THE STAFF ROOM FOR A QUICK CUP OF TEA before her next student arrived. She was back at school for the next few days, helping the Advanced French class students prepare for their oral exams.

"G'day, Karen." Dan van den Berg was sitting at one of the tables with a stack of papers in front of him.

"Hello, Dan. Grading papers? That's an unusual sight."

He laughed good-naturedly, used to the humanities teachers giving him a hard time. "The boss talked me into one seventh grade math class. How are things?"

"Good, thanks." It was a lie but Karen wasn't prepared to talk about the big black brick sitting permanently in her chest—the culmination of her worries about Libby and Alice and, more recently, Jess.

"You must be stoked about Alice getting that artist-in-residence gig."

"Artist in residence?" Karen had no idea what Dan was talking about. "I'm afraid you've got an advantage over me."

Surprise and embarrassment flickered on his face. "I'm sure I read about it in the *Gazette*."

These days, Karen read the *Gazette* every Friday afternoon going directly to the Dear Alice column to try and work out what on earth was going on with her younger daughter and her life. Since their argument when she'd told Karen to butt out, Alice had told her less and less. She came and went from Pelican House giving few details, although always politely letting her know if she'd be home for dinner and continuing with her share of household tasks. Karen was depending on Peter, and to a lesser degree, Libby, for information, but neither of them had mentioned an art project. So how did Dan know?

"I think I would have remembered reading that, Dan. Better yet, I'd have remembered if Alice had told me. Exactly how do you know?"

He shifted in his chair, squirming like a student put on the spot. "Alice mentioned it."

Something about the way he said the words told her the conversation hadn't been bar chit chat at the RSL. Karen didn't know which was worse—Alice securing yet another short-term job keeping her in Kurnai Bay or Alice dating Dan. She sat down. "Tell me you're not dating Alice."

"Jeez, Karen. Thanks for the vote of confidence."

"Can you blame me? Your track record's hardly reassuring and Hil despairs of you ever settling down. After what Lawrence did to Alice, she deserves—"

"A friend," Dan said with uncharacteristic firmness. "And that's what we are. Good friends who have fun together."

His declaration didn't reassure her. "Surely, it would only be a special friend she'd tell about her new job ahead of her family?"

"Maybe she wanted to tell someone who thought it was good news."

His softly spoken words stung. "Alice needs a real job and a real boyfriend, Dan. Not a string of temporary positions or a temporary man."

"I know you changed my diaper a few times, Karen, but we're not kids anymore. Alice tried security and it vanished on her. Right now, she's embracing temporary."

Anger propelled her to her feet. "And you're encouraging her because it suits you!"

Dan's almost permanently relaxed demeanor tensed and he glanced out the window as if needing to glimpse blue sky, green trees and turquoise sea. "Alice and I have only ever been honest with each other, Karen. I get that as her mom what you consider temporary scares you, but not everyone can be tied down."

"Of course you'd say that! Your life's a series of short-term jobs and convenient relationships. Why did this have to be the year you chose to winter in town instead of working on the ski fields?"

"The point I'm trying to make here," Dan continued, ignoring Karen's rudeness, "is that you and Libby are very similar, but Alice is ..." A soft smile lifted his lips. "Alice. You can't press her into a mold that doesn't suit her."

Except Dan didn't understand Alice like Karen did. He hadn't spent years helping her achieve things he'd taken for granted only to almost lose her to a dark and terrifying place. He hadn't been the one worrying about her for another decade until she'd finally found her feet and established herself in a career she loved. The only thing that protected Alice from that dark place was the mold of security and permanency. As her mother, it was Karen's job to make sure she found it again.

Libby was sprawled across a picnic blanket on the beach and concentrating on nothing but her body. The breeze on her skin, the pressure and release of the salt-laden air entering and exiting her lungs, the touch of rough sand on her feet and the kiss of spring sunshine radiating through her hat.

Remembering what she'd learned at the couples' workshop, she'd been striving each day to carve out some time to just be. Usually, it was a struggle to manage ten minutes, but on this glorious Tuesday afternoon, she'd been gifted twice as long, because Alice was running late. Afternoon clinic started at 2:00 so if her twin didn't arrive soon, she'd miss lunch completely.

"Sorry."

Libby felt Alice plonk herself down on the rug. She rolled onto her side, letting the hat fall, and squinted at her sister. "Don't be sorry. I've had a blissful and demand-free break."

"In that case, I totally planned to give it to you. It had nothing to do with me getting so engrossed in planning my first public mural that I lost track of time." Alice's stomach rumbled. "Did you leave me some lunch?"

"In the cooler." Libby sat up, slid on her sunglasses and pulled her hat down low as Alice bit into her sandwich. "Al?"

"Hmm."

"I'm sorry I overreacted about Jess and the winter solstice thing."

Alice stopped chewing and swallowed, unable to hide her surprise. "Thank you."

"I should have apologized weeks ago."

"Hmm. What made you decide to do it today?"

"Nick and I have been learning about how we react to things. For a while, anything to do with that woman flooded me with so much anger I couldn't differentiate between innocent parties and guilty. Everyone got caught up in my personal thunderstorm, including you." Libby twiddled her wedding band, gathering her words. "Relearning trust is hard, but I need to apologize, especially to you, because you've never let me down. You're my twin. You've always been there for me."

"Right from the start." Alice hugged her. "And I still am. So how are things between you and Nick?"

"Improving." The word felt wrong, not seeming to account for the massive distance they'd travelled in the last six weeks. "Actually, things are a lot better. I have whole days when I don't think about her and what she did to us. I'm sleeping better."

"That's got to help."

"Yeah. We still have our moments. It's embarrassing to realize we'd always congratulated ourselves on our communication, but Dom's death showed us we had no idea. We're trying hard to use the tools they taught us at the group. We're working on really hearing what the other person is feeling instead of pretending to listen while we plan what we're going to say the moment the other stops talking."

"Is it helping?"

"I think so. There's less blame. I know it sounds grandiose, but some days we're doing marriage better than we've ever done it before. The girls are definitely more settled."

"That's got to be a relief. And Leo too?"

Everything inside Libby tightened. "Right now, he's not my concern."

Alice chewed her bottom lip. "But he will be?"

"Nick and I are having sex again," she said, desperate to change the subject. The moment the words rushed out she remembered how Alice always got embarrassed talking about sex, which was why she'd always talked to—Her mind recoiled from the thought.

"That's wonderful." Alice's smile wobbled a little at Libby's expression. "Isn't it?"

"It feels a lot like make-up sex."

Alice laughed. "How can that be bad?"

"It isn't bad. It's just ... different. Before all of this, we never argued enough to need make-up sex. Sometimes it feels like we're trying too hard."

"Don't beat yourself up for trying."

"Thanks." Libby hugged her knees. "Thing is, even in my darkest times, when I hated Nick and I didn't want him to touch me, it wasn't the intimacy of sex I missed the most. It was sleeping in the same bed. You know, feet and legs entwined and the weight of his arms wrapped around me, keeping me warm and safe."

Alice made an odd sound and quickly turned her head, staring out to sea.

"You okay?"

Alice sniffed. "I miss that so much."

"I thought you and Dan—"

"That's just sex! Rule Four is no snuggling allowed."

Libby hurt for Alice. "Keep dating. Like you say, it's a numbers game and eventually you'll meet someone."

"The one guy I fell for makes Nick look like a saint." Alice's voice thickened. "And now I'm never going to find anyone, because the tea leaves and the tarot cards—"

"Stop right there!" Libby hated this sort of nonsense and she hated it even more for upsetting her twin. "Alice Hunter, there's no science behind tarot cards or tea leaf readings. Those people listen and ask you questions based on what you say and what you need to hear."

Alice bristled. "Explain this then. I didn't tell Tansy Donovan I was sick, because I didn't know. But she predicted this months ago. Anyway, why would I want to be told I was sick!"

"Sick?" Libby scanned her twin's healthy complexion. "You're not sick. What are you talking about?"

Alice pulled some creased papers out of her bag and shoved them at her. "I've got ... p-p-premature ovarian insuff—My eggs are stuffed! I can't ever have a b-baby."

As Alice sobbed quietly, Libby's gaze frantically sought the three most important results on the page. She rechecked them—the high follicle stimulating hormone level, the low estradiol and the normal thyroid function. Her heart sank.

"Oh, Alice. I'm so sorry. I—" Her eyes landed on Alice's blood type. "Hang on. This is wrong. It says here you're B positive."

Alice blew her nose. "Is that bad too?"

"No, it's just wrong."

"How do you know?"

"Honestly, Alice! How do you not remember your blood group?"

"Honestly, Libby! How do you not remember that cerise is reddish pink? Oh, right, it's because it's not important to you. I don't need to know my blood group."

Libby didn't agree, but for the sake of not arguing she got to the point. "I'm A positive and so are Mom and Dad. It means you can't be B positive."

Alice's hand shot out and gripped Libby's wrist. "Are you saying these aren't my test results?"

"No. I'm saying sometimes mistakes are made. Keying in errors. Maybe the lab technician got distracted and typed in the wrong blood group. And if that happened, we're going to have to report it, because if you'd been about to get a blood transfusion, a mistake like this could kill you."

"They must be someone else's results. I told Lacey Chu I still get periods," Alice said triumphantly. "So, what do I do? Last time it took ages to get a second appointment with her."

"I'll write you a slip for the same tests."

Alice was already scrambling to her feet. "Can you do it now? Please?"

Libby checked the time. "I've got my bag in the car so I'll take your blood and phone the courier. You'll just have enough time to catch him."

"Thank you! When will you get the results?"

"Usually by this time tomorrow. I'll call you."

"It will be good news," Alice said firmly. Defiantly.

"Al, wait. Don't get your hopes up when the only mistake might be your blood type."

But it was too late. Alice's eyes shone and Libby could tell she was back chasing rainbows and unicorns like only Alice could.

ALICE GLANCED AT THE KITCHEN CLOCK FOR THE TENTH TIME IN thirty minutes as if looking forced the hands to move faster. She'd called the clinic at two o'clock, but Penny said she didn't have the results and Libby would call. Three hours had crawled by since then. Alice understood her twin's job could go from mundane to high octane in a second, but why did there have to be an emergency today?

"That's right, Alice, it's all about you," she told McDougall and a loudly meowing Tubby. Both were mooching at her feet hoping for fallen treats from the kitchen counter.

She thought about Brutus, who needed the food but wouldn't eat, and Dan's fussy cat who ate only tuna. Neither of those pets exactly welcomed her into their homes. The night before, Dan's cat had hissed at her. Granted, it hadn't been a Thursday, but after Libby's discovery of the wrong blood type, she'd gone to Dan's seeking some celebratory sex. Not that she'd told him the reason. And he hadn't asked.

Dan not asking suited her perfectly.

The few times she'd experienced a hot flash in Dan's company, he hadn't seemed to notice, which was exactly as it should be. Exactly as she wanted it. Just thinking about the excruciating afternoon with Harry sent violent heat scudding all over her again. She tugged open the freezer, welcoming the cloud of icy cold. Lacey had given her a prescription for hormone replacement therapy patches, but she was yet to get it filled. Initially, she'd been lost in shock over Tim and her diagnosis but after Harry's comment about HRT, she'd been planning on going to the pharmacy. Then Libby's awesome news about the incorrect blood group had her delaying again. After all, she might not need HRT.

Then why do you have a bag of peas on your neck?

For some other reason. One that won't affect my ability to have a baby.

Alice dropped the peas back into the drawer and closed the freezer. As horrible as it was that Harry had recognized the hot flash, she was grateful to him for showing her a fast way to halt them. Not that she'd ever tell him that. One didn't talk about such things with the boss! She was still smarting about being paid to listen to Holly and advise on periods. At the celebratory dinner, she'd initially felt uncomfortable, but nothing about Harry's behavior or the children's indicated she was anything other than a family friend. It was so confusing.

As usual, they'd drawn her into their world of jumbled

conversations, momentary squabbles and laughter. Normally, she'd have insisted she pay for her share, but she'd been too cross with Harry to offer. She'd never met anyone before who invoked in her such a conflicting array of emotions. Whenever she was in his orbit she found herself lurching from annoyance to laughter to sadness and gratitude then back again. The man drove her bonkers.

So why are you putting up with him?

Holly and Hunter.

The thought landed uneasily. She grabbed a knife and cubed the chicken in preparation for the five-spice skewers she planned to barbecue for dinner—if she could wrestle the tongs from her father. The meal was an unspoken apology to her parents for days of being morose and asocial.

The back door slammed and Karen walked into the kitchen, her eyes taking in the honey and cream cheese residue from the cheesecake that Alice was yet to wipe up. Karen wiped every spill as it happened whereas Alice cleaned up at the end. She tensed and waited for Karen to say something, but her mother merely breathed in deeply.

"Hello, darling. Have you invited Dan for dinner?"

The knife caught the edge of her finger and Alice flinched. A pool of blood formed and Alice sucked it, her heart racing. How did Karen know about Dan? The staged dinner at Hilary's that she'd reluctantly attended had taken place months earlier. It turned out to be surprisingly easy to argue with Dan over their disparate political views. In fact, it had been exhilarating not censuring herself to be polite. The sex after had been some of their best.

"You were sensational, Twin Two," Dan had told her when he'd caught his breath.

"Are you talking sex or my performance at dinner?"

"Both. You're the best mate a bloke can have."

But the dinner was long past and Hilary hadn't invited her again, so the parents couldn't have been discussing the possibility of them dating. The only person who knew about the FWB arrangement was Libby and she'd never say anything.

Karen opened a cupboard above the microwave, pulled out the first aid kit and wrapped a Band-Aid around Alice's finger. "I ran into Dan at school yesterday. He told me about the arts council grant. I think he assumed that since you'd told him, you'd have told Dad and me."

Hurt rolled through her mother's voice and guilt stirred. "I was going to tell you, but last week was ..." *Don't say anything about that until you know for sure.* "... difficult."

"Were you going to tell us about the job or about Dan?"

"There's nothing to tell about Dan."

"Oh, Alice!" her mother snapped. "I wasn't born yesterday. You deserve so much better than Dan van den Berg."

The need to defend Dan rushed in so fast she gripped the edge of the counter to avoid swaying. "Are you saying I don't deserve an honest and true friend? Because, that's what Dan is and as far as I know he's never once lied, cheated or misled me. That's more than I can say for Lawrence or Tim or most of the men I've met through dating apps!

"Of course, Dan's not my future, but he's my now. And thank God too, because he doesn't judge me, he isn't disappointed in me and he doesn't hover and find me wanting in every area of my life like you do!"

The landline rang shrilly and they both jumped. A pale Karen answered the call and Alice, who was shaking hard, poured herself a glass of water. Damn hormones! She'd never been this brutally honest with her mother.

"... wonderful, thank you, darling," Karen was saying. "I appreciate it. Thank Nick too. See you soon."

"Is that Libby? I need to talk to her." Alice held out her hand for the phone, but her mother had already hung up.

"She's coming over." Karen smiled brightly. "And staying for dinner."

Alice narrowed her eyes, trying to work out what was going on. Libby had promised to call her when she got the test results and that should have already happened. Now her twin was coming to dinner at Pelican House on her own? Libby never came to dinner on her own.

"It will be nice just the four of us, won't it?" Karen said. "Like old times."

Libby, no! You wouldn't. "Is this an ambush?"

Her mother looked momentarily flustered. "I don't know what you're talking about."

"I think you do. It's what American television shows call an intervention. You called Libby and asked her to come to dinner especially to—"

"I phoned Libby because we're worried about you. She suggested coming for dinner so we can have a good talk without being interrupted by the children."

Alice's blood chilled and just like that, she knew this wasn't about Dan. Her twin was bringing her bad news.

KAREN MET LIBBY AT THE DOOR. "THANK YOU FOR COMING, darling. I'm sure between the three of us we can convince Alice—"

"Mom, how about I just get inside the door. Hi, Dad." Libby kissed Peter. "Got any tonic water?"

"Always. Do you want some gin with it?"

"Goes without saying. Where's Alice?"

"Murdering chicken in the kitchen. I'll send her out to fire up the grill."

"Actually, I think it's best if we all get a drink and sit down. Dinner can wait," Libby said firmly as if she was talking to patients not her parents.

Karen had thought the conversation with Alice would work best over dinner. But given her failed attempts to get Alice to reconsider any of her life choices—her head throbbed every time she thought about Alice with Dan—she was willing to try anything. If Libby thought drinks would work, she was on-board.

"I'll get some nibbles."

Karen entered the kitchen and Alice, who'd been mute since she'd found out Libby was coming to dinner, walked out. Grabbing the dip platter, Karen hurried back to the living room. The girls were on the other side of the room. Alice's head was tilted in close to Libby's, their strands of blond hair indistinguishable from each other's. They were talking softly.

"Just tell me," Alice hissed.

Karen strained to hear Libby's reply but it sounded like, "Trust me. It's better this way."

"Here we go," Peter said jovially, handing around the drinks. "Always lovely to have my girls home together. Cheers."

Peter had returned home from work five minutes before Libby's arrival so Karen was yet to explain the point of the gathering. Part of her was loath to do so. When it came to Alice, Peter didn't always agree with her.

"Actually, Dad, it's more than happenstance. There's something we need to discuss as a family," Libby said.

Peter's bonhomie faded. "I thought you and Nick were finding your way through your problems?"

"We are. This isn't anything to do with Nick and me."

Peter blew out a long, relief-filled breath.

Karen put her hand on his thigh. "It's Alice."

"It's not just Alice, Mom. This is about all of us."

"Of course it is." Karen heard the uncertainty in her voice as she tried to fathom Libby's plan of action. "We're all worried about Alice."

Alice remained silent, her gaze fixed on Libby. "How sick am I? Is it leukemia?"

Sick? Karen's fingers sank into Peter's skin as a thousand terrifying scenarios for her beautiful Alice assaulted her.

"You're not sick." Libby grabbed Alice's hand. "Mom, Dad, a colleague of mine in Bairnsdale recently ordered some routine blood tests for Alice. Why is up to Alice to tell you. The important thing is, when I saw the results I thought the lab had made a mistake. I repeated the tests and today they've come back exactly the same."

"So, this is good news?" Karen's racing heart made concentration difficult.

"It's confusing news."

"How?"

"Alice's blood group is B positive. You, me and Dad are A positive. That means there's no possible way Alice is my twin or your biological child."

The air around Karen solidified, pressing hard on her chest like a ten-ton weight. She tried to breathe in, blow air out, but nothing moved. Like a rusty saw being dragged through her chest, excruciating pain followed, bringing with it the horrors of the past.

ALICE WAS FLOATING, ADRIFT FROM EVERYTHING THAT HAD EVER anchored her. She was Alice Hunter of Pelican House, only Libby had just said she wasn't a Hunter. Wasn't her twin. No! That was impossible. Utterly untrue. Sure, they weren't identical and they had different personalities, but growing up, they'd looked enough alike for people to confuse them. And they had twin radar.

It doesn't always work.

It works enough!

Alice looked to her father, seeking reassurance. He'd tell her Libby was wrong. He'd explain. He always explained things to her in exacting detail whether she was interested or not.

"Dad?"

But Peter's attention was focused on Karen. "Take slow deep breaths, darling. Come on, breathe in ... and ... out."

"I'll get a paper bag," Libby said.

Don't leave me, Alice silently yelled to Libby, but she was already on her feet and racing to the kitchen.

Everything around Alice—the art on the walls, the throw rugs on the knotted red gum floorboards and the view over the expansive green lawn down to the sea—all of it was as familiar to her as her own thumb. For the first eighteen years of her life, Pelican House was the only home she'd known. It had been her bolt-hole whenever things in the big, scary world battered her. It was a place she came to vacation. To draw. To live. It represented love, security and safety. Family.

Now as she looked at Libby and her father fussing over Karen, all that security mocked her.

They were a family of three.

Who the hell was she?

Without knowing how she got there, Alice was standing with her hand on the door handle. She opened the door and walked into the yard, along the path, out between the lacework iron gates and into the twilight.

"Pick up, pick up! Please!" But Alice knew that, despite throwing the plea into the universe, Dan played basketball on Tuesday nights. His phone would be buried in his gym bag and he wouldn't be home for hours. She turned off her phone and walked with no other intention than the overwhelming need to put one foot in front of the other and to keep moving.

The beach called her. The soundtrack of her childhood was the roll and thump of the waves—sometimes as loud and vicious as thunder, sometimes as soft and gentle as a caress, but always there like her family. But as she crested the dunes, the salt-laden wind whipped and buffeted her—the physical manifestation of not being who she thought she was. For thirty-four years, she'd been anchored by her place in the family and now she was adrift, blown in every direction.

She wasn't a Hunter. How was that even possible?

Alice had no idea how long she walked along the cold, wet sand. Nothing existed outside of her disjointed thoughts and half-formed questions that squawked as loud and unceasing as the raucous cry of the silver gulls. It was the airborne sand, blasting her skin and stinging her eyes, that eventually drove her to take the next set of steps off the beach and back over the dunes, seeking the protective break of the tea tree and paperbarks.

The vegetation sheltered her from the wind but not from her thoughts. She wanted Libby. God help her, she wanted Karen and yet she didn't want either of them. She needed explanations, but she wasn't ready for them. Amid the war zone in her head—the shrieking thoughts that exploded when they hit—some sort of survival instinct told her that talking to Karen tonight would be dangerous. She kept walking along the track, her hands pressed to her ears as if that would be enough to silence the noise in her mind.

"Bit nippy to be out without a jacket, love."

Startled, she glanced up at the voice. At some point the track must have finished, because she was standing on a wide expanse of grass in a street and a man was putting out his trash. She didn't know him but she recognized the old-fashioned tea tree fence behind him. She'd parked outside it often enough. Somehow, she was standing on Seaspray Avenue, three miles from Pelican House.

The man was already walking back through his gate when she heard her name being called. She turned and saw Harry. He had one hand on his trash can and the other raised in a wave.

"Nice night for a walk."

Was it? She hadn't been aware of the light fading or the appearance of myriad silver pin pricks that darned the black sky. She hadn't noticed anything about her surroundings until now, but Harry's welcoming smile beckoned her like the spill of a porch light. Shaking, she walked straight to him and lost her battle not to cry.

"Crikey." Harry's arms wrapped around her. "You're freezing. Let's get you inside."

Between shivering and sobbing, she couldn't form any words, but she let him usher her up the steps and into the house. Once on the couch, he tugged an old woolen Aran fishing sweater over her head and tucked her up in the blanket the kids used when they watched TV.

"Will you be right for a sec?" He peered at her, concern bright in his eyes. "I'll be back with a hot drink."

She sucked in some breaths, desperately trying to find a kernel of calm to grab onto, but it only spiraled her into another noisy, snotty crying jag. Brutus, who always gave her a wide berth, wandered over and rested his head on her lap. Her tears splashed onto his nose, but he didn't seem bothered and he stayed put, his soulful brown eyes gazing up at her. She reached for some tissues and realized she'd left the house without her handbag.

Harry returned and pressed tissues into her hands, tucked a heat pack in behind her and pulled her still-shivering body against his warmer one. "Where's that unwanted heat source of yours when you need it, eh?"

Alice didn't know if it was because she couldn't be any more vulnerable or sink any lower than this total emotional collapse, but she laughed. Given she was so full of snot and tears it was more like a bubbly snort.

Brutus barked and licked her face. Alice ruffled his velvet ears. "Totally gross, Brutus."

Harry laughed. "There's nothing Brutus loves more than a good messy cry, right, mate?"

Between the heat pack and Harry's body temperature, the cold she hadn't been aware of seeping into her bones started to lose its icy grip. Her trembling limbs slowly stilled and her noisy gulping breaths returned to normal quiet ones.

"You think you can safely hold a mug now?" Harry asked.

She nodded and he handed her a hot chocolate with a marshmallow melting creamily into the frothy liquid.

"The kids love this, but I can make you tea if you prefer?"

"This is perfect. Thank you." She drank it, feeling its sugary warmth streaking into her and bringing with it a measure of control. "Where's Holly and Hunter?"

"Mid semester disco and scouts. Brutus has been pining all evening so you dropping in like this has really helped him out."

Alice set down her mug. "I didn't actually set out to visit you. I needed to get out and I just started walking and ..."

"Well, I'm glad your feet brought you here, but it's not the night to be walking in a sleeveless top. Want to talk about it?"

"Not really."

"Are you safe? Do you need to call the police?"

"The police? Why would I need to call the police?"

"Alice, you never go anywhere without lugging that giant bag of yours. You're half-dressed for the weather and you're in bare feet. It looks like you've run from a date gone very wrong."

She stared at her feet, surprised not to see her shoes. "It wasn't a date."

He moved slightly and her shoulder shifted against his chest, but he didn't let go of her. "If you don't want to talk to me about it, then please promise me you'll talk to someone. I hate the idea that you might find yourself this distraught and alone again."

Whether it was his obvious worry for her or his calm force field and comforting bulk nestled behind her, the fact she wasn't facing him or that over the preceding months he'd already learned most of her secrets—or none of those things—somehow it seemed perfectly natural to tell him.

"It's messy. I don't really understand it myself."

"That's okay. Telling me might help you make more sense of it."

"Ha!" She blew her nose then sucked in a long breath. "Okay. Here goes. When I last saw you, I was reeling from the news I couldn't have children, because I'm defective."

"You are not defective, Alice."

"We can debate that another time. Anyway, when I showed Libby the results of the blood tests there was some confusion over my blood group so she repeated the tests. Everything came back the same. I'm still in early menopause but my blood group was right after all. It means my parents aren't my parents." Her voice cracked. "And Libby's not my twin."

"Bloody hell." He breathed the heartfelt words into her hair. "No wonder you've been wandering around in the dark and the cold. You're in shock."

"I feel numb but it hurts like hell too." She turned and looked at him. "I mean how can it be true? I was raised on the story of my birth. I was the undiagnosed twin. Their surprise special baby girl. But it's all lies!"

"Did you grow up feeling loved and special?"

"Yes, but—"

"Then it's not all lies."

"But it's not the truth either."

"No." His arm, which had been slung casually along the length of hers, moved and he gently squeezed her hand. "What did your parents tell you?"

"Nothing. When Libby told us what my blood group meant, my mother collapsed. It was like everything was happening a long way away and I was watching it through a pair of binoculars. Da—Peter was fussing over Karen and Libby was in doctor mode, but I was detached from it all. I just walked out and—Oh!"

She sat up, throwing off the heat pack and the blanket and pulling off the sweater as the fiery flash vanquished all traces of her chill. "I really hate this!"

"At least you don't have hypothermia." Harry picked up a magazine and fanned her.

"Small mercies?"

"Yep." Harry's phone rang and he frowned at the screen as if he didn't recognize the number. "Sorry. I need to take this. It might be to do with the kids."

"Of course."

He stood up. "Harry Waxman ... Ah, yes ... No. Yes, of course. Hang on, I'll ask her." He pressed the mute button. "It's Libby. She sounds exactly like you."

"Utterly devastated?"

"That too. She wants to talk to you."

The calm that Harry had instilled in Alice vanished and when she accepted the phone, her hand shook. "Hi, Libs."

"Oh, thank God. We've been worried sick. Are you alright?"

"I don't think so."

"But you haven't hurt yourself?"

Alice glanced down at her feet and saw dried blood on them. "Maybe a few scratches. I didn't realize I wasn't wearing shoes." It suddenly occurred to her Libby didn't know Harry. "How did you know I was here?"

"I didn't. We thought you'd go to Dan's. Nick drove over there and then found Dan at the sports center. They're both out looking for you. I've called everyone you know. It was Dad who suggested Harry."

The mention of Peter drove a knife into her heart. "How are they?"

"Dad's beside himself and Mom's asleep. She was in such a state, I had to sedate her."

"Libs, I don't understand any of this."

"Me neither. Dad's refusing to talk about it until Mom's ready. I'm angry with them and my mind won't stop spinning. "

"I'm that and more."

"Oh, Alice, I'm sorry. When I got the results, I thought I was doing the right thing telling everyone together. I didn't want to upset you with unanswered whys and hows. I honestly thought that if I showed them irrefutable evidence, Mom and Dad would tell us the truth. I never imagined Mom would fall apart. I mean she's a rock. I've *never* seen her like this."

"No." When it came to Karen, Alice was flailing between devastating betrayal and anxiety. How was it possible to be furious with someone and worried about them all at the same time?

"I was panicking that Mom was stroking out and I didn't realize you'd left," Libby said. "That's when I lost it. We've all been frantic. I didn't know if you would—Please come home."

"I can't go back to Pelican House."

"Then come to Burrunan. Please. I need my twin."

Alice's hand fisted around the blanket. "But I'm not your twin, am I? I've never been your twin."

"You will *always* be my twin."

The tears, which were never far from the surface, spilled over then, choking her words. Harry lifted the phone out of her hand and spoke to Libby. Brutus bounded onto the couch, all long, sharp limbs, and licked her face before doing his best to sit on her lap. She cried into his silky-soft coat.

Harry ended the call and ordered Brutus to his bed. The dog rose but he didn't jump down. Instead, he settled on the other side of her and lay his head in Alice's lap.

"Now you're milking it, Brutus," Harry said.

The dog stared him out. Harry sighed and sat down. "This is why we have a big couch."

"I never realized Brutus had a super power."

"Oh, yeah. He's great at empathy. Lately, we've been far too happy for him, but tonight he's in his element. It's very kind of you to have a personal crisis and help him out."

"I'm good that way." Alice laughed, wondering how she could swing from black despair to amusement and back again in a heartbeat.

"You're good in lots of ways."

The sincerity in his voice circled her but she didn't know what to do with it. Last time he'd said something like that to her, she'd felt a spark of unreliable attraction. Later, he'd paid her for her help. With everything going on right now, she didn't trust herself to understand anything so she did the easiest thing—she stroked Brutus's head.

"Libby wants me to drive you to Burrunan."

"I know."

"Do you want to go?"

"I ..."

"If you decide you don't want to go, there's a spare bed here. If you decide you do, just say the word and I'll drive you. But there's no rush, Alice. Take all the time you need. In the meantime, what do you want? Tea? Something stronger? Food? The distraction of crap TV?"

Her arms and legs felt like they weighed more now than they ever had before and it was too much effort for her to even hold her head up. She let it fall onto his chest and closed her eyes. "Can I just sit here a bit and regroup before we leave?"

"Sounds like a plan."

"Thank you."

He gave her arm a gentle and reassuring squeeze. "Any time, Alice. Any time at all."

CHAPTER TWENTY

Harry let her sleep for an hour before waking her. Despite the obvious wet patch on his shirt, he didn't mention that she'd dribbled on him. This time, instead of being burned with acute embarrassment, Alice had pointed it out and laughed.

"All in all, I'm a nightmare employee."

But Harry hadn't laughed or joined in the joke with a fast rejoinder and she'd experienced a pang of disappointment. Instead he'd offered her a hot grilled cheese toastie before driving her to Burrunan. When they'd arrived, Nick had hugged her hard then vigorously shaken Harry's hand. Libby hugged Harry and then Alice when Nick released her, but Libby didn't let go of her hand, clearly worried that, if she did, Alice might vanish again.

"It will be okay," Libby kept saying after Harry had left.

"Will it? They've kept an enormous lie for thirty-four years! I mean, Karen was open and honest about *everything* and she expected us to be too. God, all those excruciating talks about sex and contraception and drugs and drinking. How she insisted if we had a question about anything we ask her. You did, I didn't. Everything was a teaching moment!"

"Nothing fazed her. She was the most progressive mother in the district."

"But it's all a sham, isn't it? For all her talk about the importance of honest and open communication, she hasn't been honest with me. Why did Karen and Peter lie to me?"

"To us! I don't know, but there must be a reason. Whatever it is, they're still Mom and Dad."

Alice flinched. "They're your mom and dad. I have no idea who my parents are. I can't even start to wrap my head around it. Are you sure neither one of them can be my biological parent?"

"The blood group says it's impossible and their reaction confirmed it. Tomorrow, we'll demand answers. They can't not tell us."

Alice wanted to learn the truth as much as she feared it. "They can. I mean, they've lied this long."

"If they do, we'll test your DNA and start searching for answers that way." Libby squeezed her hand. "But I doubt it will come to that. Now the secret's out, there's no reason not to tell the whole story. I get the feeling Dad's relieved we know."

Alice's heart ached. For all the times she clashed with Karen, Peter was always in her corner. Even though he wasn't artistic, he wasn't quite as organized as Karen. He liked to take his time and mull on things, unlike Libby and Karen, who specialized in making fast decisions. For as long as Alice could remember, she'd treasured the understanding she was more like him.

"Maybe all of this explains why I'm so different from you and Karen."

"Look in the mirror. You're not very different."

"You know what I mean. I'm the disorganized Hunter. The vague and messy one. The one everyone worries about."

"Only because we love you."

Alice pulled her hand out of Libby's, not ready to have that conversation. "I just want to sleep." And forget.

"Do you need some help? I can give you a sleeping pill."

Alice thought about how easily she'd fallen asleep with Harry and

Brutus pressing comfortingly against her. "I'll borrow Monty for company."

In the end, she'd tossed and turned, listening to a large chunk of an audio book, but never able to fully silence the question loop. Who were her parents? Why had Karen and Peter never told her she was adopted? Was she adopted? Who the hell was she?

By 6:00 a.m., she'd given up on sleep. She got up to the sweet caroling call of the magpies, borrowed Libby's running gear and went for a jog. Not a natural athlete, she welcomed the assault on her body as she struggled to get breath into her lungs and oxygen into her cells, leaving her mind blessedly quiet. Alice wanted to keep running and never stop.

When she returned to Burrunan, the household was stirring. Her nieces, who'd been asleep when she'd arrived the night before, threw themselves at her in the way only children can, their joy innocent and unfettered. They begged her to make pancakes. She rolled around on the floor with them first, letting them sit on her, and then she made them breakfast, thankful for their distracting chatter. It kept the worry at bay that today's explanation from her parents might be worse than yesterday's shocking news.

As Libby slung her work satchel on her shoulder and walked to the door, she announced, "Dan's here."

Alice's pancake caught in the back of her throat. "What?"

"'Dan the man' is walking down the side of the house. He'll be here in three, two, one. Morning, Dan. Hello, goodbye. I'm late for clinic."

"Oh, ah, hi, bye, Libby." After Libby rushed past him, Dan stepped inside holding a cardboard coffee tray full of drinks.

Alice blinked. "You brought me coffee?"

"Skinny latte extra hot, right?"

Dan knew her coffee order? "Thank you. Um, shouldn't you be at school?"

"I had to see you first." Dan wrapped his arms around her, hugging her so tight it was hard to breathe. "You know how to worry a bloke, Twin Two."

Alice flinched and immediately felt bad. It wasn't Dan's fault his nickname for her no longer fitted. "Sorry."

"Don't be sorry. I'm sorry I wasn't there for you. I saw the missed call, but I assumed it was a pocket dial, because Tuesday night's game night and, well, you know, we usually only text. It wasn't until Nick showed up, worried as all get out and you'd turned off your phone that I panicked. Libby said there's some stuff going down with your parents ..." He uncharacteristically ran his hand through his hair, messing the style he would have spent time perfecting. "The thing is, I broke a rule of engagement. I told Karen to back off and let you live your life your way. I'm sorry if that's made things difficult for you."

"You're very sweet and, yes, Mom did go ballistic, but you're not the problem."

"Are you sure you're okay? Libby was terrified you might hurt yourself."

A whoosh of indignant heat hit her. When was her family ever going to accept she was no longer a confused, angry and frustrated fourteen-year-old? "I might have just been told I can't have children and that my parents are not my parents, but I'm not going to hurt myself!"

Dan stared at her, momentarily speechless. "Shit, Alice. That's a lifetime of crap in a few days."

"You know me. When I do something, I'm all in." But her voice wobbled.

"No one can fault you on your commitment." Dan hugged her again, but this time when he let her go, he gently cupped her cheeks and then he was kissing her.

It was a vastly different kiss from the hello and goodbye pecks he'd been casually dropping on her cheek for months, but it was absolutely nothing like the erotic kisses he pressed all over her body during sex. This kiss was soft, non-urgent—a lot like tender affection.

"Do you want to have dinner tonight?" Dan asked. "No pressure. I get you'll be over talking and not feel like sex but we can eat and watch a movie ..."

Her heart rolled at his thoughtfulness. He really was a true friend. "Thanks, but I've got no idea how today's going to play out."

"I get it. But I'm here if you need me. Don't hesitate, okay?"

"Okay. And thanks for the coffee."

"Too easy. Catch you later." With a wave, he was out the door and jogging back to his car.

Alice's phone buzzed and she opened the MMS. It was a lopsided attempt at a selfie of Harry and Brutus. The dog was wearing a regal black and gold brocade Martingale collar and the message read, *Brutus dressed to impress. Thinking of you.*

Alice laughed. But when she thought back to the previous night and how both dog and man had given her exactly what she needed, a fluttery feeling beat in her chest. She couldn't quite decide if it was gratitude or something else entirely.

Karen stared out the window, watching the pewter ocean foam white under a gunmetal sky. The cold front that had moved in was lingering, a momentary return to winter after weeks of spring. It was almost as if the weather knew exactly how cold and dark things were inside her. How her worst fears had slipped their knot, releasing toxic secrets into the safe life she'd created and staining it a dirty blood red. Soon the girls would know the secret she'd dedicated her life to keeping so it couldn't hurt anyone again.

"This wasn't supposed to happen," she said yet again, as if it could change anything.

"But it has." Peter's hand touched her shoulder. "And the girls will be here soon."

Telling the girls would tear her in two. Answering their questions might sink her. "Can't I just tell Alice?"

"We've talked about this. We raised them as twins. We tell them together and we deal with the fallout together." He took her hand. "Come on. I heard a car."

"Hi, Mom."

Libby kissed her, but Alice hung back, her eyes gray with shadows of anguish and pain. Karen would have done anything to erase them, but she was all too aware that by the end of the day she would have darkened those shadows to soot.

"I thought it might be nicer in the sunroom," Peter said, leading the way there despite the gloomy sky.

"I don't care where we sit." Alice lowered herself stiffly onto the *chaise longue*. "I just want to know who and where are my parents."

Peter winced. "Sweetheart, I know it's difficult—"

"Difficult!" Alice shrieked. "It's—"

"My fault," Karen said jerkily. "I insisted we raise you as twins. Your father always thought we should tell you the truth."

Libby glanced between them, her gaze searching. "Why didn't you?"

Karen caught Alice's hands. "I thought it was the only way I could protect you. I'd have given my life if I thought it would keep you safe."

Alice's hands ached under Karen's iron-tight grip. "Who am I?"

"You're my beautiful Alice. From the moment, I saw you, I loved you."

Alice pulled away, angry that her beloved birth story was now tainted beyond recognition. "I don't want the lie."

"Ally-oop, it's not a lie," Peter said softly.

"Who is my mother?"

Karen's fingers worked the lace on an old handkerchief like it was rosary beads. "My sister."

"But you're an only child," Libby said, echoing Alice's thought. "You were orphaned at seventeen when your parents died in a car accident ..."

Karen took a sip of water. "I had an older brother, Damien and a younger sister, Lisa."

Lisa. The name triggered something. Alice trawled her memory, not knowing exactly what she was searching for. She gave up—and immediately remembered.

"The Lisa you gave that copy of *Anne of Green Gables*?"

Karen nodded, her eyes fixed on Alice. "Like you, she adored those books. I used to read them to her."

Alice felt a complicated mix of abandonment and grief, despite only just learning of Lisa's existence.

"So, Alice and I are cousins," Libby said.

"You're sisters." Karen's voice cracked. "You were born on the same day and you're our beloved daughters."

Peter cleared his throat. "Girls, please hold the questions and give your mother and I some time to tell you how and why our family was formed."

"But then you'll answer our questions, right?" Libby asked in her very direct way—so much like Karen, so unlike Alice.

Peter glanced at Karen and she nodded. "To the best of our abilities."

Alice looked at the woman she'd never once doubted was her mother, but who was her aunt, yet really her mother. Her head ached. "Please just start."

"Lisa was my baby sister. Unfortunately, she was nine years younger than me. If we'd been closer in age, I might have ... I'm sorry. Bear with me. I'll try to précis." Karen lifted her glasses and wiped her eyes. "My father was a charismatic but damaged man. He had long periods of being calm but then he'd explode without warning. This meant he inevitably lost his job and we'd be forced to move off whichever farm he'd been working on. Damien and I were a tight unit, knitted together by constant moving and having to start at new schools. We didn't have friends but we had each other."

Karen hauled in a deep and shuddery breath. "He died in a farm accident when I was eight and my life changed. My father moved us to the Dandenongs on the edge of Melbourne and my parents joined a church. Suddenly, there were three or four prayer meetings in the house during the week and Sundays were consumed by services. I was sent to Sunday School. None of it filled the hole left by Damien's death but when Lisa arrived a year later, she brought the light back into my life. I adored her. My parents said she was a gift from God, but even then I struggled to make sense of a God who would take Damien away but then give us Lisa. Why couldn't we have both? By the time I was thirteen I was questioning God and my father a lot.

"My father didn't like questions. In our house, his word was law and he qualified all his actions with 'it's God's will.' He channeled the cruelty of the Old Testament hiding it behind a twisted version of the more loving New. I was a teen wanting to do normal teenage things but my father wanted to control what I ate, what I wore, what I read, where I went, who my friends were and what I thought. My mother, either through fear or agreement, supported him and often carried out the punishments. I endured the hunger, being locked in my room and the strap, hoping it would stop him from carrying out his biggest threat, which was the one I feared the most: withdrawing me from school."

Alice noticed sweat on her mother's top lip and a chill ran over her skin. She didn't want to think about what the cruelty of the Old Testament meant. Religion in her own upbringing had been virtually non-existent. Once, when Alice was nine, she'd asked to go to Sunday School, because Amy Lark talked about the fun art and craft activities. Karen had said a very loud and aggressive, "No."

The response was so unexpected, Alice had yelled, "It's not fair!" Peter had hustled her out of the house but instead of reprimanding her for talking back to Karen, he'd taken her shopping for art supplies. Instead of giving her the usual five-dollar budget and making her choose carefully, that day the funds had been unlimited. For years, Alice had treasured it as a golden moment of her childhood. Now it fell under a long, dark shadow.

"So I stopped questioning and complied," Karen continued. "On the outside, it looked like I'd become the dutiful daughter he demanded, but school was the only place in my life I could be me. The only place I could escape and dream. I lost myself in study and it saved me. As soon as I finished high school, my father got me a job in the office at the firm where he'd managed to hold onto a job for five years.

"Between home, work and church there was no getting away from him. When I told him I didn't want the job, he came close to hospitalizing me. I knew the only way to stay in his house and survive would be to hand over control of my life and endure a living death. I couldn't do it. Not even for Lisa."

A shiver shot along Alice's spine. *Sometimes it's important to put yourself first.* How could she have lived for so many years and never once twigged that her mother's childhood had been one of deprivation and abuse?

Karen blew her nose. "I hated leaving Lisa, but the one thing that reassured me that she'd be okay was my father had never hurt her like he'd hurt me. He called her his angel and me the devil incarnate. He loved her and he hated me. I was seventeen and I stupidly believed that her angelic blond hair, cherubic curls and easy disposition would always protect her from his anger. I've never forgiven myself for that."

"You did your best, Kaz," Peter said softly. "The naivety of youth was no match for a bully like your father."

"After I left home, I tried to see Lisa but he withdrew her from school, got me banned from the church and called the police on me when I tried to see her at home. A year after I'd left, I received a letter from Lisa telling me how much she hated me for abandoning the family and God. I knew then the bastard had succeeded in poisoning my beautiful sister against me. I was dead to my family, and that's when I started calling myself an orphan."

Peter squeezed Karen's hand. "Girls, I don't know if this helps you understand, but I'd known your mother for over a year before she told me she had a sister."

Karen cleared her throat. "When Lisa was sixteen, she contacted me completely out of the blue. It was a miracle I got the letter, because I'd moved several times, married your father and changed my name. I immediately called the number she'd given and she told me she was staying with a church family at the beach. I wanted to visit, but she asked me not to, saying the family would only tell our father and then she'd be sent home.

"I should have twigged something was off. I just wish she'd told me she was struggling."

"She hadn't seen you in eight years, darling," Peter said. "Plus, she sent you those photos."

"Photos I should have questioned."

Karen extended a trembling hand and Alice accepted a discolored Polaroid. It was an eerie sensation to be looking at a woman Alice had never met, yet felt she knew. Apart from the 1980's bikini and hairstyle, and the fact two young men were gazing at Lisa with lust bright in their eyes, it was almost identical to a framed photo of Alice that Karen kept on display in the family room. "She looks happy."

"Perhaps in that moment she was and that's why she sent it to me. She wanted me to believe it too. Of course, we found out later how desperately miserable she really was. I didn't know she was pregnant until you were born." Karen smiled for the first time since she'd started talking. "I don't believe in God, but I've always believed it was meant to be that you and Libby were born on the same day."

Libby's hand slipped into Alice's. "Told you we're twins."

"How did you find out about me?" Alice asked, trying to piece everything together.

"After Libby was born, I went home for a shower," Peter said. "There was a message on the voicemail from a social worker at the Royal Women's Hospital. Lisa had listed Karen as her next of kin, but she'd vanished three hours after giving birth to a premature baby. I raced back to the hospital."

"It was awful," Karen said softly. "One minute I was in my private room, sipping wine and gazing in awe at my baby, and the next the police were standing in the doorway. I thought they'd come to ask me if I knew where Lisa might have gone. One look at their faces told me it wasn't that." Her fingers thrashed the lace. "They were very sorry, but they'd found Lisa dead in a squat with a needle in her arm. I couldn't take it in. My beautiful baby sister was dead from a heroin overdose and her baby was fighting the same addiction."

"Oh, God, Mom. How awful!" Libby hugged Karen.

Heroin? Suddenly, Karen's long teaching moments about the evils of drugs by using horrifying pictures that had given Alice nightmares made some sense. It had left her with a strong aversion to taking Tylenol, let alone anything stronger, A bubble of anger permeated her shock. Her birth mother had used drugs when she'd been pregnant with her! That drug habit was the reason Alice was born so underweight. It was the reason for the years of catch-up therapies and tutoring. Why she'd spent her childhood feeling like she'd never be good at anything.

Alice's fingers released the photo of Lisa and it fluttered to the floor. "How could she do that to me?"

"She was obviously sick," Libby said kindly. "Drug addiction's pretty complicated."

"She loved you, Alice," Karen said.

Alice didn't want to know. "How can you say that? She took drugs and abandoned me!"

"She didn't!" Two red spots burned Karen's pale cheeks. "She made sure you were safe."

The words poured over Alice like molten metal, encasing her in unwanted information. "Maybe I can understand why you didn't tell me I was the child of a drug addict, but why didn't you tell me from the start that your sister died and I'm your niece? Why lie and tell us you're an orphan? Why fabricate the story about Libs and me being twins? For years, I've whipped myself that Libby turned to Jess because I wasn't a good enough twin. Thanks a lot!"

Karen visibly sagged. "Alice, everything we've done comes from love."

"We moved down here to keep you safe," Peter said quietly. "We had two little babies born on the same day and everyone assumed you were twins. We went along with it, because we thought it gave you added protection."

"But Nanna and Grandad?" Libby asked. "How did you get them to agree?"

"Wait!" Alice was shaking her head. "This sounds like something out of a TV show. Who were you protecting me from?"

Karen looked to Peter and then back to Alice. "From my father."

"He was a very damaged man," Peter added.

"He hated to lose," Karen said. "When he expelled me from the family he still had Lisa. When she ran from his abuse, he lost her too. He'd have been ashamed of her drug addiction so he wouldn't have tried to find her, but if he'd learned she'd had a baby and that I was the guardian, he'd have moved heaven and earth to get you. He'd tried to control my life and he ruined Lisa's. I wasn't going to let him anywhere near you."

Alice shuddered. "Is he still alive?"

"Thankfully, no."

"Then you should have told me the truth when he died!" Alice's mind whirled. "Hang on, what about my father? Why did you deny me the right to know him? Maybe he wanted to be involved in my life? Maybe he was the artistic one?"

"You got your artistic talent from Lisa," Karen said with some of her old briskness. "She drew beautifully just like you do."

"But what about my father?"

Karen's gaze, which had been fixed on Alice for the entire conversation, suddenly dropped to the tessellated tiling. Alice's stomach dropped with it.

"Peter's your father."

"Who is my birth father?' Alice asked doggedly, avoiding looking at Peter's sad eyes.

"Oh, Alice. Does it matter? Let it go. You've got a loving father right here in front of you, who'd do anything for you."

Hot irritation prickled and stung. "That's got nothing to do with it. You don't have the right to ask me to let it go and I'm not going to do that. You've lied to me all my life about who I am and it stops now. I deserve to know who my father is. If you won't tell me, I'll get a DNA test and search for him myself!"

Karen's hand rose to her mouth.

"Mom, Alice deserves to know," Libby said.

Peter wrung his hands. "It's not easy for your mother."

"Then you tell me," Alice demanded, fast running out of patience. "I might have half brothers and sisters out there."

Peter looked to Karen for guidance.

"Oh, Alice, I never wanted you to know."

"Just. Tell. Me!"

Karen made a sound not dissimilar to an animal in distress.

Peter sighed. "We're sorry, Ally. Lisa was a very troubled young woman. From what we've managed to piece together, she'd been living rough for months. Doing whatever was necessary to ... survive. She left a note."

Alice leaned forward, eager to hear. "And?"

Peter nervously licked his lips. "Lisa—" He cleared his throat. "She didn't know who your father was."

Doing whatever was necessary to survive. Alice gagged and spots swirled in front of her eyes. Her mother was a heroin addict. Her father was a man who'd paid her mother for sex so she could buy her next hit. Or worse still, her dealer, using her. Either way, he was scum.

Libby's arms wrapped around her, but Alice could barely feel them. Her mind was consumed with the horror of her conception and the revulsion for the DNA she'd inherited.

"No!" she spluttered. "No, *no.*"

"Alice, hold on. This doesn't change who you are. Libby's rapid words bounced around her. "You're still funny, quirky, loving, caring, amazing Alice."

But Alice had an overwhelming urge to take a loofah to her skin and scrub hard.

CHAPTER TWENTY-ONE

OCTOBER

Jess sat on a park bench waiting for the usual Thursday transfer. It was a new month and a warm and sunny day after the unseasonal cold snap that made everyone regret packing away the winter woollies. The people in the park—the stragglers from the earlier library story time, five elderly Italian men playing a spirited game of bocce and a couple of runners—were all wearing shorts and T-shirts. Not Jess. She was in yoga pants and a hoodie, struggling to keep warm.

She almost hadn't come. The day hadn't started well. She'd woken up on the couch— again—heavy limbed and with her head banging. She'd been drinking a hangover cure and checking her email when the fulminating anger hit. It had been bubbling inside her ever since. According to the time stamp, the email had been sent late the previous evening and it was as brisk, rude and to the point as ever.

Rosa and Rick will be doing the pick-up and drop-off.

No greeting or sign off. No "Is that okay with you, Jess?" No explanation. Nada.

Jess didn't even know if Leo had ever met Nick's parents. Jess had only met them a couple of times and that had been years earlier. She didn't want to freak Leo out by sending him off with strangers. Libby would never allow her children to go off with people they didn't know, yet Jess was expected to do exactly that without comment or complaint.

Being angry with Libby was now a permanent state, but Jess couldn't believe Karen would let her down like this. Karen was the saving grace of this whole access nightmare. For weeks, she'd faithfully met Jess in the park, picked Leo up and returned him home to her at six o'clock. Last week, Karen had said, "Don't worry about daylight savings. I'll still bring him home to you."

Jess knew Karen cared for her and Leo. Unlike her spoilt princess of a daughter, Karen was doing her best to make things as easy as possible. So why hadn't Karen told her she couldn't come today? Why did it have to be an email from Libby ramming home yet again that she called the shots? But Jess knew it was more than that—it was another test to push Jess to her limits so she'd pull the pin on the access visits and conveniently leave the Hunter-Pirellis' lives.

No way in hell, bitch!

Jess had typed the words, "any change of plans requires twenty-four hours' notice," but sense had prevailed and she hadn't sent it. Libby could keep pushing but Jess wouldn't crack. Still, it didn't mean she wasn't anxious about meeting Rosa and Rick or worried about Leo's reaction.

"Mama, swing!" Leo tugged on her hands, having lost interest in driving his back hoe in the garden bed.

But the thought of standing up and pushing a swing was all too hard today. "Let's have a cuddle."

She gingerly picked up Leo, trying to avoid the ligament twinge she often got now he was heavier. It didn't work—the hot twisting pain froze her for a few seconds as she braced herself for the next wave of pain that would come when she breathed out. She really needed to see a physiotherapist and get this fixed.

Leo wasn't in the mood for a cuddle and he wriggled and

squirmed. Jess was about to put him down when he flung himself forward, arms outstretched. "Pa-Pa!"

Jess looked over his curly head, struggling to bring the couple who were walking toward her into focus. "Who's that?"

"Pa-Pa." It was Rick.

"And who's the lady?"

"Non."

Leo was kicking now, struggling to get down. Every bone in Jess's body ached and her arms felt floppy so she let him slide off her lap and watched him run to Rick. Nick's father scooped him up and swung him around and around. Once, she'd watched Nick do the same thing. Leo giggled and squealed like only happy children can.

Joy and relief swooped through Jess, momentarily dispersing her general malaise. Leo knew his grandparents! Despite Libby's refusal to have anything to do with her son and Nick's failure to stand up to her, he'd involved his parents in the life of their son. Jess blinked back tears as Rick adjusted Leo on his hip and Rosa kissed his chubby cheeks.

She raised her phone, capturing the moment of two doting grandparents making a fuss of their grandson—a boy Libby hadn't been able to give them. She instantly emailed it to her ex-friend. *Suck on that, sweetheart.*

"Jess." Rick now stood above her, but he didn't extend his hand.

"Is this Leo's?" Rosa picked up the brightly colored backpack.

Their aloofness chilled some of Jess's euphoria. It was obvious their enthusiasm for her son didn't extend to her, but she aimed for conversational, hoping to bring them around.

"Yes. I put his swim trunks in today. I thought perhaps Nick might take him swimming. Do you know what he's got planned?"

"We'll bring him back here at 6:00," Rick said.

"I meant, as in the activities?"

Rick and Rosa exchanged a look. "We don't know."

"Like hell you don't."

Angry at the obvious lie and their lack of consideration for her, she stood wanting to neutralize the power imbalance. Her head spun and the ground tilted. She threw out an arm, trying to regain her balance, but red hot pain seared her, sucking the breath out of her lungs. She staggered forward.

"You're drunk!" Rosa pushed her back onto the bench.

"No." But the word was cotton wool in her mouth and unspoken sentences a jumbled mess in her head.

"Sort yourself out," Rick said. "You've got four hours to sober up."

They walked away. Jess lay down on the bench and closed her eyes.

LIBBY'S CELL RANG WITH NICK'S RING TONE SO AS SOON AS SHE'D said farewell to Lucinda Trioli, she called him back. For years, Nick had only ever phoned during clinic hours if there was a domestic crisis, but these days, most of his calls had nothing to do with the girls and everything to do with him telling her how much he loved and appreciated her. They'd taken up the suggestion of their counselor, who'd pointed out that as they both put notes of love in their daughters' lunchboxes, why not extend it to each other? Initially, it felt forced, but now instead of dread, Libby got a buzz of anticipation whenever Nick texted or rang her at work.

"Hi." Nick's voice was unexpectedly serious. "Mom and Dad are here and they're pretty upset. They're saying when they picked up Leo, Jess was drunk."

Libby's hand tightened around the phone. For weeks, Nick had honored her request that she didn't want to hear any details about Thursday afternoons. Although the girls sometimes chattered about seeing Leo, the topic died away quickly enough once she redirected the conversation. Now, despite their agreement, that child and his mother were being shoved into her face.

"And you're telling me this why?"

"Leo might not be safe."

"Call child protective services then."

"That's a big leap, isn't it?"

"You just said he might not be safe."

He was silent for a moment and then he said, hesitantly, "Can't you—"

"No!" Angry and devastated that Nick was asking her to intervene, she hung up and strode down the corridor to the waiting room. "Mr. Tran?"

Libby threw herself into work, thankful it kept her too busy to think of anything other than the patient in front of her. Three hours sped past and she was just following up on some results when Ramesh stuck his head around the door.

"Sorry to disturb you. I have sent Jess Dekic to Bairnsdale Hospital for tests."

"She's not my patient."

"Ah, no." He looked uncomfortable. "But she was very insistent that Nick is her next of kin."

In her dreams! The urge to scream, hit, punch and destroy had her gripping the edge of the desk. "Tell me you didn't call him on her behalf?"

"I told her I would contact him. I did not specify how I would do this," he said in his precise English.

"Thank you. Was she drunk?"

"I did not do a blood alcohol reading. However, she has a UTI, is febrile, dehydrated, nauseated and has abdominal guarding. I inserted an IV, gave her an antiemetic and analgesia and started her on antibiotics. I am certain BRHS will keep her in overnight."

"As I said before, I'm not her doctor. I don't need to know the ins and outs of her treatment plan."

Ramesh gave her a tight but sympathetic smile. "This means her son will be in your and Nick's care overnight."

Libby punched for an outside line and dialed the social work department of BRHS.

For the first time in a week, Alice wished she'd accepted Dan's offer to stay with him for a few days instead of fleeing Pelican House for Burrunan and Libby. Not that she'd told Dan the exact reason she was taking time out from Peter and Karen and he hadn't asked. However, he had taken her on an overnight hike in Croajingolong National Park. It had been the perfect distraction. The physical exertion the walk demanded, the beauty of the coastal scenery, the delicacy of the wild flowers and the wildlife—all of it had filled her mind and pushed the distressing truth of her conception aside for a while.

"We're really friends, aren't we," she'd said as they lay on a groundsheet gazing up at the space haze floating lazily in front of the Milky Way.

"Did you doubt it?"

"Our parents are friends, but don't you think when we started this, we were more acquaintances?"

"No."

She elbowed him. "We're way past a charm offensive."

He sighed and rolled over to face her, his features cast in shadow. "I've always considered you a friend, Alice. Don't you remember the summer I broke my leg? You sat next to me on the beach every afternoon."

Alice did remember that summer. Peter and Karen had refused to let her stay at home alone and she'd hated being stuck on the beach while Libby did lifesaving training. "I remember sitting next to you, but I don't remember us talking much."

"We didn't say much, but I liked watching you draw."

"I found being a teen pretty confusing. Books and art were the only things that made any sense to me."

"Well, you were the only person who bothered to keep me company. It took the edge off my frustration that I was sidelined for the summer."

She laughed. "And the moment the plaster came off you abandoned me."

"Yeah. Sorry about that. Fifteen wasn't my most introspective period."

"Fifteen?" she teased.

"Despite the stories the gossips like to peddle, I'm not that shallow."

"You know, I could always tell people the true story of Dan van."

"Nah." He grinned, his teeth flashing white in the dark. "Happy to leave it as our secret."

Cocooned in her sleeping bag, she'd slept well that night. She'd woken to find they'd rolled into each other for warmth. It was as close as they'd ever come to breaking the "no snuggling" rule.

Now, standing in the family room at Burrunan with tension dripping down the walls as Nick and Libby engaged in a stand-off, Alice missed Dan's uncomplicated company.

"I'll take the kids out for a while," Alice offered. "Give you time to sort this out."

Libby muttered something that sounded like, "There's nothing to sort out."

"Thanks, Alice." Nick's strained face, which had been absent for weeks, was back in full force. He dug his key fob out of his pocket and handed it to her. "Leo's diaper bag's by the door."

Alice bundled Leo and the girls into the car answering their questions about where they were going with a vague "It's a surprise!"

As she adjusted the driver's seat so she could reach the accelerator, it started raining. Bugger! That ruled out the park, the beach and the pier. The library had just closed and the ice-cream parlor hadn't started its summer trading hours. Normally, Pelican House was the obvious answer, but since she'd fled with Libby a week earlier, she was yet to sit down with Karen and Peter on her own. Could she take the children to Dan's?

"Hurry up, Alice!" Indi demanded.

"What's the surprise? "Lucy asked.

"Tractor!" Leo announced, clearly convinced that must be it.

Alice glanced at the three expectant faces in the rear-view mirror and knew although it was Thursday and technically a Dan night, his neat and very adult townhouse lacked anything the children would consider a surprise. And Dan wouldn't welcome her arriving with three kids in tow.

Thankfully, there was a kids' CD in the car's player and she turned it on. With the children momentarily distracted by the music she tapped out two texts before driving the hundred yards out to the road and heading west.

"Sorry to do this to you," Alice said for the second time as she accepted a glass of sparkling water. "Bit of a domestic crisis at Burrunan. I offered to take the kids out to give Libby and Nick some space, but the weather's stymied me."

"Nothing to be sorry about. It's good to see you after—" Harry glanced around, noticing the proximity of the children. "It's just really good to see you."

Alice knew by the earnest look on his face that if the children weren't there, he'd be asking her how she was going. As much as she appreciated Harry's concern, she wasn't ready to disclose the sordid story that surrounded her conception and birth. "Thanks for all those silly photos."

"Did they make you smile?"

"They made me laugh."

"Job done then. Mind you, I'm not sure Brutus will forgive me any time soon for the cow costume."

"I should thank him for his sacrifice. Where is he?"

Harry rolled his eyes. "You arrive with three new and noisy children and you ask me that?"

"My bad. He's in your office under the desk, isn't he?"

"Got it in one."

"Big bird." Leo pointed to the pelican. He'd been staring at it ever since they'd arrived.

"You can touch it." Hunter demonstrated by wiping his hand down the long and regal beak. But Leo kept a good foot gap between himself and the sculpture that dwarfed him.

"Look, Alice!" Indi was clutching a wand, wearing a tiara in her hair, a rainbow-colored T-shirt of Holly's that fell to her knees and a Superman cape. She spun around and around, fascinated by the flow of the cape.

"You're a very good twirler, Indi," Harry said. "Just like Alice."

"Alice doesn't twirl." Indi almost took out Leo with the wand.

Harry steered the little girl away from Leo and the coffee table. "Alice twirls. I've seen her do it."

"When?" Holly and Hunter asked almost simultaneously and equally suspicious.

"In Bairnsdale. You two were at school."

"You didn't go go-karting, did you?" Hunter asked accusingly.

Holly crossed her arms and pouted. "It's not fair you went to Bairnsdale without us."

Alice hadn't seen Holly do the dramatic teenage gesture before. Were the kids upset they'd missed out on a trip to Bairnsdale or was it something else? "Your dad and I didn't go to Bairnsdale together. I just bumped into—"

"Alice twirled into me when I was coming out of the bookshop."

"So, can we go go-karting this weekend?" Hunter asked, clearly relieved he hadn't missed out.'

"Show me?" Holly demanded.

"Show you what?" Alice was fast losing track of the conversation.

"How you twirled into Dad." Holly was pushing back furniture.

"There's really nothing to sho—"

"Come on, Alice." Harry laughed. "Give the audience what they want."

Hunter started slow clapping and Holly chanted, "Twirl. Twirl. Twirl."

"You're all mad," Alice said.

But Harry was grinning at her from across the room and his arm was extended toward her, encouraging her to spin. The little girls had joined in the clapping and the chanting and Leo had plonked himself down on the rug as if he expected a command performance.

"It's really not that exciting, but if you insist ..." Alice took off her scarf, unfurled it and held it above her head. "Drum roll, Hunter."

The boy grinned and trampled his feet noisily on the bare boards.

Alice rose on her toes and spun, her full skirt billowing around her. As she twirled the length of the long room, lightness trickled through her. The horrors that had tried to bind to her over the last week, and define her existence as shameful, loosened. Her parents loved her. They'd kept her safe from a brutal man and given her the best chance in life to be happy. They'd shielded her from being tainted by her conception and birth.

Even though she still believed they should have told her the less sordid part of her story—that she was their niece—she wasn't certain if it would have helped or exacerbated her teenage feelings of inadequacy and the pain of being different. The three of them had worked long and hard to overcome the deficits her mother's illness had inflicted on her and she owed it to her parents and herself not to let the truth taint her life.

She was Alice Hunter. That was all that mattered.

She could have happily kept spinning and soaking up the freedom it offered, but the room ran out. Harry caught her around the waist and she tumbled into his chest. Light headed and laughing, it took her a moment to realize he was holding both her hands in a dance position and then she was twirling out again and spinning back.

"Again, Alice. Again," her nieces called.

Harry twirled her in and out three more times before he spun her into him. With her arm across her front and his firmly on her waist he tilted her back. Trusting him not to drop her, she willingly fell into a deep dip. Laughing, she looked up into Harry's face and their eyes locked. His moss-green gaze, usually full of worries and concerns, was lit with longing. A delicious and unambiguous shiver shot through her.

"Can you teach me that, Harry?" Lucy asked.

Harry's mouth twitched wryly and then Alice was back on her feet, feeling the loss of his hands on her.

"Me too!" Indi said. "Teach me too."

"I didn't know you could dance, Dad." Holly sounded both accusatory and impressed.

"Glad I can still surprise you. When you grow up in a household obsessed with ballroom dancing, you don't have a choice not to learn how to foxtrot, waltz, tango and swing."

"Dance, Harry." Indi positioned herself in front of him, holding out her hands.

"It was my idea. I should go first," Lucy said.

"I'm hungry," Hunter announced. "When's dinner?"

Leo inexplicably burst into tears, adding to the cacophony of sound. Alice scooped him up, kissing the top of his head.

"I'll teach you both how to cuddle dip," Harry told the little girls. "And while you wait your turn, Holly can paint your faces if you like. Right, Hol?"

"Sure."

Indi immediately dropped Harry's hands. "Can I be a lion?"

"What's for dinner?" Hunter repeated.

Seemingly unfazed by the chaos she'd brought into his house, Harry said, "What do you reckon, Alice? Will we order in pizza?"

"Great idea. Thank you."

"Cool. Can I have meat-lovers?" Hunter looked as if all his Christmases had come at once.

"Pizza!" Her overstimulated nieces cheered.

"And garlic bread," Holly said.

"And a big bottle of Coke," Hunter added.

"No," Alice said as Harry's deeper voice chimed with hers.

Harry winked at her. Despite being surrounded by noisy children, Alice got an undeniable rush of lust.

Hunter grabbed a menu from somewhere. Holly started making a list of pizza choices and Harry took a niece in each hand and spun them around and around. Leo snuggled into Alice's shoulder, his soft curls caressing her cheek, and his thumb snuck into his mouth. Alice stood in the middle of bewitching hour—every parent's least favorite time of day—with her heart expanding and cramping all at the same time.

Don't wallow. With what felt to her like superhuman strength, she tried focusing on living in the moment. The impromptu dance party. The seriousness of choosing pizza. The way Harry made her feel. The weight of Leo in her arms and the softness of his sleepy body against hers.

"Mama?" Leo said.

Alice bit her lip. That was the problem with living in unexpected moments—real life always came rushing back.

THE MOMENT THE CAR DISAPPEARED BEHIND THE TREES WITH Alice and the children in it, Nick broke the taut silence that had stretched between them since Alice had walked in on their argument.

"Libs, this is a one-time situation. She's in the hospital so of course Leo will stay the night with us."

Libby didn't think there was any of course about it. "I don't know what's wrong with her, but whether it's appendicitis or the result of hitting the bottle, a social worker needs to be involved. He's better off in foster care until she can look after him again."

Nick's eyes darkened. "He is *not* going to foster care."

Libby felt their hard-earned détente slipping away. "You better talk to Rosa and Rick then."

"They leave for Queensland in the morning."

"Then you better think of someone else, because he is *not* staying here."

"Libby, please. I'm begging."

"Don't you dare make me out to be the bad guy. You know how I feel about this. You shouldn't even be asking me!"

"For God's sake. I didn't plan this. It's just one of those things."

"And how many more will there be? She listed you as next of kin! This is the thin end of the wedge, Nick. If we give in on this, she'll use it to push for more. This is a line in the sand moment and you might not be prepared to draw it, but I am."

"This is nothing to do with you and her, or me and her. It's everything to do with a little boy. Leo's usually home with her by now and we've sent him off with Alice."

"He's more than safe with Alice."

"Yes, but she's not his mother. I'm not adding to his confusion by putting him in the care of strangers. I mean, Jesus! You'd never suggest the girls go to foster care. You realize you're pushing me to sleep on *Freedom* tonight with him and the girls."

She crossed her arms and dug in. "The girls are not having a sleepover on a school night."

His nostrils flared. "Libby, I've respected your wishes on all the access arrangements and under normal conditions, I was willing to keep doing it for as long as you needed. But if you can't make one concession in extenuating circumstances for an innocent little boy, I'm wondering how you can keep working as a doctor."

"That's got nothing to do with this."

"First do no harm, remember?"

"I phoned the social worker! I'm making sure he's safe."

"That's the bare minimum at best. Where's your compassion?"

He turned to leave and panic skittered in her chest. "Where are you going?"

"To pick up the kids and get them into bed on time on *Freedom*."

"I said I don't want—"

"You can't have it all ways. You don't want Leo here when you're here, fine. I respect that. But I'm not prepared to send a message to the girls that I love them any more or any less than Leo. It's up to you."

The cold steel of old betrayals shot down her spine. "Remember to pack their toothbrushes."

CHAPTER TWENTY-TWO

Alice let herself into Pelican House. The kitchen lights were low, the sink gleamed and even for Karen it was insanely tidy. Alice got a pang of remorse for not having contacted her parents sooner. She plucked some specialty glasses out of the cabinet and carried them along with a bottle of port into the living room. Karen's school computer was open on her lap and Peter was reading a book.

"Hi."

"Alice!" The laptop tumbled as Karen jumped to her feet. She hugged her before moving her hands over her as if she was checking her daughter was real and in one piece. "Libby said we needed to give you space but ..." Tears fell down her cheeks.

"We've missed you, Ally-Oop."

Peter's arms enveloped her too, sandwiching Alice between them just like she'd begged them to do when she was a kid. It felt ridiculously good.

"I'm going to drop the port."

"Can't have that." Peter rescued the bottle and poured them all a drink.

She sat between them on the couch. "I just needed some time to—"

"Try and make sense of it." Peter said.

"It's too sad to ever make sense of."

Karen squeezed her hand. "Alice, you're the innocent in all of this. I didn't tell you because I never wanted you to be burdened by something you have no control over. All I wanted was for you to grow up feeling safe and loved. To be free of shame and fear so you could be happy and meet your potential. I wanted everything for you that your mother didn't get to have. What she wanted for you."

The prickle of tears made Alice blink. "How do you even know what she wanted for me?"

"The police found a letter in her pocket written on hospital paper. I still have it. Do you want to read it?"

Alice's instincts warned her to protect herself. "No. Maybe you can paraphrase it?"

"She said she loved you. She wanted to be a mother but she knew she couldn't be until she got clean. She asked me to keep you safe until she could." Karen took in a ragged breath. "You were so sick and her pain and shame must have been so acute ... I just wish I'd known. I'd have rescued her from the streets, I'd—"

"Lisa didn't want you to see her like that," Peter said softly. "How sick she was ..."

Alice took her mother's hand and held it as understanding unfurled inside her. The secret grief Karen had carried all these years drove everything she did, from the way she'd raised her to her current push for Alice to live a safe and secure life. "I can't imagine how you did it."

"Did what?"

"Overcame your own childhood deprivation and loved us so well."

Karen rested her head against hers. "I was lucky. I met your father."

"You worked bloody hard," Peter said.

"Yes, but I had all the Hunters loving me and making me feel safe. It's easier to be the person you want to be when you see your best self reflected back to you through others' eyes. And your grandmother was special. With grace and an innate understanding and a lot of guidance, she and your dad showed me how to be a mother."

"You're a wonderful mother. And because of you and Dad, I'm relatively happy and healthy. You don't have to worry about me as much as you do."

"I've been telling her that for years," Peter said.

Karen kept her gaze on their intertwined fingers. "It's hard for me not to worry, Alice. As a child, you were so much like Lisa, living in your own make-believe world of rainbows and your cast of fairy friends. You clung to your childhood so much longer than Libby and that worried me. You were naive and innocent and easily hurt. When you dropped out of everything then refused to go to school and the psychologist said you were at risk, I was terrified. My worst fear has always been that one day, just like your mother, you might find everything too much."

Anguish for Lisa and Karen morphed with her own needs. "I've grown up, Mom. You and Dad got me here by loving me and giving me every opportunity to overcome my tough start. I'm sorry about my big wobble in the middle, but that was everything to do with aching to be a regular kid who didn't need extra help. And probably a bit to do with living in Libby's shadow."

She gave her mother a wry smile. "I'm sorry I was slow to find my adult feet but, hey, I was slow in everything, right? The thing is, I've survived having my heart broken, being told I can't have children and that my parents didn't create me. I've cried about the babies I'm not going to have and I'm sure I will again, but I can honestly tell you that not once have I ever thought about hurting myself, or worse. I'm not Lisa, Mom. I've only ever known love and I've got you and Dad to thank for that."

Karen's tears intensified. "I'm so relieved."

"So, you'll stop worrying?"

"Are you content?"

Alice considered the question. "I'm all sorts of things at any given moment. I'm angry at my body and now I can't help thinking that my ovaries don't work because of the toxic cocktail I floated in as a fetus—"

"I'm so sorry, Alice. I know how much you wanted children."

"Thank you." She bit her lip, using the pain to hold herself together. "And while we're being honest with each other, I need you to understand that I don't want to go back to Melbourne."

"But you loved—"

"Kaz," Peter said gently. "Listen."

Alice threw him a grateful look. "I thought I loved my job. But it turns out designing catalogs to showcase artworks for the rich to buy didn't come close to giving me the job satisfaction I'm getting now. I love using art to help people remember their lives and remind their families they weren't always old and frail. The mural I'm going to create as part of my artist-in-residence position means I can bring joy to people by representing why they live where they live."

She thought about how Holly was drawing her way through her grief and how Harry was using Alice's painting of the old Clarendon homestead to remind him of how far he'd come. "I want my work to be about using art to improve people's lives on an everyday basis, not helping someone with a lot of money elevate his social status. And I want to do it here in Kurnai Bay and the surrounding district. It's my safe place. I've got you and Dad and Libby. I've got friends."

Her mother's mouth tightened. "You mean Dan?"

"Yes, and you need to apologize to him. He's been amazing this week. But he's not my only friend. There's Missy at Pirellis' and Jim from the *Gazette*."

"And Harry Waxman?" Peter asked.

A rush of heat scuttled through Alice as it did every night at nine o'clock. So much for the new HRT patches she'd been using for a week. "And Stacey at the nursing home and many others. Sure, I came back to the bay because I was hurting, but I was over Lawrence by Christmas. I know you're worried I'm spinning my wheels and at first that was probably true, but it hasn't been for months. I've learned that I didn't lose everything in Melbourne. In fact, I've gained far more by coming back here."

"So, it's an active choice?" Karen asked, clearly struggling to let go of her vision for Alice.

"It is." Alice thought about tonight and twirling with her nieces. "And now I know I can't have babies, I want to be close to Lucy and Indi and share their childhood. And if you still need proof this is where I belong, it's this: even in the middle of all this turmoil, I've experienced moments of joy. Isn't that what you've always wanted for me?"

"She's right, Kaz," Peter said.

Alice threw him a grateful smile. "And now I've fully committed to the bay, it's time I moved into my own place."

"You don't have to," Karen said.

"Yeah, Mom, I do. I love you to bits, but we drive each other nuts."

"If you were just a little tidier ..."

Alice laughed. "If you were just a little messier."

"We're always here."

"I know. I've always known, but today when I was twirling with the kids, I came to truly understand how incredibly lucky I am to have you both."

The three of them sat, lost in their own thoughts, and then Alice broke the silence.

"Mom, I didn't lose the newborn baby photos of Libby and me, did I?"

Karen sighed. "No. But I wasn't lying when I said film was expensive. We had a couple of hospital photos of Libby, but I destroyed them so there was no chance either of you would find them."

"How long was I in the hospital?"

"Eight weeks. The moment you were discharged, we moved down here. Two weeks later, I took you both to the studio for that photo you love so much."

"And the *Anne of Green Gables* book?"

"It was in the plastic bag of Lisa's possessions at the hospital. I couldn't believe she'd kept it or that our father never found it and burned it. It doesn't make a lot of sense, but I hope it gave her some strength when she needed it." Karen shifted forward. "Would you like to see Lisa's box?"

"Was it the one I saw you with a while ago?"

"Yes. There's photos and some letters."

"Maybe another time." Or maybe never.

"I understand. Ask when you're ready." Karen sat back. "Are you heading back to Burrunan tonight or staying here?"

"About that. Things are a little tense over there. Jess is in the hospital—"

"Hospital?" Karen sat up straight. "What's wrong?"

"I don't know, maybe appendicitis? Whatever it is, Ramesh thought she needed to go to Bairnsdale. The thing is, Jess put Nick down as next of kin, so you can imagine the state Libby's in."

"Leo." Karen sighed, her face twisting in despair. "Please don't tell me Libby's being difficult over Leo."

"I want to, but I can't. Nick's taken the kids to sleep on *Freedom*."

"And who's with Jess?"

"I have no idea."

Karen lurched to her feet. "This nonsense has gone on long enough. I'm calling the hospital and then I'm talking to your sister. It's time she understands exactly what she's risking."

Alice couldn't face any more drama tonight so she texted Dan.

Any chance I can come over, just be a friend and get some help with a Dear Alice?

The porch light's on.

ALICE MADE HERSELF A CUP OF TEA AND SAT OPPOSITE DAN, WHO was reading on the couch.

"I've left this one, because I don't know how to answer it."

"Hit me with it."

"'Dear Alice, I'm single and I run a small business. Recently, I've developed feelings for my employee. I think she's single, but how do I tell if she's interested in me as a person or if she's just being a friendly employee? I don't want to jeopardize our working relationship, but if she feels the same way as I do, I'd hate to let the opportunity pass us by. Awkward.'"

Of Alice's many and varied dating disasters, none involved an office romance. She'd gone to work for the Cahills after she'd met Lawrence. The romantic in her wanted to say, "Ask her out," but the feminist in her knew the power imbalance could put the woman in a difficult situation.

"Any suggestions?"

"I've asked a woman out who I worked with."

"But were you her boss?"

"No. And this dude's right about awkward. One ski season, when I was working at Mount Hotham, this woman and I had amazing chemistry. Eventually, we acted on it. The next day I rocked up to work and she was a completely different person. Either my lust had camouflaged her crazy or sex activated her neediness. It made for a long and difficult three months."

"So your advice is don't do it?"

"If he was in the big smoke I'd say that, but let's face it, this is the bay and choices are limited." He winked at her. "With a bit of planning, it's easy enough to run into people."

She laughed. "That's your modus operandi, is it?"

"It worked with you."

"I was at work."

"Yeah, but thankfully I wasn't. It's been a great few months."

Summer was fast approaching. Dan's surf school would be gearing up to full strength and their arrangement would finish. Although she'd miss the benefits, she hoped the friendship would continue, because he'd become one of a few unexpected rocks in her life.

"How's this then for a reply?" She started reading. "'Dear Awkward, This is tricky! So often we can confuse friendliness and a *conscientious and enthusiastic employee with something else. During your week, do you ever see her socially? Away from the office might be the best place to cautiously gauge her interest. Good luck and I hope it works out. Alice.'"*

"Sounds fair to me. It's a shame there are so many small businesses in the district. I'd love to know who the poor bloke is."

Alice laughed. "You say that every time."

"And so does the rest of the bay."

As Jess clutched the back of the hospital gown and maneuvered herself out of the wheelchair and back into bed, she decided it was the most undignified piece of clothing ever invented. She fell onto the pillows, dizzy from painkillers, nauseous from antibiotics and ridiculously exhausted from lying on an examination table for an ultrasound.

Before today, the only ultrasound she'd experienced was when she was pregnant with Leo and it had been joyous. The radiographer had rubbed warm gel on her belly before pressing the probe over her baby bump. Jess had laid back in delight, watching tiny Leo floating contentedly inside her and sucking his tiny thumb. Today's ultrasound was nothing like it. Who even knew it could be done vaginally, let alone be so painful and uncomfortable? It made the previous day's blood tests, where the nurse had jabbed her three times before finding a vein, feel like a walk in the park.

Apparently, they'd ruled out appendicitis. Other than that, Jess couldn't get much more out of the doctor or the nurses than Ramesh had told her the day before: "You have a fever and a urinary tract infection. This other pain you're describing needs investigating."

The pain that was never far away twisted sharply. Jess gripped the edge of the mattress, not daring to move in case she made it worse. Very slowly, she let go of her breath and the pain eased, receding to the familiar dull ache that was a permanent background presence. She suddenly wished Libby was here. Libby would have found out what was going on and explained it to her using words she understood. Libby would have sat by her bed, keeping her company and making her laugh.

At least, she would have—once.

Loneliness plucked at Jess. Should she call Patrice? She wasn't certain their friendship had attained the level of keeping a sick friend company, especially as the French woman worked six long days a week. The accountant Jess worked for once a week was just down the road, but as they only ever discussed the account she managed, he wasn't someone to call on either. She picked up her phone and for the tenth time opened the most surprising and unexpected text she'd received. Alice Hunter had sent her a photo of Leo. His eyes shone with delight, his face was wreathed in an all-encompassing grin and he looked so much like Nick that Jess's heart turned over in painful delight each time she looked at it. Alice had added underneath, *I hope you're home soon.*

The night before, desperate to hear Leo's sweet voice, Jess had immediately texted her thanks and asked Alice for Nick's phone number. Alice hadn't replied, but at nine o'clock, Nick had sent his first ever email on the dedicated account.

Leo is doing okay and settled to sleep without any fuss. You know I can't be your next of kin. Please give the hospital another name.

Jess didn't have another name to give.

Despite the lateness of the hour and knowing her little boy was asleep, she'd emailed back: *I want to talk to Leo.* Nick hadn't replied and eventually Jess had fallen into a fitful sleep. She'd woken at 6:00, anticipating a call around 7:00 when Leo woke up. It hadn't come. Neither had a call after breakfast. She'd still been waiting when the orderly had wheeled her off to ultrasound.

Jess retrieved her phone from the bedside locker. There was a new email from Nick.

Leo ate breakfast and happily went to daycare. Do I need to pick him up? Please advise your ETA back so I can plan accordingly.

A tornado of disbelief blew through her. Where was the "How are you?", the "Hope you're feeling better soon?" The basic humanity?

She typed fast. *If you were my next of kin or gave me your phone number you would know this information already!*

How could Nick think two brief emails telling her Leo was eating and sleeping were enough when he sent Libby videos of the girls whenever she went away for medical conferences? How could Libby, who never went longer than twelve hours without talking to her children, deny Jess the opportunity to talk to Leo? It defied understanding. It was evil.

Childhood memories rushed her and once again she was a second-class citizen, undeserving of what other people took for granted as a basic right. Well, to hell with that. She punched in Libby's phone number and when the automated voice asked if she wished to leave a message, Jess vented in four-and five-letter words, finishing with, "Rot in hell!" Next, she called the daycare center and asked to talk to Leo. The director put her on hold and then one of the staff in the Wombat Room came on the line.

"Hi, Jess, Leo's playing happily in the sandpit."

"Can I talk to him?"

There were a couple of beats of silence. "The thing is, talking to him will remind him that you're not here. It might upset him. You don't want that, do you?"

Frustration almost stole Jess's breath. Of course she didn't want to upset him, but she was his mother! She hadn't seen him in eighteen hours, she was in limbo, waiting for test results and more than anything, she needed to hear her son's sweet, piping voice.

"Can you at least send me a video of him?" She heard the unsteadiness in her voice.

"It's not something we usually do—"

"Being in the hospital's not something I usually do!"

"Oh, right. Sorry. Yes, I'll take one and send it to you. What's your number again?"

Somehow Jess managed not to yell that her number was on every piece of daycare documentation to do with Leo. Tightly and slowly she dictated her number.

After the hustle of an orderly and a nurse taking two women to the OR, the ward settled into relative silence. Jess checked her phone for the video but it hadn't arrived. Unable to settle and lacking the concentration to read, she looked at photos of Leo and channel surfed. Whenever a nurse came in with medication or to take her temperature or check her IV, Jess asked, "Are there any more results?"

Each time, the nurse replied, "Your doctor's in the OR. He'll be around later this afternoon."

"This afternoon?" Jess heard her voice rise. "Does that mean I'll be staying another night?"

"Not necessarily but highly likely."

For the first time since arriving at the hospital, Jess felt tears starting to well. "I miss my little boy."

"It's hard, isn't it? I've got two boys—two and four—and they're intense. Sometimes I think I'll go mad if I don't get some breathing space, but after a couple of hours away from them, I get all fidgety." She patted Jess's arm. "You look pretty washed out. Try and sleep."

After the nurse left, Jess heard her talking to someone in the corridor and then Karen walked into the ward carrying a vase filled with vivid gerberas. Jess blinked, wondering if she was imagining her, but as her eyes came back into focus, it was definitely Karen. Surprise was followed by relief and this time, her tears spilled.

"Hello, Jess."

"Hi," she said thickly.

Karen set down the vase and rummaged through her handbag, producing a packet of travel tissues. "Here."

"Thanks." Jess wiped her face and blew her nose. "Sorry. It's just I didn't expect you or anyone else to come."

"I would have come earlier, but I didn't know you were here until Alice mentioned it around 9:00 last night." Karen pulled out the visitor's chair and sat facing her. "How are you?"

"Woozy. I've had an MRI and an ultrasound but the only thing I know for sure is I have a UTI. I've had them before but I've never felt this rotten."

"Sounds like you're in the best place then."

Another wave of nausea rolled through Jess and she grabbed for the vomit bowl. She had so many questions she wanted to ask Karen— did Libby know she was visiting? Had Karen seen Leo this morning? Was Libby being kind to him? But instead she heard herself asking, "Why did you come?"

"Because no one should be alone in the hospital."

Jess heaved, bringing up bitter yellow liquid.

Karen passed Jess a glass of water. "I'll get the nurse."

Jess rinsed and spat, trying to rid her mouth of the heavy metallic taste and then Karen was back, offering a damp face cloth. The nurse arrived with an injection to stop the vomiting and after that, Jess lay back and closed her eyes.

She wasn't sure how much time had passed when the sounds of the curtain hooks whizzing around the metal rail roused her. Karen was still sitting beside the bed and Jess's doctor was pulling up a second chair.

"Sorry to wake you," he said.

"If it's to tell me I can go home, then you're forgiven."

He gave a tight half-smile and looked inquiringly at Karen. "And you're Jess's mother?"

"No, just a friend." Karen stood up. "I'll give you some privacy and come back in a few minutes."

"No." Jess shot out her hand, catching Karen by the wrist, not totally understanding why but knowing implicitly she didn't want to be alone. "Please stay."

"Are you sure?"

"There's no one else."

Karen nodded wordlessly and sat down, sliding her book into her bag.

Dr. Jenkins cleared his throat. "As you know, we've been running some tests to work out if there's more going on making you sick than just a urinary tract infection."

"And is there?"

"Unfortunately, yes."

A chill raised goose bumps and her mouth dried. It was like she was seeing Doctor Jenkins for the first time since he'd appeared by her bed. On earlier visits, he'd been chatty but now the tone of his voice and the gravitas of his body language screamed bad news.

"Would you like me to explain the results to you now?"

No! Karen's hand slid into hers and Jess felt the reassuring squeeze. Okay, so it was bad news, but bad news had a gradient. There was no reason to leap to catastrophe. Obviously, a doctor wasn't going to joke about her needing surgery so why put off knowing? The sooner Jess knew how long she'd need off work to recuperate, the sooner she could set things in motion for Leo and contact Centrelink for income support and ...

"Hit me with it."

His shoulders tensed. "I'm sorry, Jess. The results tell us you have cancer."

Cancer. The word flung itself around her head, slipping and sliding, banging and crashing. Instinctively she wanted to curl into a ball and hide. "Wh-what sort of cancer?" she heard herself ask, the words echoing back to her.

"Ovarian cancer."

Thank God she'd already had Leo. "You'll get it out of me by taking all my baby-making bits?"

He leaned slightly toward her. "I'm afraid it's far more serious than that, Jess. The tumor's spread to your liver, lungs, bowel and your spine."

Over the noise in her head telling her that the surgeon couldn't possibly remove all those body parts, Jess heard Karen gasp. "So, surgery and chemo?" Jess asked, remembering some of the stories from Relay for Life events. "Will you operate today or—"

"Jess," Karen said firmly. "Let Dr. Jenkins explain."

"I can see this is a huge shock," he said. "I'm so very sorry, but at this point, you've passed the time when surgery, chemotherapy or radiotherapy can help you. We will do our absolute best to keep you comfortable, but now is the time to get your affairs in order."

Jess saw his mouth moving and heard his words, but every part of her was screaming to reject them. "No! No! You don't understand. I'm thirty-four. I've got a toddler to raise."

"I'm sorry," he said helplessly. "Ovarian cancer is like a sleeping giant. Often, by the time the symptoms are obvious it's already too late. Sadly, this is what's happened to you. I know it's not fair and the next few weeks will be difficult but—"

"Weeks?" The room spun around her. "Are you saying that's all I've got?"

"No one can predict exactly, Jess, but it's looking very grim."

"So, you could be wrong?"

"Based on my experience—"

"I want a second opinion!"

"Of course. I'll arrange it." He produced some papers and placed them on the over-bed table. "I'll leave these here for you to read and a social worker and nurse from palliative care will visit and explain the services on offer. I promise you, Jess, we'll do our absolute best for you."

"Your best doesn't sound anywhere near good enough if it means I'm going to die!"

"Thank you, doctor." Karen's voice trembled. "Can we call you later when Jess has questions?"

"Absolutely. And I'll drop in again before I leave for the day." He placed his hand over Jess's and fixed his gaze on her face as if no one else existed. "I'm so very sorry."

His sincerity wrapped around her like a python, squeezing her. She fought it with everything she had. "I won't die. I refuse to die!"

He neither agreed or disabused her—he didn't have to. His sadness-laden silence spoke louder than any words.

CHAPTER TWENTY-THREE

LIBBY STRUGGLED TO CONCENTRATE. SHE'D BEEN DOGGED BY THE problem from the moment she'd woken, stretched out her foot to tangle it with Nick's and hit cold bedsheets. After a run and a shower she'd made breakfast, but the entire time she'd been bracing herself for Nick to walk through the door with the children for breakfast.

It hadn't happened.

At seven thirty, Nick's nautical tune had played on her phone. "Hi, Nick."

"Mommy, we're having café pancakes for breakfast!" Lucy said excitedly.

"How lovely!" Somehow, Libby managed to sound enthusiastic, despite the disparate emotions flooding her.

"I want to talk to Mommy!" Libby heard Indi demanding in the background. The usual wresting of the phone from her sister followed. "Hello, Mommy. Leo did a poo and it stinks."

"That's enough, Indi. Give me the phone, please," Nick said.

"Me! Mine!" Leo's voice drifted into the mix and then Nick was on the line. "Hey." The word was infused with wariness.

"Hi." The distance between them seemed so much farther than the actual two and a half miles separating them.

"Lucy's saying it's yellow day at school, but I thought it was next week. Can you check for me?"

"Wear a color" days at school were the bane of their lives, especially yellow and orange. Neither color suited the girls so there was little in their closet to use as an emergency backup when they forgot.

Libby read the note on the fridge. "Oh hell, she's right." Her mind raced, canvassing various options like dropping a scarf at school so Lucy could tie it around her waist, but Nick was already saying, "I'll drop the littlies at daycare and then take Lucy to Target before school. I might just buy a polo shirt in every possible color so we're not caught short again."

"Good idea. Did the girls sleep okay?"

"The girls *and* Leo slept like logs. I was the one left staring at the deckhead half the night."

His criticism of her was clear, but she refused to apologize. They had an agreement and he'd tried to change the rules without warning. "Hopefully, you'll sleep better tonight."

"I have to go or Lucy will be late for school."

The line went dead. Libby felt like the bricks were back, stacking up fast between them.

Despite a busy clinic, she hadn't been able to shift the feeling all day. She'd half-listened to the abusive message from Jess before deleting it and she'd been checking the email account each hour, but there'd been no new messages since Jess's reply to Nick seeking more information.

Had Jess finally tracked down Nick's new number? If she had, surely Nick would have told her? A dormant doubt niggled and her fingers itched to call him and ask, but instead she texted, *Can you bring chai latte in thirty?*

As she completed a standard insurance medical report for Felicity Longmuir, the words of their counselors, Teresa and Chris, came back to her: *Do you commit to revisiting this when you're stronger as a couple?* The "this" being Leo.

Right up until the previous evening, Libby was convinced they were strong again—stronger than they'd ever been. But that didn't mean she was anywhere near ready to deal with that child beyond knowing he existed and keeping her side of the agreement that Nick spend time with him once a week. This time, she wasn't waiting for the cement to dry on the wall between them before seeking help. Even though it involved babysitting and a trip to Melbourne, she booked an emergency session for them to meet with Teresa and Chris.

Nick arrived with afternoon tea and despite exchanging a greeting kiss and a hug, she collided with his implacable tension.

"Have you heard from Jess?" she asked.

"Other than email? No. Of course not! I think it's time to phone the hospital and find out what's going on."

"That's giving in! It's exactly what she wants."

"Jesus, Libby." He blew out a long breath. "I know she's played games, but she's obviously sick or she'd be out of the hospital. Right now, Leo is our priority."

Your priority. Libby felt her teeth grind. "I'll call Alice and ask her to take him tonight."

"That's not fair to Alice or Leo."

"Don't be silly. She loves kids."

"That's not the point though, is it?"

A kernel of shame pinched her that she'd forgotten Alice was dealing with the grief of not being able to have children. "True. I'll ask Mom."

"Libby." Her name sounded like a warning shot. "If Jess has to stay in the hospital then Leo needs continuity with us."

Anger fizzed. "Don't push this onto me. I'm not ready!"

"I'm sorry you're not ready," he said quietly. The words weren't reassuring and the unspoken "but" hung between them, loud and uncompromising.

"I doubt you want me to call the hospital," Nick said eventually. "I probably wouldn't understand what they told me anyway, but we need to know the state of play. If Leo is going to be with us for the weekend or longer, I need to pick up more clothes and buy diapers—"

The office phone buzzed. "Yes, Trina?"

"Libby, your mother's at reception. She says it's urgent. Do you want me to ask Ramesh to see Mr. Ruben for you?"

Karen never said things were urgent unless they really were. "That would be great, thanks."

"I'll send her down."

Libby hung up. "Mom's here to see me. She told Trina it's urgent. God, I hope Dad's okay."

"He'd be here if he wasn't," Nick said.

"Maybe." But Libby's mind was already darting to car accidents, which bypassed the clinic entirely, going directly to Bairnsdale.

Nick glanced at his watch. "Indi and Leo can stay at daycare until 6:00 if necessary, but school finishes in ten minutes. Can you call—"

"Hello, darling. Nick. I'm glad you're both here." Karen dropped distracted kisses on their cheeks before sitting down.

"Sorry, Karen. I'm about to take off and pick up Lucy," Nick said.

"No need. I've asked Alice to do that for you," Karen said with unusual firmness.

Libby instantly felt vindicated that she hadn't been thoughtless of Alice's feelings when she'd suggested her sister look after Leo. But her mother's actions confused her. "Is Dad okay?"

"Your father's fine. It's Jess. I've just driven back from visiting her."

"What?" Betrayal scorched Libby so fast her skin hurt. "How could you?"

"Oh, for heaven's sake, Libby," Karen said irritably. "You of all people should know that no one deserves to be alone in the hospital."

"But she—"

"Do you know what's wrong with her?" Nick asked.

"Yes."

For the first time since Karen walked in, Libby scrutinized her mother. The remnants of the previous week's emotional whiplash were sketched in the lines on her face, but Alice had called late the night before reassuring Libby she'd spoken to their parents. "We had a long talk and things are good, Libs. When I think about the crapshoot of life, do you know how lucky we are to have them as our parents?"

Libby had opened her mouth to say she'd known that since she'd met Linda Dekic, but that memory brought back the permanent problem of Linda's daughter and her child. Fury had cut off her words along with not wanting to give Alice an opportunity to comment on the fact Nick was sleeping on *Freedom*. She'd murmured her agreement instead.

For the first time in a very long time, Libby knew her mother's stressed demeanor wasn't about Alice and a creeping sense of dread crawled through her. "What's her diagnosis?"

Karen's eyes filled with shadows and she took hold of Libby's hands. "It's not good. She's riddled with cancer."

"Shit." Nick's face drained of color.

Libby pulled her hands away from Karen's, struggling to feel anything. She fell back on doctor mode. "Where's the primary?"

"They're pretty certain it's ovarian cancer. The blood test comes back tomorrow, but does it even matter?" Karen's voice trembled. "I thought she'd let herself go. Thought she was drinking too much because of everything, but her weight gain is fluid—"

"Ascites," Libby said automatically. "It happens when the cancer's in the liver."

"It's not just in her liver. It's in her bowel, her lungs, her bones. It's everywhere!"

"But they can treat it, right?" Nick asked.

Libby didn't need her medical knowledge to answer the question— one look at Karen's face told her everything. "They'll keep her comfortable."

"So, you're saying she's—" Nick's voice was strangled. "How long has she got?"

Karen blew her nose. "They've told her weeks."

Nick swore.

Libby stared out the window, watching the whitecaps far out to sea. The emotions of the others eddied around her, but none touched the dead weight inside her that held all her feelings for Jess: anger, pain and hurt. Regret? No. The only regret was that Jess had jettisoned their friendship and her trust on a selfish whim.

"She wants to come home," Karen said.

"Is she well enough?" Nick asked.

"Palliative care will organize things," Libby said flatly.

"Only if Jess has support in the bay," Karen said. "Libby, you need to talk to her."

"No."

"Jess is dying."

And death trumps everything. The thought tasted bitter in her mouth and she chose her words carefully.

"And I'm truly sorry she's dying, but it doesn't change the fact she lied to me, betrayed me, used Nick and not once has she ever apologized or even hinted at any remorse. Life isn't a movie script, Mom. This isn't the tear-jerking moment where I conveniently forget everything that's happened and forgive her."

"What if she wants to apologize and ask your forgiveness?"

Libby turned around slowly and faced her mother. "Did she tell you that?"

"No." Karen sighed. "But I think you should forgive her."

"When hell freezes over."

Karen glared. "Libby, my father was a cruel and bitter man. I hated him. His need to control everything and everyone around him damaged the people he professed to love. He's the reason I brought you up to put others first and to care. I thought if you didn't know about him or ever meet him, he could never leech into you. But this anger you're holding onto has changed you. You've become as hard and intractable as him. It's terrifying."

Libby hated the unwelcome words. "For thirty-four years you kept your father a secret from us and now, when it's convenient, he's a lesson?"

"Unless you deal with your rage, Libby, it will become a permanent part of you and you'll lose everyone you love."

"I'm only angry with Jess!"

"You're not. You're angry with everyone who doesn't agree with you. You're angry with Leo too, but he isn't Jess. He's blameless of the sins of his mother. He needs you. It's time to step up."

Nick gently squeezed Libby's shoulder. "Think about it, *tesoro mio*."

She shrugged away his touch, furious with them both. "Why can't you see my side? If I go and talk to her, she wins."

Karen's body sagged into the chair. "Oh, Libby. It's not a competition."

Nick stared as if he didn't recognize her. "For God's sake! Didn't you hear a thing Karen just said? Jess was your best friend and now she's dying. Think about it. She's not going to see Leo grow up."

But we will. In death, Jess was inserting herself into the heart of Libby's family, just like she'd done for years, and had been trying to do for months. In the process, she was ripping away any choice Libby had about involving Leo in her life.

"How can you have forgiven her?" Libby heard herself yelling. "She almost destroyed us. And now, just as we're back on our feet, she's firing a final salvo and getting exactly what she wants."

"For pity's sake, Elizabeth Jane," Karen said sharply. "I want to slap you! Jess didn't plan this as a piece of one-upmanship over you."

"I wouldn't put it past her," Libby muttered.

Karen stood up. "I can't talk to you when you're like this. I don't like you when you're like this. I don't even know who you are anymore! Jess deserves to die with dignity. I'm going to talk to Alice and your father about how we can bring her home and give her that. If you wish to be involved then come to dinner tonight."

"I'll be there," Nick said.

"Thank you."

When Karen left the office, Libby wheeled on him. "You don't owe that woman anything!"

"I owe her exactly what I owe any fellow human being: empathy, compassion and kindness. I have to live with myself when she's gone and I regret enough already without adding more to the pile. When Leo's older, I want to be able to look him in the eye. How can I do that if I let his mother die alone?"

"She won't be alone," Libby snapped. "She'll be well cared for."

His face filled with pitying sadness. "You might have forgotten the times you've cried when patients died with just you and Penny by their sides, but I haven't. We owe Jess this."

"We don't. She's not even family."

"You considered her family for a long time and Leo has made it real. I know she's not our favorite person, but I can't in good conscience walk away from her now. Not when I know she has no one else to turn to."

This was the honorable man she'd fallen in love with. The man who'd admitted his mistakes, worked hard to re-establish his integrity and, in the process, won her back. But right now, she didn't want honorable. She wanted someone in her corner, someone to see things from her point of view. More than anything, she wanted someone to understand.

Why did she have to forgive when she was the one who'd been hurt the most?

Duty, heartbreak and self-righteous protection knotted like fishing line. "If she asks for my help to die at home, I won't refuse her."

"Can you live with that if she doesn't ask?"

"I'm going to be living with the evidence of what she did to me for the rest of my life."

Nick grimaced. "That's not what I asked."

"I know."

But Libby didn't have an answer to his question.

CHAPTER TWENTY-FOUR

NOVEMBER

Alice sat on a large towel, staring out to sea as Holly and Hunter tore down the beach, chasing the marauding seagulls who'd tried valiantly to pinch their fish and chips. Earlier, they'd all been rock pool rambling as part of Alice's preparation for the mural. Initially, Alice had called Harry asking to borrow Hunter.

"I want to capture what kids see and he's got the perfect mix of enthusiasm and interest."

"He's also reckless, plunging his hand in first and looking second. So, if it's okay with you, I'll tag along too."

Alice could hardly say no and she found she didn't want to. She kept remembering the way Harry had looked at her the night he'd dipped her. The way he'd winked at her and how her body had reacted with a rush of delight and lust. But sexy Harry was absent this evening and Alice kept wondering if she'd imagined the whole thing.

They'd spent a companionable hour exploring the rock pools and both she and Harry had grabbed Hunter by the back of the T-shirt at least once to avoid disaster. Holly, who now had occasional moments of being a disdainful teen, had been a kid again and equally as enthusiastic as Hunter about their finds. "How about this, Alice?" They'd held up all sorts of things while Alice rapidly sketched outlines and scrawled notes she hoped she'd be able to decipher later.

"Penny for them?" Harry asked.

In the distance, Holly caught her brother and tackled him to the sand. "I was just thinking how normal this is."

"You mean the constant negotiations over who has the most chips and the three of us telling you in no uncertain terms exactly what you should draw in your mural?" Hunter's shout of protest as Holly sat on him drifted on the air. Harry sighed. "And violent sibling affection."

Alice laughed. "Yeah, that's pretty much it."

She pushed her hands into the warm sand and thought about Jess. She'd been discharged from the hospital and although she had little physical stamina, she wasn't completely bedridden—yet. Karen had drawn up a care roster and Alice wasn't certain if her mother was shielding her from too much one-on-one with Jess or giving her space while she could still have it.

So far, Alice's role was taking Leo out for a few hours each day and it wasn't a chore. He was a delight unless he was tired and he didn't have a monopoly on that. Alice took him to the park and the pool and sometimes she just walked him along the coastal track through the tea tree while he napped in the stroller. She loved it, but it felt wrong to enjoy her time with him quite so much. Shouldn't she be devastated that a woman of her own age was losing the opportunity to live and watch her son grow up?

She turned toward Harry. "Do you ever feel guilty that you're here and Helene isn't?"

In usual Harry style, he took time to consider her question. "At the start I did, when I was learning how to work and be a single dad. But not anymore. It sucks that her body let her down, but I'm just thankful I'm here for the kids."

"Leo is not going to have that."

"Isn't your brother-in-law his father?"

"Yes."

"What does Jess want to have happen?"

"For Nick to raise him. But Libby's still so angry, we're worried she'll inflict more harm on Leo than Nick's love can heal. Mom and Dad and I have tried talking to her. Tried explaining this situation's so awful there are no sides anymore, asking her what she'd say to a patient in a similar situation, but she closes down as tight as a clam."

"No kid should suffer for the sins of his parents."

Alice nodded, grateful that Peter and Karen had protected her so well from that. "I know that intellectually Libby believes that, but with Leo she has blinders on."

"Give her time."

"Unfortunately, there really isn't very much time to give."

Harry poured sand through his fingers. "You look at the little guy and see the child you can't have, don't you?"

She was horrified by his perceptiveness. "Is it that obvious to everyone?"

"Probably not. I was just watching you with him at my place." He cleared his throat.

"Let's have dinner."

"Um ... We just consumed an entire month's fat intake."

"I mean a real meal."

She rubbed her belly. "I don't think I could even manage an ice cream."

"Not tonight, Alice. Another time, at a restaurant."

"Like when we celebrated with Holly?"

The tips of Harry's ears glowed red and he swore softly. "Without the kids and Brutus."

Realization slowly dawned and a zip of excitement fizzed around her. "You mean, like a date?"

"Yes!" His breath came out ragged as if he'd just run a race. "Would that be something—"

"Dad!" Sand flew as Hunter slid in between them. "You said we could fly the kites."

"It's getting a bit late. School tomorrow."

"But—"

"Dad, can I have a cell phone?" Holly plonked down next to them. "I'm the only girl at school who doesn't have one."

"I doubt that."

"It's true!"

"We'll talk about it later, okay?"

Holly faced Alice. "You think I need a phone, don't you?"

Alice was still buzzy from Harry's convoluted attempt at asking her out. "I—um. I think it's something you and your dad need to discuss."

"I thought you were my friend!" Holly pouted.

"That's enough, Hol," Harry said firmly.

"I thought we were flying kites," Hunter whined.

"And I thought we were having an enjoyable evening until you two started behaving like brats." Harry shot to his feet, one hundred per cent father. "Come on, pack up. We're going home."

"But, Dad—"

"Do. It. Quietly." Harry folded up the picnic blanket and clipped the lead on Brutus before giving Alice a wry smile. "Kids, eh? Catch you later?"

"Sure. Text me."

"Text you?"

For a man who seemed to read her like a book, sometimes he had serious lapses of social clues. "You know, about that idea of yours …"

It was like watching a movie in slow motion. Confusion gave way to comprehension and then his lips twitched into a smile reminiscent of the one he'd given her when he'd dipped her. Butterflies flittered in her stomach.

"I'm not the best texter. How about I call you?"

"That would be great."

ALICE SAT BACK ON HER HAUNCHES, ROLLED HER SHOULDERS AND ignored the pain in her knees. A rainbow of chalk colors streaked her hands, her loose work pants and likely her face and hair, but finally, the mural was ready to be sealed. Drawing it had been a mental escape from the confronting reality of Jess's diagnosis and Libby's intransigence.

Alice used her finger to smooth out the color around a sea star but she knew it was an act of procrastination. The council members had all trooped past ten minutes earlier, unanimously approving the large pavement mural. Now Lionel, one of the maintenance blokes, was waiting with the roller and a can of clear coat to make it permanent.

"It's incredible, Al," a familiar voice said.

She glanced up to see Dan standing behind her along with a large group of onlookers. Most of the women were looking at him, not the mural, and Alice understood why. The late afternoon sunshine lit his hair golden like a crown and the rest of his good looks and toned body dazzled the mortals. But the cheeky grin he usually cast widely was absent, replaced by an appreciative smile that was focused on her work.

"Thanks, Dan. I'm pretty happy with how it's turned out."

"You can see every feather on the swan."

"It's amazing, isn't it? But I can't take any credit for that. Holly Waxman pointed out that a mural depicting Kurnai Bay must have a swan. She wowed me with her preliminary sketch so I said have at it. But the rest is all me."

"It's like standing on the reef at low tide with Neptune's lace squishing between your toes."

That was one of the unexpected things about her friendship with Dan—he was a natural cheerleader and it gave her a warm fuzzy feeling every time.

Hunter appeared, wriggling his way through the crowd. "Hi, Alice. You drew the blue-ring octopus!"

Alice laughed at his delighted incredulity that she'd taken his suggestion. "There are two so people know what they look like before they light up."

"That's so cool!"

"Dan, this is Hunter Waxman," Alice said. "My rock pool guru."

"G'day, Hunter. Do you draw like your sister?"

"Nah. I play soccer and cricket."

"Excellent," Dan said easily. "Great swan, Holly."

Holly, who'd just arrived with Harry, flushed bright pink but she didn't look down at her feet. In fact, she seemed pleased by the compliment. "Thanks, Mr. Van."

Alice hadn't connected the fact that Dan might know Holly from substitute teaching, but judging by the teen's blush, he was obviously popular. Harry was glancing between Dan, Alice and his daughter, clearly uncertain of the connection. Dan shot out his hand.

"Dan van den Berg. I've been teaching Holly math while Kira Lester's on leave."

"Harry Waxman." He shook Dan's hand. "So, it's you I've got to thank for her sudden enthusiasm for the subject?"

"Dad!" Holly blushed.

"What? You told me the other day how much you love math."

Alice hid her smile. Poor Harry. He'd told her over dinner earlier in the week that being a father of a teenage girl was more bewildering than string theory. Their date, if you could call it that, had been an odd evening. Harry had insisted on picking her up, opening doors for her and pulling out chairs, but their usually effortless conversation often flagged. Alice had found herself wishing they were at the beach or back at his kitchen table or on the couch surrounded by the noise of the household. Perhaps the children and Brutus filled holes between them she'd never noticed existed. That thought had torpedoed her fledgling moments of attraction.

When Harry drove her home, he'd surprised her by walking her to the front door of Pelican House. Peter had whipped it open the moment their feet hit the veranda, insisting Harry come in for a nightcap. Alice had wanted to die on the spot, and not only because her father was channeling 1950. Harry had been a formal stranger all evening and she anticipated the following twenty minutes would be excruciating. But for the first time since he'd arrived to pick her up, the Harry whose company she enjoyed so much appeared and they chatted easily.

When he'd said goodnight, neither of them had suggested another date.

"You ready, Alice?" Lionel was levering the lid off the can of clear coat. "It's just the wife's got wine club tonight and I need to get two coats done and get home for the kids."

"I guess so." Her hands itched to keep working on the mural.

"It's awesome, Alice," Holly said.

"It really is," Harry added. "Glad to see my sea cucumber suggestion got a thumb's up."

"So, you all think it's ready?"

"Yes," four voices said.

"Okay, then." Alice signed it with a flourish and prepared to stand.

Two familiar hands belonging to two different men dangled in front of her. Momentarily discombobulated, she hesitated for a second before sliding one hand into Dan's and the other into Harry's, allowing them to pull her to her feet.

Standing between them, with her hands resting lightly on Hunter's shoulders—mostly with affection but with some cautious restraint—she watched Lionel expertly roll on the clear coat and seal her art into a bay fixture.

"Alice and Holly's first piece of public art," Harry said proudly. "This calls for a celebration. You up for dinner at the Thai, Alice?"

"Can you come, Mr. Van?" Holly asked breathlessly.

Surprise flitted across Harry's face but he reiterated Holly's invitation. "You're welcome."

Dan looked at Alice. "It's Thursday."

"Is that a problem?" Harry asked.

"Alice and I usually—"

"We'd love to come to dinner, wouldn't we, Dan?" Alice said

quickly. She wasn't certain if her insistence they go was because she really wanted to celebrate with the Waxmans or to prevent Dan from outing their arrangement to Harry. Or both.

Harry was now looking straight at Dan, his face a study of concentration as if he was trying to work out exactly what was going on. "Totally understand if you can't make it, Dan."

"I'd love to come. We have to eat first anyway, don't we, Al?" Dan's arm dropped casually across Alice's shoulders.

What was he doing? Flustered, Alice stepped forward and busied herself packing up her gear.

"Do you like satay, Mr. Van?" Holly asked.

As Dan told Holly about eating satay in the streets of Malacca, Alice risked a glance at Harry. His previously open face was closed and his body radiated a new wariness. With a stomach dropping thud, she realized she'd foolishly intersected two of her three very separate worlds.

ALICE SPENT THE FIRST PART OF THE DINNER FEELING LIKE SHE was a referee. In the end, she gave up trying to find topics that both Dan and Harry would find interesting. It didn't take long to realize that Holly had little interest in talking to her while Dan was in the room and he didn't disappoint. For a man who professed not to want children, he was great with them and he drew Holly out to the point she was almost gregarious. Alice focused on Hunter, doing the back-of-the-menu quiz with him while Harry seemed to move between the two conversations with a distracted air.

The moment Hunter finished his last mouthful of deep fried ice-cream, Harry said, "Righto, you two, time to go."

"Aw, Dad!"

"School night."

"I know for a fact Holly's got math homework," Dan added with a smile.

"Can we give you a ride, Alice?" Harry asked.

"You're in the opposite direction, aren't you?" Dan said before adding firmly, "I can drop you home, Al."

Harry faced her. "You sure?"

For a second, Alice wondered if he was asking her about more than just the ride home. "It's probably easier," she said lamely. It felt like no matter the answer, she was letting one of them down.

"Can you come to cricket on Saturday, Alice?" Hunter asked.

"I'll try."

"Alice is probably busy." Harry dropped cash on the table and ushered the kids toward the door.

Alice picked up the money, quickly working out he'd paid for all of them. "Harry!" But the door was closing and if he heard her, he didn't look back.

"Nice kids," Dan said later as they walked back to his place. "Harry divorced?"

"Widower. His wife died a couple of years ago. Cancer."

Dan shuddered. "There's too much of it about."

They were quiet for a while and then Dan broke the silence. "About Saturday. It's my last free weekend until the end of January. I was hoping we might walk to Talbot's Gap."

"Surf school starts that soon?"

"School camps are headed my way first. I'm sure Hunter will be fine if you turn up another week." Dan opened the front door and marched straight to the fridge. "Champagne?"

"Ah ... sure. But why?"

"Your mural."

As Dan grabbed the bottle from the door, she caught sight of a seafood platter on the second shelf. Flabbergasted, she realized he'd planned a much fancier dinner than their usual Thursday stir-fry or risotto.

She pointed to the food. "Why didn't you tell me?"

"Because then it wouldn't have been a surprise."

Dan didn't do surprises. "But if I'd known you'd planned ..." She trailed off as his brows rose, reminding her they'd eaten dinner together every Thursday night for months and he hadn't expected tonight to be any different. Neither had she until Harry had suggested dinner, Holly had looked at Dan with shining eyes and Alice hadn't wanted to disappoint anyone, including herself.

Dan popped the cork and filled two champagne glasses before handing one to her. He raised his own. "To more Alice Hunter art in Kurnai Bay."

"Aw, thank you." She clinked her glass against his, took a sip and then didn't quite know where to put herself. Usually they cooked, ate and had sex. This was new territory.

She followed Dan into the living room, kicked off her shoes and tucked her feet underneath her.

He sat next to her. "How's the house hunting going?"

"It's not. It's what my family says is typical Alice. My momentous decision to move out has coincided with the looming tourist season. Rents are back to being sky high. I'll have to wait until February."

"You can always move in here."

"That's kind, but with summer coming, I don't want to cramp your style."

"About that." He set down his glass and faced her. "You wouldn't be cramping my style at all. It turns out, Alice Hunter, you're very much my style."

Champagne bubbles fizzed up her nose and she coughed. Dan laughed, patting her on the back. Finally, she caught her breath. "What do you mean, I'm your style?"

"Exactly that. I love you, Al."

"You love me?" Shock bounded her heart into overdrive and it thundered in her chest.

He grinned. "You should see your face."

"I—we—you—" Words failed her.

"Yeah, I was pretty stunned too, but I've had a few weeks to get used to the idea. It's not that far out there. You're funny, great in bed and my best friend. What's not to love?"

She blew out a breath, trying to make sense of what he was saying.

Dan loved her? Easygoing, uncomplicated, relaxed Dan, who'd never committed to anyone, loved her? But amid the rush of delighted disbelief, she managed to ask, "What exactly does loving me mean, Dan?"

He picked up her hand. "Move in with me."

"For how long?"

He frowned. "What?"

"Dan, have you ever been in a relationship for longer than a year?"

"Alice, I don't see us having an end date. We can get married, if that's important to you."

"You're proposing?" Disbelief made her voice squeak.

His brow wrinkled momentarily and then he grinned. "I guess I am."

"But ..." Her thoughts spun so fast she was dizzy. "But you said you never wanted to get married."

"I didn't, but you changed my mind. Just think, we can travel the world and have sex in every city."

He was smiling at her and his eyes sparkled with desire. He cupped her cheeks, kissing her quickly—the touch a combination of love and lust. Then he was wrapping his arms around her and cuddling her in against him.

"You're breaking the no-cuddling rule," she teased, but tried it on for size anyway.

He stroked her hair. "I've wanted to do this since the night at Croajingolong."

"That night did feel different."

"Yeah. By then I'd given in and allowed myself to love you."

Alice thought she understood. In the past six months, she'd experienced the occasional moments where she'd wondered if her feelings for Dan were stronger than just friends. But despite her delusions about Tim, she wasn't a total masochist when it came to her heart. Dan had been very clear on their rules of engagement. No commitment. Just casual. They were friends with benefits and she'd taken him at his word. He wasn't anyone's man, except right now he was saying he wanted to be hers. Did she want this? Did she love him enough?

"What changed your mind?"

"There's no longer a reason why we can't be together."

A reason? Alice revisited the rules. Each one had imposed emotional distance. Then the memory slammed into her. *I'm not interested in commitment or kids.* Spikes of heat jabbed her toes, spreading up her legs, before hitting her torso and drenching her.

She sat up, moving away from him. "Are you saying you allowed yourself to love me because I can't have kids?"

He had the decency to look uncomfortable. "It doesn't mean I'm not sad for you, Alice. I know you wanted kids, but think about it. It's removed the only non-negotiable point of difference."

She shook her head so fast her brain hurt. "Not wanting to have children and not being able to have them is completely different."

"How?"

"I want children in my life."

"I get that. You'd make a great teacher."

"What's that got to do with it?"

"It's a way of having kids in your life. You've enjoyed tutoring Holly Waxman, so why not formalize it? I'll happily support you financially while you do a master of education."

His love and care both caressed and stung. "Dan, I want more than being on the periphery of kids' lives. We're only thirty-four. We could adopt or foster."

He suddenly looked as serious as she'd ever seen him. "Alice, I said from the start, I don't want to have kids."

"Yes, but now you love me."

"I do love you. I want to spend the rest of my life with you, but there's more than one way to get what you want out of life. You can get your kid fix teaching during the day and we get to enjoy the evenings, weekends and vacations together." He stroked her cheek. "Just think about the trips we can take, the places we can visit and the fun we'll have together. It's win–win."

He was offering her love and commitment—two of the three reasons she'd put herself through months of disastrous dates. But the chunk of her heart that still bled so easily whenever she thought about her inability to have children dripped red again. She couldn't have kids. Dan didn't want any. Was he right? Did that render their insurmountable difference moot?

Did Dan have a point? Tutoring Holly had brought her a lot of joy and shown her teaching was something she could do. Was teaching the solution to involving kids in her life? Before she'd learned she was infertile, she hadn't wanted to pursue single parenthood. Now, there were absolutely no guarantees she'd ever meet a man who'd want to venture into adoption with her. Fostering kids brought its own set of challenges too, and was she really up for that?

Her thoughts strayed to Lucy and Indi—and Leo. "What about my nieces and nephew?"

"What about them?"

"How do you feel about them sleeping over?"

He gave her an indulgent smile. "I don't hate kids, Al. I'm happy to have them here now and then. I just don't want them underfoot every weekend."

He pulled her back into him and the heady feelings of being adored rendered her momentarily boneless. He was very dear to her and they were definitely compatible in bed. He was offering her love and a life filled with travel and the outdoor pursuits they both enjoyed. She wouldn't be lonely again. He was hers for the taking. All she had to do was say yes.

FROM THE HOSPITAL BED IN HER LIVING ROOM, JESS WATCHED Leo clapping his hands and squealing as Alice pretended to be a bull and chased him into his bedroom. If she squinted, it was easy to pretend it was Libby showering Leo with love. At first, Jess had only done it occasionally, but as her stamina failed her and Alice's presence in the house became a daily event, Jess spent large chunks of time imagining what she desperately wanted to see.

Jess had been home a few weeks now and Libby hadn't emailed, texted, phoned or visited. Unlike the many other times when Jess had asked for a meeting, this time she hadn't left pleading or screeching voicemails or sent begging emails. She hadn't tried to contact Libby, assuming her old friend would come to her. But it appeared not even dying was enough to persuade Libby to make contact.

She picked up the white envelope and pulled out the contents. Again. The high dose of her pain medication blurred the words on the pages of her will and medical power of attorney. They'd been the first items on her "get your affairs in order" list that she'd tackled. Peter had helped her. Nick and Karen had been at the meeting too and Nick had agreed without argument to her request that he raise Leo. But that had been when Jess was convinced Libby would come running. Now she was having second and third thoughts, and time was a ticking bomb.

Jess still had so many things she wanted to do, like finish writing twenty birthday cards for Leo. Karen had suggested it and bought the cards for her, but she could only manage a few each day. The early ones were easier, but the teenage ones were almost impossible. Who would Leo be then? What would he be interested in? The questions rammed home exactly how much she was losing and how much she was going to miss.

Initially, she'd railed violently against the diagnosis and had spent a week lost in the depths of the internet, chasing miracle cures. It was Karen who'd said, "Don't waste the precious time you have."

Jess had hated her for it. "What the hell do you know? Get out!"

Karen stayed seated. "You can yell and scream and call me every name under the sun, but I'm not your mother and I'm not leaving you."

For some reason, that had been the moment Jess truly understood she was going to die. She'd crumpled then, sobbing uncontrollably for the first time since she'd been twelve and determined tears were a waste. Now she was only chasing one miracle—to still be alive on Leo's second birthday.

Alice reappeared in the room. "All that fresh air in the park this morning and he's out like a light."

"Thanks for taking him."

"Too easy."

It was unusual for Jess to be alone with Alice. Usually there was someone else in the house too. Apparently, when death circled, so did people and casseroles. Karen had set up a schedule so Jess wasn't exhausted by visitors and she checked if Jess wished to see them. She'd said yes to everyone, even Genevieve Lawry, who'd made her life hell. The woman had sobbed over her, apologizing for ostracizing her and seeking her forgiveness. Jess couldn't help feeling Genevieve's visit was more to do with the woman's terror that if she didn't apologize, Jess might haunt her.

It surprised her who chose to visit, but outside of her care team, the only person she really wanted to see was Libby. The only thing holding Jess back from asking her to visit was the dread Libby would refuse. It was one indignity she refused to suffer.

In the early afternoon sunshine, Alice looked like a big kid or a children's entertainer. Once Jess had dismissed Alice and her signature bright clothing choices as immature, clownish and completely lacking in style. But the specter of death had given Jess new eyes. Over many days, she'd watched Leo's wondrous delight as he hid under Alice's rainbow print circular skirt or drew his finger over the elephants on her pants.

"I can't play with him for long before I'm exhausted, but I love watching him with you." Jess plucked at the light cotton blanket. "I didn't expect you'd want to help ... We've never been close."

Alice made a sound that held the nub of a laugh. "That's an understatement. When you and Libby got together, I always felt I was in the way."

Jess felt responsible for that. "I think I was jealous of you."

"Me? I was gangly and insecure while you and Libby owned the school."

"You had parents and a sister who loved you."

An odd look crossed Alice's face. "You're right. I got lucky."

At least one Hunter girl realized that. Something crystalized. "I want Leo to know love like that. When I watch him with you, I know he has it. I want you to co-parent him with Nick."

Alice stared at her, eyes wide. "But you've made your will ..."

"I'm still breathing, Alice. I can change it."

"Right. Of course." Alice tugged on her hair and Jess half expected her to suck on the ends like she'd done when she was a teen. "Jess, you know I love Leo to bits just like I love the girls, but I'm not sure me co-parenting him with my brother-in-law is the best solution."

Steel coiled in her belly. "It's better than Libby hating him."

"She doesn't hate him."

"I'm not stupid, Alice. I'm dying and I don't have time for bullshit. Leo is my priority. Nothing else matters."

Alice stared out the window for a long time and when she eventually turned, her eyes were overly bright. "I recently found out that I can't have kids, so your offer's a tantalizing gift and an honor."

For the first time since being told she had weeks to live, Jess wondered if Alice's situation existed to ease her own. Relief spilled through her. "Thank you."

Alice nodded, but shadows dimmed her eyes. "But I don't think you asking me to co-parent him is in Leo's best interests."

"I think *I* know what's best for my son."

"Perhaps." Alice's face was unusually determined. "But you said no bullshit, so here it is. When I was thirteen, you wedged yourself between me and Libby. By choosing to have Leo, you wedged yourself between Libby and Nick. If I raise Leo, it will put a wedge between me, Nick and Libby and the effects will spill out into the family. Everyone will suffer, including Leo. I'm not prepared to let that happen. If Leo is truly your priority, the only way to protect him is to sort everything out with Libby."

Jess's chest cramped. "It's not all on me, you know."

"I know. But it will be all on Leo."

"You make it sound like I'm being difficult."

"You're choosing to hear that."

"Will you at least ask her to come and see me?"

Alice shook her head, her obstinacy always so at odds with her pixie looks. "You're the only one who can ask her, Jess."

"She won't come."

"You don't know that."

"I do. It's something I might have done. The ultimate revenge."

Alice winced. "A friend of mine told me that parenting takes you to places you never expected to go and then abandons you in the mud without a compass. This is your compass and your way out of the mud. You need to do this for Leo. Email Libby and ask her to visit you. It's that simple."

Only there was nothing simple about it.

CHAPTER TWENTY-FIVE

LIBBY POKED AT THE COLD MEAT AND SALAD SHE'D PUT TOGETHER for lunch and eventually pushed it away.

"If you lose any more weight, you'll get sick," Nick commented.

It was Wednesday and they were eating lunch at Burrunan. Nick had suggested they meet at a café, but the last time they'd done that, a stream of people had paused by their table wanting to talk about the "terrible news."

"Just shocking," Genevieve Lawry had said, shaking her head. "I mean, it really makes you think ..."

Libby hadn't inquired as to exactly what it had made the notorious gossip think.

Nick had countered with, "It's a difficult time for everyone," and when Genevieve realized that was all she was going to get from them, she'd finally left them in peace.

Nick passed Libby some strawberries. "First of the season. Dad picked them this morning."

She shook her head.

"Jess doesn't have an appetite either."

It was the first time he'd mentioned her in a few days. Weeks earlier, when Jess was first discharged, Nick had invited Libby to the meeting with Jess and Peter where formal arrangements were being discussed regarding Leo. Libby knew there'd been subsequent meetings, not only because Nick had asked her to attend, but because he always went to great lengths to reassure her that he never saw Jess on his own—Karen, Peter or Alice were always present. Libby loved him for that as much as she hated his lack of understanding that Jess's diagnosis didn't mean her instant forgiveness.

Her mother gave Libby terse updates about Jess's condition whether she wanted to hear them or not. Libby hadn't mentioned her unknown grandfather or her mother's brutal assessment of Libby's behavior to her therapist. Teresa had suggested that the fact Libby listened to Karen talking about Jess meant she either cared enough to want to know or was using it as a form of flagellation. Acutely uncomfortable with all scenarios, Libby had tartly told Teresa that she had little choice but to listen, because Karen in full flight was an unstoppable force.

According to Karen, Jess was no longer able to spend a full day out of bed. She was having ascites drained to relieve breathlessness, her pain medication was being increased and other than cuddles and stories, she could no longer care for Leo. Alice was doing the lion's share of caring for the child and Nick covered the weekends. Although in deference to Libby, Nick wasn't on the sleepover roster. He hadn't even suggested it.

"The thing about Jess's appetite," Nick continued, "is she can't do anything to bring it back."

And they were back to the circular argument. "I can't forgive her."

"I'm not asking you to do that."

"That's a first."

"No. It's your mother who wants you to forgive her. I've never asked you to do that."

She did know that. Just like she understood his loyalty to her. Although Nick took responsibility for his part, he hated the act of betrayal Jess had inflicted on them both. But he no longer hated Jess. Libby found that a hard pill to swallow.

"Libs, you keep saying if you go and see her, she'll win."

The familiar tension inside her tightened a notch. "She will."

"I think if you don't go and see her, she'll win."

"That makes no sense."

"Hear me out." He interlaced his fingers with hers. "I know in an ideal world, you should have all the time you need to work through your anger, loss and betrayal for your friendship. But Jess is losing ground and we're almost out of time. Leo is my son and I can't and won't shy away from that. He'll be living here sooner rather than later and we need to prepare for it. We need to prepare the girls. If you don't talk to Jess before she dies, I'm terrified her legacy will be that we won't survive as a family."

"I wouldn't give her the satisfaction."

"Perhaps you already have."

"What?"

Nick flinched. "You're barely speaking to your mother and you're refusing to see Leo ..." He didn't say, "And we're not out of the woods yet." He didn't have to—it was clear on his face.

Unless you deal with your rage, Libby, it will become a permanent part of you and you'll lose everyone you love. She heard her mother's unwanted prophecy and this time she couldn't ignore it. Her heart kicked up, rushing agitation along her veins as she glimpsed two different versions of her future—neither of them what she wanted. "I hate this so much."

"I know. We all do. There are no winners, but Libs, we can try and prevent there being any more losers."

Libby knew he was thinking of Leo. Of the girls. Of their marriage. Their future.

And that's when it hit her, reverberating through her like shock waves and upending the mess of emotions she'd been so desperate to hold onto to keep her safe from ever being hurt again. She might be a doctor, someone who cared for a living, but Nick was the better person.

"You're far kinder than me."

He shook his head slowly. "I didn't lose as much as you did."

LIBBY WAS FAMILIAR WITH A PALLIATIVE CARE SET UP, BUT THE shock of seeing a hospital bed in Jess's small living room made her sway. The thin and emaciated woman with the huge belly and sunken eyes didn't look anything like the vibrant woman who'd once been her best friend. Anguish rode alongside her anger and her feet refused to move beyond the doorway.

"Hello, Jess."

"Libby?" Jess turned her head. "Are you trying to outdo me at looking like death?"

It was typical Jess and it wounded Libby, reminding her of how close she'd once thought they were. How far apart they were now. "I'm sorry you're dying."

"Yeah. Me too."

"Is there anything I can do for you?" The question came out automatically, honed by years of doctoring.

Jess barked a laugh, which turned into a coughing fit.

Libby hastily poured her a glass of water. "Here."

Jess managed to take a couple of sips through the straw before sinking back onto the bank of pillows. "Do you mean that?"

"What?"

"Doing anything for me?"

Libby felt the pull of a trap. "Some things are unforgivable."

Jess closed her eyes for a moment and took in some deep breaths. "You forgave Nick."

"He's my husband."

"And I'm your best friend. Why can't you forgive me?"

That Jess needed to ask defied all understanding. "You hurt me more."

For a moment, the only sound was the loud tick of the kitchen clock. "I didn't mean to hurt you."

Libby felt herself clench and unclench her hand. "You make it sound like it was all just an accident."

"In a way it was," Jess murmured. She was quiet for a bit and then she cleared her throat. "Did you know Nick was the only guy you never told me about?"

Had the cancer reached Jess's brain? "What are you talking about? Of course I told you about him. You were my bridesmaid."

"That's not what I mean. For years, you told me about every guy you liked. I helped you get ready for every first date. Hell, I even went on first dates with you, but you didn't mention Nick until after your night at Bunga Arm."

"I think you've just forgotten."

"I haven't forgotten a thing."

"I'm sure you have. It was ten years ago."

"I know *exactly* how long ago it was."

Annoyance rode up Libby's spine. "Then why are you only asking me about it now?"

Jess's dark gaze, full of the shadow of death, nailed her. "Because, I'm running out of time and we need to be honest with each other."

"Honest? That's rich coming from you. I've always been honest."

Jess's mouth tightened. "You haven't and it started with Nick. I know why you didn't tell me about him. It was the same reason I never told you about him. Neither of us wanted to share him."

Libby opened her mouth to deny it, but the past rose like a wraith, bringing their university years sharply into focus. Far away from the confines of Kurnai Bay and the watchful eyes of her parents, Libby had embraced freedom. She'd knowingly pushed the boundaries of the rules that Peter and Karen had instilled into her and Jess had happily taken her on the ride. Back then, their friendship was the most important thing in her life. Outside of classes, they did everything together, including sharing boyfriends. It avoided the problem of one of them dating a guy the other didn't like. Dylan had been great fun—a sexy extension of their friendship. But their second attempt with Eric hadn't been a success. Libby had realized she'd grown up and that she shared her parents' values after all. But she hadn't told Jess that, preferring to say that Eric was hers if she wanted him. Jess had shrugged but, a month later, Eric was out of the picture.

Libby had met Nick on one of the few times she was home in the bay without her best friend. Entrusted with the job of picking up the oysters for Dot's eightieth birthday, she'd been walking out of the fish co-op juggling four white boxes. The top box had started to slide and Nick caught it, staving off disaster. He'd relieved her of half the load and they'd stood next to her car talking until Peter had telephoned asking, "What's the hold-up?"

The following day, she'd gone sailing with Nick then promptly delayed her planned return to Melbourne. During her daily phone calls and texts to Jess, she'd deliberately avoided mentioning Nick. If she had, Jess would have driven to the bay to vet him, just as Libby would have done if the situation had been reversed. It had been the first time in their friendship that Libby didn't want Jess's opinion. Nor did she want her charismatic presence around Nick in case it turned his gaze away from her.

"I see you've remembered," Jess said.

There was no point denying it. "I wanted him for myself."

"Yeah." Jess's fingers fiddled with the sheet. "And you're everything he ever wanted, whereas I remind him too much of the wild years he wants to forget."

Libby sat down, shocked by the look of pain and yearning on Jess's face. "You loved him before I met him, didn't you?"

"Since I was fifteen. No one else has ever come close.'

"But ..." Libby grappled with this new information. "No. If you'd loved him, I would have known."

"Seriously, Libby?" Jess laughed, the sound derisive. "Only people who've never known rejection wear their heart on their sleeve."

Slowly, things started to fall into place. Jess's many short-term relationships. Her refusal to commit to anyone. Her on-off friendship with Will. The very first time Jess had ever dented their "friendship first" pact.

"When we got engaged and I begged you to take the Melbourne job, you chose Sydney."

"I stayed away to protect our friendship."

The words snapped Libby out of her confusion. "I don't believe you."

"That's your choice, but it's true." Jess let out a long, rattily sigh. "I love you, Libby, you're the sister I never had. But there are times when it's not easy to love you. You got everything: the best parents, a sister, cute kids, a house on the point, a worthy career *and* the man I love. Do you have any idea how hard it is sometimes to listen to you prattle on about Nick, whining about his stinky socks, how he dresses the girls in mismatched clothes, but then how he always nails your birthday present? Sydney gave me the space I needed so I didn't lose both of you."

The banked coals of Libby's fury flared. "If my friendship's so precious to you, then why the hell did you risk it by having sex with Nick?"

"It was never deliberate."

"I find that hard to believe."

"I'm dying, Lib. Can you just listen?"

The words bit and Libby forced herself to use the listening tools she and Nick had been taught. "I'll try."

Jess took another sip of water as if readying for a long story. "If Nick had fallen in love with anyone other than you, I'd have done everything possible to break them up. But I loved you both. I didn't want to lose either of you, so I moved to Sydney. We talked and had our girls' weekends and when I didn't see you with Nick, I could pretend nothing had changed.

"That year after Dom's death, I ached for you. I wished I could do something to make you feel less gutted. I knew the anniversary was going to be tough so I flew down to surprise you. But when I arrived at Burrunan, you'd taken the girls to Melbourne and Nick was home alone and a mess. I couldn't believe you'd left him when he needed you. It was such a princess thing to do and I got mad. How could you not see what you had in him? So I borrowed Nick, just like we borrow stuff off each other all the time. And I gave him back to you, except for one tiny part of him. I got Leo. You got everything else. It's a fair trade."

It's a fair trade. It's what they'd always said to each other when they were teens and negotiating a swap of possessions. Her guilt about leaving Nick alone collided with her disbelief. "Nick isn't a *Dolly* magazine or a T-shirt!"

"Neither were Dylan or Eric."

Old regrets chilled her. "We were young and stupid."

"Eric didn't cause us any problems and we lived with Dylan for a year without ever fighting over him once."

Libby's mind melted. "Are you saying you thought Nick ... that the six of us could be one big polyamorous family?" Her own incredulity was answered by the look on Jess's face and Libby sat down hard. "Oh my God, that's why you wanted Sulli's house."

Jess stiffened. "I don't get why you're so surprised. You begged me to come back to the bay. You told me over and over how I was a sister to you and that Nick and you were my family. How our kids would grow up together and Leo wouldn't be an only child. It was everything I wanted for him. Everything I wanted for me. Of course I came back and took it. I didn't have the strength to refuse it."

"And what? You never thought I'd be upset when I found out who Leo's father is?"

"*Mi casa es su casa.* Friendship first."

It was the pledge they'd made at thirteen. An immature commitment before either of them had any idea how complex and difficult adult life could be. But they'd grown up and recognized the naivety of such a declaration, hadn't they? Libby had. It was unimaginable that Jess still believed in those simplistic adolescent words.

Except the wounded look on Jess's face clearly told Libby she not only believed the words, she blamed Libby for breaking the pact and damaging their friendship.

The lunacy of it spun her head. Why would Jess think this was normal? Who thought like that? She groped for examples from family and friends and came up empty-handed. Patients? A few snippets of faded psychology lectures dribbled into her mind—arrested emotional development due to childhood trauma. Her mother had survived. Her mother's sister hadn't. Jess was like Karen—tough, a survivor. But Linda hadn't beaten Jess, she'd just drunk herself to death. Jess wasn't traumatized and damaged—she'd got out and thrived. By twenty-two, Jess had left life with Linda and poverty far behind.

Except now, Libby wasn't so sure. Were the deprivations Linda had inflicted on her daughter more than just a lack of food and money? Libby had applauded Jess for being a rebel and for not putting up with crap from anyone, but had she misunderstood completely? Was it really lack of conformity or more the lack of a role model? Was it growing up without a clear understanding of what was acceptable behavior inside a friendship, or any relationship for that matter? Was this why Jess had stuck to their juvenile rules?

The entangled wreckage gutted Libby. "You really believe you've been a good friend to me, don't you?"

"I've been the best version of myself with you."

Libby wanted to yell, "But that's nowhere near good enough!" but the futility of saying it crushed her.

For years, she'd embraced their differences, loving what they offered each other. She'd often said they were two halves of a whole and that was why they were such good friends—they complemented each other. Their strengths fused them together into a tight circle and they didn't need anyone else. Not once had she conceived that Jess could hurt her. Best friends never did that to each other.

Best friends.

The thought barreled into Libby like a runaway truck, bringing with it flashes of memories, like the BFF they'd carved into wet cement when they were thirty. Thirty, for heaven's sake! The many, many times she'd put Jess ahead of Alice and Nick, because Jess made her feel like she was on top of her life and kicking goals. Libby winced as the truth rained over her. God, she was blaming Jess for being juvenile and yet she'd believed every inspirational quote about best friends. She'd mythologized their friendship, not Jess. They'd both demanded and expected unconditional love from the other, only her idealism of the perfect friendship and her need for rules and boundaries had run headlong into Jess's pragmatism and survival instincts. The differences she'd embraced were also the reason they were in this nightmare. They were best friends who loved the same man. Jess had survived the only way she knew how.

Jess grabbed the bed bar and struggled to pull herself up. "I won't ever apologize for Leo. He's my gift. The only part of Nick I got to share. But I regret what it's done to us. I'm sorry for that."

The unexpected apology disarmed her. "I loved you."

"I know. I love you too."

If you love me, how could you do what you did? "I thought we had the perfect friendship."

Jess's thin shoulders rose and fell. "Nothing's perfect, Lib. If it was, I wouldn't be dying. And I wouldn't have to ask you this." Supplication filled her dark brown eyes. "Can you find a way not to blame Leo for me hurting you?"

Flames of anger curled around what she'd long believed their friendship to be. The heat rose, cracking the two perfectly connected halves open and searing her. Vengeance oozed out thick and black before catching alight and filling her with acrid smoke and the bitterness of broken trust and faith. When the black cloud eventually dissipated, she glimpsed in the ash something closer to the reality of their friendship—flawed but with love, however misguided, at its heart.

Libby hugged herself hard, trying to hold herself together. "My family's right. I've let bitterness and revenge get in the way of everything I believe in. Along the way, Leo got tangled up in my hate for you and my grief for Dom. He should have been immune from it all." She heaved in a breath and felt something inside her cleave. "I'm truly sorry for that."

"Thank you." Jess sucked in her lips. "And you and Nick?"

"We've learned a lot."

"Will you be okay?"

Libby wished she knew. "We want to be."

"You *have* to be."

"We're getting help with the speed bumps. We owe it to the girls —" She corrected herself. "We owe it to the children to honor our mistakes, learn from them and live the best version of ourselves. I promise Leo will grow up in the heart of our family surrounded by Hunter and Pirelli love, exactly as he deserves."

Jess pinned her with the lioness stare of a mother protecting her child. "And you won't change your mind?"

"No."

"Not even when he's fifteen and running wild?"

"By then Lucy and Indi will have taught me a few tricks and I'll be prepared."

"You'll give him the 'I love you but not what you're doing' talk like Karen gave me?"

Libby tried to smile but her mouth wouldn't work. "I promise, I'll tell him I love him every day, just like I tell the girls."

"Thank you." A tear slid down Jess's cheek. "Can you do something else for me?"

"If I can."

"Can you tell Leo I was his mother? Tell him some of the good things I did, not just the bad."

"Oh, Jess."

Her chest ached. For so long Libby had believed she was the aggrieved victim who'd suffered the most hurt. Now shame filled her at the many and spiteful ways she'd inflicted pain on Jess since March. She hugged her friend's emaciated body and gave in to the tears she'd battled for weeks not to cry. This ovarian cancer, this silent killer, was stealing so much. Jess's right to raise her child to adulthood. The chance for a little boy to remember his mother's love. The opportunity for Libby and Jess to build a proper adult friendship ... and a thousand other everyday yet momentous things.

"You're Leo's mother, Jess. You will always be his mother and we won't ever deny you to him." Libby swiped at her tears and snorted in a deep breath. "I've got a thousand good stories I'll tell him."

"There's things I want to say to him too."

Libby fished out her phone and opened the camera, sliding it to video. "Tell him."

Jess grimaced. "I look like a corpse already. I want him to hear what I'm saying not be scarred for life."

Libby understood. Jess had always taken the time to do her face and hair before stepping out the door. "What if Kathy comes and does your nails, hair and makeup?"

"She's always booked a month in advance. I may not have that much time."

"I'll make it happen."

"Pulling in those privileged doctor favors, are you?"

"Doing it for a friend."

CHAPTER TWENTY-SIX

DECEMBER

Alice was happy to be back working at Summerhouse. The routine of the last two weeks had changed now that Libby was taking leave to spend as much time as possible with Jess.

Alice was happy her sister had finally exorcised the fulminating rage that had consumed her for months, and she was extremely relieved to see the old Libby back, interacting with Leo with the same degree of care she'd lavished on him from birth to sixteen months. In the worst of situations, it was the best possible outcome for everyone, but knowing that didn't prevent a seam of loss from opening inside Alice.

When Jess had asked Alice to raise Leo, she'd experienced one perfect moment—her chance to love and raise a child. It lasted a split second, before the real cost of such a decision had opened out in front of her, revealing its stark and uncompromising truth. Jess was the perfect example of the high price that came with taking something that wasn't hers and losing everything. No matter how much Alice wanted a child, she wasn't prepared to risk Leo's wellbeing or the love of her family.

What about Dan?

Or Dan! Of course, Dan. That went without saying.

She was still wrapping her head around thinking of her and Dan as a couple, because on a day-to-day basis not a lot had changed. In fact, for only the second time since they'd started their arrangement, she'd missed Thursday night dinner. With everyone focused on making Jess's last weeks count, it seemed wrong to announce they were together. As she'd told Dan, "With Jess and summer, I don't have the headspace to move."

He'd told her not to stress. "I get it, Al. We're both busy, busy. Let's wait until the end of January when we've both got more time and then we can enjoy telling everyone."

So that was the new plan, and although she'd intended to leave a toothbrush at Dan's, she hadn't gotten around to that yet either, as she'd been sleeping at Jess's most nights. They managed to grab a quick lunch every few days at the hamburger joint next to his surf school's storage container and she'd told him that Libby and Jess had reconciled, but she hadn't mentioned how much she was missing her daytime jaunts with Leo. It wasn't something she felt comfortable talking to him about, but then again, she hadn't told anyone else either. She'd planned to tell Harry two nights earlier when he'd dropped Holly off for tutoring, but by the time she'd listened to Hunter telling her about his wicket-taking ball at cricket, Harry was saying, "No time for lollygagging, Hunter. You'll be late for practice."

When he'd returned to collect Holly, instead of hopping out for a chat, he'd tapped his horn and Holly had run to the car. Harry hadn't done that for months. It had taken Alice by surprise, but then again, nothing had felt the same between them since their lackluster date, and she'd hardly seen him since the uncomfortable mural dinner. She kept telling herself it didn't matter.

Except it did matter. Harry was the only person she could talk to about Leo.

His withdrawal ticked her off. Okay, so their date had proved that despite the delicious zips of attraction that had arced between them, none were strong enough to survive an evening alone together without Holly and Hunter to fill the awkward moments. And really, it was good she knew and understood that now. If they hadn't gone on the date, she might still be wondering if there was something between them, and then she couldn't have committed to Dan, and her love life would still be in the holding pattern it had been in for fifteen months.

But it wasn't and she and Dan had a plan. She smiled at the rhyme. And Dan, unlike Harry, wasn't serious and deep and uncannily perceptive. What you saw was what you got with Dan—an uncomplicated pleasure seeker. And more importantly, he wanted her.

But damn it! She and Harry had shared a lot this year and she thought they were close friends. Maybe she should go and see him and ask him what was going on? Except ... was that crossing the boundary line Harry had obviously drawn after their failed date? Was she back to being the tutor?

She suddenly remembered she'd been paid for the mural and she pulled out her phone.

Hi, Harry, Alice here.

Duh! He'd know it was her, because her name was in his phone. She hit the backspace.

Hope all is well?

This was business. Again, she pressed the backspace.

I have $100 for Holly's work on the swan. Can I stop by and drop off the cash? Alice

Immediately, pulsing dots appeared on her phone as Harry typed. Anticipation fizzed. Tingling delight spun through her and her thighs automatically tightened. Horrified, she hastily put the phone down. It didn't mean anything. It was just the communication method triggering a response that had been established during all those weeks of texting Tim. After all, it sometimes happened when Dan texted.

It's supposed to happen when Dan texts. It's not supposed to happen with Harry.

"Hello, Alice, dear. You look pretty. Pink cheeks suit you." Elsie Gregson and her walker stopped in the doorway.

A line of walkers banked up behind her and Roy Barton called out, "Hurry up, Elsie, you're gumming up the works."

"Patience is a virtue, Roy," Elsie said.

"Bugger that. I've got too much to do and not enough time." Roy winked at Alice. "Good to have you back, love."

"It's good to be back."

"How's your sick friend?"

Once Alice would have said, "Jess is Libby's friend," but the correction didn't seem important anymore. "She's fighting hard. It's her son's second birthday tomorrow."

"That's something worth fighting for."

Alice nodded and blew her nose. "Let's get started."

With the usual friendly wrangling from the residents, it took a few minutes to get everyone settled into their seats. Then Alice took time to look at each of their projects, checking for any progress during her absence.

"Trudi did her best," Cynthia offered when Alice tried to hide her dismay at some of the pages. "She's a much better nurse than she is a scrapbooker. Can you weave your magic?"

"Absolutely."

It took Alice some careful work to remove Trudi's misguided enthusiasm for butterflies. After the morning tea break, she sat next to Elsie and carefully positioned the sixty-five-year-old wedding photo onto the page. It had been taken outside the Catholic church and the bride's magnolia brocade train draped elegantly across the stone steps. A young Elsie held a bouquet of roses and her groom stood tall and dignified in a new suit, gazing at his bride as if he couldn't quite believe his luck. Despite the passage of many years, bearing five children, losing one to cerebral palsy and grieving for the man she'd shared her life with for sixty years, the essence of the young bride was still evident in the 88-year-old woman.

"How's that?"

"If you straighten it, we can put the invitation on an angle." Elsie's hands were crippled with arthritis and although she couldn't physically place the scrapbook items where she wanted them, she had a very good eye for design.

Alice did as she was asked, positioning the beautiful wedding invitation with its silver print on heavy—now yellowed—paper. Its existence suggested a love match and Alice realized that when Elsie had been her age, she was in her second decade of marriage. "So, Frank was the love of your life."

"No."

Alice stared at the woman who'd only ever spoken in glowing terms of her husband.

"Close your mouth, dear, the flies will get in."

"But?"

"Frank was a good man, but he wasn't the one who swept me off my feet and made me dizzy with excitement. He was the one who caught me when I fell. Good men don't always make your heart race the first time you meet them, but they're there for the long haul." Elsie's quivering fingers touched Alice's wrist. "Don't settle for anything less than a good man."

Alice thought about Dan and sex. He made her heart race and now he loved her and wanted to spend his life with her. That was the trifecta. "Just between you and me, I've found my good man."

Elsie's rheumy blue eyes sparkled. "There's nothing better than a man who loves you and wants to give you the world."

"We're going to travel."

"That's lovely, dear, but I wasn't being literal. I meant you need a man who wants to give you your heart's desire. My Frank was ahead of his time. He knew when I'd finished school, I'd wanted to be a teacher, but I didn't have the opportunity. When our Douglas died, he encouraged me to enroll in teacher's college even though it meant he was running the farm and dealing with the kids when I was studying. That's love, Alice. That's someone giving you the world. If you and your young man have each other's best interests at heart, you'll be very happy."

"Thanks, Elsie." But as Alice created the page she struggled to move past the words "heart's desire." Her heart's desire was a child and Dan's was a carefree life. But she'd made her peace with that, because even if Dan had wanted children, he couldn't give them to her. No one could. And, just like Frank had encouraged Elsie to teach, Dan was offering her financial support so she could become qualified. That was care. That was love. That was giving her a new version of the world. Besides, she had Lucy and Indi and Leo to shower with love on the weekends.

Happy to have them here now and then. I just don't want them underfoot every weekend.

The large piece of banana bread Alice had scarfed at morning tea suddenly sat like a lead weight in her belly. Exactly what did "now and then" really mean?

After the session, Alice drove straight from Summerhouse to Dan's place, grateful for the rain and stormy seas that had closed the surf school for the afternoon.

"Dan?"

"In the bedroom."

As she stepped into the room he walked out of the master bath. His hair was wet, his chest glistened with droplets of water and he wore a towel wrapped low around his hips.

"Perfect timing." He caught her by the hand and pulled her in close to kiss her.

She came up for air as the backs of her knees hit the mattress and she felt herself about to tumble backwards. "Dan. Stop."

He drew back. "What's up?"

"I need some information."

He sat on the bed next to her. "Shoot."

"Remember when I asked you about my nieces and nephew coming for sleepovers and you said as long as it wasn't every weekend?"

"Yeah."

"So how often were you thinking? Twice a month?"

His brow furrowed. "Not quite that often."

"So once a month and then during school vacation?"

"Alice, I work all through summer vacation and we'll be traveling during the others."

"So once a month when school's open?"

"I'm not keen on tying ourselves down to a permanent arrangement. If the weather's good, we want to be able to maximize that. I don't want to miss out on a blue bird day of skiing or perfect hiking conditions, because we're tied down to babysitting."

The weight in her stomach turned to stone. "The problem is, being tied down by kids and pets is exactly what I want."

"But you said—"

"I know." Alice bit her lip, hating that she was about to hurt him. "And when I said it, I believed it. But now I realize teaching kids won't be enough for me. I'm worried we'll end up resenting each other."

He rubbed his face. "What about compromising on weeknights? The kids could visit once a month then?"

She shook her head, remembering Lawrence. "It never works when there's a fundamental difference. You want a kid-free life and I don't. It will always be our stumbling block."

His usually bright blue eyes dulled. "So where does this leave us?"

Her heart fluttered. "I hope as dear friends."

"With or without benefits?"

The full scope of her decision suddenly came home with a deafening crash. "Oh, Dan. I want to say "with," because it's fun and easy and you're great company. But if we keep going, it's only going to prolong the inevitable." She cupped his cheek. "I'm so sorry. I never wanted to hurt you."

"You're really sure about this, aren't you?"

She blinked rapidly, wishing she could live the life he wanted. "I'm sure."

His handsome face sagged, pulled down by sadness. He hugged her. "Good for you, Al. You've finally learned to demand what you want."

A sob escaped. "A good friend taught me how."

"He sounds pretty awesome," he said, but his voice wobbled.

"He is. He truly is."

Leo stared in wonder at the candles on his birthday cake. Patrice had made a cake in the shape of a number two and decorated it as a racing car track complete with cars. As much as he loved anything with wheels though, right now the candles were the highlight. "Twinkle, twinkle star," he said.

Jess leaned in, her head close to his. "Blow out the candles."

Leo blew raspberries. Nick laughed and tousled his hair.

Indi said, "I can do it for him."

"No." Libby restrained her younger daughter. "It's Leo's birthday."

"I'll help." Jess blew with Leo and the candles flickered then died.

Leo burst into tears.

"Hang on, mate, they're not gone forever. I'll bring them back." Nick struck a match and relit the candles.

Leo's tears stopped and he clapped his pudgy hands. "More stars."

Jess's throat thickened. If only someone could light a match and bring her back when she was dead. But she'd be gone forever and Leo wouldn't understand. Eventually, he'd forget her. She buried her head into his curls as she'd always done when her love for him overwhelmed her. This time though, it hid her tears.

The previous two weeks had been difficult, but in a completely different way from the months that had preceded them and the weeks since her diagnosis. The joy of having Libby and Nick back in her life was equal to her despair that it would soon end. Since the afternoon when Libby had arrived unannounced, she'd been in organizational overdrive. She'd filmed Jess trying to pass on some of her hard-learned life lessons, but it had been almost impossible to work out what to say. In the end, they'd decided to make a video for when Leo went through puberty and was likely questioning who he was. Jess had studied photos of herself and Nick at twelve and created an image of Leo at that age. She held it in her head when she spoke to the camera, telling him about her side of the family and how lucky he was that Nick was his father and Libby his stepmother.

Libby had suggested filming and recording her singing Leo's favorite songs and reading stories. The picture books were quick and easy, as were some of the early elementary books Lucy enjoyed—neither taxed her too much. Jess dearly wished she had the energy to record the entire Harry Potter series, but yesterday when she'd barely had enough energy to sit up, she'd momentarily questioned if she could even get to the end of *Harry Potter and the Sorcerer's Stone*. But she would. She'd made it to Leo's party and Christmas was only two more weeks away. After that, there was New Year to aim for.

"Who's for cake?" Alice deftly slid the knife through the chocolate delight and passed a huge slice to Leo. "There you go. Share that with Mommy."

But as much as Jess adored cake, she knew she wouldn't be able to keep it down. She'd had trouble keeping anything down since yesterday, not that she'd told Libby. Sometimes, seeing the doctor in her friend's eyes was too confronting. It was easier to mention things to Alice, Karen and Nick.

Libby held up her phone. "Leo. Jess. Look at the camera."

"Daddy, when are we playing pass the parcel?" Lucy asked.

"I want to hit the piñata," Indi said.

Karen lifted the phone out of Libby's hands. "You and Nick and the girls go and stand behind Jess and Leo. I'll take one of you all."

Jess's lips felt like ten-ton weights but she smiled, because it was one more photo—one more reminder for Leo that she was his mother and she'd been the center of his world for the first two years of his life.

"You've got more cake on you than in you." Nick lifted Leo off her lap and wiped his hands and face before organizing the children for a game of pass the parcel.

As the children ran outside and the noise levels dropped, the room swayed. Jess's hand closed around the edge of the table. "Karen."

"Time to lie down?"

"It's that or fall down."

Karen helped her back to bed, lifting her legs up onto the mattress and expertly stuffing pillows behind her so she could watch the games through the sliding glass doors. Libby had insisted on bringing her to Burrunan and Jess hadn't objected. She loved the house and the people in it. Each morning they wheeled the bed into the airy family room with its views to the water.

Jess pointed to Leo, who was wielding the piñata stick. "He looks so happy."

Karen laughed. "He's probably on a sugar high. I know Indi is. There's going to be tears."

"Lucky, I'm off the hook for dealing with that. I knew there was an advantage to dying."

Karen winced and Jess did something she'd never done before—she slid her hand into Karen's.

"It's okay. I'm not dead yet."

"You've always been a survivor. I recognized that in you the first time I met you."

"We're kindred spirits." Karen had told her about her parents; about her sister Lisa and Alice. "You were far more of a mother to me than Linda."

"I tried to fill the gaps. I wish I'd done more."

Jess shrugged. She'd had a lot of time to think about the choices she'd made and the cost of her mistakes. "You did more than enough. The rest is on me."

Karen huffed. "Linda has a lot to answer for."

"And my grandmother, but how far back do we go? The important thing is the cycle's broken and Leo has only known love. When everything went to hell with Libby and me, you were there. More than once it was thoughts of you that stopped me reaching for the rum, so thank you."

"You don't have to thank me."

"I do. I hurt your daughter. Other mothers would have hung me out to dry like most of the town, but even though you hated what I'd done, you didn't hate me. It meant a lot."

Alice came back inside, her fairy wings lopsided and her tiara askew. "It's getting a bit wild out there. Thought I'd calm them down by reading some stories."

"Can you spare me a minute?" Jess asked.

Alice glanced questioningly at Karen. "Ah, sure."

"I'll get the books." Karen walked over to the library tub and grabbed some books before taking them outside.

A sharp spasm of pain caught Jess and she fisted the sheet.

"Are you okay?" Worry filled Alice's voice. "Do you want me to get Libby?"

Jess shook her head as the pain faded and she released her grip on the sheet. "I want to thank you for loving Leo."

"There's nothing to thank. He's easy to love."

"So easy. It cuts me that you can't have one of your own."

Gratitude crossed Alice's face. "Thank you for thinking of me when you're dealing with ..."

Jess laughed—it was that or cry. "I'm late to the empathy party, but at least I got here."

"I'm devastated you won't see Leo grow up."

"About that ..." Jess took a moment to ride the wave of despair rolling through her. Now wasn't the moment to give in to tears—this was too important to say. "Libby's a brilliant mother, but sometimes she gets tunnel vision on the practical stuff, whereas you—Well, every kid needs an Alice fairy queen, pirate king or a penguin princess in their lives. Promise me you'll steal him away sometimes and surround him in paint and glue and glorious nonsense?"

Alice was silent and then her face contorted and she was gulping in air and crying hot, messy tears. Eventually she blew her nose and stared at Jess through panda eyes, black from run mascara.

"Is that a yes?"

"Of course it's a yes. A great big yes. I'm on the lookout to rent a place with a shed where mess is no object."

"Alice!" Indi wrenched open the door and stood on the threshold with her hands on her hips. "Come and twirl."

"Go," Jess said, feeling Alice's hesitation. "You know she's as obstinate as you are. She'll only badger until you give in."

"Do you want me to send Libby in?"

"No hurry. I might catch a quick nap."

Jess's eyes fluttered closed. The birthday party was everything she'd hoped for, and tomorrow Libby and Nick were putting up the Christmas decorations. She planned to watch Leo while it happened, soaking in his delight. She'd even string some popcorn. Lucy had seen it on an American television show and had begged Libby for a live tree and popcorn garlands.

She heard the heavy tread of familiar footsteps and opened her eyes. Nick was crossing the room with a trash bag in his hand. "Where's Leo?"

"On Libby's lap listening to Alice doing all the voices and actions for *Wombat Divine*."

It was the first time she and Nick had been alone together since Libby found out about Leo and he was glancing outside as if he was hoping someone would walk in. Even with death hovering, the old pain of him never loving her still managed to beat, accompanied with the pain of how much she'd hurt him. Having gone through life never saying sorry for anything, her apology to Libby had unleashed a need to make amends—as much to secure Leo's happiness as to leave earth with fewer regrets.

"Thanks for today, Nick."

"Too easy."

"It's not easy though, is it? I threw an incendiary into your life."

"Yeah."

"Me dying's probably the best apology I can give you."

His face blanched. "Jesus, Jess. Don't say things like that. Don't even think them."

"Why not? If I wasn't dying, I'm not sure Libby would have ever spoken to me again—or accepted Leo."

"You don't know that."

He sounded just like Alice, but then again, Alice and Nick always looked for the best in people. "I do. I love Libby to bits, but she and I share some less-than-stellar traits. Holding onto a grudge is one of them."

"She loves Leo."

"I know. I'm not worried anymore."

"And he's the best sort of incendiary on the market. My parents are besotted."

She managed a smile. "He's got everything I wanted him to have."

"Except you." Nick put the trash bag on the floor and came and sat by the bed. "I'll always tell him how much you loved him and how much he's loved. And when he's old enough to understand, I'll tell him Libby and I were having problems when you got pregnant and although I regret my behavior, I have never regretted him."

"That's incredibly generous."

Nick shrugged. "It's what we told Lucy and it's what we'll tell Indi when she's older. It's all they need to know."

"Thank you." She wanted to tell him she loved him, that she'd always loved him and she'd hoped for years he could love her too. But she knew her love was a burden he'd never wanted and if she truly wanted to die with as few regrets as possible, she couldn't tell him. "Can you bring me Leo, please?"

"Sure."

A few minutes later, Libby walked in with Leo on her hip. "Here's Mommy."

Libby lowered him onto the bed and he pulled at Jess's blouse just as he did whenever he was tired. "I'll get his bottle."

Jess nodded, unable to speak. Of the ever-increasing list of things this demon cancer was stealing from her, it was being forced to wean Leo that had driven home her new reality.

"Bottle's coming." Jess stroked his head, too weak now to lift his thirty pound body off her.

"Here you go."

Leo crawled off Jess's chest and snuggled in next to her, sleepily holding the bottle.

"Lib?"

"Yes?"

"I've made a list of things I want Leo to know. It's on my iPad. It's stuff like how much I love his cuddles and his gurgly laugh. How I love standing in his room watching him sleep. Please tell him I took him out jogging in the stroller and how we spent ages on the pier watching the fishermen. And when he's older and he's no longer scared of ducks, tell him even though he was terrified, he refused to give in to his fear, saying, 'Duck okay,' and—" A spasm caught her and she stiffened, losing her breath.

Libby took her hand. "I promise I'll use the list. I'll ask Alice to match it with photos and make it into a book."

New pain gripped Jess, circling her belly like a steel band and bringing a new sense of urgency. "But there's stuff I haven't written down. Tell him I love him more than I ever loved anyone. That education changed my life. That you and Karen showed me what was possible. Tell him to work hard and stay in school—" She gasped, bringing her knees up to her chin as if that would stop the agony. Leo sat up. "Show him what I couldn't."

"Shh, stop talking. I'll get you something for the pain."

"No, listen!" Jess struggled to speak. "Love him ... so he learns ... how to love ... the right way ... not like me." The edges of her mind fuzzed red as violent pain exploded in shock waves of agony. "Show him ... to be kind so ... he doesn't hurt ... people who love him ... I—"

"Jess!" Libby's voice sounded a long way away.

"Hurts ... take him."

She registered the loss of Leo's warmth and for the first time ever, she gave in to the pain.

⚓

In many ways, the old master bedroom at Burrunan resembled a hospital ward, although the toy box beside the bed clearly stated that it wasn't. Everything else did though, from the catheter bag hanging on the side of the bed to the syringe driver continuously administering medication. It was two days since Leo's birthday party and the onset of the complete bowel obstruction that had finally beaten Jess. Today, she'd barely been conscious and Libby was doing everything possible to keep her comfortable.

Nick's hands massaged Libby's shoulders. "Take a break? Alice and I can—"

"No."

"If it was Ramesh, you'd tell him to take a break."

"His best friend isn't dying. I want to do this for her. I need to."

"Fair enough. Do you think she can still hear?"

"It's the last sense to go and Jess always loved a good eavesdrop." Libby applied some lip balm to Jess's lips and then to her own. "She asked me if we were going to be alright."

His hands stilled. "What did you say?"

The hesitancy in his voice sounded like worry and she raised a hand to cover his. "I told her we wanted to be okay. We had three kids depending on us so we had to be okay."

"And we know where to get help when we need it."

"That too."

He dropped his head close and kissed her.

Lucy walked in wearing her school uniform. "Mommy, can I give Jess a kiss before I go to ballet?"

"Of course."

They'd discussed how best to handle Jess dying at Burrunan and had wondered if the children should go to Pelican House. In the end, they decided it was better for them to be involved and see Jess slowly fade away, so it didn't seem like she just suddenly vanished. That said, Libby didn't want them terrified when Jess's breathing deteriorated to rattling rasps. It was a fine line.

"If you're sure you don't want a break, I'll take Leo and Indi to the park for half an hour to blow off some steam while Lucy's at ballet. Alice is here and the palliative care nurse is due—"

"Go. It's fine."

He nodded and kissed her again. "Love you, *tesoro mio*."

"Love you too."

"Come on, Lucy-Goose, time to go."

A few minutes later the running feet and banging doors ceased and the house fell quiet. Alice wandered in holding a bowl of warm water and with towels tucked under her arm. "I found a bar of that lemongrass soap you said she liked."

"You really are the best."

Jess's favorite music played softly in the background and together Alice and Libby carefully washed the unconscious woman. The fresh scent of the soap lingered long after Alice had carried the bowl and dirty sheets away.

Libby sat down again, fatigue running like glue in her veins. It wasn't a new feeling—it had been part of her life since her intern year. She squirted Sorbolene moisturizer on her palm and gently massaged Jess's hand. "Remember my first year at the Alfred Hospital? The night of my first death? I called you up and you drove in to meet me. It was midnight but you insisted we go dancing.

"You dragged me onto the floor and said, 'Dance like there's no tomorrow.' I thought you were nuts and I only danced because you'd gotten out of bed to be with me. But slowly my anger at not being more experienced and not being able to do more for Jenny Reid shifted. I knew I'd given her a dignified death and I got this sense of peace. You gave that to me. Over the years, you gave me a lot. I hope I did that for you too."

Jess's fingers flexed, trapping Libby's fingers tightly against her palm. Amid the sound of a noisy rattling exhale, Libby thought she heard the word, "Yes."

It was an excruciatingly long minute before Jess breathed in again. Then her breath shuddered out. "Be ... hap ..."

Libby's tears fell onto their hands. "I'll miss you so much."

Jess's eyes remained closed and her pretty mouth slackened as each breath shuddered in and out of her wasted body. She suddenly gasped as if she wanted to say something and Libby leaned in close. But Jess didn't make a sound and her fingers slackened in Libby's hand.

"Jess?" Libby's own breath hitched in her throat and she closed her eyes for a moment, gathering strength. Gently, she pressed her fingers on her friend's throat, seeking the rhythmic beat that determines life. It had been faint all day. Now it was gone.

Jess was gone.

The feisty woman, full of perfection and flaws, who'd walked into her life and changed it in the best and worst ways was lost to her forever.

Libby lay her head down next to Jess's and cried for her friend. For herself. For Leo and the utter unfairness of it all.

CHAPTER TWENTY-SEVEN

A week after Jess's death, Libby, Nick and the children packed up *Freedom* and disappeared for six days, leaving Alice at Burrunan minding Monty.

"Are you sure you want to be on your own?" Karen asked Alice as they stood on the pier waving to the departing yacht.

"I haven't spent any time on my own in a month. I think it might be nice."

"I guess you can always invite Dan over if you're lonely," Karen said brightly.

Alice appreciated how hard her mother was trying to accept her life choices and her arrangement with Dan, so she decided to put her out of her misery. "About Dan. He proposed."

Karen stared at her openmouthed. "Dan van den Berg? The commitment-phobe asked you to marry him?"

"In a roundabout way. And you know how worried you've been that he'd hurt me? Well, it turns out I'm the one who did the damage. I said yes, because we get on so well and I didn't want to be lonely. Then I realized even though I can't have kids, we still want very different things. I hate that I've hurt him."

"Does Hil know?"

"I doubt it. And please don't say anything. I'd hate for the gossips to catch hold of it."

"And it's just the sort of thing they'd latch on to now Jess is dead and there's nothing left to say." Karen hugged her. "I'm sorry for Dan's heartache, but if he doesn't make you happy, darling, then you've done the right thing."

"Thanks, Mom."

"You and your father are right. I've wasted far too much energy worrying about you when you know exactly what you want and need."

Alice laughed. "That might be overselling it just a tad."

"I don't think so." Karen kissed her. "I have to go. I'm on setup duty for the U3A Christmas lunch."

They headed off in different directions and Alice slowed at the mural, held up by a group of Japanese tourists taking photos. She got a jolt of pride watching them and her heart turned over at the sight of a little black-haired child squatting down and patting the swan.

Oh God! The swan! With everything that had happened with Dan and then Jess, it was more than a week since she'd promised to pay Holly. Harry had sent a brief email a few days earlier, telling her Holly was at school camp so there was no need for tutoring. Alice had been too busy to reply, not to mention piqued that he hadn't asked her how things were going.

He always asked her how she was—his question matched by his intense green eyes seeking answers beyond her words. Of course, when he'd sent the email, he might not have known Jess had died, but he certainly knew she'd been deteriorating. Then again, perhaps Jess's situation brought back difficult memories of Helene so he couldn't ask. And it wasn't like he knew Jess, so there'd been no reason for him to write to her expressing his condolences.

But he knows me! She shrugged away the feeling that was part annoyance, part disappointment, part hurt and part something so intangible she had no hope of explaining it.

"This is ridiculous."

A couple of tourists turned around, giving her a confused look before bowing politely. Alice bowed back, embarrassed she'd been caught talking to herself in public. She crossed the road, walked to the ATM, withdrew Holly's money and drove to the Waxmans'.

Harry's car was in the drive but Brutus wasn't in the yard. Alice knocked on the back door and waited. After the third knock and still no reply, she sat on the steps and rummaged through her tote bag, finding a crumpled envelope and a pen.

Hi Holly, here's your money for the swan. The tourists are loving it so I hope you visit it and see their joy. I bet camp was awesome fun. Looking forward to hearing all about it. I'll see you over vacation. Love Alice x

A wet nose shoved its way onto the envelope in her lap before two dark eyes gave her a doleful stare.

Alice ruffled the dog's ears. "Hey Brutus."

Harry's black walking shoes came into view and Alice looked up, taking in his bare legs, rust-colored shorts, an unfamiliar but new blue and white T-shirt and a battered sunhat. He looked exactly like Harry —part on point, part disheveled and undeniably attractive.

Despite the HRT patch on her thigh, she suddenly felt hot.

"Alice." His intonation was neither friendly or unfriendly.

Flustered, she stood up. "I was just dropping off Holly's money. With everything going on, it slipped my mind. Sorry."

He shrugged. "Don't worry about it."

She didn't know where to put herself and Harry wasn't helping. "Are you okay?"

"Fine."

All she had to do was hand him the envelope and leave, but every other time she'd visited he'd been welcoming and insisted she come in. Suddenly she wanted to sort out where she stood in regard to his family. Subcontractor to him and friend to his kids? Just an art tutor?

"Can I come in?"

Surprise flickered on his face. "You know the kids are at camp, right?"

What did that have to do with anything? "Yes."

"And you still want to come in?"

"Yes!"

He walked past her and unlocked the door. Brutus bolted inside, claiming the couch.

Alice followed them. The house positively sparkled, a sure sign Harry was worried. "You're not stressing about camp, are you?"

"No. They love camp."

"So ...?"

"I can offer you tea or coffee or would you prefer something cold?"

The excruciatingly polite invitation flayed her like a whip. "Harry, what's going on? First you were weird on our date—"

"Terrified."

"What?"

"I wasn't weird. I was terrified."

She laughed, but immediately sobered when his expression matched his words. "Why were you terrified? You asked me out."

"Because it mattered, Alice."

"It was just dinner."

He shook his head. "I wanted it to be more than dinner. I wanted it to be the beginning of something, but I stuffed it. Then I saw you with Dan ... I can't compete."

"Dan's just a good friend."

Harry snorted. "It's pretty obvious he wants to be more than friends, Alice. And he's young and unencumbered. I'm this scruffy bloke ten years older than you, barely keeping up with two kids, a dog and a mortgage, whereas you're a twirl of color and light that takes my breath away. But I can only offer you chaos and baggage."

She wanted to hold onto "you take my breath away" but she'd let declarations like this lead her totally in the wrong direction with Tim and to a certain extent, Dan. This time she was using reason and logic and ignoring lust. "What's the baggage?"

"You're joking, right?"

"No."

"The kids, the neurotic dog, the mortgage." He spread out his arms. "My life."

"None of that's baggage." Her eyes strayed to the pelican—the ever-present memory of his dead wife and the children's mother. "Do you mean Helene?"

"No." He kept his eyes fixed on Alice. "I loved H. We had eighteen mostly happy years together and she'll always be part of our lives. But the kids and I have learned to live without her, which in some ways is sad but in other ways is healthy. It's exactly what she wanted for us. This year's shown us we can be happy again. You've been a big part of that, Alice. The kids love you."

Her heart rolled. "I love them too, but that's not enough, is it?"

His dark brows drew down. "What do you mean?"

"Honest to God, Harry. How can you be so perceptive with some things and so hopeless with others? Are you attracted to me?"

"What the hell do you think 'takes my breath away' means?" He ran his hands through his hair. "I love you, Alice, but what about you? Any chance you can love me as well as my kids?"

The question brought into stark relief her own concerns. "Sometimes I think you and I are perfect together and other times ..."

"When do you think we're perfect?"

"That night I arrived with my nieces and nephew. The rock pool ramble."

His shoulders sagged. "So, you think we're only perfect when there are kids everywhere?"

"Not just then. You've put up with my erratic emotions and you were incredibly kind to me the night I fell apart."

"Kind?" He grimaced. "That sounds *very* platonic."

"No, I didn't mean it like that. There've been moments when I thought there was a definite spark between us. Like the time you dipped me."

"There's definitely a spark from me."

She licked her lips, sensing this was too important to get wrong. "But sometimes, when I feel that spark, you do something that makes me think I've imagined the attraction."

"Like what?"

"Like paying me for talking to Holly about periods. I mean, jeez!" She threw up her arms. "That's something a friend does, Harry. You don't pay for that."

"I didn't want to be accused of taking advantage of you! It's bloody complicated when money's involved. That's why I wrote to Dear Alice."

She stared at him. "You were Dear Awkward?"

"Pretty apt when it comes to me around you." He gave her sheepish grin. "I followed your advice and asked you out."

She thought about everything he'd said but their unexciting date kept coming back to her. "Harry, I think we need to have sex before we can decide anything."

He blinked and swallowed. "Did I just imagine you saying 'we need to have sex'?"

"No. You heard right."

"I want to say hell yeah, but I feel I should ask why."

"To make sure we're compatible. I mean, we didn't meet and have that big bang, did we?"

"Speak for yourself."

The surprises kept coming. "You found me attractive from the first moment we met? That's not possible. You could barely look me in the eye and when you did speak to me, half the time you were rude—Oh ..."

Harry's ears glowed red. "Happy now you know you've discombobulated me for months?"

"I thought you were grieving."

"Mostly I just had no idea how to be around you."

"At least you know your weaknesses," she teased.

"I also know my strengths." He wrapped his arms around her, pulled her in close and kissed her.

⛵

"I THINK IT'S FAIR TO SAY WE'RE COMPATIBLE," ALICE SAID LATER, snuggling into Harry.

His fingers played in her hair. "Nothing like putting a guy under pressure."

"You more than rose to the occasion."

He grinned. "At least I finally did something right."

She suddenly wanted to know all about the casserole-bearing women. "Have you had sex since Helene died?"

"I had grief sex with H's best friend a couple of times. It wasn't a good idea."

"And since you came down here?"

"Nothing, unless you count me fantasizing about you. I imagine your year of dating has been a lot busier."

She propped herself up on an elbow and looked at him, knowing that whatever lay ahead for them, the first step was telling him the truth about the last eleven months. "Not really. When I met you, I was in the middle of a stupid crush that involved quite a bit of sexting."

"I think I've seen his dick."

This time she flushed. "Yeah, that's him. Worse than that, it turns out he was married with kids."

"Bastard."

"Yeah." She sighed. "And I don't know how you're going to feel about the next bit of information, but I need to tell you that from May to November, Dan and I have been weekly friends with benefits. It's over now."

He blew out a long, slow breath. "You have had a busy year. Why did it end?"

"We wanted different things."

"Like what?"

"He wants a child-free life. I don't."

Harry's face fell into serious lines. "So, here we are back at the crux of the issue. I know you can't have kids but you want them. I love you, but do you have feelings for me or just for Holly and Hunter?"

It was a fair question and one that deserved an honest answer. She thought about something Elsie Gregson had said: good men don't always make your heart race the first time you meet them, but they're there for the long haul.

"Do you remember earlier in the year when we ran into each other at the coffee shop over the river?"

"You were speed dating?"

She nodded. "You walked in and Zadie told me you were cute in a shaggy dog sort of a way and maybe you'd make a good project."

"Next time I buy coffee there, I'm not tipping."

"It gets worse. I said I didn't want a project, I wanted a fully functional man."

"Ouch."

"But that's the thing. You look a bit scruffy and sometimes you annoy the pants off me, but underneath you're one of the most functional men I know. You encouraged me to go back to drawing. You quietly dealt with my hot flashes and me crying all over you without making me feel foolish. You listened when I needed advice and when I arrived unannounced at your house with three kids in tow, you danced with me.

"I thought I wanted someone who just accepted me saying 'yeah, all good' when they asked me how I was. At first, I hated the way you dug just that bit deeper and how sometimes you seemed so serious, but when you went all old school taciturn on me, I missed you."

Alice interlaced her fingers with his. "I've missed the silly photos, the very precise and grammatically correct texts and even the number jokes, although I only get half of them. But most of all, I've missed you and the way you're in my corner. Love snuck up on me somewhere between that first hello on the pier and our rock pool ramble."

He was grinning up at her. "So that's a yes on loving me?"

"That's a yes. But I want a do-over on the date with the serious yet often very entertaining Harry Waxman."

"You're on." He kissed her.

Suddenly, the mattress dipped and Brutus's face appeared above them.

"If it isn't kids, it's hungry dogs," Harry grumbled.

"It's the rich tapestry of the life I want."

"And you're sure? Because the kids—"

"Don't need any more heartache and disruptions. I get it, Harry. I don't want those things either. I'm willing to do everything to make us work, including dealing with this dog who is really taking advantage of you. Brutus! On your bed!"

The dog gave her a melancholy stare before reluctantly jumping down.

Harry laughed. "You look like a sprite but you're remarkably tough, aren't you?"

"I prefer 'resilient.' So how are we going to handle this with the kids? I mean, they see me as their friend not your lover. Remember how upset they got when we said we ran into each other in Bairnsdale? They might not be so thrilled that we're dating."

"They only got upset because they thought I'd gotten to spend time with you and they'd missed out."

"But outings are different from everyday routine. I'm not fun Alice all the time."

He stroked her hair. "We'll take it slowly with them, but that said, they don't get to call all the shots. We'll work it out together. Meanwhile, lucky we both work flexible hours because, initially, school hours are about the only time we're going to be alone."

"Summer vacation starts in three days."

He wrapped himself around her. "I told you my life was chaos. Are you still in?"

"I'm there with bells on."

NEW YEAR'S EVE WAS IN FULL SWING ON THE WATERFRONT AND although it was still daylight, the carnival's Ferris wheel was lit up as brightly as the massive Norfolk Pine the council decorated each year with Christmas lights. The scent of hot oil and sugar wafted in the air from barbecues, food trucks and the ubiquitous cotton candy machine. Locals and tourists mingled among the family-friendly festivities, enjoying the summer night.

Hunter bounced up and down in excitement. "How long to the fireworks, Dad?"

"About an hour. Let's play some Finska to pass the time."

Holly, who was sprawled on the picnic blanket and full of dinner, groaned. "Do we have to?"

"No, but don't blame me if Hunter and I break your winning streak," Harry teased.

Holly shot to her feet. "Bet you can't."

"You in, Alice?"

She inclined her head toward Libby. "I'll be there in a bit."

"Okay. See you soon." Harry kissed her on the cheek.

"Dad!" Holly looked scandalized. "You're too old to be kissing outside where people can see."

Harry laughed and caught Holly around the waist before trying to plant a kiss on her cheek. She shrieked and squirmed away.

"They're always kissing now," Hunter said matter-of-factly to Karen. "I think it's gross but Dad's happy."

Karen tried to keep a straight face. "Are you happy?"

"Yeah. Alice and Dad took us go-karting. And next week we're going on one of Nick's boats. Alice says she knows all the good fishing spots."

"They're top secret, Hunter," Peter said. "You'll have to fish blindfolded."

Hunter gave him a sideways glance, then grinned and took off after his sister and father.

"Who'd like a ride on the Ferris wheel?" Peter asked.

"Me! Me!" Indi and Lucy jumped up and down.

"Twinkle lights go round," Leo said solemnly.

"Come on then." Karen lifted Leo out of Libby's arms. "Little girls, hold Da's hand. Big girls, we'll be back soon."

"Be good," Libby called.

"Will Nick make it back in time for the fireworks?" Alice asked.

"He texted ten minutes ago. He's pulled the hapless tourist off the sandbar so he should be back in twenty minutes." Libby started packing up the leftover food from their picnic dinner. "I really like Harry, Al."

"Me too."

"And he got through a Hunter-Pirelli Christmas and he still wants to be here."

"Yep, he's a keeper."

Libby's week sailing the quiet waterways of the lakes had started the slow process of coming to terms with Jess's death. She and Nick understood the impact of grief better now and they'd talked a lot. The days on *Freedom*, without the distractions of work, gave her precious time with the children as she started the adjustment of being a mother of three. Initially, Nick had overcompensated, jumping in and doing more for Leo. She'd told him she was the one needing to do the extra things to bond. The girls behaved as they'd always done with Leo, either loving him to death or getting annoyed with him, and for that Libby was grateful.

When they'd berthed back at the marina, Alice had greeted them with her news. Libby hadn't seen her twin so happy in a long time and she was both relieved and thrilled. But it didn't stop her heart aching that Alice couldn't have a child of her own.

"Will you and Harry consider overseas adoption?"

"By the time we jump through all those hoops, Harry will be too old and Holly will be sixteen. Anyway, we don't need to adopt a baby."

"But you love babies."

"I know. And I used to think not having my own child was the end of the world, but life teaches you things you never thought possible. Watching Jess die helped me put things in perspective. I'm healthy and happy and now I've got Harry, Holly and Hunter." She laughed. "Even if Holly is just hitting her stride as a teen."

"You're diving in at the deep end, that's for sure."

"I dunno. I look at you and Nick and Harry, and I think parenting is the deep end period. At least we've got Mom and Dad as role models. There's parenting gold to mine."

Libby thought of Jess. "The older I get, the more I appreciate how much of who I am is because of Mom and Dad."

"We got lucky. And my 3H's are gifts I didn't expect. Besides, I've got your gang whenever I need a little kid fix. Jess made me promise to shower Leo in glitter and glue and paint and clay."

"He painted his first elephant the other day."

"Wow, really?"

Libby laughed. "It's a blob of color, but every time he walks past the fridge he tells us it's Elmer."

"That's one of the books Jess read, isn't it?"

"Yes."

Alice hugged her. "How are you?"

"Yeah. Sad. But it's nothing like when I lost Dom." Libby fiddled with her wedding ring. "And don't roll your eyes, but somehow having Leo makes it all a little bit easier to bear."

"I don't think that's strange. I know he looks a lot like Nick, but there's quite a bit of Jess in there. I guess in a way, it keeps her close. Are you and Nick going to try for another baby?"

"I think we need a year to blend our new family before we add another one. And there's always the challenge of getting pregnant."

"Oh, God, are you perimenopausal?"

"No."

"That's good news then."

The words chastened Libby. In a year when betrayal had derailed her life, revenge had skewed her beliefs to an unrecognizable point and forgiveness was a dark lesson in humility, Alice had been there for her, even when she disagreed with her actions. And now, despite Alice's own disappointments and heartache, she was still wanting the best for her.

"Thanks for being my sister."

"Thanks for being mine."

Nick dropped down next to them. "Honey, I'm home and I'm starving. Any food left for a volunteer coast guard?"

"Nope, we ate the lot."

Nick grinned. "Guess it's a Dagwood Dog for me then, with a jam donut chaser."

Libby shuddered and lifted a container out of the cooler. "Mom made your favorite chicken salad."

"Where is everyone?"

"The carnival and the beach. They'll be back in time for the fireworks."

Alice shot to her feet. "I'll take one for the team and go and get hammered at Finska so you two can have an unexpected canoodle on the picnic blanket."

"We don't deserve you, Alice," Nick said.

"Pay me more," she teased before making her way toward the top of the beach path.

A FAMILY OF FOUR WAS WALKING UP THE STAIRS, TWO BOYS preceding their parents. Their mother was obscuring their father and it wasn't until the woman drew level that Alice saw the man. She recognized him immediately.

"Tim." His name shot out of her mouth before her brain could censure it.

The woman looked at Alice then turned to Tim, whose expression was a combination of stunned surprise and intense wariness.

The boys had run on ahead but Alice checked they were out of earshot. She held out her hand to Tim's wife. "Hi, I'm Alice. You must be Tim's sister, Sasha. He told me all about you." She turned and indicated the retreating boys. "Joel and Rufus, right? You must be so glad your brother's not the cheating bastard your husband is."

Sasha stared at her as if she was talking gobbledygook.

"I think you've confused me with someone else," Tim said quickly, moving forward as if it would encourage Sasha to resume walking.

"No, I haven't. I'm Alice Hunter," she said, stressing her surname in case Sasha wanted to contact her. "I live here in the bay. Anyway, I better not hold you up. The fireworks are starting soon."

Alice ran down to the beach and immediately met the Waxmans, who'd packed up their game and were heading back.

"You're all pink. Must be close to nine o'clock," Harry teased.

"That means fireworks! Come on, Holly, race you back." Hunter took off like a rabbit chased by a greyhound. Holly followed.

Alice slid her arm around Harry's waist as they walked. "Remember the two-timing texting bastard I told you about? I just ran into him and his wife. After I got over the shock, I didn't second-guess a thing and I introduced myself to her. She might choose to believe whatever tale he spins her, but for the first time since I found out he was cheating on her with me, I feel clean."

"Good for you. I reckon you should write a book about the perils of online dating."

"I'd rather spend my time painting."

He gave her a quick squeeze. "About your art. How would you feel about a studio in the backyard? It's not like we don't have the room."

"Holly would love it."

"That goes without saying, but what about you?"

"I'd love it too." Ideas started popping. "I could start an art school."

"Is the bay big enough?"

"The bay's perfect for people from Melbourne wanting to take some time out to paint and draw and throw clay."

"Alice! Dad!"

Holly was standing with Alice's family and waving to them from the growing crowd. Karen had her hands resting gently on Hunter's shoulders and he was animatedly telling her something. Libby's hand was in Nick's and Leo sat on his shoulders, his hands dug into Nick's curls. Indi was on Peter's shoulders.

Lucy raced over to Harry. "Can I sit on your shoulders?"

"Sure." He scooped her up. "How's that?"

"Look!" Lucy pointed to the first explosion in the indigo sky, delighted by its white cascading light. "Happy New Year."

Holly wriggled in between Harry and Alice.

"Happy New Year, Hol," Harry said.

"Duh, Dad. Bit early."

"I reckon this one might be worth celebrating twice, don't you?"

Holly slid her hands into Alice's and her father's. "I s'pose."

Harry winked at Alice. "Sounds like it just got a gold-star endorsement."

Holly rolled her eyes but she leaned into him and smiled.

Alice thought about the difficult year they were putting to bed. She wasn't so starry-eyed that she believed the new year would be devoid of heartache or challenges for her and everyone she loved. It was love that drove them to muddle through life, but even with the best of intentions, they'd make mistakes.

No one ever said out loud that love was as impossibly difficult as it was deceptively easy. That the exhilarating highs came with devastating lows that forced a person to question everything they believed about themselves and the ones they loved. That love meant sacrifice and sometimes, like her parents, that was generously given. Other times, like with Libby and Nick and Jess, it was extracted by force. All those uplifting quotes about forgiveness people liked to blu-tack to their walls seemed glib compared to the mammoth task true forgiveness demanded. Letting go of anger and pain was a task that involved as much energy as a seismic shift.

The oohs and ahhs of the crowd circled Alice. She watched the joy on the faces of her family—the children's wonder making the adults, who'd seen fireworks many times before, exchange looks and view them with unjaded eyes. That was empathy and gratitude. That was love.

Harry grinned at her over the top of Holly's head and she smiled back before lifting her gaze to the sky. The spectacular display rained color over her and she gave thanks for that moment and the many more to come.

ACKNOWLEDGMENTS

Another year, another book and another reason to thank the people who have generously supported me as I wrote *Just An Ordinary Family*. To my dear sister, Sue Peterken, who dropped everything to read the first one hundred pages when I feared this book didn't have legs. She then told me to hurry up, because she wanted to read more. That reassurance was gold.

Kerri Sackville's book *Out There: A Survival Guide for Dating in Midlife* was a most excellent resource and helped me write Alice's adventures in the online dating world. Real-life stories from my niece Tahlia Lowe also helped. Signing up to three different online dating sites to understand how they work was illuminating as were the looks on my adult sons' faces when they found the apps on my phone. I promise I didn't engage, ghost or neg anyone.

Thanks to Kate and Phoebe Parsons for all their information on bronze casting. I'm seriously jealous of your pelican and I'm so excited that it has such a special place in this novel. Thanks also to fellow author and artist M.J. Scott for the drawing tips and Lauren Harbor, author and dog lover, for all things greyhound. Dean Fuller answered my questions about working on an oil and gas platform, Alan Collett helped me out with some accounting terms and Serena Tatti advised on Italian terms of endearment and their spelling. Peggy Howden gave me information on growing vegetables in Gippsland and tennis mate Penny Radalj came up with the great idea of using community events to connect a year. I ran with it, recalling years of wonderful festival experiences as well as the family's annual summer barefoot bowling night. Years of my parents regaling me with U3A stories came in very handy and I borrowed, with permission, the term "director of Homeland Security" from Eliza Harvey, after hearing it on her excellent podcast, *Long Distance Call*. Sandra Nieuwenhuis guided me through scrapbooking and Kerri Coghlan shared her experiences at Relay for Life. Dr. David Brumley patiently answered my questions about palliative care and dying at home.

This book was the reason we enjoyed a fabulous family sailing adventure on the Gippsland Lakes—research! Thanks to Kerry McKendrick for filling in my knowledge gaps about the area and providing me with wonderful photos to add to my collection. Using the silt jetties in the novel was her idea.

Many thanks to Rachael Donovan and Annabel Blay at Harlequin who are always equable and calm when I am not. Thanks to Kylie Mason, my editor, whose skills lie in both the big picture and the minutiae even if we don't always agree and to my agent Helen Breitwieser, who is always a wise source of counsel. Special thanks to Norma Blake and Norm Lowe for 'Americanizing' this edition and a shout-out to Laura Helm and her friends for their information on what is considered 'expensive food' in the USA.

I'm indebted to my wonderful publicist, Amy Milne, who has brilliantly and enthusiastically supported me with my previous three books and she had hoped to work with me on this one. Tragically, she passed away leaving a huge hole in our lives. My deepest sympathy goes out to her family, friends and colleagues.

Heartfelt thanks go to the men in my life for their love and support, for the research road trips and the story ideas, no matter how outlandish—like being captured by aliens who built the pyramids. To

Norm and Sandon, all the love for staying up late and brainstorming with me so I could dig myself out a big plot hole three weeks before deadline (GAH!) and of course to Barton Lowe—Boy Wonder—who is my graphic designer for banners, mugs, business cards and all things fionalowe.com as well as fixer of PowerPoint presentations.

Last but by no means least, a huge thank you to you, my generous readers. The choice of books is enormous and the book budget limited so I appreciate the time and effort you expend on my books. I love meeting you on book tours, Facebook, Twitter, Instagram and email. Please sign up to my newsletter at fionalowe.com and sign up to my newsletter at fionalowe.com and stay in touch; your enthusiasm keeps me writing.

ALSO BY FIONA LOWE

Daughter of Mine

Birthright

Home Fires

Just An Ordinary Family

A Home Like Ours

Coming in 2022

A Family of Strangers

Join My Newsletter

For a free novella, *Summer of Mine;* Doug and Edwina's summer of 1967, please join my VIP Readers newsletter. You'll also be the first to hear about new releases, book sales, competitions and giveaways. Register at

fionalowe.com

Did you know **BookBub** has a new release alert? You can check out the latest deals and get an email when I release my next book by following me at

bookbub.com/authors/fiona-lowe

ABOUT THE AUTHOR

FIONA LOWE has been a midwife, a sexual health counselor and a family support worker; an ideal career for an author who writes novels about family and relationships. She spent her early years in Papua New Guinea where, without television, reading was the entertainment and it set up a lifelong love of books. Although she often re-wrote the endings of books in her head, it was the birth of her first child that prompted her to write her first novel. A recipient of the prestigious USA RITA® award and the Australian RuBY award, Fiona writes books that are set in small country towns. They feature real people facing difficult choices and explore how family ties and relationships impact on their decisions.

When she's not writing stories, she's a distracted wife, mother of two "ginger" sons, a volunteer in her community, guardian of eighty rose bushes, a slave to a cat, and is often found collapsed on the couch with wine. You can find her at her website, fionalowe.com, and on Facebook, TikTok, Instagram and Goodreads.

BOOK CLUB QUESTIONS

BOOK GROUP QUESTIONS

- Fertility is a theme across the novel from the arrival of the first period, through to menopause. Discuss the emotional impact of a monthly period, missing a period, and the loss of them on women's lives.

- Online dating has replaced the weekly dance/disco/nightclub as a way of meeting people. What are the pitfalls and the positives of online dating? Do you think being "friends with benefits" ever works?

- Experiencing grief can distance us from the life we know by changing our thinking and our emotional responses. What are some strategies to help us connect again?

- Love and trust go hand in hand. When someone we love betrays us, they inflict incredible pain, leaving us questioning not only everything we believed about the relationship but everything about ourselves. Can you forgive someone and still not trust them or does true forgiveness come from learning to trust again?

- Inspirational quotes lead us to believe that sisters are each other's best friend. Do you agree? Do sisters have a special bond that is stronger than friendship with another woman?

- A popular phrase at the moment is "toxic friendship." Do you think Libby and Jess had a toxic friendship? If not, how would you describe their connection?

- Many women have one "bestie." Have you ever fallen out with a best friend? What were the ramifications?

- Do you think expectations of best friends can be higher than that of family? Why?